WATER LILY
DANCE

Also by Michelle Muriel

ESSIE'S ROSES

WATER LILY DANCE

a novel

MICHELLE MURIEL

LITTLE CABIN BOOKS

LITTLE CABIN BOOKS
2025 Zumbehl Rd, #252
Saint Charles, MO 63303

WATER LILY DANCE

www.littlecabinbooks.com

Printed in the United States of America

ISBN 978-0-9909383-5-4 (hardcover)
ISBN 978-0-9909383-4-7 (paperback)
ISBN 978-0-9909383-3-0 (eBook)

Library of Congress Control Number: 2019905648

For Mommy
I miss you.

One's better off alone, and yet there are so many things that are impossible to fathom on one's own. In fact, it's a terrible business and the task is a hard one.

CLAUDE MONET

PROLOGUE

Sophie

~

St. Louis, Missouri
March 2012

After the second knock, I peer out the window at the police officer pounding on my front door. Three light knocks, a polite folding of his hands, two hammers, three, and four. "Hello?" he calls. "Open the door please, ma'am." He catches me at the window.

I check my cell; still no answer from Blake. I grab my keys and slowly open the door.

"Are you Ms. Noel? Sophia Noel? Blake's wife?" the officer asks.

"Yes." I stare past him, searching for my husband's car to pull into our driveway. The drizzle ends offering thick, warm air and a hazy sunset. *Tonight I will tell Blake, lavender and faded denim fills the sky.*

"I love our sunset game," Blake says, smiling. "I love your eyes, what you see."

"Tell me again about my eyes," I whisper.

"You see what no one else sees. I love that about you. There's no one like my Sophie."

"Miss?" the officer says, waving his hand for my attention.

"No one?" I say to myself.

"Ma'am?" the officer says louder. "There's been an accident. Is Blake—"

I rush past him, barefoot, splashing in puddles, through wet grass, into my car speeding down the street.

I know where Blake is.

I know the street, the address . . . 1135 Cherry Blossom Lane . . . three blocks down the road, make a right, a slight left, three minutes, maybe four.

She wanted to live close to me after her divorce. "Sophie, I'm all alone," she said. "One more chance—it will be different this time."

She needed a friend.

I drive through the neighborhood, flashing red and blue in the distance, sirens rising. The smell of damp earth no longer calms me or cherry blossoms mingled with pines. I see Blake's car on the other side of the street.

There is nothing left for my heart to do.

It does not beat.

I cannot breathe.

The drizzle returns. A wash of tears covers my eyes. I didn't see the little boy, the little boy standing next to his bike. The boy curious as a little boy would be.

He takes one step.

Why did he have to take that step? Why did I leave my house? Why did I go after Blake? Why did we argue? Why did I have to be right?

"God, please!" I slam the brakes and turn the steering wheel missing the sidewalk. I throw it in Park, shut off the car, and rush to him—the little boy now curled up on the grass. I kneel beside him. "He's all right!" I scream, trembling. "He's all right!"

An officer runs to us. I search past him to Blake.

The sirens stop.

They cover my Blake.

The cold blue lights' endless swirl cast shadows on his wrecked green car.

Silence.

"He's gone," I cry, kneeling next to the little boy. I cradle my face in my hands, unable to look at him, unable to move.

Silence.

"He's gone," I cry again, without breaths, without pause. Through my streams, through my fingers, two muddy sneakers step in front of my knees. "He's gone," I sob. "He's . . ."

The little boy's hands fall over my shoulders—warm, tiny fingers wiggling across my arms, stretching over my body into his soft hug. The boy fills the silence for me with his tender sigh. One pat, two . . . his mother rushes in to take her child home while I tumble to the grass into no one.

1.

Sophie

The quiet of a first snow.

Five seconds.

Softly close the door.

It sticks.

Try again; slam it shut—I want to rip it off and Hulk it out the window.

Breathe. Too late. A staggered breath ricochets inside my chest, tight, heavy, tumbling. I take pills to settle my heart. My shower of tears fall; it's hard to swallow, impossible to hold them in. My eyes close to a movie of fast motion thoughts, blurry colored scenes, faces past and present, blinding white at the end of the reel. Black . . . midnight.

When I close my eyes, I see you. I see light and a thousand colors swirling in the air above us. Bits of colors land. We stand in the grass our toes between thin blades of lime green holding tips of gold, lemon, and cream. I notice this because you taught me how to see, truly see.

We come alive, laughing. I run behind a fat oak, its bark patches of melon, milk chocolate, periwinkle cracks. You laugh at me. Admire me in the twilight. I twirl in a pomegranate chiffon dress swaying the grass around us turning the shadows bronze and crimson. The cool air bounces off my cheeks; I breathe in rain, wet grass, and daisies stretching up through the earth. We stare up at the sky, its drifting clouds teasing, hiding the stars, revealing twinkling jewels. The moon casts white light over the trees until the seashell clouds tuck in their hidden pearl. Bathed in soft blue, you still see my smile, my rose lips saying goodnight. Tears tumble down my cheeks, you catch them, and with a soft kiss on my forehead, they end. You bottled them all. When I close my eyes, I think of you—in sunshine, starlight, and color—because when I open them, I see you in gray and it frightens me.

~

The marble tile on my bathroom floor should feel cold; I'm melting. A flush pricks my skin at thoughts of death, loss, fear. I scan the touches in my new bathroom: my husband's perfectly set tile, fluted window trim . . . the his and hers sinks. "It's beautiful," I whisper, stretching across the floor. "But you never got to finish."

I'm wearing my husband's favorite outfit: a ruffled, green blouse and black slacks; it reminds him of our first date. I don't care about the drywall dust or paint splatters on the floor; it feels good to lie down, disappear.

"You're Irish, aren't you?" Blake snickers in my thoughts. Our memories float above me as letters caught up in a gust of wind that need saving. I catch one. *Our first date.*

"Irish? How did you know?" I egged him on.

"You mentioned that clogging show, Riverdance, you have auburn hair and green eyes."

I couldn't stop smiling. Blake was so handsome, the way the corner of his eyes crinkled when he flirted. "Full disclosure, brown eyes, in case this leads to a second date."

"In case?"

I tugged at the tablecloth nearly spilling my wine. "Most people see a black and white tablecloth, it's blueberry."

"Sophie, you're changing the subject, but I'll play." He bit his lip puzzled at me, noticing the tablecloth tracing a square. "It matches the blue flowers in our vase."

"Sweet peas. Technically, my mom insists my eyes are honey wheat with silver rims." I hid my blush, tracing squares with him.

His hand crawled over mine. "Interesting."

"My mom's an artist. So am I . . . I think."

"That explains it—in a good way," he fired off.

"My best friend talked me into wearing these stupid green contacts. One sec." I rushed into the bathroom fumbling to remove my lenses, contemplating the hideout. I thought I blew it until I returned to our table. Blake gave me the same enamored gaze on our wedding day. "Will it disappoint you if I'm not Irish?" I asked. We looked away and back into each other's eyes, snickering and corny as a love-struck couple in an old Hollywood movie.

"Yes. I really need to impress you. I plan on becoming a top-notch attorney." He raked his fingers through his hair. *"I read people. It's what I do."*

"I see." I bit a hunk of bread to keep from laughing. "Using your logic, you're Swedish. You have aquamarine eyes, lemon chiffon hair, and you mentioned that movie Meatballs."

Blake leaned back in his chair, arms folded. I mimicked him, laughing. "Touché. I don't think—no, I guarantee no one has said I have aquamarine eyes or lemon chiffon hair."

"Welcome to my world."

He stared into my eyes with his confident grin, leaned in close and said, "Sophie, don't ever wear those green contacts again." And kissed me.

"Technically, avocado."

When I told Blake my mom was French, he tried to impress me with a few French words. He said them all wrong. "If you would have said wee-wee one more time, I would have lost my mostaccioli," I confessed to the ceiling, wishing I could live inside that memory forever.

A rap on the bathroom door dissolved nostalgia. I stayed quiet, noticing a crack in my ceiling. Water stains invaded my bathroom ceiling. Stains that should have been primed and painted and cracks. Blake called it settling.

"How do you feather out Crisco paste again?" *Drywall compound, goofy.* Blake's imagined laughter covered the silence. *I'll fix it, Sophie. I'll fix everything.* "It's too complicated," I said to no one. "It's too late."

Blake added a speaker in the ceiling. "For your *smooth jazz*," he said, making faces. He hung my crystal chandelier where I insisted—now it looks off-center. The cabinets need pulls. I caved on the brushed nickel. I wanted bronze. We knew how to pick our battles. The bathroom was our last project together, that, and repainting our orange front door Blake claimed was never an argument but a miscalculation. He promised to fix it. He promised he would fix it all.

I fell in and out of sleep hoping my friends would leave, imagining my unfinished bathroom as a corner of nature Mom would have painted. That's what I did.

Imagine.

Blake said if I were a superhero, my imagination would be my super-power because I possessed this strange ability to create beautiful things from nothing and watch them come to life to make the ugly disappear. *"Beauty for ashes,"* he said.

"You mean I'm an artist." I laughed.

"It's more than that. It's how you see the world. How you determine to see it."

My colorful imaginings served a purpose only I knew, but after ten years of marriage, Blake understood exactly why I needed the escape. He knew.

The bathroom rug sprouted grass tickling my ears, steel-blue walls: my sky, missing base trim: a crevice in the mud where earthworms sleep. Three taps on the door: an intruding woodpecker. "Fly away," I shouted, staring at a rainbow of soaps on the tub's ledge. "Mother soap fresh and fat rests on tub's edge, watching slivers of her children used, forgotten, cast aside, stuck to holes on the dull silver drain. French soaps—stellar gift, Blake."

"Sophie, you pick a scented soap based on how you feel?" Blake laughed.

"It's called aromatherapy," I said, defending myself.

"A stupid therapy. Make your case." His smug smile declared I had none.

"My hotshot attorney always thinks he's right. Fine, unscented ovals for so-so days; cocoa butter bricks: happy days." He rushed behind my back, pretending his hands were mine tossing my hair, waving jazz hands. *"Minty evergreen loaves: tired days."*

His fingers stroked my chin. *"You need a shave."*

"Lavender cakes: sexy days, creamy coconut bars: sad days." I closed my eyes imagining the warmth of my husband's arms wrapped around me now.

"I'm throwing them out." He pressed my body into his. *"Except for lavender cupcakes and chocolate bars, so my wife feels happy and sexy every day."*

"Lavender cakes and cocoa butter bricks," I whispered.

"Sophia?" I faintly heard Mom's call. I stayed quiet, drifting. She understood my complicated history—disappearing into bathrooms—a Houdini trick I mastered as a kid Mom somewhat inspired. I locked myself in a bathroom at ten when my parents divorced, when we left Paris for California. I locked myself in a bathroom when my first crush Tommy moved away, when a kid spread lies about me in school, a blind date went south, Blake and I argued.

And I locked myself in this bathroom at thirty-blah years old because two weeks after my husband died, my stoic facade crumbled.

I sat up and clutched Blake's cell phone. The bottle of well-meaning

Valium teetered on the sink's edge. The drip from the faucet: lip smacks, our soft air kisses. I rested my face in my coconut palms noticing Blake's cell again through my fingers, the laughing phone.

Sophie: Come back. I'm sorry :(
Blake:
Megan: You're so hot. Come over.
Blake:
Sophie: I checked out. You're right.
Blake:
Megan: I'll make you feel so good.
Blake:
Sophie: I love you. Can't we bring it back to before?
Blake:
Megan: You'll love it. You'll love every beautiful minute of it.
Blake: I'm driving—

The quiet after a first snow.

Two seconds.

Drip. One Mississippi. Two Mississippi.

Kiss. One Mississippi. Two Mississippi.

"Blake, you should have fixed that drip. You promised you would."

Blake: I'm driving—

"Mother soap fresh and fat cleans debris."

Blake: I'm driving—

"Mother soap wishes men would not waste children. Men would not leave children to waste away."

Blake: I'm driving—

They stormed into my house—my bathroom. A row of grim faces hovered above, a slow pan on the actors in this Hitchcock flick: Mom, my neighbor Mr. Elders, his wife Maudie, my college bud Joe, his friend "the cop" and my coworker Jacey. Last week, Maudie taught us how to make cherry scones at one of Mom's get-togethers. Joe and I listened to Mr. Elders and Mom trade war stories, history about my grandparents—stories I never heard, about things I never asked.

"She was so happy last week," Mr. Elders whispered. I floundered as Mom's protégée but proved master at painting on a smile.

"I thought she was doing better," Maudie said, holding wet smears of mascara on her fingertips. "Gossip from the news again; they're so cruel."

"Sophie said she dealt with that about her dad in Paris," Jacey whispered.

"It sucks she has to deal with the press now," Joe said through his teeth, shooting them a scowl demanding silence. *That's my Joe*, I thought.

"She just lost her father," Mom told them in a quiet aside. "Not a good time. I don't blame Sophia."

"*Little Girl of the Garden*," I mumbled. "Remember, Mom? What's the headline today: *Wife of a Cheating Dog Lawyer Dead Husband*?"

"Shh, honey. It will be all right," Mom whispered, shooing them away. Her soothing scent of chamomile and lilies brought me back to our moment.

"Never been one for those rosy-colored glasses. Noel needs tough love. She tried to kill herself, Josephine," Mr. Elders whispered.

"Ed," his wife snipped. "And stop calling her Noel; it's Sophie."

"She's all right," Mom insisted, waving a hand to quiet the two. "Sophia promised me she didn't take all those pills. I trust her. My daughter has a beautiful imagination. It helps her, that's all. She needs time."

"To disappear," I whispered to her. "Mom, make them go away."

"She's in shock, ma'am," the police officer said. Mom crinkled her nose at him.

"I love you, Sophia," Mom said in her storytime voice. "It's going to be all right, *ma petit chère*." The others—meshed collective chatter in an underground tunnel.

"Ms. de Lue, the ambulance is here," Joe said. "I'll take her." He cradled my arms, guiding me along as he used to in college after one of his frat parties.

I fell into him. "Trash can punch. Joe, you should've never let me drink trash can punch in college or let me wear that go-go outfit. Remember?"

He squeezed my hand. "Hippie lush." His *shhs* whistled across my ear.

I loosened my grip. Joe wouldn't let me go. "Mom isn't a miz. *Mrs.* Noel—no, that's my dad's name . . . and mine. My maiden name, the only thing Dad ever gave me. Wait, Mom *is* Ms. de Lue, the artist." I wobbled between Joe and Mom as a lazy pinball between bumpers.

"Come, *ma fille*." Mom held me now.

"*Ma fille* means my daughter," I said. "Mom's not saying my feet. That's what my dad used to think she was calling me. Remember, Mom?"

"*Oui.*"

"See, isn't that cute? Mom's French and a famous artist. What am I now?" She couldn't catch my tears fast enough.

"Our Sophie," she said, stroking my hand tender, careful. I traced my finger as her little girl over the blue veins squiggling across her thin bones stretching and squirming as she moved her long fingers. I watched my life unfold upon her hand: a memory of Blake making a snowman at midnight on Christmas Eve. "*Next year, Paris.*" *He laughs, eyeing the white fluff, takes my hand; we land with a thud, fanning crooked snow angels in crunchy snow.*

"*Mon trésor*, time to go," Mom whispered. My treasure. My image of my husband melted with a splattering of tears atop her hand. I closed my eyes drifting, floating farther away like a snowflake on an unknown journey, swaying, swirling in an indigo sky.

"Everyone in your life is a gift, Sophia Noel, even your enemies. It's up to you whether you receive them as a gift into your life or not." Mom's recited whisper led me out of the bathroom. It's what she always said, what she always used.

"Blake was my gift," I whispered, squirming to hide in the bathroom again. She felt my body stiffen for the flight holding me close. Mom eyed the officer squeezing in to move us on. She held up a hand to stop him. I paused at a row of photos on the wall: college dates, our wedding, anniversaries. "Why does God give gifts if He's going to take them right back?"

"God doesn't take anyone He receives them." Mom stared into my eyes, I barely into hers. She straightened my blouse as her child, floating her fingers across my cheek.

She left me alone, my tears dripping on the floor. I watched them splash and huddle together in tiny puddles. "God doesn't take anyone He receives them," I whispered her words erasing fearful images of the past days. "But I'm still alone."

"Miss?" The officer held out his hand; his blurred into Mom's.

"Orange. We're the only house on the block with an orange front door," I mumbled. "The paint swatch said Cinnamon Squares, brick red. Blake knew I wanted Peace, sky-blue with a hint of gray. He wanted Cinnamon Squares, sounds like a breakfast cereal."

"Let's go, ladies." The officer herded us forward.

"There's no one like me Sophie Dot Dot Dot." My body pulled away from Mom collapsing into Joe's. "I didn't take the pills, Joe. I wanted to."

I wanted to close my eyes and sleep, swallow pills—one, two . . . twenty.

"I know, you crazy girl." Joe's kiss to my cheek, soft as I remembered.

"It's been a long time since you kissed me like that. Joe's from Paris, London, and Kenya . . . my Kamau, remember?"

"*Mpenzi wangu.*" Joe revealed a handkerchief and wiped my tears. "Shh."

"*Mpenzi wangu,* my love . . . I remember." I sighed, squeezing his hand. "They still make men's handkerchiefs?" I said to myself. Joe heard me and smiled. He always heard me.

"And gentlemen still give them to ladies," he said in the soothing tone I adored. "Shh, you will be all right."

You will be all right. Not a piece, not half. All. Right headed. Right hearted. I will be . . . that means someday, not now. "What about now?" I asked.

Jacey wrapped a red silk scarf around my neck. "It's vintage French. It will make you feel better. We're all here, Sophie. We're coming with you."

"Lavender." I breathed it in, burying my face into the cool, fragrant fibers. "I'm not going to the nut house am I, Mom?" I tried to shake myself awake. "Just exhausted, you guys, sorry for this. Plumb burned out, if I was in a John Wayne movie. Plumb. That's a funny sounding word. Plumb. I need to repaint this door."

Mom nudged me along. "They said you're dehydrated, honey. We're taking precautions."

Mother soap scrapes up children to put them together again to be useful. "Dehydrated in a bathroom." I laughed, leaving tender eyes, shaking heads, and that *tch tch tch* people make with their tongues on the roofs of their mouths. The star of the freak show Megan directed. "You're wrong, Megan. They love me. *This* is true friendship." They all heard it. Even if I didn't say it as much as I should, even if I shut them out again. They all heard it, and I hoped someday, I could believe it again.

Mother soap—bathrooms aren't meant to be bunkers, but they're perfect for hiding from the world.

2.

Camille

≈

Paris, France
April 1865

It started with a dream—of water. I am nine. Papa tucks me underneath
the covers; Mamma says goodnight. I close my eyes and see the meadows of
Lyon. Tiny white flowers, Papa and I cannot name, fill the countryside come
spring, violets, too. Fuzzy, pink blooms intrude upon our path sticking to
our fingers as spun sugar. Papa and I run through the fields warmed by the
sun with my little dog Raphael. Raphael is only a pup, a white fluff bouncing in the field of green; I can always find him. And then, the water comes.

It covers me.

At first, sky-blue water so cool and refreshing, as if I float upon the lake
in the early morn. I drift through mist as one of those little bark boats and
to the sea. Water splashes warm and soft over my skin. The mist rises to fog,
and I no longer see the sun, meadow or Papa. In an instant, the water churns
thick and yellow, thrashing about me, swelling into a purple wave washing
over my body, burying me beneath its crest. My throat fills with water as
I scream for Papa, but he cannot find me. The beautiful, blue water, now
putrid dense with mud, makes it hard to breathe.

My legs drag clumsy and weighted. Papa calls for me, to run for higher
ground. In the night, the river disobeys its Creator and comes to swallow us
whole. The hem of Mamma's dress, a golden ruffle washes past. I reach for
her hand; she looks at me and turns away. She turns away.

Papa rescues me. My petticoat catches the railing preventing me from
falling into the river as the others. Papa said it was an angel holding me tight
until he could reach me. So, I pray for hundreds of angels to save those lost.

"Mamma's in shock," Papa whispers. But I know Mamma clutches the baby inside her. I cuddle safe in Papa's arms, but the screams and thrashing of neighbors in the water below, tree limbs and livestock, too, pieces of homes, our entire lives—swept away in the night. Papa covers my eyes; I, my ears; and he sings soothing songs to silence the horrors.

When I awake, I'm ten, eleven, twelve for this dream is as water. It holds no age, knows no time, no boundaries, and yet it brings no restoration. I huddle in Papa's arms; he knows this dream—the great flood we survived when we lived in Lyon, France, my birthplace.

Papa sings his lullaby to hush me back to sleep, a tune about our saving angel. "Papa, will our angel find us since we moved from Lyon to Paris?"

"Indeed, angels are forever about us offering gifts at the right moment. Though we may not see; they help us to see when we need them the most."

"But, Papa," I say, shifting out from his bundle. "God promised Noah He would never again flood the earth. Have our rivers disobeyed Him?"

Papa sits up, bristling at my question. "*Ma fée*, God promised He would not destroy the whole earth with flood but made no conditions as to Lyon, nor our home, and when the waters recede He will build anew," Papa says, doing his best to tuck me in, but I wiggle and squirm as a fish tossed into a skiff. "But without us."

"But, Papa—"

"Hush, my daughter." Papa's soft, big palm strokes my hair. "Seek the good in the worst times." His voice trembles. "God lifts us out of the mire, and we have arrived in Paris to start a new journey, perhaps one greater than in Lyon, *oui*?" His brown eyes glisten with hope, resolved. He smiles, caressing my hair. "God has blessed my daughter with raven hair and a curious disposition. Shall I worry, Camille?"

I snicker, but dare ask, "Papa . . . is it fair?"

He sniffles and wipes my tears. "My family is safe. God will not give us more than we can bear." He pulls his best handkerchief from his pocket and turns away to wipe his slender nose. Mamma claimed it silly, but we all fancied Papa's nose, how beautiful it was for a man. His broad shoulders and stature, olive complexion and handsome mustache—my papa glimmered as my angel inside and out.

"Can we carry this, Papa?" I ask, snuggling into him.

"We don't have to," he whispers. "Let nature be fickle," he says louder. "God shall never be. We must not waiver now."

When Papa's tune does not calm me, nor his sermons settle my thoughts, he walks me to the window to view the moonlight on the cobblestone streets of Paris. Gaslight mingles with moonlight washing the stones gold, crimson, and amber. He offers the satchel of lavender Mamma hangs in the window; we take turns savoring its scent. "Paris is France," he whispers. "There." He points out the window, and, from our high tower, we watch the tranquility of the Seine, unafraid. "There is our future."

I settle. Papa explains again our hardship to rebuild in Lyon. How the Emperor sailed to rescue us, tossing his gold coins, and Papa caught many—that's what Papa tells me, that we have family in Paris and a fresh start. He even fancies a famous painting he feigns is us, Papa holding me tight on our roof when the Emperor traveled by boat to rescue his people. "The painting is of Tarascon, far from Lyon," I say, yawning. Papa's story lulls me to sleep, for I believe I'm the child in the painting, but insist the artist has incorrectly painted me as a peasant and in the wrong costume for we're much more fashionable.

I close my eyes to dream about this grand Paris, where everything is changing and so must we, but Papa still cannot tell me why Mamma never comes to my room when I cry, and why she turns away from me in my dream, why she has always turned her eyes from me.

When I grew older, my dream of the flood came less until forgotten. Papa visited my room on occasion when he caught me awake at my window. Sometimes, he sneaked us slices of Mamma's butter cake, baked for next day's lunch. We whisper about our new dress shop in the Batignolles, Napoleon's progress on the new quarters, the people of our village, the artists, and writers. How our emerging village flourished as a hub of modernity, opportunity, and creative insurrection. How he thrilled, though now older in years and to Mamma's consternation, he brought us here to play a part in it.

On my eighteenth birthday, the dream of the flood that carried us to Paris strangely returned. After the birth of my sister, and as I neared the age of marriage, I began to see why Mamma had turned away, why turning away from me was her own measure of survival. For perhaps I as Noah's flood glimpsed an impure thing that needed a rush of water to erase.

3.

Sophie

~

January 2014

Denial. Anger. Bargaining . . . Rage. If you convert three months into hours, it rings as a longer time to live, minutes even longer. Two thousand, one hundred and sixty hours to say I love you, one hundred and twenty-nine thousand, six hundred minutes to laugh. We fought together our entire lives, a divorced mom on her own from Paris making a splash in the California art scene with her eleven-year-old daughter. We battled through the miscarriage of her second child and her will to paint again; resurrected her success in a small town near St. Louis; and survived the loss of her second husband, my dad, and Blake. It wasn't pretty, but fighting never is.

This fight we never expected—a jump from behind dirty blow.

They promised her three years and stole them back for three months. If I knew walking into this place would disintegrate three months into three days, I would have taken my mom to Paris. With one brushstroke, Mom refused the murky gray and evil blacks and painted our days with lavender. As she summoned sunrise, I saw it in her eyes: her final wish and those important things she said a mother should have told her daughter years ago.

She never said them.

I wanted to ask, but we were too busy using up our minutes slaying monsters, pretending this wasn't happening.

I requested the lilac room; they gave her generic putty. Orange disinfectant screamed welcome. "Putty walls," I moaned.

"For the sake of argument, almond cream." Mom reached for my hand.

"At least Monet prints are everywhere."

"Oh, *mon trésor*, if I could only see Monet's garden once more. You must see it again not like before. Baby, our trip to Paris." She gripped my hand, allowing the weight of the world to drop on her shoulders. Together we could hold up a thousand worlds, not this one, not today. "Not again." Tears crept in her voice. "We have so much to share. My journals . . ."

"I don't want to talk about the past," I whispered, clinging to her.

"You never want to talk about the past, Sophia." Her body stiffened; she released me. "*Ma fille*, your exhibition . . . I will miss so much. You will paint again and go to Paris?"

Paris. My dream with Blake and promise to go back with my mother; the City of Light shimmered for her. It was my mother's birthplace full of fond memories and artistic revolutions. The City of Light scarcely glowed for me. My forgotten childhood lingered in dreams on its cobblestone streets, and family secrets remained hidden in its past. I lost my parents in Paris, maybe even a piece of myself. "Remember how we wished together? The wishing flowers," Mom said, smiling. "Do you remember our stories, *ma fille*?"

"Sleepy fairies." Memories played inside our eyes. "Shh, *Maman*."

This time she held me using her last bit of strength for the day to squeeze me tight. "You haven't called me *maman* since you were a little girl." She wiped away her tears before I could catch them. I wanted to hold them in my hand and never let them dry.

"I remember the words sometimes. You need a cup of sleepy tea, Mom."

"Gimbletook has already visited. I'm so tired, Sophia."

"Gimbletook. How do you remember her?" I stared into her eyes sharing silent memories; Mom and I never needed many words.

We held hands scrutinizing the sparse, sterile room. Mom dammed her tears, gazing into another Impressionist print. My posture deflated as I stepped into the room. Mom eyed the large bathroom, plush pink robe, and winked. "I look like a hag," she grumbled to herself in the mirror.

"You do not." I searched the empty room, her. I had never seen this look on my mother's face before, apologetic, done. "And when did you start talking like Phyllis Diller?"

"When my hair turned into hers."

"All the nurses were asking about your beauty creams, complimenting you on your, and I quote, 'gorgeous complexion and silky, black curls.'"

"Again," she snipped, nose in the air.

"Black raisin, intruding steel . . . your bangs laced with platinum."

"*Bien.* Just because I am in here, doesn't mean you get to be lazy. See, Sophia. See."

"I try, Mom."

"And when you don't see something you like . . . repaint it."

I turned away unable to stop my tears from falling. At her sigh, I toughed up to face her. "Mom . . . you're so beautiful."

She swirled her fingers over her cheek as if confirming she was still all there and gave me a brave smile. "How did my Sophia get wavy auburn hair? Your dad had copper in his hair, *mon trésor.*" *My treasure.* I loved it when Mom called me her special names in French: *mon amour,* my love; *ma petit chère,* my little dear; *ma fille,* my daughter. We stared at each other in the mirror. Mom held onto the countertop for balance, rearranging her makeup. "You look pale, honey." Her delicate, cool hand kissed my cheek and forehead. "Did they really ask about my creams?"

"We did." A nurse popped in with a hospital mug of ice water.

"Antiaging creams in this place." Mom slipped into bed. I tucked her in.

"We can do better than this." I brought the floral pillows we made last year and her crocheted masterpiece we dubbed "The Beast," a blanket in retro lime, turquoise, and orange squares bordered with black scalloped trim. The Beast followed us from California to Missouri, on a plane to Paris, and back again to Mom's couch where it engulfed us while we watched old movies. I hung a few of our paintings and filled the room with fresh sunflowers and lavender. "One last touch." I held my breath, calming the flutter in my chest, revealing my surprise.

"My easel." Mom turned inward, gazing out the window. "You didn't have to bring that."

"Of course I did." I placed an Eiffel Tower statue on her windowsill.

"Leave it folded for now."

"I brought you canvases . . . your brushes and paints. You never know."

"It's like when I brought you to college, isn't it?" she said, falling asleep.

"Ms. Noel," the nurse whispered. "Join me in the kitchen for tea?"

"We weren't prepared for this." I froze, searching her with my blank expression. "She was ready to fight," I whispered, edging us back into the hall. "My mom's a fighter."

"I can tell when we had our chat. She has a strong spirit. And her faith—"

"Yes," I interrupted. "My mother is the strongest woman I know."

"It makes it harder." The nurse scribbled her notes. "What's important now, enjoying your last days together, and when the time comes, assure her it's okay to let go."

Let go? Mom and I never used the words. In our family letting go meant giving up. The de Lues never gave up, not Grandma in Paris during World War II, not her mother or her mother before. It was *Press on, Sophia. We will rise higher.* "Mom couldn't get the chemotherapy drug they promised," I said, seething. "Her doctor told us they didn't have it. No one did . . . a national shortage. He stamped 'done' on her chart and moved us on."

"We understand you couldn't take care of your mom at home?" The hospice nurse asked in a low voice. They all spoke like golf announcers here.

"I only felt a prick of the dagger today now it's a thunderbolt." I twisted my Silly String hair into an overstretched scrunchy.

"A recent widow, so young—we know this is hard on you. This is why we're here." The nurse's raspberry readers slipped down her nose as she studied me, wrote on her clipboard, and looked back at me with her angelic grin.

"Caring not curing, you've said that a hundred times." I stared into the orange rhinestone brooch on her collar. "Do you like pumpkins?" I asked, unamused. "It's after Christmas."

"My pin?" She patted the gaudy thing. "Flowers. It does look like a pumpkin, doesn't it?"

I studied the pin as the nurse did me minutes before, losing myself in the gleam of amber and rose sparkles. "I have no one," I managed. "No help. I wanted to take care of her . . ."

"You don't have to explain. Her at-home nurse told us you—"

"Affirmative . . . I had a nervous breakdown—downs." I saw the "family" restroom across the hall. *Another place to hide.* I claimed a rocking chair in the small library, leaving my blanket and a copy of *East of Eden* on the seat. Nobody went in there. Surrounded by old books made me feel safe, made me feel my dad Ironic, all the knowledge in that room couldn't offer one answer, only the comforting smell of libraries, bedtime stories, and home.

"Ms. Noel, don't blame yourself."

Blame. I hadn't thought of the word. It hid under the words guilt, anger, and exhaustion—words fueling me staying in this place, standing in front of her. My heart's flutter returned; I pressed my chest to steady it. "We've never given up on anything in our lives. Mom refused an ambulance. I drove her here in my car . . . alone." I grabbed a box of tissues wishing for Joe's soft handkerchief.

"What can I do for you, Ms. Noel?"

"Give us back our time. Get her that drug."

She hung up her clipboard. "Come with me. We'll have the kitchen to ourselves."

I held my chest and closed my eyes. *Breathe, Sophia.* "My British step-mother believes a cup of tea cures everything. It never worked for us."

"I happen to think a cup of tea can do wonders, especially for you now."

I stood inside my mother's doorway watching her rest. *I wanted to paint with you again,* I thought. *We could have at least painted the clouds.* Her chest rose and fell; her dainty form buried under a mountain of white sheets. "What if she gets better?" I asked, turning to the nurse for a dose of hope. "It happens, right?"

The nurse checked her clipboard and sighed. "Let's have that cup of tea."

The putty walls found whimsy covered in Mom's art: her famous sunflowers, lavender fields, and little girl wearing a sunhat running through a meadow of poppies. The scent of lavender and spearmint tea filled the room. She held me close. "I'm ready, Sophia. I'm not afraid to die, but it scares me to see my daughter afraid to live. Make peace. It's time to move on."

"I'm too old for unresolved issues, is that it?" I asked, holding her as she stroked my hair.

"Blake's death stirred things up. You won't find the truth unless . . ."

"I dig deeper? Why?"

"We have our answers, *ma fille.*"

"You mean you do." She reached for the Eiffel Tower statue. "I'm sorry, Mom." I tucked her in. "You don't deserve that. Not now." They did their best to make the place look homey, wood floors, Monet prints, oak panel-ing—but it wasn't our home.

"Sophia, we've come so far. You're on a path, and I can't be there with you to finish." Her blank stare frightened me; her sullen skin no longer pearl, and then she smiled, her eyes hints of sparkling sea doused all fear.

A kiss to her silky cheek, I breathe in rosebuds. Your gray-blue eyes glisten with a million hopes and dreams for your daughter every time I walk in the room. Licorice hair in Gatsby waves, impeccable posture, strutting in an airy sundress and floral heels. I can still hear the click of your heels in your gallery, marching to the front door to open and close. "This is how I will remember you," I whispered to myself, sitting beside her.

"Promise you'll finish. You won't give up." She reached for my hand. "You have to—"

"Face her?"

"*Oui* . . . or let it go."

"I don't need to."

"That's the problem, *mon trésor.* You have a solution, but you don't want to take it. Make peace and move on." *Move on.* Mom and I weren't seekers of truth regarding the hardships in our lives—we *moved on.* I learned early, it was easier for us to skip over our tragedies, family secrets, and move on without explanations, without winning our apologies. Mom used to say, *"In Occupied Paris during World War II keeping secrets for the de Lue family meant the difference between life and death, food on the table and starvation, artistic freedom and bondage. I'm sorry, ma fille, a mother's gift at keeping secrets traveled through the generations to us now."*

"It will hurt forever missing you," I whispered.

We held each other tight.

I spent the night at Mom's house, a place where we cemented new memories, her independence, my life after Blake, and where her art displaying the years embraced me as old friends. It smelled like Christmas—the aroma of toasted pecans, browned butter and butterscotch chips from the cookies I baked, hoping Mom could savor one bite. I loved the openness of her house. Tall arched windows flooded her living room with light, a sprinkle of Hollywood Regency in one room, French Country in the next. Walnut floors, airy mint walls, lavender throws, and silk pillows, every touch a treasure hunt I remembered.

Mom's rosy perfume kissed me as I walked into her bedroom. I lingered among her things, sat at her dressing table as her girl, playing with brooches and pearls left waiting. Her prized cedar hope chest sat ready for me at the foot of her bed. Inside: floral silk scarves framed a stack of colorful journals decorated in ribbons and charms—the journals she asked me to bring to her days ago. A pink fabric journal sat on top; a lavender ribbon held Mom's note: *For My Sophia. Read first.* "If I leave you in here, if I don't open you, this isn't real." I passed my hand over the stack of journals, grabbing a cashmere scarf instead. "*Maman,*" I whispered, wrapping the scarf around my neck, lowering the lid.

Patches of New Year's Eve snow frosted the corners of Mom's windows displaying the perfect Christmas card. January snow offered quiet, and I stood wishing for September when cicadas outside her window filled her room with buzzing. "*Cicadas sound like a chorus of steady tambourines,*" she would say. "At least we rang in the New Year, Mom." I tossed the leftover streamers off her bed, wandered into the living room, grabbed the Beast, and left the lights off savoring the last bit of daylight.

The sunset melted into peach and strawberry, and I ached to watch it fade from Mom's studio. I couldn't take one step near it, not tonight. I scanned the decorative touches we added months before. The reality that standing in my mother's living room alone would be my new normal shot a jolt in my stomach I couldn't absorb. I threw myself onto the sofa with a guttural groan. My chest tightened. I sucked in a deep breath, as my doctor instructed, but the steady stream of tears made my heart quiver.

Wrapped in the Beast, I moved to the window seat, my favorite hideaway in the house—a vintage Hollywood nook in lavender Mom created for me. I sunk into the lilac velvet cushion surrounded by maroon pillows and baroque linen window shades. A crystal angel waved at me from an end table. A photo of Mom and me dressed as hippies made me smile. Yesterday, Mom gave me one task. One I procrastinated doing for weeks because it would force us to discuss the subjects we skillfully avoided for years. The last few months, we didn't have time for regrets and blame; we didn't have time for many things.

I looked around at the soundless house; anger kept the floodgates closed, distance enabled me to pretend I was strong enough for this. The sting of growing up without my father, and my mother's silence, were bitter thoughts I entertained because I knew if for one second I dwelled on our years of love, her endless love, I would shatter into a million pieces and there would be no one here to glue me back together again.

The house turned dark and quiet now. I hit the CD player and listened to Ella Fitzgerald sing "'Round Midnight." *"It's so smooth and sleepy,"* Mom *would say, cuddling me.*

"You don't think it's a sad song?" I asked.

"She's a woman who realizes how much love she has for him."

"And now that he's gone, she can't stand the memories."

"It's only a quarrel; she longs to make more memories waiting for his return."

"Let's pick a new favorite song. This sounds like the sad story of our life."

"I never waited for your father's return. We parted that's all. It always comes to that."

"Mom, you're not the one in the song. You're the listener. I'm the woman who 'hasn't got the heart to stand those memories.'"

"We make our own midnights, ma petit chère. It's a beautiful song and still my favorite. Listen to the piano . . . so beautiful."

"It is, Mom." I softened Ella and dimmed the lights enough so I could still read. The pink journal teetered in my hands. It wasn't as old as I remembered, but I hadn't looked at them in years. I stroked the silky fabric smiling at the crooked glued edges on the inside cover and set the card next to her waving angel. The lavender ribbon slipped off; I wrapped it around my wrist watching the pink and red rhinestone heart twist and turn.

Throughout my childhood, I caught my mother scribbling her thoughts, talking, laughing, and crying. She said she wrote in the journals for me because unlike her mother and grandmother, who shared few stories near the end of their lives, Mom wanted me to remember our triumphs and tragedies not to inflict pain but to deposit hope. "When times are at their worst, my journals remind me they are only temporary," Mom said. "The heartache will not last forever, *ma fille*. It doesn't have to."

I stared at the journal now resting on the table's edge guarded by Mom's angel. "Cicadas," I whispered, "swish as a jazz brush swirling on a snare." I curled up on the window seat and let the smooth jazz of a 1960s nightclub sing me to sleep.

4.

Josephine de Lue

January 3, 2014

Today my daughter asked me about faith. Now, while I sit here frail and fading.

"What is faith, Mom?" she asks. "I don't know anymore."

"Sophia, that is the easiest answer I will ever give you," I say. "Faith is what you're persuaded to believe is true. Do you believe that I love you?"

"Of course, Mom," she says.

"Are you persuaded beyond all doubt that I love you?"

"Yes."

"This is faith."

"Mom, is it really that simple?"

"Yes. Now, it's whom and what you place your faith in that makes all the difference." I understand what my daughter is asking me: If I have faith, why am I not healed? So I answer, though she hasn't asked. "Honey, I'm not afraid or angry with God. I have peace," I whisper. "No more tears, ma petit chère. No pain."

Sophia looks away, sighs, and clutches the steering wheel staring down the highway. I'm surprised she lets the quiet fall. "What is faith for if this is what it gets you, oui?" I ask. "This is what you're thinking." What I'm thinking is how strange it is I'm not in an ambulance with tubes, oxygen, and gadgets, but I'm driving to a hospice house in my robe and slippers with my daughter in her car. "Have I given you everything you've ever asked me for?"

"No, Mom."

"But you're persuaded, without a doubt, that I love you and would do anything for you, anything to keep you safe, oui?"

"Yes, of course."

"This is faith." Sophia sighs again, turns up the heat. I close my eyes to the sudden smell of madeleines: vanilla, buttery and soft as my mother used to make.

I see Lewis, my first husband, standing at the front of our little French church as I walk down the aisle with Papa. "Wedding cake," I mumble. "One bite covered in thick almond buttercream."

"I'll make your favorite cookies," Sophia says, perking up. "Maybe you can try a bite."

"We'll see." My hands shake and wiggle; I hide them one under the other. I'm upset I cannot concentrate on my daughter's questions or her smile, but only my breathing and I have no stomach for sweets.

As I look up at the clouds in front us, the clouds turning into silver shapes with golden edges, a thousand memories rush into my mind. They shuffle and swirl as a deck of cards on a card shark's table, memories jumbled with people I don't remember; I wonder if they are even mine. My finger traces shapes on my leg while I study another cloud, purple and soft. Sophia guzzles water to swallow away tears. I'm angry my once sharp wit is gone, my measured reasoning is unclear, and I'm thinking as a child.

"Mom," I barely hear her say. "What are you thinking about?"

I will miss my baby's tender voice and honey wheat eyes with the silver rims, her strawberry blond hair she had darkened, and watching her mature as a woman, as an artist, find love again, find hope.

"God did not make me sick to teach me some lesson, Sophia," I add, though she knows I would shout this over and over again. "Why do healthy people judge the dying as not having enough faith to live? Shame on a fool's need to be right before the broken-hearted."

"Who judged you?" My daughter rears up; her chest rises and falls in a huff of breathing.

"Asinine," I blurt out, making my daughter laugh. "When I broke my foot, God didn't make me fall so I would learn patience—I was stupid for wearing four-inch heels in an ice storm."

"You got it, Mom," she says with a laugh, pleased her mom has come back to her.

I'm proud of my daughter. I look at her and see the years: my brave little girl, the wife she was to Blake, the daughter she is to me and her father, despite everything, the kind woman she is, and I find myself praying, with a deep-seeded hope, Sophia will see how valuable and beautiful she truly is.

Now I am quiet.

My daughter holds her tears, fussing and fearful, asking if I'm all right. She's doing her best to remain brave and strong; we both are. I feel my heartbeat skip; it's hard to breathe. We snicker at an ambulance speeding past us; we cry, too.

"Why the hell didn't the nurse have us take the ambulance?" I say, and our tears turn to quiet laughter. It's what we've always done; inappropriate laughter has brought us through many tragedies, too many.

"I want you to have my art," I finally say, and I cannot stop my tears now. I look away, straining to recall the important things, the list I worked on for months.

"What about the relatives?" She tries to help me. "Dad's family? Your sisters?" She makes it matter-of-fact because she knows I need lists and tasks as if readying for one of my art exhibitions.

"No," I answer. "Only you. I want you to have my art . . . to inspire you."

My anger rises because I'm not thinking clearly, but what comes to the surface are my final wishes that my daughter will have everything that is mine. I'm happy these wishes are not covered in silver clouds glittering with guilt or obligation.

"I have your will, Mom. It's okay."

"I want Georgie to have the lake painting; the small lake painting with the boy with the blond curls . . . unless you don't want him to have it."

"Whatever you want, Mom."

And we go back and forth repeating these stupid lines, and my paintings become a blur as I stare at the porcelain cheek of my daughter wishing I could paint her one last time.

"This is too much," I say, and my daughter smiles and sighs, this time in relief, because I sound like her old mom, not the pale, tired woman with the swollen belly on her way to a hospice house I hope is decent and nice, not for me, for her.

And I will do my best to tell her it's all right. I will do my best to hold on as long as I can. "This is what I want," I swallow it down. "This is what I need. It's all right, baby." My wall has crumbled, and I cannot stop my quiet sobs.

Sophia leaves me alone. I, her. We continue staring at the road ahead, a hospital on the horizon. For a moment, she makes up stories and questions and tries to amp me up with the special things she has planned.

"Shh," I say a bit angry. I hear tears in her voice, and I no longer have the strength to hush them away.

I'm staring at my daughter seeing her disappear right before my eyes in a blurry haze; it frightens me. I want to ask her if she's all right, but I know Sophia will not tell me the truth. She runs from it. She wants to stay strong for me. I know. I know we will have another cry. We will never say goodbyes because we're not ready. But she will have these words.

Sophia, you will have my words. And I pray, in them, you will always remember: faith is not wasted.

Faith is never wasted.

5.

Camille

Before the shopkeepers' brooms brushed their monotonous rhythm on the freshly paved walkways of our new Paris, and the splash of our water buckets dissolved evening's dust. Before the first whiff of gingerbread and chocolate, when the soft purple light of Paris bids us good morning, Papa and I sneak away from our dress shop for a quiet walk along the rue de la Paix. On special days, we may even take a cab.

We don't prattle about our fine boutique, the gowns requiring pressing, the window display, or lace I purchased from the nunnery. Rather, we take turns guessing lines from Shakespeare or Balzac between bickering about the marriage proposals I have rejected.

When the air is warm fragrant with citrus, browned butter, and pastry, Papa reminiscences about his boyhood in Lyon, I the orangery of its garden and our picnics on the banks of the Saône when I was a little girl. We marvel at our new Paris, Emperor Napoleon III's improvements, palatial parks, and boulevards lined with horse-chestnut trees and gaslights. Often, we gaze upon the soul of our city: its trees, gardens, cobblestone streets, and people.

"Paris is France," Papa declared every morning as we exited our shop. We inhaled the damp morning air. Papa adjusted my shawl. I smiled, folding my hand into his. "Camille, what will you do with your life nearing nineteen?"

"The Comédie-Française holds auditions for fine actresses." I raised my chin, floating my hand across my shoulder feigning innocence.

Papa rolled his eyes. "Ah." He snickered. "My daughter's in a jovial mood to rile her papa so early." He shuffled the dust off his feet shaking his head at our neighbor's dirty stoop.

I pulled him along before he started sweeping. "The troupe is a high honor. I have modeled for three artists this spring. Monsieur Bazille believes I will make a striking actress. I'm tall, slender, and possess much patience."

"A trait from your mamma as you are trying mine."

"And lovely carriage—as you."

"Flattery? My daughter is too beautiful, *oui?*" He chuckled, masking worry. "I'll strive to keep the dandies away."

"You said yourself, as Monsieur Bazille, I'm not as other models."

"And respectable, *oui?* I dare say he recognizes you come from a proper family. I didn't raise you to play Venus to a group of artists."

"Papa." I stopped our stroll to face him.

He tucked my hand inside his forearm shuffling us along. "Good. You're paying attention, your head forever in the clouds."

"I rather Flora." I muffled my giggle watching Papa hold his temper in his cheeks.

"Why I agreed to such foolish notions at all." He slipped away admiring a tobacco shop window its attraction whimsical carved pipes and jeweled snuffboxes. "I very much want to waltz into that shop for a cigarette. Will you tell your mother?"

"Scorched linen, asafetida and glue." I snubbed him. "France's most terrible weapon." He paused, tipped his hat to a passerby, and moved us along. "Frédéric Bazille is a serious student."

"A student of what? He cannot decide on painting injured companions or mending them."

"He said I exude a softness and sincerity."

"Did he? The charming medical student from Montpellier, who rather paint and play the proverbial patron of the Comédie-Française and flit in and out of every ball as a gangly crane, counsels my daughter on life and profession? My daughter holds an excellent education and moral character, unlike the tarts on the walls of the Salon. Do you wish to soil your name among them?"

I shrugged off his temper. "Such gossip, you sound like Mamma."

"You forget, *ma fille*, women enter our shop daily with a hatful of gossip. I have a daughter," Papa mocked in a lilting tone, "a little-known oddity about Paris who loves fashion and attends church." He flipped his handkerchief at my nose. "And whispers about the scandalous love affairs of actresses she now wishes to emulate."

"You are being dramatic, a worthy performance." I laughed.

"I'm too soft with my daughter who mocks me now." Papa's red cheeks cooled to blush. "I favored selling common drapes and fabric to nunneries, not lavish dresses and flagrant accoutrements to every manner of woman in Paris. It might have suited my daughters better."

I squeezed his arm, hoping for a calmer demeanor. "I will never regret our Elegance Shop."

"Make amends, play your mother's harp tonight before it turns to dust."

I let go of his arm, scuffing my heels behind him. "It has been years, Papa." He stared into my watery gaze offering his arm. "*Oui*." I nodded. "I promise to play at Geneviève's party."

"You make me happy."

The morning stillness we loved infused the air about us. Hints of Paris awakening: shutters opening, a breeze whispering through the trees, coaches in the distance. "Why shouldn't I be considered for a part?" I asked softly.

Papa nestled my hand into his forearm, leading our stroll without an answer. We nodded to a handsome couple in evening dress appearing as if sneaking into their apartment after their long, sordid night. "My point precisely," Papa said through his teeth, eyeing and tipping his hat to the couple giggling at us, flying inside their love nest.

"The Brohan sisters encouraged me for years. Letters of introduction from two stars of the Comédie-Française are worthy of your attention."

"Ah, the virtuous Brohan sisters."

"You cannot hide you fancy them as all of Paris."

Papa's eye twitched. "I suppose the Brohan sisters and Monsieur Bazille arranged your choice of three husbands, roles at the Comédie-Française, summers in the country, and every foolish whim spewing from these artists scouring our city as the rats we are at last rid of."

"'A rotten carcass of a butt, not rigged, nor tackle, sail, nor mast. The very rats instinctively had quit it.' *The Tempest*, in case you search your mind."

"You gave me no chance! Don't distract my point. Play your theatricals at home, but as every respectable woman in France, which I shall remind Monsieur Bazille and your Brohan sisters you surely are; you will soon marry a husband suitable for this family."

"But, Papa—"

Papa reared his head rolling his eyes like a challenging stallion. "I arrange a profitable match, Camille. A worthy husband proves a noble ambition."

"It is not my ambition. It's yours."

"*Oui*." Papa removed his hat and swiped his forehead with his handkerchief. "I forgot my odd daughter; my fault in how I raised you."

"Must I now apologize for the independence you prized in my youth?"

"I wish this match, Camille. This path you entertain leads to shame and ruin. No woman without her reputation survives in Paris. Would you break your papa's heart—your sister's?"

Papa's words stung worse than any creature's bite for truth graced his words. "'The more one judges, the less one loves.'"

"And in time—you may not use Balzac so. 'It is a wise father that knows his own child.'"

"Balzac ill-used."

"Ah, you are wrong, *ma fille. The Merchant of Venice*. I win." Papa glanced back at the tobacco shop as if he deserved an award. A morning fruit seller greeted us with his cart. Papa swiped a cluster of grapes winking at me, waving away the seller as a prince, but I knew he paid the merchant in advance. Papa loved his games. We circled a chestnut tree and headed home.

"Must you always win, Papa?" I asked defeated.

We breathed in our Paris, sighing, exhausted by our morning joust. Papa noticed my lazy steps, smiling, surprising me as he led us away from our shop to walk a bit longer. A flower shop in sight, a buxom hussy with blonde curls piled high as a heap of macaroni waved. "*Bonjour*, Monsieur Doncieux, young Camille," Madame Pontray shouted. She buzzed outside her flower shop stocking her stand with spring blooms, the best in the Batignolles.

"*Bonjour*, Madame Pontray," we replied, lost in the scent of lilacs.

Madame Pontray's flower shop exuded fairyland. Lilac trees, scarlet geraniums, and buckets of white carnations bordered her walkway. A table blanketed with ferns showcased piles of pink and red roses, gold baskets brimmed with violets, and shelves stuffed with choice bouquets. Inside, ivy dressed gilded trellises, palms and exotic flowers encased visitors in a storybook garden. Murals of clouds and cherubs drifted across the ceiling. The perfume of her notorious beauty elixirs added romance kissed with the essence of damp soil and spicy flowers. Madame Pontray's flower shop was a treasured escape for her flowers and listening ear.

"A timely visit, monsieur," she gasped, fluttering her lashes at Papa. "You always rescue me from the struggle of this umbrella." Madame Pontray stretched to install the oversized shade to the top of a flower stand. Papa rushed to save her, adjusting the umbrella in place. She snuggled next to him. "This heavy umbrella, though I fancy the purple, my Virgil, bless his soul, knew how to set the old one right."

"The handle teeters in its slot. That is all." Papa slipped out from her entrapment. "I'll fix it tomorrow." She perked up at his promise clutching his hand, winking at me. Flustering Papa was Madame Pontray's cherished diversion. Papa cleared his throat, darting his eyes from her to the umbrella. They stood under its shade diffused in violet light. "Beware, madame, the wind may topple it," he said, untangling his hand from hers.

"I shall anticipate your visit and relish our calm spring morning." A breeze raced through the trees at her words. We watched the umbrella dance. "Well, I cannot fault the trees for their morning stretch." She led our laughter, clinging to Papa. Today, I pleasured in his squirming.

Older in years, underneath her overdone costume Madame Pontray possessed an alluring beauty. Refraining from her typical gaudy toilette, she appeared refined in a pink silk dress, ruffled collar, and lace belt fitted to burst. Remnants of her long-ago extravagance, swags of pearls, draped her neck. She smelled of violets, Papa's favorite. Her ploys proved scandalously entertaining, yet I idolized her freedom and genuine charm making everyone feel adored.

"You're early," she said, stuffing a curl into place. "I have no time today. No time." As a vaudevillian skit, she entertained us with her ongoing flurry. She waved her hands in the air like a circus chimp, rushing into her shop bounding back holding a handful of silk ribbons. She wriggled her eyebrows puzzled, finger on chin striking a regal pose, and dashed into her shop swiftly returning balancing a stack of shifting white paper and a mound of pink roses.

"It will be fine, *ma chère*," Papa said, turning her cheeks to cherry.

"*Merci*, Monsieur Doncieux." Her wobbly curtsey nearly toppled the umbrella.

"As life must be fine and in order," I said, recounting Papa's indifference toward my artistic endeavors. "Madame Pontray, what is your opinion on women's rights?" I asked, gathering a bundle of forget-me-nots.

"Child, an ill-timed subject," she whispered, shaking her head, nodding toward Papa.

"Papa, have you no Shakespeare as your answer?"

"I'm contemplating a pipe. A short cutty, mind you, as I inspect Lafarge's window. Some reasonable timepieces; he's late this morning."

"Papa would rather suffer a shave from Mamma's hurried hand than throw in with us," I whispered to Madame Pontray. "We may speak freely."

"I'm busy, child," she sighed, sorting ribbons. "If mademoiselle wishes her flowers to be ready on time, I must work. And your mother, heavens. The fit she'll have if they are late."

"You forget, my daughter," Papa said, "I run a dress shop where I hear women's chatter on independence all day. Must you subject me to it now?"

Madame Pontray tucked a pink rosebud in my hair ensuring solidarity. "Exquisite against your chocolate tresses; Camille needs a touch of rose lip salve; a drop of angel water, divine. Come this afternoon; I have a cucumber pomade to brighten your complexion."

Beaten, Papa strolled away. "I ponder at Lafarge's window a bit longer."

"I knew the talk of toilettes would rub him," she snickered. "Now, what ails you today?"

"Suppose a daughter," I began, "a child no longer, wished to dream of endeavors that excluded a match by her father to one muley gentleman—"

"Why, Monsieur Valentine is a handsome soldier. I know well his family. Oh, my Virgil was a dashing lad with a copper head; his fair complexion mapped nary a freckle. A regimen of walnut water dulls the amber glow."

I squinted at her to Papa's laughter. "A man she scarcely knows."

"*Oui*, a two-week courtship shall allay your fears."

Papa's laughter fueled me on. "Only after marriage, France will then declare me a French national. What am I now without a husband? A woman by birth, and for this, my country will not claim me unless I tie myself to a man. Am I not its citizen alone?"

"I married Virgil at seventeen, your mother married at sixteen—forgive me, monsieur."

"Papa cannot hear us. He's memorizing prices to haggle with the shop-keeper at lunch."

"Dear, you're wise in business and fashion beyond your years, but you long to remain Papa's girl, no? *Ma chère,* this will never change." She watered her geraniums. "Fine coloring."

"Is it fair my husband will own my property, dowry, comings and goings?" I paced in front of a frantic Madame Pontray. "France permits Amiable Husband to wander Paris carousing—"

"Camille," Papa and Madame Pontray squealed.

"Squandering a useful education, whereas, Suitable Wife will have none."

"To the point, child," she moaned, sweeping her stoop.

"Amiable Husband may have his sordid affairs." I chased her, hopping and dodging puffs of dust. "They jail Suitable Wife for the mere thought of Flaubert's *Madame Bovary.*"

"Enough." Papa returned. Madame Pontray raised an eyebrow at me to continue.

"If for a moment, a daughter declined this match I would live the life of a man, free to roam, work, love, and embrace the truth: my eyes are not sinful stirring at the sight of vibrant fashions or actors on a stage. I wish to act, own a dress shop as my papa, make women beautiful, and look beautiful not for a man for myself, daring to live as a modern woman in our new Paris." Madame Pontray tossed her broom for timid applause.

Papa swept in. "Madame, I apologize. We'll expect our arrangements this afternoon."

"But Papa, you and Mamma married without a contract."

"You shame our family in front of Madame Pontray?"

"Love holds no shame. I am not in love, Papa."

"Peace." Madame Pontray raised a bundle of roses as a sabre quieting our fray. "Time alone, monsieur. *S'il vous plaît.*" She tamed Papa's temper, ushering him back to Lafarge's window. "*Ma chère.*" She sauntered toward me. "I run a sliver of a shop with pride. Oh, I hear what they say about me. So what," she whispered, tying perfect ribbons around roses without looking. "They gossip about lots like us who make noise because *they* are jealous."

"They?"

"Ladies who wish to do yet do nothing. Rebellion holds excitement and danger."

"More is a word I regret I ever learned." I fussed with ferns on her cart.

She quieted my hands. "More for yourself is futile; more from yourself—

why, surely your papa claims this as a noble endeavor. Give him time, Camille." She handed me a basket of lilacs juggling three. We arranged them on a table. "'White hair often covers the head, but the heart that holds it is ever young.'" I smiled, impressed. "Ah, you didn't know I knew some Balzac. Take heart." We stared at Papa. He turned around thumbs in his vest strolling back. "Your tall, handsome father makes it difficult for a woman to refrain from coquetry, no?"

"Papa is the kindest soul in Paris. Mamma knows his handsome, gray eyes invite mischief, but he has never strayed."

"Periwinkle, dear." She caught herself with her first knotted ribbon. With a hearty laugh, she resumed spying on Papa. "Shall we abandon your charming father for a stroll in my greenhouse? My son Charlie finished it, a fine home for my azaleas. We'll bellow our hearts to the flowers; they will not quip back." Her laugh rose and fell toward Papa. "Camille, in time you will learn your father only wishes to protect you."

"You always cheer me, Madame Pontray." I welcomed her gentle embrace.

"It's time you call me Elise. We address each other as equals, though no others shall."

"Elise." I plucked hairpins from my satchel and tamed her stray curls. "Times are changing." I grew melancholy again unable to win a true supporter of the cause.

"Do not seek the approval of men. If conviction leads your heart, if it is worthy, pursue it. Don't expect a certain society to receive you. Walk among your own, be happy thus."

"I cannot marry a man I do not love."

She spotted her reflection in the window approving my handiwork. "What do I know? I'm a middle-aged widow forced to work; this hardly makes me base but happy. One may not always have a choice, but one may always choose happiness."

We admired Papa stuck to the glass at Monsieur Lafarge's window. "*Merci.* Your rosebud in my hair sweetened my morning."

"'That which we call a rose by any other name would smell as sweet,'" Papa said.

With an alluring smile, Elise handed him a pink rose tied with a lavender ribbon. "This may serve as a peace offering. Who won today?" she asked.

"Papa. He always wins." I craved Elise's company, divulging matters I could no longer share with my mother. Mamma discussed only marriage contracts, money, and the Paris salons she must invade for the Doncieux's self-preservation. "Social prominence ensures survival in Paris. Opportunity, my daughters." Upon our arrival in Paris, Mamma climbed the ranks of French society, no longer satisfied with our station at the bottom of the bourgeoisie. "Paris," she said, toasting her champagne. "Where pleasures are born, tasted, and die before sundown." She carried her letter of introduction and reinvention, made a successful showing at her first soirée, now judged eligible guest and invited to the fêtes of the season. While most daughters cling to their mother's instruction, I fled mine, wishing for the simple life of Elise and her flowers.

Elise nudged me awake. "Take care of your papa, Camille. He looks a tad peaked."

"He craves a cigarette, Elise." I fancied our newfound friendship.

"Savor a violet; it will bring you tranquility—a mug of ale works too. *Au revoir.*"

During our laughter, a handsome gentleman approached, scrutinizing her peonies. He lifted the flower pondering it in the light, tilting it as a looking glass as if searching for a prism of color. Next, he examined, as the most pressing tasks, a basket of lilacs, cradling a cluster as a maiden's cheek. He glanced at me, this dandy with dark hair and olive skin as Papa, flaunting his tailored frock coat, fiddling with the lace cuffs dangling from his shirtsleeves.

"Garish," I whispered, eyeing his lace. The man stared again, no longer at the lilacs, me, under the watchful glare of Papa. The young man smirked, indifferent, inspecting wildflowers, noticing me again—this time as his study. His handsome, brown eyes crowned with dark lashes traced my face, my form. He tipped his hat to Papa, staring back at me without careful measure.

"*Bonjour*, monsieur, mademoiselle," he said, holding a bundle of peonies.

"*Bonjour*, monsieur," Papa said, tugging my arm. "*Au revoir*, madame."

"Not you," Elise said to the young man. "You owe me three portraits."

"An artist," I whispered, lingering behind; Papa walked on. "I forgot to ask Elise about the sugared violets, Papa." I caught up with him. "A present for Genèvieve."

Papa looked back at Elise; she wiggled her fingers inviting us back. Papa declined, waving her off. "Settle your business with Elise while I pick up Genèvieve's cake."

My heart raced at his answer and the chance to learn more about the artist perusing the flowers. "Remember, my father, my sister fancies lemon."

"My father? Flattery once again?"

"Mamma insists I'm too old to call you Papa." I glanced back at Elise. She argued, flailing her arms while the handsome artist stood patiently.

"I fancy Papa." He handed me my rose. "Go. Spend your time with Elise. Lemon cake? Your mother insisted on a strawberry tart; I shall buy both and take the scolding."

"Papa, how we press your patience." I gave him my hug and rose.

"A houseful of women, but I should have it no other way." He kissed my forehead and looked back at Elise. "The dandy riles Madame Pontray. Perhaps, I should accompany you."

"And spend our morning fixing umbrellas and arranging flowers?" I smoothed my hair fidgeting to leave. "I will study the draper's window for ideas and design an attractive display for our sale today. Wait for me at the patisserie. You must give me another crack at Balzac."

"My daughter makes a fine point." Papa stuffed his thumbs into his vest and studied me as the artist, not so intrigued. "Be careful there." He eyed the dandy looking into me. Papa flagged down the pastry cook now sweeping his stoop. "Monsieur Allard!"

"Lemon cake, Papa," I called out.

6.

Camille

I hovered near Madame Pontray's, searching in the neighboring draper's window. "His lace is poorly displayed," I said to myself, glancing back at the artist cradling his flowers.

He tipped his hat to me and smiled, turned back to Elise and said, "Madame, you're mistaken. I paid my account in full."

"Do not stumble to me from your midnight ball with your demands. Lad, go back to bed."

I muffled my snicker, edging closer.

"Madame, is it not an honor a famous artist as I, Claude Monet, chooses to paint your flowers, the finest in Paris? Colors so pure, the gods must deliver these blooms entrusting them to your care. I'm doing an important work and could visit any stand—"

He dodged Elise's wet towel as she wiped her windows. "Do what you must." She took his bundle of her prized peonies and arranged them back on the table.

The artist searched the sky for his next words. He scratched his head; his dark hair fell in careless waves to his chin. Unlike the other artists in the Batignolles, he wore no beard but the shadow of a missed shave, his face flushed with impatience now. "Elise," the artist blared with a clap as if a marvelous idea. "I will title my work *Madame Pontray's Spring Flowers*." He grabbed her hand twirling her to his imaginary music. She giggled as a girl soon turning skeptic. "You may hang my painting in your shop window until it's sold. Why, a crowd will gather. Wouldn't you welcome your name and shop recognized by all of Paris?" he asked, nearly hitting Elise's shifty umbrella with his grand gesture.

"Serves you right if it crushes your dull topper." I held my laugh spying behind a tree.

"You've never been accepted by the Salon," Elise snapped, unmoved by his charm.

The young artist lowered his head admiring the flowers. Elise spotted me lingering. "I thought you believed in me, madame. You're wrong," he said, sniffing forget-me-nots.

"Their fragrance blooms in the evening, monsieur." Elise came to him, touching his arm softly. "You will smell nothing now."

"And who else but Madame Pontray would tell me this? The Salon accepted two of my marines this year. I bring your flowers to the dinner in my honor boasting about Madame Pontray's bouquets. My benefactor and his wife fancy your roses shopping nowhere else, *oui*?"

"Now you shame me into offering you my flowers." Under this artist's spell, Elise wrapped his bundle of peonies, added a basket of lilacs and a cone of white roses and violets.

"Monsieur, you should be ashamed of yourself." I burst in. I was certain Papa would have obliged. I snatched the basket of lilacs from the charlatan to his amusement.

"Mademoiselle Doncieux," Elise scolded.

"I would have taken you for a gentleman," I continued. "If you haven't a sou, shoo."

"Shoo?" He laughed, folding his arms impressed with my manner.

"I'm sorry if I offend, but we deal with your types. One as you never intends on paying."

"Such boldness, mademoiselle, but you know not my arrangement with Madame Pontray. I paid twice the cost for these flowers compared to the market."

"Go there." I winked at Elise. "Look." I showed off a small bouquet. "Rosebuds, sprays of mignonette, a sprig of myrtle tied with a fine ribbon elegantly arranged for five sous."

"I have lost all reasoning to my once quiet morning," Elise declared. "Under the scolding I shall surely receive from your father, Camille, I'm leaving—Monsieur Monet, to fetch you a fresher geranium. I'll expect you for a sitting to paint my son's portrait this afternoon."

"*Oui*, madame," the artist said, grinning at me.

With all reluctance, Elise made introductions. "Monsieur Claude Monet,

Mademoiselle Camille Doncieux and her father yonder who watches with all diligence—as do I." She plucked the basket of lilacs out of my hand, handed them back to Monsieur Monet, and skipped away in one of her flurries. "Too busy. Too busy."

The young artist set his basket down and placed his bundle of peonies on the table waiting for me to speak. I rushed to a corner of the flower stand rearranging the ferns jumbled in the tussle of baskets and bouquets. "Mademoiselle, you offer me no chance to retain my honor?"

"Elise is like a mother to me. I don't fancy seeing her swindled." I handed him a bundle of orange pansies. "The warmth you need for your painting, monsieur. Her hydrangeas hold a shade of blush that brightens in the light."

"I planned to return for them. But now—"

"I apologize for my boldness, not the defense of my friend."

"In painting my pictures I lose all reason, seeing nothing but the subject before me until I finish. Let's start over. I am Claude Monet, the artist."

I abandoned the ferns, snickering. "An artist—as if I didn't know—cobalt on your fingernails, yellow smears on your jacket." I muffled my laugh fussing with Elise's crooked umbrella. "You state your name as a constellation Cassiopeia or Hercules."

He smirked, studying the purple umbrella against the turquoise sky. "Mademoiselle, I don't mind your independence when it's not seeded in rudeness. Women's rights, did you say?"

I spun around to him biting my tongue. He searched me for my reply, and when I offered none, he chuckled, inching closer, studying the umbrella. I took in a hurried breath as a soft wind swirled between us. "'This rudeness is a sauce to his good wit, which gives men stomach to digest his words with better appetite.'" I pounded my fist on the flower stand to Papa's imagined approval—Elise's umbrella came crashing down upon us.

I closed my eyes, opening them to Monsieur Monet's, free of harm as he made haste to catch it. "It seems we are caught under the grip of a monster," he said. Pleased with himself, he lifted the umbrella shielding us in purple light, smirking at my reluctance to leave out from under it. We huddled underneath the shade; a violet shadow dressed his button nose. *A childish nose*, I thought. *Yet he's no boy.* His face shown no stubble but was clean-shaven splashed with lemon, spearmint, and cloves. I could not move; I did not want to.

"'If my dear love were but the child of state,'" he said, readjusting the rosebud in my hair. "'It might for Fortune's bastard be unfather'd / As subject to Time's love or to Time's hate, / Weeds among weeds, or flowers with flowers gather'd. / No; it was builded far from accident.'" He smiled, gesturing to our umbrella making me laugh. I soaked in his tender gaze. He bowed and repositioned the umbrella over Elise's stand. His sonnet won me. "I welcomed staying under it," he whispered, "but alas, Madame Pontray's flowers demand a cast of lilac shade."

Perhaps he was a famous artist accustomed to loose women begging for their portraits. *I am not one of them*, I thought. "Monsieur, I come from a good family and do not play about on whims with dandies, frolic during odd hours in the night at brassieres, and I don't go into ateliers alone with eager artists proclaiming themselves a rising star in our wondrous heavens."

He snickered to himself, fueling my anger, waving his hand to calm me. "Mademoiselle, I meant my friends think as you. I embrace independent thinking, breaking from the confinements of antiquity. Perhaps you would enjoy meeting them. But, *mon amie*, you must leave your scowl at home." He backed away feigning fear, coaxing my smile.

"I fancied your use of the sonnet, monsieur."

"The good fortune of our accident with that umbrella; I watched it teetering above you."

"You are odd, Claude Monet, the *artist*." I laughed. "As opposed to butcher or baker?"

"Perhaps you would have dined with me if I introduce myself as ragpicker? Don't laugh. I know many wealthy ragpickers. Fortunes abound."

"Songbird sellers make a fine living." I enjoyed our play. He no longer fiddled with shirt cuffs, yet I now tugged at the fringe on my shawl. "Lucy Lamb." I settled my hands. "She rears and tames songbirds, teaches them tunes if you can believe such a thing."

"I don't believe it." He moved closer studying me as he did the peony in the light. He tilted his head eyeing my lips, my hair, spotting the lick of black hair curled near my ear I never tamed. Not a trace of shyness exuded from his stare. I followed his gaze, his dark, brooding eyes transfixed upon me as a hypnotist waving a trinket on a chain.

"It is true," I said under my breath.

"How much more successful she would be as Lucy Larkspur." He took liberties turning my head into the light as his flower, his rough fingertips brushing lightly across my chin.

"Lucy Linnet," I whispered, leaning into him. "Monsieur?"

"Tell me more," he said, eyeing my dress. "You are exquisite." We exhaled together. Releasing me from his spell, I backed away turning my eyes downcast, hiding my smile. "That is the pose. You have modeled, no? I have seen your face."

I caught my breath at a flutter of nerves. "Songbirds dread thunderstorms, and a rusty nail in water improves their health, the iron you see." He grinned amused. "You mean to mock me."

"No, mademoiselle." He touched my shoulder to stop me from leaving. "Your Lyonnais accent . . ." He smiled to himself. "Reminds me of my mother's."

"Your mother is from Lyon? She must miss it, as I."

"My mother is gone." He snatched his flowers. "The blame of my unruly nature, for my aunt now sees to my taming, but alas, the pleasures of Paris ruin me. Forgive me."

We stood in silence admiring the tables strewn with a rainbow of flowers.

"Monsieur, my condolences; your mother must have been beautiful as my mother. They say women from Lyon—I would be bold to continue."

"Women from Lyon possess more beauty than any in France. Lyon knows nothing other than dark hair, fair skin, and calf's eyes on their women which make for exquisite beauty."

"Calf's eyes? Do we all moo, too?" He welcomed our laugh. His hand brushed mine.

"Is he your father? The man waves you on as frantic as Elise."

"Papa assures my sister receives the lemon cake she wanted for her party."

Monsieur Monet admired me again, this time I did not look away. He smiled, stroking his chin for his missing beard. "Near the Madeline is a bakery," he said. "Madame Busque and her specialty of pumpkin pie, an

American treat that's tolerable. She makes a hearty apple pie and doughnuts for the Americans who invade Paris."

"Papa calls them savages."

"I know well this name."

"This pumpkin pie might serve for great amusement at our table, but my mother requires perfection and tradition."

"Is she judge at the Salon? I'm impatient at my own imperfection. I enjoy observing imperfect things, yet, strive to paint them perfectly."

"I confess I have no idea what you said. But I can assure you if you seek perfection, the peonies you have selected will make poor models."

"How so?"

"The pale pink flowers are stunning, but they quickly fade to white. They will not hold their color and will frustrate you who seem astute as to the light and color that stirs you."

"It is not so much what attracts my eye, but how it makes me feel."

"Feel, monsieur?"

"The blush of these pink roses offers me the sensation of peace."

"Innocence . . . I think of my sister as I savor these, how innocent she is about everything. Flowers are innocent. They simply grow; provide us beauty and fragrance, and that is all."

"I beg to differ. Flowers mend arguments; they invite love and comfort hearts." He offered me a sprig of forget-me-nots from his bundle.

"Festiva Maxima boasts a white bloom with flecks of crimson sturdy for your constant repositioning, yet it may not suggest the delicacy you require for your picture."

"I don't mind strong flowers."

I traded his bundle for a cone of white peonies. "Madame Lemoine meets your desire for a sturdy peony. White blooms, a hint of yellow, and a rose perfume that will permeate your studio. How the light will dance off those petals, monsieur."

"And yet, the one I held from the start." I looked inside his first bundle of peonies; they were the same. "But, mademoiselle, I took great delight in your argument."

"Don't you value the proper use of color in art?"

"Proper? How should one measure a sunset? Does God proclaim He shall only yellow with azure one day—crimson and vermillion the next? No. The sky is a swirl of wonderment: honey, apricot, cherry, plum, and cider."

"You sound like you're making a wonderful punch."

"As is our sky, a variable taste of refreshment to quench the thirst for a pure, simple thing. We must not confine beauty to a mere scheme of minimal color. It is why the sunlight reflects as many colors as combinations of notes on a piano. God has ensured the painter, as composer, is left with no shortage of inspiration from His array of colors from nature."

"Surely one must possess a measure of taste, for all notes played at once ring horrid."

"I see you're are a woman of cultivated fashion; your rule may stand for costume and floral adornments in a salon, but if an artist dare not attempt anything beyond the confinements of technique, one's school of dictation, there will hardly be any new art imagined or created. One may be lazy in seeing and doing, but an artist lazy in both is no artist and plays at painting."

"'If we could but paint with the hand what we see with the eye,'" I whispered, wrapping his forget-me-not sprig around my wrist.

"Sweet lass, you quote Balzac as my mother," he said, tying the knot. "You are graced with surprises."

"This is not the draper's window," Papa interrupted.

"Monsieur Doncieux," Elise bellowed, rushing out of her shop. "I have your geraniums, Monsieur Monet, and your sugared violets, Camille, with an extra bunch for your father. Monsieur Doncieux, come inside—settle your account and review your flowers. I'm behind already, and we shall not declare whose fault this is."

Elise rushed Papa into her shop before he could say no. "Camille, come child," he said, scowling at Monsieur Monet.

"I've seen that look before." Monsieur Monet laughed. When Papa and a giggling Elise disappeared into the shop, I paused as Claude Monet lifted my wrist tenderly and kissed it. "I shall paint you," he whispered.

I thrilled at the thought, his touch, his breath tickling my ear and swiftly left the artist at the flower stand with his thoughts of colors and light.

7.

Sophie

The most exotic place I visited on my vacation was the patio furniture section at Hardware Haven at seven a.m. I wandered to the paint department around seven fifteen. Six seemed too desperate. Seven fifteen, the place was empty, and my nerves didn't have to dodge an over-aggressive mallet pounding on paint cans. "Nostalgic Evening." I contemplated the stormy-blue swatch, swaying to Lenny Kravitz belting "Fly Away." *Another at-home vacation*, I thought. "I'll pitch that at the travel agency." I rolled my eyes at my staycation over Paris. "It's cheaper." A woman with frizzy hair smiled at me pointing to her cell. I spaced at the pinks. Frizzy distanced herself picking through paintbrushes. "Pink front doors are for fairy tales."

Frizzy groaned. "You're losing it," she said, glaring at me.

"Excuse me?" I blushed.

"Cuckoo, Eileen." Frizzy lurched behind a pyramid of primer. "Wait, this woman—"

"Dot dot dot." I pondered Wild Violet. "I thought you were talking—" Lenny's *yeah, yeah, yeah* cut out, so did Frizzy. The curse of satellite radio struck early. I drifted to the neutrals. "Timid White, Polar Bear, Frost."

Silence.

There's a difference between a silence that signals a beginning and one that declares the end, Mom whispered in my thoughts. *In a painting, white is a powerful silence.* "Is that what this is?" I asked no one.

"White signifies anticipation, possibilities, madame."

"That restless excitement before the curtain opens at a show. I can't feel it," I said to myself. "I don't want to." I stared at a handful of white swatches, struggling to see the minute differences Mom taught me: cotton, snowfall, eggshell. *Silence.*

I rustled the cards to get rid of the quiet. My thumping heart took over. I concentrated on the static of a deep breath through my nostrils, a swirling winter wind on its release. "Not now," I whispered, inhaling another gust of wind. Maple Leaf drifted to the floor, Stormy Cloud. I closed my eyes waiting for the sounds I needed to come back in tune. "Not here." A flush washed my skin. *Inhale.* Cedar replaced wet paint taking me to Mom's back-yard deck: summer parties for her patrons, my wedding reception, our last talk sipping wine in the moonlight.

I used to long for silence, hold it in my hands as a child cradling a baby chick, absorb the things no one takes the time to listen to anymore, strive to see clearly, deeply. *See. Sophia.* "I'm drowning in ugly choices, Mom." I opened my eyes to a strip of yellow.

Since I was five, my artist mother taught me how to "see." To observe minute details in nature, people, moments in life: colors, emotions, the slightest variations catalog, remember, paint them, *see*. While other kids made whistles out of blades of grass, Mom and I dissected the colors: lemon to an eggshell line center fanning out to lime sherbet ending in green bean. My brain houses an almanac of painted memories, good and bad, whether I want them or not. No one wants to remember death, why we say passed and loss. Death is too midnight. "Indigo Rapture?" *Warm blueberry syrup, melted butter over a stack of Mom's pancakes.*

"Too gray, madame."

Now I do what I can to fill the silence. It's easy. I've done it since I was ten in the way we all do because we can't absorb the quiet—it's too compli-cated . . . painful.

"Magical." I found my smile, staring into the lavender swatch picturing myself nestled on Mom's window seat. *Magical thinking isn't a problem—it's a gift. My Sophia has a gift.* "Stellar intro to your "friend" Dr. Arnold, Mom," I said, seeing her lavender clad living room, my heart racing. I closed my eyes, recalling the last time we were all together.

~

"It's one session, *ma fille*," Mom said. "A harmless chat, that's all."

"Mom, you're the queen of 'that's all,' which is never that's all."

She dragged me to her sofa upholstered in a vibrant chinoiserie print of birds and flowers. I buried myself under the Beast tracing magenta peo-nies. "Talk to him." Mom revealed her latest masterpiece *Sunflower Field,* a painting of a field of sunflowers in the distance, sunny yellow petals floating against a turquoise sky, rows of lavender swaying off the canvas.

"You're still painting the little girl with the sunhat."

She pinched my cheek, leaving a dot of blue. "You will always be *ma petit chère*."

I wore her crocheted blanket as a cape. "This isn't on you, Mom."

"Sophia, you lost your husband. We're still working through your father's death."

"When you say lost, you mean my mind, don't you?" I dropped the blanket on the sofa and held up a box of microwave popcorn and a movie. "*The Wreck of the Mary Dreary*."

"*Mary Deare*. You never want to talk about painful things, but I see."

"Dreary is better. Come on, Mom, Gary Cooper."

"You carry too much." Mom rubbed her nose leaving a dot of blue matching my cheek. "Talk to him. I'll make dinner and my scrummy vanilla pound cake. A chat."

Dr. Arnold dinners and chats at Mom's house every Thursday. Mom tried to fix it all.

"Hiiii. I'm Dr. Arnold, Soophhiahh. Nice to meeet youuu."

I hate limp handshakes, and I would rather have a colonoscopy right now. "Sophie," I said, tracing a parrot on Mom's chinoiserie sofa. "And I have twenty-twenty hearing."

"Sophie," he said, scanning Mom, me. "It suits you."

A fist bump. Seriously? Mom folded her arms giving me the stink eye. I hunkered down under pillows. "Dr. Arnold, what does it mean when someone says the name you've had your whole life suits you?" I asked. "How do you know if it doesn't suit you? What do you do when someone says you're not a Sophie, you're a Lucy? This is troubling to me now."

"Sophia, don't show your mean side, it's too soon." Mom ushered Dr. Arnold to the couch across from me, leaving a cheese and fruit tray. He sunk in, attacked by purple pillows.

"Beautiful home, Josephine." He dug out from under the pillows. "Clean as a whistle."

"I never understood that expression, Dr. Arnold," I said. "Whistles aren't very clean, are they? Where do you even buy whistles? Are they only for coaches and cops?"

Mom slipped a laugh.

"Well, Sophie." He smashed his praying hands to his lips. "It references the idea for a whistle to work it must be clean of all debris. Your mom's house simply works."

"Dr. Arnold, look closer you'll see debris. No house is spotless."

His nose twitched and he did that middle-finger-pushes-up-your-glasses tick, that made me wonder if he was secretly flipping me the bird. "I like you're intuitive, Sophie."

He had one heck of a penetrating stare. *A charmer, good for Mom.* "Inquisitive." I popped a hunk of cheddar in my mouth. "*Merci*, Mom." She scurried away.

"Of course."

Middle finger number two.

"Let me be honest," he whispered. "Jo thought I could help you. I don't usually speak with patients outside my office, let alone with the daughter of a woman I'm dating."

Jo? "Wait a minute . . . *you're* Brian?" I choked on a grape. "OMG, *magical* Brian?"

"She said that?"

Middle finger number three.

Mom rushed in with two glasses of iced tea. "What are you two smiling about?"

"I'm getting to know Brian." I toasted Mom with my glass. "I mean . . . Dr. Arnold—he's *magical.*" I blew out a laugh. Dr. Arnold crawled under the Beast.

"Sophia's a master at changing the subject." Mom pelted him with a pillow and vanished.

"All right, Sophie." He slipped off his glasses. I caught Mom's attraction. He had a strong chin like my dad, clean-shaven, fit and a gorgeous head of chestnut hair with gray patches. "I'll be honest with you if you think you can be straightforward with me."

"Do you know if this bird is an olive-headed lorikeet?" I asked, pointing to Mom's sofa.

Psychobabble, intrusive questions and "chats" to help with my inability to express pain, inefficiency to face the truth, efficiency at holding onto my hurtful past, abandonment issues, anxiety, dissociative disorder, depersonalization dot dot dot. It took five hippie dinners for Dr. Arnold to turn me into a dot dot dot. Detachment this, regret that, Sophie Noel Dot Dot Dot.

"Are you ever going to show me what you've been writing?" I asked him.

"It's your turn." He handed me a lavender journal—Mom's creation, Mom's idea.

It teetered limp in my hands. Its blue ribbon held a bedazzled sunflower charm dangling across the spine. My heart fluttered and I dropped it.

"Are you all right?" Dr. Arnold asked, handing it back.

"Ribbons. Mom has this thing about covering ugly things with ribbons."

"Is this journal ugly to you?"

I read her inscription: *For my Sophia. You have much to say. It's time. Love, Maman.* I closed the journal and threw it on the table behind me. "I don't do journals."

"It's a gift from your mom." Dr. Arnold dropped the journal over my head onto my lap.

I held it. "Would you like to see her painting *Carousel*? It's my favorite."

"Think of it as a sort of brain dump," he continued without a hitch.

"Dr. Arnold, I've confided things about my husband I haven't shared with Mom. But unanswered questions—that's the game of life, isn't it? I made my peace years ago with the apologies I'm never going to get."

"Have you?"

I thumbed through the journal's blank pages. "I don't know how to fill these," I said, surprised tears invaded my voice.

"There's no right or wrong way, Sophie. Is there anyone you can talk to?"

I stared at Mom's words again, the lavender journal our favorite color. "I used to talk with Blake until he started talking at me." I adjusted Mom's picture frames on the fireplace mantle. I smiled at the first photo: gangly, twelve-year-old me in a red dress at Christmas. "She kept this one of us, that's my dad. I didn't know it was up here." I stared at the second photo: me, Mom and Dad in front of the Eiffel Tower. "I can't even remember who took the photo."

"Would you like to talk about Paris?"

I swallowed, going for another hunk of cheese. "I'm a firm believer not everything happens for a reason. Things happen. The past is the past. There's nothing I can do about it. Move on. Mom's been telling me to move on since I was ten—when we were on our own."

"You mean after your parents' divorce?"

"Does talking to God count? Mom encourages it." I adjusted a beaded frame with a photo of Mom and me at her art gallery. "Her grand opening here . . . special day." I ambled back to the couch and stared at Dr. Arnold. "Dead people can't answer questions, so you move on."

"Our sessions don't have to end. Your mom's worried about you. Your friends—"

"I don't have any friends."

"What about your coworkers Joe and Jacey?"

I wandered to Mom's latest painting: a canvas washed in sky-blue, a drifting pink balloon, and Mom's little girl wearing the sunhat stretching for the sky. "This one's creepy to me. Mom doesn't do creepy. She can't have all this negativity around here. It's our last session."

"Visit me at my office."

"Do you like her paintings? You never mention them. Most men in her life rarely did except my dad. He loved her paintings."

"Are you still having panic attacks?"

I escaped to the kitchen, poured two glasses of milk, and grabbed the Oreos. "If you want deep, ask Mom to let you read her stack of journals in her hope chest. She thinks we're related to the artist Claude Monet—well, his first wife, Camille. My Dad believed it. I did too. Many people claim a famous distant relative. Mom imagines it for her art; it connects us in some way."

"What if you view your journal as letters to say . . . an imaginary friend? Have you ever had an imaginary friend, Sophie?"

I offered Dr. Arnold his glass of milk. He grabbed an Oreo and dunked. "If I say yes, you'll dot dot dot me." I filled my two front teeth with cream.

"Many children have imaginary friends," he continued, eyeing me.

I dunked an Oreo. He waited. "My best friend growing up Megan Hilly killed her."

"Let's talk more about that."

"I figured you'd want to."

Dr. Arnold downed his milk and wiped his lips with his sleeve. Catching himself, he smiled and nodded for me to continue.

"Gimbletook . . . a princess fairy," I mumbled. "This is embarrassing, kid stuff." I held up an Oreo, studying its dark chocolate wafer. "What are these hieroglyphics on the cookie? Are they florets, crosses, or four-leaf clovers?"

Dr. Arnold examined the cookie and snickered. "What happened to Gimbletook?"

I set my cookies aside. "Gimbletook was a fairy tale I playacted. All kids pretend."

"Talking to ourselves is completely normal."

"Okay. I was thirteen. Mom got a letter from Dad . . . bad news. I ran to the park. Megan saw me talking to an empty swing; Gimbletook turned human for the day. 'You're nuts,' Megan said. 'Gimbletook's dead, weirdo fairy girl.' I ran home and bawled to Mom, but I should have raced from Megan my entire life. Mom said, 'Sophia, you're too old for an imaginary friend.' It stung Mom siding with Megan. I didn't have the easiest childhood. It wasn't normal."

"Keep going."

"I didn't care about Megan killing Gimbletook; Megan did it to hurt me. She knew how hard it was for Mom and me: a new town, school. How could a best friend be so cruel?" I sipped my milk, wishing Mom would walked in to save me. "I sound childish. It doesn't matter now, does it?"

"This wasn't the first time Megan hurt you?"

"Hurting me was Megan's hobby. I was an idiot, a thirteen-year-old, twenty-year-old, and thirty-year-old idiot to let Megan back into my life."

"This friend Megan . . . is she still around?"

"No, she has nothing left to take." I gathered my things to leave, clutching the journal. "Thanks. I don't mind being a dot dot dot. Maybe in a year or so I'll lose a few. Take the Oreos."

"The journal, write a few pages." He handed me his card. "We all talk to ourselves. Talk out loud when you feel anxious. So anxious, you start having those problems with your heart."

"Dr. Arnold, isn't this grieving? I lost my dad and husband in a row. Everything caved in on me. I thought going away—"

"You mean killing yourself?"

I turned back to Mom's photos on the mantelpiece: her happy daughter, proud graduate and over the moon bride; Mom stood by my side in every one. "We make an unbeatable team." I had no idea who that happy person was, the woman who was supposed to be Sophie Noel, and it frightened me. "I would have never done it. I wouldn't have done that to my mom."

"You've suffered a traumatic experience. I'm assured now more than one. Sophie, it's not about going back to the past to revisit old wounds. It's about finding something you may have lost along the way, and—"

"Getting it back," I whispered.

"So you can freely 'move on' as you say. Don't you want to do that?"

"When I do, I smash into another roadblock. I'm tired of car crashes and losing people."

"Playact again, Sophie, vent the painful stories of the day. Purge them on paper. It's one step. Journals are wonderful expressions for grief, anger, and resentment."

"You always sound like a negative feeling store." Depleted, I headed for the door. "Haven't you ever wanted to be left alone? I've had a lifetime filled with people, and now I'm there. I just want to be left alone."

"You believe you're invincible, the strong one. You're above having another nervous breakdown. You're going to have to trust again."

"Weren't you supposed to tell me how to do that?"

"You must find out for yourself. If you don't give yourself permission to heal, you may have another breakdown. You need to find your way back home." He handed me his card again.

I took it this time, a placid white card, a few silver words. I read it. "'We know what we are, but not what we may be.'" I stared into him, swallowing tears. "Shakespeare."

"*Hamlet*, Ophelia. Your mom loved my own motto: Healing hearts and minds."

"Can you, Dr. Arnold? Can you heal a heart?"

"Time can, Sophie. Give yourself time."

"I lost two people I love. I didn't always understand them, but I knew how to love them."

"What about yourself?"

I folded the card in my coat pocket wondering if I would ever use it. "*Au revoir*, work calls. I'll write, talk it out, and brain dump to conquer my dot dot dots."

"Sophie." Dr. Arnold slapped my back and slipped the lavender journal I left on Mom's couch back into my arms. "You're going to be all right."

"She's already all right." Mom entered. "Are we done here?" And in Mom and Sophie Noel fashion we buried it. I buried it. Mom grabbed her proverbial "You're going to be all right" stamp, stamped it on my forehead, and we "moved on." Just like Dr. Arnold warned me not to.

I clung to her, our painting lessons, teas, dinners, goodnight phone calls, and movie nights. When Mom became sick, I was Sophie Noel Dot Dot Dot again, and I met Claude Monet.

I still talk to God, but I met Monet because I would have stepped off the planet.

8.

Sophie

"Thank you for visiting Hardware Haven. Don't forget to check out our power tool sale in aisle six." The announcement startled me back to the present. A misty paint swatch display in view. I gazed into the prism of cards, and at the whirl of a fan, their edges flapped and fluttered as a rush of butterflies, brushing my chin, fingertips, landing on petals and puddles. I closed my eyes breathing in nature, the scent of mowed grass and lilacs gone.

A cold chill shot through my body reminding me of this winter.

The static of R&B faded in and out over the loudspeaker spastic as my breathing. "Morning Sky," I said, shifting my thoughts, imagining my door covered in blue cotton candy.

"No, madame, too garish."

"Antique Peony? I can't find Peace. Wild Sun—"

"Blue is more durable, madame," Monet said with his critical stare. "Welcoming as a cobalt sky strewn with sunlight."

"I love a cloudy day, a bit of gray in my blue, *très magnifique.*" I studied another lavender swatch. I know why I need to fill the silence. Maybe it's a dream now because I can't remember the last time I embraced the quiet as that child cuddling the chick.

I turned back to the display overwhelmed by the simplest choice of one color, one color to transform my orange front door into something sublime, one stupid, inconsequential color to *move on.* "Cinnamon Squares." Anger seared my chest. "Blake, you picked it to annoy me. You knew I wanted Peace." I scanned the reds, halting at a slice of orange. A flush singed my cheeks as I stared at the offending swatch. Examining the color, I understood why Blake chose it. Cinnamon Squares wasn't my putrid pumpkin door at home, but warm, inviting. "The color on this swatch has nothing to do with my front door," I mumbled, wishing the quiet resounded with jazz, customer's chatter, mallets pounding on lids. "You wanted to fix it," I whispered. "I needed you to. I need you to right now. Mom's gone, Blake, and you're not here to hold me."

The rainbow display blurred into streams of muddy watercolors. "Damn it, Blake." I grabbed a handful of orange cards and pitched them. *That would feel so good*, I thought, imagining myself chucking Cinnamon Squares swatches to the floor.

I wasn't imagining.

My hands attacked the offending orange as Chaka Kahn roared, "I'm Every Woman." The slot for Cinnamon Squares exploded. I couldn't stop now. One, two . . . twenty.

"Miss?" I faintly heard the paint guy from behind his counter.

"I'm sorry, but you need to rename this color," I said over my shoulder to no one. Paint Guy either ran for backup or ducked and covered.

"Huh?" He resurfaced. "Be right there," he shouted over a hairdryer.

"No brick red in it at all. My front door is the monstrosity of my neighborhood thanks to . . ." I held up the swatch as Charlie Bucket's Golden Ticket. "Cinnamon Squares!"

"Vermillion, madame," Monet added.

"Orange as a traffic cone."

"Madame, orange offers sweetness, fire, and light."

"Not this orange. At least have the common decency to trash the swatches that scream Metamucil and baby aspirin." A Cantaloupe card landed in Frizzy's tumbleweed; she blew away.

"May I help you?" Paint Guy asked, his paint-speckled fingertip scratching his forehead.

"I'm helping *you*." I tossed Carrot Baby Food above his head. "Not an ounce of red in any of these. Orange as a tangerine, orange as the middle of a candy corn, orange as—"

"An orange?" Paint Guy stared into me as his thumbs texted on his cell.

"Orange is useless unless the proper mix of red sets it off as energetic and vibrant. These look grossly brown and yellow." I tossed the stack of Blazing Autumn in the air like confetti. "They'll drive people insane. I'm protecting you from lawsuits." Paint Guy stared at me while his thumbs tap-danced on his cell. "You're sending a bunch of emojis, aren't you? My husband and I used to do that. My favorite is grit-your-teeth dude which you're nailing at the moment."

He searched for backup. "FYI, I'm texting my manager on how to deal with *you*."

"What if I'm a secret shopper? Isn't the customer always right?"

"Right."

"Good. Rusty Gate, unequivocally dog poop. Blazing Autumn, dried blood."

"Miss, that wasn't a 'you're right' but wow-this-chick-is-scaring-me right."

"Wow, in this lighting your eyes shine a hint of violet—like Elizabeth Taylor's." I gnawed my thumb as a child caught stealing candy. "*Chick* not great; Miss okay."

"You're changing the subject, and that's not a compliment. I didn't print these, but yeah . . ." He plucked the swatch from my hand and held it to the light. "My bad, Blazing Autumn does look like dried blood." He crouched down and opened a cabinet door, grabbing a stash of orange swatches. "Mother f—fraction." He wobbled, catching himself, clinging to the display. I glimpsed his prosthetic leg.

"I didn't mean to . . ." He glared at me bored, scratching the stubble on his chin with his cell. "They flew out on their own—like a poltergeist thing."

"You're scaring our customers. I'm gonna have to ask you to leave."

"There's no one here." I snorted. "Okay, let's make a deal. You don't bother me, and I won't blab on you and your Millennial rudeness texting and ignoring customers who question the reliability of your Cinnamon Squares—*orange*—paint swatch."

"Chip. You seemed so quiet standing there, all Mary Hatch."

"You're too young to know *It's a Wonderful Life*?"

"It was my mom's favorite movie."

Was. I stared into the swatch, Canvas, picturing Mom and I snuggled under the Beast watching *It's a Wonderful Life* on Christmas Eve. Sugar cookies, a mug of her hot apple cider warmed my palms. We didn't need Dad there with us; Mom was parent enough for both of them.

"Hey, space cowboy." Paint Guy poked my arm waking me. "Are you going to faint?"

"I'm fine." I gathered myself. "I'm sorry," I whispered. The soothing sounds of smooth jazz settled my heart. I locked eyes with Paint Guy. *True empathy. Thanks.*

"The orange set you off," he said, waving away his manager and the security guard marching toward us. "Why? It's just . . . orange." Paint Guy holstered his phone.

My heartbeat rattled; no deep breaths could settle it now. "Or maybe it was that frizzy-headed woman blabbing on her phone." I crammed blue and green swatches into my purse.

"I heard you talking to some guy named Monet. I didn't see your cell."

"Spewing her insensitive remarks about how people die already." I burned my glare into the empty orange display. "Move on," I whispered. "Get over it, Eileen," I said louder, shoving crumpled orange swatches back into place. "Maybe she can't get over it. Maybe Eileen is scared and freaking out she's so sad all the time when she used to be a happy person. Maybe Eileen has seen enough death to last her a lifetime. Frizzy could yell her move-on-it's-only-death speech in her car, at a restaurant, not here while I'm trying to find a freakin' paint swatch called Peace."

"Chip." He slipped me a few tissues.

"Please don't say that again."

"It says it right here." Paint Guy shoved the back of Lemon Meringue in my face. "'For best results, view paint *chip* in light where paint will be used.'"

"Exactly! Cinnamon Squares is a fraud."

"Noel? Is there a problem here?" Only two people in my life ever called me Noel, my seventh-grade Shop teacher and my neighbor Mr. Elders. This retired drill sergeant had the gift of popping his nose into my business at the right moment. He could sniff me out if I sat buried under a snowdrift in Nova Scotia. "Maudie needs another tarp," he said annoyed. "Wish she'd figure out how to repot a damn houseplant without destroying our carpet."

"Sounds like a big houseplant, sir," Paint Guy said. "Aisle five."

"I know where it is," Mr. Elders snipped, throwing off his hood. "Noel?"

I kicked a few swatches under the display, biting my lip to stop my tears from falling. "I'm conducting an artistic conference on color theory." I blurted, attacking my thumbnail.

"Well, I don't know about that," Mr. Elders said, swishing in his puffy parka, "but I do know a yellow door sells a house."

"Am I selling, Mr. Elders?"

"Are you, Noel?" He poked his needle nose closer as if ordering me to drop and do fifty.

"I have an Indigo Rapture to shake," Paint Guy said, tossing a handful of Orange Popsicle in the air, returning to his counter.

"You do that, jackpot," Mr. Elders said, winking at me. He stood observing the scene, rustling and ready to bust out of his parka balloon. "Blue is more durable," he insisted, plucking a country blue swatch from the display. "Forever Lake Blue." He placed it in my hand and held on. "Your mom would've liked this one. I told Blake you wouldn't like the orange."

I slipped my hand out from his and stared at the comforting blue square watching Mom nod in agreement. A thousand memories danced across my eyes: birthday parties, holidays, how special she made our days as a single parent, never a complaint, forever, a wonder.

"Noel?" His puffy sleeve brushed my shoulder.

"Thanks, Mr. Elders." I dropped my coat onto a pile of orange swatches at my feet.

He picked it up and handed it back, my coat stuck with Cinnamon Squares. "I told Blake you wouldn't like that color. I felt bad about that, honey."

"Bad?" I smiled inside it took ten years for him to call me something familiar as honey.

Paint Guy crouched behind his counter sucked into his cell phone, laughing at the screen. "The guy's pulverizing a mound of cherry jello in the air with a tennis racket in slow-mo."

"I thought it brought charm," Mr. Elders said. "Maudie didn't so I knew you wouldn't either. I told him." He blew his nose. "Damn cold coming on." He fidgeted with his coat pocket.

"Yes, Mr. Elders, you told me." I bundled up turning to leave.

"Then . . . Blake left." He choked up again. "I'm sorry, honey, this is unpleasant."

"Left?" I spun around to him.

He slipped a toothpick out of his mouth, gnawing it, contemplating his next words. "Blake said he was coming here to buy that blue paint you liked. He was going to repaint the door while you were at work, took the day off. He didn't tell you?"

"Blake didn't tell me a lot of things."

"Maudie warned me. Damn it. I'm being an old man in your business. I'm sorry." He searched the ceiling as if the tarp he needed hid in the rafters.

"And Blake never took a day off," I whispered.

"I'll paint your door." Mr. Elders toughened up. "The surface has to be fifty degrees. Exterior paint, not that glossy crap—interior wall paint won't work. Did jackpot tell you?"

"I'm on vacation, Mr. Elders. It's winter, just trying to decide before spring."

"Long way to go." He searched down the aisle. "We've missed seeing you, Noel."

"We'll chat again soon." I buttoned my coat overdue to leave. Mr. Elders gestured for me to fix my misaligned buttons. "Got it."

"Of course." He grinned and studied me, concerned. "Is your father coming to visit?"

His question caught me off guard. "Dad died a few months before Blake."

"Sophia Noel." He sighed. "Forgive an old man's memory." He blew his nose again.

"You're forgiven." I tugged at my buttons unable to look at him, ready to flee.

"You'll be all right, Noel." He offered a firm pat on my back. "Takes time, yeah? Come around. Maudie baked a fresh batch of those cherry scones you like." Mr. Elders waddled past the mess of paint swatches, threw a salute to Paint Guy, and left.

Cinnamon Squares killed my husband.

"Can't pick the right color, huh?" Paint Guy asked, handing me a paint brochure called *Tranquility*. "For real, death sucks. I lost my mom three years ago. I'm Guy."

Close. I took his brochure. "I'll come back tomorrow." *I'll never come here again.* "I'll try samples of Nostalgic Evening, Saving Grace, Wild Sun, Dolphin, and Magical. I'm Sophie."

"Cool." He grinned, proud of himself—nutbag lady situation, defused. "You lost someone." He stared at his computer. "You're that woman on the news; it's your red hair."

My stomach jumped at the mention. "Auburn."

"You look like Superman's girlfriend, Amy Adams, way sexier, taller, less freckles."

"I don't look like her at all, do I?"

"Better. I'm older than I look. I served in Afghanistan. If you ever wanna talk in between color choices, I'm down." He scratched his mountain of sandy hair.

"Thank you for your service."

"I just came home. I get it. Why I didn't say anything. Frizzy's a perm gone wrong."

"It's something I . . ." For the first time in months, I warmed up to someone to trust. A vet might understand. PTSD. Though my Air Force father said it was a disservice for civilians to compare everyday emotional trauma to that of war. But that's what they told me—nothing I could handle alone, but I could do alone oh so well. "The essence of the motif is the mirror of water, whose appearance alters at every moment. Did I say that out loud?"

"Yep," Guy said, punctuated by the ding of his cell. His thumbs free to fly.

"A quote . . . from Claude Monet."

"Monet? Interesting."

"Do you ever feel like water, as if you're changing every minute?"

"No, I'm a dude. I'll always be a dude."

Trust potential over. "I'll come back for the samples tomorrow."

"Looking forward to it, Sophie. I'm sorry for your loss."

"Thanks."

"Sophie," Guy said with a playful smile. "I think that color's over there."

"What color?"

"Flirt. Not quite cherry popsicle as your cheeks more raspberry sorbet."

I grabbed a paintbrush and tarp, I didn't need, pausing in front of the orange swatches. "Sorry about the mess. I . . . my mom usually helped me with colors. I can't see them anymore."

Guy was either lost back into the jello smashing videos or he didn't want to touch it. And I didn't blame him one bit.

~

I examined swatches in my car grabbing my cell to call Mom. I already planned how to change the subject from me dating again, to raindrops. It rained instead of the forecasted three inches of snow. Mom loved contemplating nature, rather, testing me to see if the daughter of a famous artist remained observant.

I almost dialed.

"I see only clear raindrops falling from the sky mixing with snow."

Clear. What a horrible word, Sophia. Look closer.

Raindrops. Deflating balloons translucent against the blue sky: clear, empty days; gray, sad days; golden dew landing on cheeks: happy days. *Tears come in different sizes, Sophia.* "I wish I could stop crying to notice." Tiny pools: the onset of sadness; thick globs: pain; flat pancakes: laughter; penciled streams: sad movies.

I cracked open my new lavender journal for a test ride, my pen shaking over the page:

Everyone I have ever loved is in a "better place," as if the better place was me not in it. People float around me; I barely see them. I try, I do. Look forward, "move on," but I'm stuck, frozen to the earth like a broken flower, no chance to grow, no idea how.

I slammed the journal shut as if the words started flying off the page forcing me to face them. "Mom, you know I don't do journals."

See, Sophia.

All I see is darkness, that blue-black screen with fiery red specks when I get up in the middle of the night. There's nothing, no one. I'm groping for corners of furniture, doorways, you. Mom, where's the sun? Make the storms go away. I'm tired of clear raindrops on a drab, dark day. Paint the overcast into a sunset, a sunrise. You can; you always do.

Show me how to see clear as colorful again. Show me.

9.

Camille

On the corner of the Quai du Louvre stands a modest café where, for the price of a cup of coffee, young artists sit atop the mezzanine for hours painting pictures of our new Paris. An artist's friend stops a passerby—their game begins. He tips his hat. "What is the time, monsieur?" the artist's comrade asks, tricking the man into holding a pose during chitchat, unbeknownst to the artist who paints them.

For worthy artists, all avenues lead to the Salon, the annual art competition where the Emperor's jury, in the name of protecting excellence in French art, invokes censorship of any painting daring to topple it with new techniques, motifs, and colors. *Refused*, brands an unworthy painting thwarting success. *Accepted*, introduces stars.

The new artists swarmed the Batignolles where I lived, but Claude Monet and his group captured me. I spied the popinjays strutting around the village, past our shop, this dandy and his fellows sipping champagne, clamoring about dinners in famous salons and gatherings at the Café Guerbois. They boasted a revolution armed with palette and brush, determined to frustrate the Salon and change the ways of France. The relentless study of nature their only decree, painters of parasols down on boulevard, forest picnics, and sunsets rippling the Seine, chasers of sunlight washing the countryside and candlelight glowing in a cottage.

I shall paint you," Monet whispered, but my ordered life set course.

"Model, actress—society's synonyms for mistress," my cousin Gabrielle warned.

The great renovator of Paris under Napoleon III, Baron Georges Haussmann, ignited the rebellion escorting Paris and its young citizens into modernity. If the Palace of Industry had anyone to blame for the artistic insurrection standing on its freshly paved stoop, it was he. With the demolition of Victor Hugo's revolutionary streets and dusty cafés, our new

Paris yielded modern fashion, parks demanding fashionable promenades, tree-lined boulevards aglow in gaslight, luxurious shop windows, theaters, and the new art. If Napoleon III himself decreed the modernization of Paris, why should we not expect it for ourselves?

I would never pose as the artists' models hovering as hummingbirds diving in for a taste, modeling nude for a few francs stuck on a platform in a dim workshop jeered at by students. My own—parading not flesh but the emerging fashions of Paris. I purposed to win Claude Monet's eyes, my form captured in the colors, light, and truth he revered, and impress Papa on canvas—my stage. I, as Napoleon's city, transformed into the modern Parisian woman, for she had come to Paris whether Paris was ready for her or not.

While most young women dreamed of marriage, I traded my mother's base motto of opportunity in status and wealth for a simpler decree: these bold artists would capture their new Paris, and they would capture me in it.

"You linger at Madame Pontray's to catch glimpses of those artists. I have seen that dandy, Monet, wandering with your Frédéric Bazille," Papa scolded, racing back to the shop.

"But Papa—"

"You will have a family of your own and these artists practicing portraits, squandering allowances, will discover a dozen other Floras," he finished, swiping his mustache.

"I will be happy?" I asked, handing Papa my cuff of forget-me-nots.

He slipped them back onto my wrist. "And fill my shop and heart with joy."

"And gossiping ladies craving the latest ball gowns to impress their gangly crane gentlemen." I dropped my hand from his. We watched our neighbor, Monsieur Belrose, sweeping the walkway of his cluttered shop, his wife piling cheap men's trousers and hats on tables for their sale. "He arranged them all wrong," I mumbled. "You cannot see the signs."

"You will help him."

"*Oui.*" Papa wrapped me in my shawl with a loving smile. The years had been good to my papa and his handsome looks, his mustache now speckled with gray, untidy. "You're getting lazy," I said, his tender blue eyes admiring me, concerned.

"Oh, *ma fée*," he sighed. "I'm your old papa who wishes everything good for his daughter. It is my fault you yearn for more than a husband and home to keep."

"*Ma fée*, my fairy . . . you have not called me that since I was a child."

"You remind me today you are no longer a little girl. Whatever you shall dream, I'll do my best to let you fly. I will do my best." With a kiss to my forehead, our walk ended.

We return to our boutique, The Elegance Shop, one of the finest little dress shops in the Batignolles. Shopkeepers open shutters, omnibuses take their stations, the milk woman positions her cart on the corner awaiting the pretty dresses and starched, white caps of the housemaids, cooks light home fires, and kettles boil for the morning *café au lait*. The *flâneurs* stroll, the artists paint. I rush to buy Papa his paper and secretly stash the latest *La Mode Illustrée* and forbidden novel.

Paris rises, so too the Seine River, where for five sous one can travel on a steamboat omnibus from one end of the city to the other, taking in a grand panorama of churches, palaces, and bridges. Gardens and parks crowd with lawn chairs and strollers, while the proud Parisian scrutinizes dresses, *chapeaus*, and wisps of an unruly chignon. Evening, the city glows with gaslight, apartment windows open to violins, the air swirls with burning wood, tobacco, and wine. When the last note sings, our city barely sleeps, eager to wake and busy with another day.

And each morning, whether mist drifts upon the Seine, a shadow casts on a lot of bricks or over an old woman. Whether streams of sunlight flicker shimmers of gold dust on a maid's apron, or a purple umbrella dances in the wind, I have seen these sights a thousand times, yet they still fill me with wonder, and I imagine I have scarcely even seen them at all, truly seen them.

10.

Sophie

I stared into the block of cobalt blue layered with a flowing swipe of cadmium yellow. Today it was a block. Yesterday, a flowing trickle, the day before, a shadow. *"He never painted shadows, my Sophia. Light was Monet's mistress,"* Mom corrected in my thoughts.

For the past two months, I sat, most days pin straight, in the art museum's exhibition of French Impressionist Claude Monet's masterpiece: *Agapanthus* triptych, a 42-foot long display of Monet's *Water Lilies* inspired by his garden in Giverny. Every day before work, I looked to the three enormous panels of floating color to give me answers. To anyone who knew nothing of fine art, but would challenge themselves to savor it; they would not see blocks, but genius.

Today, cobalt blue, vermilion, and madder red were blocks. Large, messy, happenstance blocks with angry swirls and desperate globs. Dingy emerald greens with intrusive swipes of orange. I hated orange. Something about the negativity the color orange brings to one's life. Staying away from orange seemed my only sane decision lately.

Monet never used a tube of orange, Mom interrupted my thoughts again. She was in there a lot since she passed away. *"Putain,* Mom," I said, prompting a look from a museum guard, a college kid so paper skinny I wondered what the heck he could accomplish if it all went down. "I wish you were here." *Putain isn't a cuss word, Sophie. It means prostitute. Your mom hates when we say it.* Dad joined the conversation in my head. It was crowded in there today. "Damn, Dad," I said to myself. *I wish I learned more French from you, Mom . . . more everything.*

When students vanished, and lovers stopped lingering, I slouched; I sprawled on the conjoined modern couches, allowing Monet's colors to transport me to his escape. I conjured an imagined Giverny to fill the room.

Summer. Prehistoric willows whisper a rustle in the wind, the scent of damp soil, marshes, and ponds. A garden escape of his meticulous design: tomato-red poppies, fuchsia dahlias with smears of golden buttons, rose trees fat with plump pink blooms, and water lilies—floating, teetering on beds of waxy green. "I still remember what it looks like, Mom."

Twirl for me, my dad says in a distant dream. *Round and round, little bug, until the sunflowers twirl with you.* A little girl twirls in a faraway garden— Monet's garden—at sunset when the soft blues and lilac melt into heather. A little girl's sunhat drifts inside my mind across a dreamy pond reflecting willows and our heather sky. This is how I remember it. This is how I wanted to.

"A grown-up vacation for a girl still in school," my fifth-grade teacher said.

"My parents are taking me to Paris," I bragged. *"That's where my mom was born. She's gonna show me the Impressionables and Money's garden."*

"Impressionists, Sophia, Monet's garden. Paint us a beautiful picture."

A little girl sits dreaming in a circular corner of Monet's private world. *"Did you have tea here, Monsieur Monet?"* I had asked no one, my tiny sandals dangling sweeping blades of grass. A sunflower rested on my lap as I sat on Monet's green, wooden bench guarded by an Empress tree dressed in violet blossoms—my Empress tree. I sat still waiting for magic. Waiting.

"Are there Empress trees in California, Mommy?"

"I don't know, Sophia."

"Why do we have to move there? Why can't we go with Daddy to London?"

"It's complicated, Sophia."

"Are there Empress trees in Missouri?"

"You're too old for fables now, Sophia. I don't know."

I opened my eyes ending childhood memories, staring into the corner of Monet's *Water Lilies,* his pond's bank slathered in hunter green. I dared to dip my fingers swirling the tan and ochre sludge. My shoes brushed the grasses; lacy ferns tickled my ankles. A trail of liquid pink carried a wisp of sunlight on its back. "I miss you all," I whispered, staring down at my shoes no longer dangling, no longer sweeping blades of grass.

On this wintery day, I sat feeling the heat of sorrow in my chest, on my cheeks, ready to melt as a plump snowman built in spring. I closed my eyes again, drifting on Monet's lilac, sapphire pond, gliding on the surface disturbing the water lilies he thoughtfully arranged. Water lilies brush my face as I float upon this pond of light. Streams of vermillion wash my cheeks and shimmers of yellow, dust my hair. I watch violet fluffs float above across patches of sky-blue. Salmon and moss grasses dance near the shore vying for attention. Across the way—Monet's Japanese footbridge. *Mom, how you could've painted it. I wish I had the skills. Today, a stroll by the water lily pond, Monet's exotic children.*

Birds singing, a deep breath of sweet peas and roses—peace. The clouds above ordered by him, a multi-colored sky of impressionistic perfection. "A mist hovers in the morning shafts of sunlight as a spotlight on your rose trees," I whispered.

Monet chuckled. "They need pruning. I ordered three hundred pots of poppies with instructions to swiftly plant the Japanese peonies if they so arrive. Now, a field of poppies . . ."

"Poppies?"

"September. French poppies . . . only French poppies will do. A lantern shade the way the light peeks through the petals. A quick dab of vermillion, deep madder . . ."

"Orange." I snickered.

"Vermillion with a touch of cadmium yellow," he corrected.

I found my smile. "The wind moves your petals."

"Fickle models, how they dance. Ever changing, my brush cannot stop. I cannot stop."

"And Camille?"

"*Oui* . . . Camille."

I wanted to see a field of red poppies flickering white light, and at dusk paint them blue—cobalt poppies with violet streaks and dabs of moonlight. Breathe in brisk, night air, grassy meadows, dirt roads, and settled oaks. This French countryside his escape, mine, only in my thoughts; forgetting myself, I closed my eyes wishing I were there. Paris called, but I hadn't the guts to go now. "You're painting indoors," I whispered.

Today I stood off to the side observing Monet obsess, visualize, and transform with every sweeping brushstroke and calculated dab in his meticulously ordered atelier. "Madame, you surmise I carry these monstrosities on my back? I devised a pulley system once to paint an enormous picture in a garden, lovely painting, wretched trench."

"You brag you never finish a painting in your studio."

Monet paused, shooting me a critical glare. He smoothed his long, white beard to a point, his white cotton suit spotless as he stood before his wet canvas pointing his brush at me as a warning. "I'll have you know, child, I, Claude Monet, never finished a painting in the studio. In the open-air, *en plein air*. Nature my atelier."

"You tell stories to build legend when your work is legend enough."

"Bah." He studied me, holding up a brush loaded with paint, one eye closed ready to erase me with a glob of French ultramarine. "My dear child, if one brought paints to imagine on blank canvas a corner of nature in the forest, by the sea, in a garden, it was because I, Claude Monet, dedicated to it first like no other."

"You did." I laughed, imaging the glob of blue on my forehead. "But you shouldn't—"

"Sophie?" Randall, my museum guard in, popped in as a warning. Set to retire, the last thing he needed was a prattling woman pawing at priceless artwork as an obsessed Monet groupie. I shuffled away from the corner of the canvas back to the couch.

Ma petit chère, sweet daughter, find your way back home.

"How's our Monet today huh?" Randall asked, trying to cheer me.

You need to find your way back home. I opened my lavender journal engrossed in fake scribbles, dropping my pencil watching it roll in front of Monet's masterpiece. "If it rolls past the taped line will an alarm go off?"

Randall folded his arms eyeing my pencil's road trip. I avoided his grimace, gnawing on my thumbnail, counting while I counted the clusters of periwinkle brushstrokes in Monet's watery sky. "Who were you talking to earlier?" he asked.

I flashed the audio tour's iPod. "Warn people about the volume on these."

"Is that right?" he asked, retrieving my runaway pencil. I grabbed a strand of hair and twirled. "Let's . . . keep it down." He handed me my pencil with a sympathetic smile.

"Thanks, Randall," I managed, chucking it in my tote.

"You're early today." He plucked an orange paint swatch off the floor. "Yours?"

I shrugged and looked behind me searching for a trail of Cinnamon Squares. "I'm on vacation."

Randall put his hands in his pockets, watching me gather my belongings. "Lily told me about your mom." His deep, tender voice cut through the silence. His twinkling baby blues admired me as he offered a pat to my back letting his warm hand linger. "Hang in there, Sophie."

I held my tears, sliding away from his affection. Randall was an unexpected friend the past few months. He didn't wear the typical museum guard uniform, so I gathered he was head of security. He mentioned he was a "specialist," as my receptionist at Faraway Travel was a communications specialist, as I wasn't a travel agent but an independent travel specialist. A handsome man in his early sixties, I wondered how many broken hearts Randall left behind in his youth. Gray feathered hair covered his head, a burly salt and pepper mustache his lip. His keen eye, determined saunter, and Texas drawl swaggered right out of a John Wayne Western.

After a week, Randall shared about his late wife, two sons he desired to grow closer to, and the black Labrador puppy he rescued on his birthday. I wasn't Sophie Noel Dot Dot Dot with Randall. I held a clean slate, no baggage, intrusions, and no explanations. I tossed my trust to this stranger and he guarded it as a priceless work of art.

Something else happened when I walked into the Monet exhibit; this flowered aquarium became a sanctuary of thought. Monet's stream of consciousness stretched across his canvas in a spectacle of color, light, and thousands of calculated, disciplined brushstrokes—mine floated to the ceiling unbridled waiting to come back to me as a beautiful picture I might understand and enjoy. "If you need anything, I'm here," Randall's voice echoed underwater. I kept my gaze on Monet's masterpiece. As it happened every day, the colors came alive as some secret animation only I could see dripping down the canvas to pools of illuminated color on the floor. "Sophie? Sparrow?" Randall's concern brought me back.

"Someday, you'll have to tell me why you call me Sparrow," I said, changing the subject.

He set the Cinnamon Squares card on my journal. "You hated Sugar."

I handed it back. "Are we still doing lunch on your last day?"

Randall pocketed the swatch and nodded. "It will be the highlight," he said with a smirk, strolling back to his hallway. He paused. "You look nice, Sophie. I'll miss this . . . our talks."

"I'm honored you would make time for me on your last day."

"I'll always have time for you, Sophie. I'll be back. The new guy has a lot to learn."

"I'm not sure I'll visit the museum much after Monet leaves. I wish this exhibition could stay here forever."

"You'll just have to go to Paris."

"Yeah," I mumbled, focusing on the iPod in my hand. "Thanks, Randall, for your thoughts about Mom."

"Wanna talk about it?"

"Not today."

He nodded and let the silence fall as I shifted in my seat, shuffling blank pages in my journal. "Duke doesn't like his new name." Randall changed the subject for me.

"He's a puppy. He'll get used to it."

"Nope, I think he'd like something else. I could use your help."

"But he's your dog. You have to name him."

"Maybe we can share him. You said you knew about dogs. I don't know why I got him."

We stared at Monet's water lilies in silence. I shook my sleepy legs awake to stand and turned to him. "Because you needed him, and he needed you."

He took in my words, rubbed his mustache, and said, "So, I should give it more time?"

"Maybe he isn't a Duke, maybe he's a . . . Cole."

"A Cole, huh?"

"Cole." I warmed up inside meeting his eyes with my smile.

"Settled. He's a Cole."

"How many dogs do you think are out there named after John Wayne characters?"

"Plenty." He tipped his imaginary cowboy hat and disappeared around the corner.

And then I spotted it.

A huge, shiny magenta purse twirling in a nearby gallery.

The hot pink purse that dangled behind a riding lawn mower at Hardware Haven, the one I spotted skipping through the museum's parking lot but told myself it was my imagination. I searched the opposite gallery again.

A little girl in lemon sneakers waved, tugging at her mother's pink book bag. I sighed, sitting in front of Monet's masterpiece, listening to the rhythm of Randall's heels as he entered a gallery and his warm voice greeting the girl.

I reached into my coat pocket, pulled out Dr. Arnold's crinkled business card, and read the back: *We know what we are, but not what we may be.* I barely caught him at Mom's funeral, but that was the idea. "I'm not crazy," I said to Monet's masterpiece. "I'm in survival mode."

≈

"Soft voices," a teacher ordered; preschoolers filed in a noisy huddle. Children plopped to the floor giggling and asking questions. The corner of a magenta purse invaded my snip of joy. A pair of glossy pink stilettos to match shuffled behind another school group and posed near Randall. "She looks like the Mona Lisa," a boy snickered, pointing to me.

Time to leave.

I looked nothing like the Mona Lisa except for the waves in my long auburn hair. I had no devilish grin, and at the boy's voice, I thought of my stepbrother Georgie. Mom would've loved to see his sly smile one last time.

I zipped through the gift shop past Lily and her offers to fix me up with her list of curators and museum guards. Lily was a petite twenty-something-year-old yogi who insisted working at the Monet exhibition gift shop was a sign because her name was Lily. "Sophie," Lily called, ignoring two boys tossing water lily coasters as Frisbees.

"In a rush," I said, throwing on my coat.

Lily grabbed my arm, walking me to the register. "Your Monet stuff is in, silly."

I lost myself in a coaster's miniature Monet painting: *Poppies at Argenteuil.* Crimson and cantaloupe poppies blanket a sunlit meadow. Sprouting with the flowers, a mother stands with her son on a hilltop. "She appears detached, indifferent, why?" I asked no one.

"My little Jean—see his smile, madame? He's my flower, no?"

"I see a mother leaving behind her child, a child wondering why," I said to myself.

"Sophie?" Lily tapped my shoulder.

"Huh?" I stuffed the past back into its place and set the coasters on the counter catching a glimpse of a magenta purse swinging toward the entrance. "I need to go." I searched for it again.

"What's wrong?" Lily asked, following my gaze. The girl in lemon sneakers swung her pink book bag pelting the innocent. "Oh, we ran out of those pink totes last week. Are you okay? You look pale and your cheeks are super hot. That's not a compliment."

"A slew of ghosts floating around here today."

"OMG, I know. That mummy exhibit freaks me out. On the non-ghost side, Philip asked about you. Boys!" Lily snapped at the coaster-throwing toddlers. Reinforcements arrived: a curator in an orange tie, eyebrow raised, and Lily's manager, Marge. Marge had a stare like a statue; she dressed as my mom put together from head to toe in a dress and matching heals. Never flats. Never pants. Always pearls. "You in? Dinner with Philip—I think he's Freeennch."

As if singing it would make me ponder. "Thanks. No." I escaped her grip.

"Sophie, he's perfect, older like you. Wait, not like that's a bad thing." Lily tightened her ponytail, her arched eyebrows headed for her hairline. "He's a curator."

Note to self: looks "older" after trying. "Thirty-five. I just turned thirty-five."

"No way." She stared at me as if I had an octopus on my head, releasing her honey hair, draping it over her shoulder. I couldn't remember the last time I fixed mine, the last time I cared.

"Sophia," Marge said, her stone-cold stare softened. "I'm sorry Felix and I missed your mother's funeral. Josephine was so talented. We all loved her."

Was.

"How are you doing?" she asked, staring past me at three lost preschoolers.

The images of Mom's final days flashed through my mind. *I'm falling apart. I'm melting onto your sticky marble floor. No one will even notice the puddle.* "Lost. I have to go."

A girl in pigtails grabbed a silk scarf and twirled in circles, a boy eyed an umbrella. "I'm sorry. Duty calls. Come back to see me." Marge made a beeline for a teacher lost in an art book. Lily and I watched as the teacher gathered her flock and left.

"Sophie," Lily said softly, "I adored your mom. I'm so sorry." She offered me a Snickers bar as a child. "I have two." She nibbled her candy bar. "Did she give you her amazing gift?"

"Gift?"

"Josephine was so excited. Journals—watercolor flowers painted on pages just for you."

"Mom brought her journal here?" I wasn't sure I wanted to know where this was going.

"She wrote in it all the time. Like you do, but you mostly stare at the pages. A teal one too, but your mom wouldn't show me that one. She was very secretive about it. It looked old."

"Teal?" I scanned the entrance again for a magenta purse. Nothing. After a hard swallow I said, "Poetry. That's a book of poetry." I searched for the time on my wrist missing my watch. *Mom's journals in her hope chest . . . I dismissed them. They were her gift.*

"Did your mom write it?" Lily grabbed her phone and showed me a photo of her, my mom and Marge. "She was happy she saved them for you."

"Yes. Thanks for the coasters and chocolate."

"Bye, Sophie. I didn't mean the old thing. I'll text you this photo if you like. Your mom looks so happy. Marge is doing a tribute in one of the new galleries." Lily tucked a golden strand behind her ear flashing her "birthday" diamonds. She didn't need to work here.

"Bye." I whispered, rushing out of the shop. I hurried through the maze of galleries, skipping my usual stop at the Expressionists; I had enough chaos for one morning, and headed for the museum's exit. Randall spoke to a group of women, acknowledging me with his salute. Behind his arm, I saw it again, bobbing around the information desk, knocking into a man's leg, and swinging past Randall: the magenta purse—luggage size.

"Sophieeee!"

I heard the echo. I knew that voice. It hit me like a linebacker at the third yard line.

"*Putain!*" I needed a bathroom. I needed one fast. "Arts of Asia." I bolted through the foyer catching Randall's glare. The magenta purse and Jimmy Choos shuffled after me. "Lord, let it be one of those stupid pink book bags." I hid behind a statue and looked. "That's not a cheesy book bag." I found the hidden door by the stairwell, rushed in, and clicked the latch.

11.

Camille

Elise sent word Claude Monet inquired about Papa's shop. His poor excuse: replacing the torn lace on his sleeve. She revealed I was neither shop girl nor model, but if one wanted to find the finest fripperies in Paris, a visit to The Elegance Shop on the rue de la Paix was paramount. She did not say which of the three rue de la Paix our shop resided. *We shall see the effort he puts forth in finding you,* she wrote. "Indeed." I tucked her card into my pocket.

Located far from the show of diamonds at Monsieur Samper's and the fashion houses of Paris, The Elegance Shop stood on a quiet strip in the Batignolles around the corner from Elise's flower shop, down the street from a patisserie, and in between a stationary shop and Monsieur Belrose's haberdashery. Papa writes the music of the shop; I make it sing. This year, I couldn't ignore business exhausted Papa's heart. Mamma pressed him to retire, move into the grander apartment she eyed since last spring, and marry me off. She boasted of a mysterious inheritance on the horizon, securing my match to the wealthy Henri Valentine—known through the associations of my grandfather, Etienne Manéchalle, captain of the cuirassiers since departed.

Nothing persuaded me to marry Henri, twice my senior. A cavalier's wife was the dream of my grandmother, not mine. Working in the shop provided a measure of independence. Once it stuck to my skin, I had no desire to unclothe it.

I waited downstairs in the shop for Papa, admiring the heart-shaped locket he gave me on my birthday. I treasured his message in precious stones: lapis, opal, verdite, emerald, and diamond—*loved.* At his voice, I slipped it back on. "Time for work," I whispered to Raphael, my little Bichon curled up as a fluff of cotton behind the counter, guarding our front door.

A skilled tradesman in textiles of Lyon, arriving in Paris, Papa sold draperies for storefronts and carriages with his brother. When his brother moved to London, Papa allowed his shop to shine the vogue colors of Paris silks. Pink, lilac, and aqua, replaced powdery blacks and grays. Soon, women's fineries, lemon parasols with cream tassels, beaded and silver purses, sixteen-button gloves with pearl buttons and embroidered flowers, hand-painted fans from Alexandre and Duvell, and antique lace.

"In Paris, every idea is a grand idea or none at all," Papa said. He was the first in the Batignolles to rent ready-made gowns for balls and portrait painting. He catered to the Parisian's appetite to appear rich to obtain riches. We sold treasures to grooms for marriage baskets, offered instruction on *la mode*, beauty elixirs from Elise, corsets from Mademoiselle Rousseau, and hats from Madame Billet. Known as the rue de la Paix Petite, for in one shop we carried the best from the luxurious rue de la Paix, Paris on the rue de la Paix, Batignolles.

To motivate Papa, I redecorated the shop: pale lavender walls, apricot sheers, fresh lilacs and freesia in chinoiserie vases, crystal chandeliers, settees in pink floral silk, and a shop window draped in lace curtains displaying the season's rage in fashion. Our private salon hosted special events: artist's invitations to sketch our latest gowns, teas, and Madame Pontray's lectures where talk of women's independence slipped in between boleros and fans.

"Camille?" Papa called, interrupting daydreams. "Model this hat for Madame Durant today." He held up a teal bonnet sprouting white feathers.

"Oh, but I fancied it, Papa." I tried it on. "Madame Durant cannot pull off this hat."

Papa folded his arms in no mood for my game. I smoothed the teal ribbons coveting the bonnet. "'In diving to the bottom of pleasure we bring up more gravel than pearls,'" he said.

"No reason to apply Balzac." I scooped off the bonnet to his snicker.

"I cannot afford you modeling our wares about Paris never desiring to sell them."

"They sell, Papa, because I model." I eyed the bonnet, foolish the thing had gripped me. "Madame Durant's head is enormous." He frowned, thinking a moment. We burst into laughter. "You price it too cheap. Mamma's right. Your will for the shop is lost; let us close today."

"Stuff and nonsense." Papa strolled to a display of lace handkerchiefs. "My daughter still uses her childish pout to manipulate me."

"I do not." I added three hats on the counter, fanning out their rainbow of ribbons.

Papa disappeared into the stockroom returning with an red bonnet crowned with white feathers. He adjusted it on my head. "You earned this with the sale of those gowns and two silver purses last week. We must appease Madame Durant."

I rushed Papa with a hug. "'I shall put my bonnet to its right use. 'Tis for the head.'"

"*Hamlet.* You used that quote last week."

"Will I ever win, Papa?"

"I dare say you conquered me this morning. Go, your mamma and sister are in the throes of party making and require your opinion."

"It will be a nice birthday party for Genèvieve, *oui*?"

"Grander than necessary, but it keeps your mother happy . . . and busy."

"What must we do to keep Papa happy?"

He inspected a table of shawls pleased. "Be more pliable, Camille."

I sighed, unwilling to look at him. "Take the bonnet," I said, gazing at the fans behind the counter displayed in a cabinet as fine porcelain.

"Keep it, *ma fée*. That's not what I mean."

"I know, Papa." Mother-of-pearl, lace, and ivory distinguished every fan as a work of fine art. Maintaining luxuries in our shop strained Papa's purse. He did not need Mamma's needling; he pondered retirement often now. I opened the cabinet, admiring a painted fan of a sunset and seascape; a sail-boat drifted before my eyes. I rocked in it alone, pleased, saddened. *Was I sailing away from Paris—Papa?*

Papa forever discerning my mood hovered near. I hid my tears, gazing at the fan, the empty boat rocking on waves. Out of the corner of my eye, Papa's handkerchief flapped as a flag of surrender. I wiped my tears, turning the fan over, losing myself in a moonlit forest.

"Your mother and I desire a good life for you." He closed the cabinet. "I will respect your choice for marriage, but you will choose."

My eyes darted from his to a show of sparkling brooches under glass domes as princely treasures. "I wish no match to an old man."

"Ah." Papa meandered away, weeding out three parasols from a stand.

"Add these to the sale. They have remained here too long. Perhaps . . . so have I."

"I didn't mean—"

"Old man. Did your mother utter those words when we married? I, the old man—your poor mamma was so young and frightened. Was I that horrid a choice as Henri Valentine?"

"No. You are handsome and good. You were in love and took care of us, her."

"Were we?" he asked himself, staring out the window as if recalling a happier time. "Regrets . . . one can never rearrange the past, so it's best forgotten." Papa bristled at my tender touch. "Enough talk. Madame Durant arrives at ten. Go to your sister."

I set my bonnet on a stand and came in closer though he began to walk away. Raphael yawned and stretched, chasing after Papa who opened the shop's front door. I headed toward the stairway. "I love you, Papa. I pray I meet a man as honorable, giving, and loving as you."

Papa stood a moment. He sniffled and hid his handkerchief back into his pocket. Raphael danced to cheer him making us both chuckle. "A noble desire, my daughter," he said, rushing about the shop in his usual manner. "Go now." He carefully turned the seascape fan back to its sailboat rocking on the ocean.

I came to him instead, offering a teacake and said, "'My bounty is as boundless as the sea. My love as deep. The more I give to thee. The more I have, for both are infinite.'"

We shared the sweets watching Raphael dance for one of his own.

∽

"Geneviève Doncieux, what do you have all over your face?" I asked, entering her bedroom. My little sister bounded toward me with a hug, her tiny face slathered in white cream.

"Cleopatra's Freckle Balm," she stated, handing me a wet towel.

"This is how you bid your sister good morning as a little princess demanding a bath and a dresser? Come now. Wipe it off before your skin wrinkles as an old maid."

"It will not!" Geneviève rubbed her face until her cheeks turned pink.

"Mamma made my curls extra bouncy so they'll last all day." She curtsied in her fluffy, pink dress and plopped on the edge of her bed, making her chocolate ringlets jiggle.

"Delicious." I snuggled next to her. "*Bonne* fête, sister." I wiped smears of cream off her face, placing my cool hands over her rosy cheeks. She closed her eyes relishing my touch. "Think twice before you sneak Mamma's potions, or your angel cheeks might turn frog green."

"Stuff and nonsense." She giggled, throwing herself back onto her pillow.

"You sound like Papa."

Geneviève jumped off the bed, searching her room. "You're trying to scare me with that fairy tale *Diamonds and Toads*." She tossed me a pillow. "Will you recite it at my party?"

"Promise to stay out of Mamma's potions." I threw the pillow back. "A hug and a kiss and you must."

"A hug and a kiss and I must." She paid her penance with a swift hug and kiss, racing to her doorway, sniffing the air. "Mamma's baking me a chocolate brioche for breakfast."

"Are you certain Louise did not make it?" Geneviève wiggled beside me searching behind my back. "Your dress is there." I pointed to the settee draped with a white silk costume.

"Louise has the day off to fetch secret gifts for my party," she whispered, ignoring the settee. "I spied a tray of cherry foams and honey puffs."

"You will act surprised, no?"

"*Oui*." Bright-eyed and fidgety, Geneviève bounced around her room, searching behind chairs and under dressers making me recall my ninth birthday at our home in Lyon.

After my party, Mamma and I walked in our garden as she shared stories about her elegant mother, how she missed her. She slipped a ring on my finger—my grandmother's. A sparkling oval sapphire encircled with diamonds. "Our loved ones are never gone," she said, "even when we leave them to live our own life. We hold memories and special tokens as this ring to treasure." *And to remember where we come from.* We stood in the sunlight, our tears splashing on the color-changing gemstone, sparkles of blue and violet flickering before our eyes.

I looked down at my empty finger, ashamed I stored the ring away years ago, trying to reconcile my feelings toward my mother with her growing distance. "I will wear it tonight in good faith," I whispered to myself.

"There." Geneviève skipped to me with her find, a violet hair comb.

"That gift was for tonight."

She rocked on her heels. "I didn't tell Mamma I saw the fairy bag."

I gathered a lump of her curls and set the comb inside. "The fairy bag is no secret. You helped us wrap the prizes for your friends."

"It's a secret. I used a green ribbon for my toy, but how will I pick it?"

"You won't. You play the game blindfolded. Show me your costume." She followed me to the settee, clapping as I held up her little white dress with puffed lilac sleeves.

"I'm a fairy," she said, twirling. "*Merci beaucoup* for my lilac sash."

"Have you found all your gifts? I'll have nothing left to give you tonight. Your dress is almost perfect." I tossed the crinoline petticoat. "There."

"But I won't look like the other girls. They'll have their skirts out to here." Geneviève stretched her arms waddling a waltz, making me chuckle. "Tilly's sister taught her how to kick like this." She danced her odd waltz, shocking me as she kicked and flailed her arms.

"To sabotage, I'm certain. You resemble a rabid goat."

Geneviève picked up the crinoline skirt, pouted a second longer, and tossed it on the bed grinning. "Mamma says crinoline is *la mode*."

"Wire cages are for birds and are happily outlawed by Frenchwomen who know. Mamma knows nothing of *la mode*. She wears boas with cloaks and handkerchiefs with scarves," I mocked, flinging scarves around my neck.

"And a fuzzy, blonde wig resembling Madame Pontray's fat cat Daisy," Geneviève giggled, wearing two bonnets.

"Simplicity and taste will invite you into the grandest circles no matter your station." I removed her bonnets, she the scarves around my neck.

"You steal Madame Pontray's words. Has she finished my fairy wings?"

"I do not. Do I not exude grace?" I placed her costume on her bed and practiced one of my poses: finger to chin, a forlorn expression, my other hand resting on a bow at my bodice.

"You hold a bragging tongue that'll get you into trouble with Mamma and the old woman at the well as in *Diamonds and Toads*."

I wandered to the window. "How wise Sister is on her *ninth* birthday."

"I know many things, and you're being too serious as Papa." Geneviève remained quiet, thumbing through her books. Nine years younger, yet she often surprised me with her maturity.

My thoughts drifted to Henri Valentine. Hardly confident as the artist. I had never been alone with a man before as Claude Monet, in the early hours when sunrise cracked the mist over the Seine, the sounds of Paris simmering. Encased in the perfume of flowers, breathless utterances of Shakespeare under a canopy shaded in violet, his tender touch to set the rosebud in my hair, the tickle at the strands he strewn across my cheek, my reluctance to move away. I spoke as a fearless woman boasting on independence to Elise but with Geneviève, longed to remain a child fearing my future.

"Sister, what are you dreaming of?" she asked, giggling.

I tucked away my thoughts and joined her. "Did you find the garland of roses?" I cheered, changing my mood.

"Pink! Are they real?"

"Real." I helped her off the floor; she took my hands for a twirl.

"I'll smell like a rose garden. Tilly shall be absolutely jealous."

"I'll pin them at the bottom of the skirt to your waist," I said, spinning.

"I'm dizzy, Sister," she shouted. We stumbled back to sit on the window seat. "What will you wear, Camille?" She cuddled close.

"A dress by Madame Angelard: lemon and spearmint satin with buttery lace icing."

"You're making me hungry." She popped up again picking a book off the shelf.

"The lace, dear sister, was threaded by the gods." I turned my attention back out the window. A group of young men huddled outside Monsieur Belrose's shop. I spotted a man with raven hair and ducked as he tipped his hat to me. "Monsieur Monet," I whispered.

"Who is that?" She pushed her way to the window, waving to the men below.

"Come down from there." I pulled her away.

"Why are so nervous? Who is he? A lover?"

"Genevieve Doncieux!"

"I'm old enough to know about such things."

"You are not. Your birthday gives you no leave for rudeness."

"I'm a child. I'm supposed to be rude."

I refolded a quilt and draped it across the window seat. "Never think of your sister so. It's not a thing to say," I snipped, peering out the window.

"Sister . . ." Her tiny steps edged closer. "It's cloudy now. The rain ruins my birthday."

"It's scarcely morning." I searched the horizon losing myself in lazy gray wisps intruding upon the bluebell sky. The wind chased them away. A golden crust made my sister smile as its sunlight landed on her shoes. "See. The sun takes its time to wake as you do."

My sister tugged at the back of my dress. "Camille . . . I didn't mean—all right, I won't wear crinoline." Her voice warbled with tears.

"Ever. A hug and a kiss and you must."

"A hug and a kiss and I must." Geneviève tugged me away from the window and held me tight. She grabbed a book in one hand, a curl in the other and scooted back onto her bed watching me. With a blink, her wide-eyed stare glistened with tears. "Papa said you'll move away from here someday . . . soon." The warble in her voice returned. "Is it true? Who will hide prizes in my room on my next birthday? Who will brush my hair and sing songs when terrors wake me? Who will share secrets when I'm old enough and help me know what is *la mode*?"

I closed my eyes, tears pooling inside my lids, opening them to a misty window blurred with the men below. I could not leave my Paris now, this intruding city, the intoxicating changes of freedom swirling about the grand monuments of progress. "You worry for nothing."

"I don't ever want you to leave. I'm sorry for talking foolish. I'm sorry I—" She threw herself onto her pillow, her soft sobs a splash of rain intruding on her special day.

"Baby sister." I rushed to her, wiped her tears, pinching her cheeks to make her smile. "Silly talk. I'll never leave you. Someday we will both be married. That is all."

"Never." She sighed away her worries as children do, burying her head inside a book.

I raised her chin staring into her sparkling brown eyes. "Someday, but we will always be together. Always. Happy birthday, Sister." I rocked her gently.

12.

Sophie

"Woman barricades herself in the art museum's bathroom, news at eleven. I'm probably going viral right now the way I rushed in here. Two security cameras watch this bathroom, or are they guarding the Joseon dynasty relics? Hospital air." That stale, cold medicinal balm soured my nostrils. "Breathe, Sophia." *Lilacs, warm cinnamon rolls, brownies.*

Seashell countertops, gray and dark brown tile, depressing brown. "Great, I picked a depressing bathroom." Lacquered mud stalls and around a hidden corner: a narrow milk chocolate door. *I could hide in there*, I thought. *Hold out for a bit before they bust down the door.* I wriggled the knob; it turned. *I bet a security alarm goes off if you open it. I bet a security alarm goes off if you're in the bathroom for more than ten minutes.*

Art museums relished muted, soft soles, not Jimmy Choo stilettos pecking its herringbone wood floors. They echoed closer. "Don't linger, Sophia." I held my breath to avoid hyperventilating, sifting through my tote: a chocolate bar, water, magazine, phone—I could stay in here all morning. "Sophia, get your ass out of this bathroom," I whispered. *My brave, potty-mouth Sophia, leave.* The imagined words of my mom fired fast and often now in my thoughts. "Ass isn't a cuss word. I'm an adult." *Then act like one.* "You're not here, Mom. Why does it matter?" *It matters to me, Sophia. I didn't raise my daughter to have the mouth of Al Pacino.*

I cracked the door open searching the foyer. "She's a freak. She's still freakin' out there." I contemplated pushing the steel trash can in front of the door and locking the latch. "Her lipstick is always perfect. She won't come in here. She hates bathrooms. I hate bathrooms."

"So do I, dear." Cranberry loafers spoke with a British accent behind a mud pie stall. "Bloody hell." They spoke again. "Excuse me. Would you be so kind, dear?"

"*Putain*," I whispered.

"Excusez-moi. J'ai besoin de papier toilette."

"I should know French but I don't," I said. "Sorry."

"You said *putain*. I assumed . . . why should you know French, dear?"

"My mom's French. I never got around to learning it. I don't have the patience."

"I'm sure you would have, dear. It's never too late. Now, about my . . ."

"I knew how to speak when I was young."

"I hope so. You speak lovely, dear. Now . . ."

"No, I knew French . . . when I was a child. I was born in the U.S., but we lived in Paris for a while. My mom was an artist. Was. I can't get used to saying that; I don't want to. Isn't it funny how women can chitchat in the bathroom as strangers?"

"If I could get—my legs are numb, dear. Toilet paper, mine is empty. I really should look before I pick a stall. I'm so used to scanning the loo for mess. Ghastly taupe and god-awful brown grout. Did I say gout? I'll turn down my iPod. What lummox picked doo-doo brown for a bathroom? They make it unattractive in here so we don't linger. Are you there, dear?"

"Yes, I'm sorry. And the whole *putain* thing . . . I thought I was alone." I handed her a roll of toilet paper under her stall. "Do you need more?"

"I hope not. We're all addicted to our cell phones, aren't we? I'm texting as we speak."

"TMI."

"TMI? Dreadful jaw disorder. My friend ground her teeth to nubbins in her sleep. She never spoke the same after the implants, ruined her voice-over career, all the lisping."

"No . . . I . . . never mind," I said over her toilet flush. *You're just washing your hands, Sophia,* I told myself. *The coast is clear. She's gone. Don't stay in here. Do. Not. Linger.*

"Thank you for the toilet paper, dear. The last time this happened, I had to use my favorite handkerchief. I wasn't bringing it home, mind you. It's unbearable when young girls hand you crap paper towels. Glad it was you." She emerged from her stall; a woman in her sixties her gray-blue eyes scanned me, a lovely gray-blue like my mother's. I gazed into her eyes while she washed her hands. Kind eyes, eyes that seemed trustworthy, friendly.

She smiled, tossing her silver hair, feathered and cropped in a trendy pixie cut and wrapped herself in a Persian shawl, stunning turquoise, brown paisleys with splashes of rose. I pretend to blush my cheeks, searched for lip gloss, something for improvement. I had nothing.

"This is as fabulous as I get," she sang. "I'll spritz my perfume outside. I hate when women do that, in case you're allergic, though I detect a hint of coconut. Lovely. I don't understand a woman's obsession with ghastly vanilla. No woman over thirty should smell like a child bathed in candy. Bye, dear."

"Some women think men like women bathed in candy. Did I make sense?"

"I'm sure you did, dear. Take care." She examined the bathroom, eyeing my tote and belongings spread out on a chair. "Brown—all the improvements at the museum and they designed a hideous, brown bathroom." She balled up her paper towel, tossed a free throw into the trash, and screamed a laugh that probably made Randall call for backup. "I'm on a committee. I'll make a suggestion. A pink Oriental cherry blossom theme sounds lovely, doesn't it?"

Pink reminded me of why I ran in here. Before the woman left I shouted, "No, wait! Will you do me a favor? I know this is strange and you don't know me."

She rushed to me and held my hands. "What's wrong? You're shaking, dear." Her kind eyes searched mine. She looked at the exit, me. "Oh, yes. I see."

"See? I'm not crazy. I shouldn't have shouted. It's . . ."

"You're ducking a breakfast date, aren't you? He's hideous, a real horse face, of course. You're a knockout, dear. That navy shirt dress is quite fetching and the long boots very sexy."

"I dusted this off. Believe me I'm not stylish at all . . . sweats, sweaters."

"Find a handsome young man. I don't know why young girls date old men. There's not enough to go around for us geezers." She pulled me to sit on a chair hugging the wall. "Plenty of us mature women can still attract an older man—and a young stud or two." Her laugh echoed in the ceiling. "They're not all into young bimbos." She teased my hair.

"Oh, you don't have to—" I popped up in protest.

She gently sat me back down and said, "I know what I'm doing. I'm in theater . . . retired I suppose. On occasion I assist a struggling production here or there and everywhere."

"My hair doesn't—"

She grabbed a hunk and twirled it releasing a soft wave. "Brilliant," she said, bouncing it into place. "I wish I wasn't too damn old to play Juliet. I truly felt another Juliet resided within me. Where were we—men." She eyed the exit again at a tap on the door. I held my breath. "False alarm, that was me, dear. I fancy common looking blokes." She examined her master-piece—my hair—dug in her purse, revealed a jar, moistened her fingers, and smoothed them over my head. "James Bond types constantly look into mirrors." She swiped my forehead and nose with powder, my cheeks with blush. "Any lip gloss?" she asked. "I have a sample I never used from one of those teenybopper shops where they gawk at you wondering why the hell *you* came in. One little dish had the audacity to tell me I needed a mask for my chins."

Before I could answer, she slathered the gloss across my lips. "Peach is your color. You're quite stunning, dear, when you fix your face. And that little button nose, glorious."

"Wow. That was . . ." I looked in the mirror barely recognizing myself. "I haven't worn makeup in months."

"Is it best to date a plain or handsome man?" she asked, gathering her things.

"Gorgeous men smell good. My husband was handsome and arrogant. I could handle it."

"Well done, you. Why would I date a man who smells better than me?"

"You have a point. You may have *the* point."

"Didn't you Google him? You ought to have Googled before you made the date."

"A friend—"

"I see. I used to meet men here on blind dates, on a Friday night, never in the morning. I've met a few nice chaps, too damn old. Sorry, dear, I hear you don't care for swearing."

I snickered at this apparently sixty-something-year-old minx. "I love your accent. You sound a little like my stepmom. My dad remarried and lived in London. I visited somewhere in the country. I can't remember where."

"Cornwall. I bet it was Cornwall. Or Buckinghamshire. Yorkshire?"

"Cornwall rings a bell, so do the shires."

"Is he that, dear?" she asked, walking to the door. "Hideous? Looks aren't everything. You might go on with the date. I find a mind, even a jester, lends more to a serious relationship than a beautiful brute." She snatched a nail file and grabbed my fingers. I pulled them away; she smiled and sawed on her own.

"No, he's . . . I . . . found out he's . . ."

"Married! Bugger. We have a great deal in common." She walked over to the door and peered out as a Bond girl. "Now . . . who am I looking for?" she whispered. "My heart is racing."

"A woman holding a huge, hot pink purse, technically, magenta—luggage size."

"And a horrible beehive? The wife. The hot pink Louis Vuitton. Right, I've spotted it."

"That's her! I know, seriously, the beehive."

"What's she got stuffed up in there, a can of Guinness?"

"Probably." I loved this woman.

"She's . . . wait . . . she's talking to a security guard. She's flirting with him, sure of that. Oh, she's too young for him. What a tramp. I censored myself for you, dear."

"Is she coming this way?"

"No—wait. Good. She's leaving. The man's ushering her out. She's throwing a fit."

"Thanks, Randall," I whispered.

"She looked at me. No, she's gone." She held her chest and shut the door. "I haven't been this worked up since I blanked onstage during a performance of *The Merchant of Venice*. Improvising Shakespeare is impossible. Zounds, Shylock, methinks you suck. Dreadful."

"Are you sure she's gone?"

She spied out the door and gave me a thumbs-up. "Absolutely. I must get over this cold. I sounded like that Rocky fellow, didn't I? My nephew learned his American accent from those boxing movies." She bundled herself back into her shawl.

"Thanks, you were great. Did you really say zounds, Shylock, methinks you suck?"

"Not precisely, but it made you laugh. Dear, I'm off." She tossed her shawl over her shoulder, tousled her hair, and turned to me with one last compassionate look. "I gave myself a faux hawk, didn't I? It's the bloody gel. I told my nephew this haircut was too young for me."

"No, it's perfect. It brings out your beautiful eyes."

"Thank you." She paused, seeing right through me. I felt my tears rising. "Coming?"

"Oh, no. Don't hold the door. I have to—"

"There's no one out there, dear. I promise." She held out her hand offering to walk me outside. "You can trust me."

Everyone in your life is a gift, Sophia, even your enemies. It's up to you whether you receive them as a gift into your life or not.

Mom, how can anyone think an enemy is a gift?

They teach us how to fight, love and forgive. It's up to you now.

"Thanks, I'm fine." I cowered back to my chair, checking messages on my cell.

"If I wasn't late for my meeting, I would take you for a mimosa. Sounds nice, doesn't it?" She opened the door. "Have a better day."

"I will. A better day, I like that. I didn't catch your name."

"My manners. Annabel. Lovely to meet you."

"Sophie. Will I see you around here again?" I asked, needy.

"I tell you what . . . I spend a great deal of time at the bookstore around the corner on Sunshine Street. Maybe I'll see you there. We can have a cup of tea. You need a cup of tea, dear. It will settle your nerves. It always does. Take care."

"I will." Annabel's kindness stayed with me. I wanted to trust her, but I wished I hadn't noticed that slim door hidden in the corner. I clutched my magazine, settling into a cozy seat, chugged my water, and closed my eyes. "Breathe, Sophia. Breathe."

⁓

A tap on the door scattered my dreams. The bathroom door opened. Another tap; this time it pinged with keys. "Sophie? Sparrow?" Randall's rich voice echoed in the hallway.

"I don't like nicknames I have no idea what they mean." I didn't realize how stuffy it was in here until I had to speak.

"And I don't like our guests locking themselves in the only women's bathroom on this floor," he said in a stern voice I wasn't expecting.

"Why did you have to say women's? Don't men lock themselves in the bathroom, too?"

"Not particularly . . . in an art museum."

"Why put a lock on the bathroom door?"

"There isn't a lock on the bathroom door. You're in my utility closet." He opened the door wider, and I popped out like a jack-in-the-box my things exploding onto the floor.

"You shouldn't barge in here, Randall." I picked up my stuff. "Do you have cameras in the bathrooms now? I know the privacy laws are all to shit—buckets."

"Buckets?"

"I haven't found my replacement words yet." I shifted on the stool looking for a shoe.

"Replacement words?" He handed me my boot.

"Swearing, I promised Mom I would stop. How did you find me?"

"A concerned woman, Annabel, told me you were in here . . . that you might be in trouble. Are you in trouble, Sophie?"

I shifted again this time kicking a bucket. "A *concerned* woman? Right."

"How about we get that cup of coffee now."

My body stiff, I stretched, shaking the pins and needles from my legs. "Tea, coffee, everyone wants to fill me with caffeine." I opened the door, looked at him unapologetic, and headed for the mirror. "I guess I could use it. I fell asleep." I brushed my hair, blowing up Annabel's masterpiece. "It was only for a few minutes."

"Sophie, you can't go locking yourself in the bathroom at an art museum."

"It was an accident. A woman needed toilet paper—brown in a bathroom? Disgusting."

Randall gave me his sympathetic smile standing beside me. I handed him my smashed Snickers bar as my silent apology. He took it. "So women don't get ideas about locking themselves in the janitor's closet," he said. "Or hang my 'closed for maintenance' sign on my restroom door. You wouldn't believe how many women meet their blind dates at an art museum." He offered one of his back pats again, this time I stayed under it. "Oh, Sophie, you had to pick the day when the news crew arrived, huh?"

I dropped my tote. "Oh. My. Gosh."

The warmth of his palm left me as he stepped away and retrieved my tote. He held on to it, opened the door, and ushered me outside. "They were shooting in the Monet exhibition." He gestured to a crowd of giddy women. "It's all yours, ladies."

"Zounds, methinks blind dates suck," I said to the mob.

"Zounds?" I shrugged and gave Randall the reassuring smile he needed. He laughed and held my hand as a child. We walked in silence. "I also deflected two teens wielding cell phones. I was a big hero for you today." He led me through Arts of Asia, down a different hallway, and into a gallery under construction. "You're a special guest. Not many people walk through here."

"Thank you, Randall. I'm sorry."

He escorted me through a tall, steel door; we stood outside facing the parking lot. "Are you all right, Sophie? Do you need me to call someone?"

I searched for my car, her purse. "I . . . someone was out there who wanted to hurt me."

"Want me to walk you to your car? Do I need to call the police?"

"No." I took my tote from him. "I wish it were that easy. You did not sign up for me."

"See you tomorrow?"

I thought about that eccentric British woman, Annabel, wondering if I might catch her at the bookstore to give her a piece of my mind for ratting me out to Randall, or maybe . . . missing another shout-out on the five o'clock news, a cup of tea and wisdom from a worldly-wise woman sounded sublime. "You're the best, Randall."

"I'm sure going to miss this."

"I keep you busy. I see you pacing around here checking out women."

"Never when you're around."

"Good. I've found my purpose." I reached into my coat pocket for my keys and pulled out Dr. Arnold's card instead. I shoved it back into my purse.

"Get some rest, Sophie. See you tomorrow?"

"If this hits the news, you might never see me here again."

"It won't."

"Is that a threat, mister?"

"Nope, fact."

"Later, Cowboy."

"Sparrow." Randall left me with his charming wink and imaginary tip of his cowboy hat.

I gathered myself, remembering where I parked. A sprinkle of snow-flakes stuck to my coat. The warm sun slipped back into hiding offering soft gray clouds and snippets of lace.

Snowflakes. Bits of stars fall to earth frosted in white and trimmed in silver, the artistry of angels. I paused and let the tender ice melt on my cheek, avoiding the urge to look up and taste childhood with my tongue. "Mom, you should have painted snowflakes."

It's all right, honey.

"It isn't, Mom. It never was."

13.

Camille

"What's this—sadness on my daughter's birthday?" Mamma strolled into Geneviève's bedroom, sipping coffee, wearing an azure dressing gown embroidered in paisleys. The scent of steaming coffee swirled about her mixing with baked chocolate and lavender. Her black, wavy hair, soon stuffed into a horrid blonde wig. Mamma glowed without it; her black tresses set off the blue eyes that escaped her daughters, for we had, as Claude Monet claimed, *calf's eyes.* My cheeks burned at the thought, the sight of him below.

I replayed our encounter, his tender kiss to my hand and unabashed gaze. He was older, twenties, young and handsome. His hubris was unbecoming and attractive. Strange, after a few private moments, his presence below tempted me to be with him now.

"What is my daughter daydreaming about?" Mamma asked, startling my secret thoughts.

I closed the curtains and greeted her with my tentative hug. "*Bonjour,* Mamma. I'm finishing Geneviève's costume for the party."

"Your cheeks are red." She eyed me and glanced toward the window. I rushed to the dressing table searching for a cool towel. "Geneviève's, dear. What mischief goes on here?"

"Camille read me the fable about the diamonds and toads. We had a good laugh and a twirl besides." Geneviève failed to hide her wink at me.

Mamma crept in sniffing for secrets flinging her dressing gown over her lap as she sat demurely on the settee examining us. "You're biting your lip, Camille, as my child caught sneaking sweets." She laughed to herself, her piercing blue eyes drowning me in judgment. "A striking fashion on you today; cream and lilac stripes complement your complexion." I tugged at my sleeves. "Exquisite taste as my mother. I'm told the death of my blonde wig ensues tonight."

"Hurray," Geneviève shouted, clapping her hand over her mouth.

I hurried to Mamma, grabbing a hairbrush, twisting her black tresses into a chignon. "Your hair is too luxurious for a wig, Mamma. You look younger without it."

"Flattery? My daughter wants something. Geneviève, go and eat your breakfast. I speak with Camille alone." My body stiffened at the mention.

I held onto Geneviève's hand, but with talk of breakfast, she squirmed away scampering out the door. "May I help in the shop today, Sister?"

"After breakfast, you may sort ribbons," I said. "And no comments to Madame Durant on her new bonnet's irregular size. We'll sort it out later."

"Hurray. I won't utter a word to Madame Giant Head," Geneviève snickered, her chocolate ringlets jiggling across her neck as she skipped away.

My feet stuck to the floor. I searched my sister's room, enduring my mother's stare out of the corner of mine. "Camille, I don't relish Geneviève working in the shop. If you insist on presenting yourself as a common grisette, don't encourage her to do the same."

"It is our shop, Mamma, and she enjoys the busywork."

Mamma sipped her coffee watching me gather the books strewn about the room. The men's voices from the street grew louder. "Such a ruckus outside this morning," she said. "What's the matter now?" She looked toward the window, starting to rise.

I rushed to her. "A few more pins." Mamma sat down. I perfected her chignon as her coiffeur. "Monsieur Belrose draws lively visitors to his shop."

"The apartment across the way is grand, is it not?"

"Papa says it's too expensive," I mumbled, clinging to the window seat.

Mamma sighed and blinked cordiality away. "Always distance. He will close the shop."

I stared into a storybook tracing its gilded spine. "Why? We are making money. This should please you. Papa loves the shop."

She bristled at my tone, poking at her hair. "I know of his promise to you, but neither of us can ignore his health suffers for it. You pressure him."

I swallowed the sharpness of her words and held my locket, staring at the horizon. A doctor's visit last year, medication, Papa grew strong again. Debt was not Papa's burden—we were—his desperation to keep his wife. The pressure Mamma declared burdened neither of my parents' shoulders; it crushed mine. When we escaped the flood in Lyon, I carried a secret. As I grew older, the power of holding this secret gripped me. With one whisper, a rush of water in the night, my mother's ruse of respectability and prominence about Paris would disappear. The answer to why my mother turned away from me as a child was clear. She was afraid—of me.

Papa stopped hiding his indifference toward Mamma, her unhappiness, unreserved. I lied to my sister; I wished to flee Paris. The vision of a fan's sailboat carrying me across the sea no longer frightened as I stood in silence with my mother—the type of quiet resounding with noise.

"Where does my daughter go?" I faintly heard her ask. "The older you become, the more you drift. The more you . . . stray away from me."

I faced her with a newfound confidence. "I, from you?" I spied at the men below.

"You seek trouble." She rang her cup with a spoon for my attention. "And find it."

"It's a day for joy." I resigned for Geneviève, making myself go to her.

Mamma looked past me. "Why did your father paint this room blue? Yellow is fetching. He wanted a son and suffers in a houseful of women." She turned inward, glancing at a book on the floor. "*Cinderella*. Geneviève adores fairy tales."

"We all do." She caught me biting my lip again, pressing a finger to her mouth, reminding me as she did when I was a child. We smiled.

"But we cannot live in them." She set her cup and saucer on the table, searching me, straining to understand a daughter she barely knew. "I don't understand this gibberish on independent women. My mother used another name for them."

My skin prickled at the sting of her words. "It is no sin to desire a thorough education, work as a man works and think thoughts apart from home life, marriage, and—"

"Family?" I lingered at the bookcase. Most daughters confided not to their fathers on walks about the city, but to their mothers in the array of a salon with tea, cakes, and doting. "Will you not reconsider Monsieur Valentine?" she asked. "A soldier's wife is noble—your grandfather—"

"Napoleon's fiercest knight awarded the Legion of Honor." I smiled at the *Three Musketeers* in hand. "For a soldier, Henri lacks confidence. He loathes talk of the theater, art, and music. I must soldier on to marry the soldier and never speak on subjects I fancy?"

"A wife is for her husband, not the other way around."

"I refuse to believe I'm nothing without a man. It was not Adam but God who created Eve."

"More claptrap from that Madame Pontray."

"The elderly man haggles for his young bride, gains his price, and moves her away from her family and friends to a country cottage under the guise of tranquility. Why? He has no power over her in society but can dominate in solitude. This is the woman you wish me to become?"

"Me?" Mamma eyed her exit, rejecting my musings on women's rights. She unraveled her hair letting the waves fall, dropping pins in her hand, a dish. "Do we suffer?"

"Your daughters do—you manage to provide for yourself extravagantly."

"Enough." She rustled on the settee, pulling up the sides of her hair, repinning them her own way. "I concede your ideas are your own, but you need a well-off husband to take care of you. Our funds will provide no future for you or your sister. It is the only way."

"It might be a way, but it is not the best way, and it should not be law."

"How will you earn your living?"

"Open my own dress shop . . . perhaps model. I have a proven talent," I insisted.

She picked up a forgotten book off the settee and waved it. "Your mind swims in fairy tales, but these fanciful notions are not the way of France."

"France is the most unchanging country in the world."

My mother stood, offering me the book in hand: Shakespeare sonnets Papa gave my sister last year. I held it tight, escaping to the window. "Conventions," she said, following me, standing at a distance letting me stew. I ignored the men below, fixing my eyes on the horizon, wondering what sort of life I could have living beyond it, beyond these walls, the choices of curtains, rugs, and husbands. "Rules proper women must follow," she said. "They build us a new Paris and pave a dark path for a woman without a sou or reputation." She sat on the settee, awaiting my answer. I said nothing.

She sighed, stiffening her posture; my hands fidgeted with the curtain's rough folds. "I see so much of my father in you." For the first time in months,

Mamma softened and came to me stroking the lick of hair near my cheek. She smoothed it back with a brush of her finger. I missed her touch. "Those little wisps of hair always tickled me."

"Women of France cannot fight as a soldier for her, but they must be soldiers in love, carrying out their marching orders without rebellion."

"A woman walking the path you desire is an outcast among the women she thought might come to her aide, understanding. The circles of Paris are cruel, yet, necessity."

"I try, Mamma. But it is hard to unlearn what I have discovered."

"What's this?"

"I do not need a man to tell me who I am . . . to give me purpose."

Her hand slid off my shoulder. She returned to her settee, I, my window. "A model? No. You have your grandfather's stubbornness, which tests me."

"I don't mean to test you."

Mamma shook her head at me suppressing a smile. "Oh, you burn with his fight and passion for art. My father was a brave man, but the scars he carried from battle; my mother and I never grasped his sacrifice. The sacrifices he made so his daughter wouldn't have to fight."

I picked up Geneviève's party dress stuffing the crinoline under the blanket. "I cannot imagine Grandfather as a hellish knight on the battlefield, wielding saber on monstrous steed, and pipe and paintbrush at home as your tender papa. Your mamma's salon filled with artists?"

"A few stars." Mamma stared at her reflection, puzzled. "You believe you compete with Geneviève for affection—my competition was my father's war horse." We shared a soft laugh.

I missed Mamma's tales of my grandfather, his love of horses and art. She lost her father at thirteen. Papa said it was the deepest wound for a child, worse, Mamma's second heartbreak, losing a son. A tragedy we never speak on, that we must understand life was unfair to Mamma.

France's law forbids a young woman from marrying without her parents' consent. Marriages in France were not romantic, but business contracts years in the making. Any hint of scandal—a contract, unlikely. "Gabrielle is a fast woman," her voice resounded out of nowhere.

I drifted. Mamma's lecture on my cousin's coming visit, muted. "Cousin Gabrielle is respectable," I said. "We plan to attend the night concert at

Frédéric Bazille's invitation." I grabbed the hairbrush. Mamma sat still while I braided her silky strands forming an intricate chignon. "A knot of pansies will make you younger than springtime."

"Flattery?" She raised an eyebrow. "Your papa knows it is the Mabille, an outlandish ball, where one may find the trouble she seeks?" She studied her hair in the mirror, grooming as Elise's cat licking and tucking hairs in place. "I suppose . . . if your company is worthy."

"*Merci*, Mamma! Gabrielle writes Frédéric is the subject of the ladies."

"His Uncle Lejosne's salon hosts the grandest soirées in Paris, a cultured, wealthy family. Monsieur Valentine will also attend this outdoor ball."

"To watch over me? Will you and Papa spy as well?"

She lifted my chin and searched my eyes. I had no window or storybooks to hide them in. "Beauty matters not if tainted with suspicion. Camille, come out from the clouds. No sensible woman marries for love. If so, she discovers it was not love at all but fear."

"I am sad you think of Papa so. I always believed you married for love."

"I was a young girl without a father; your papa was twenty-two years older." A flush of youth washed over her. "I didn't know what love was." Mamma gestured to the window. "One Monsieur Monet waits in the shop insisting you alone help him with the lace he requires for—"

"His aunt," I said, catching my excitement. "He is a particular sort."

Mamma brushed past me peering out the window. "A handsome sort indeed. Monsieur Bazille's height gives himself away. There he stands with Monsieur Monet. If dressed, I would go outside to meet him, the doctor who desires to whisk my daughter off to the Mabille."

"A group of us, I barely know Frédéric." I peered at the men.

"Frédéric? Hmm, Monsieur Belrose is having one of his fits with those unsuspecting young men—artists. They rummage through the Batignolles as a caravan. Poor Monsieur Belrose, he should've closed his shop years ago. His wife is hardly getting on." She dismissed me with a clap. "Go, you are the Beauty that tames the beast."

"Monsieur Belrose is just an old man frustrated by his forgetfulness."

"Funny, how many of us wish we could forget. How many of us *should* forget." With a fling of her gown, Mamma squeezed my hand and left the room.

14.

Sophie

Winter drifted back to sleep offering a sprinkle of rain. I prided myself in knowing how to be alone; I hadn't realized I couldn't do lonely. Instead of rushing to my car, I found a quiet park bench outside the museum, and for the first time in over a year, I dared to absorb the silence.

See, Sophia.

"I've convinced myself it isn't crying if the sky cries with you." I searched the clouds for answers, this impressionistic sky with its streaks of denim, lavender and scattered raindrops. I remembered this sky.

A year and nine months ago, my husband left the house under a lavender sky to "run an errand" and "visit a friend." I let him go without questions, questions I had for months, questions a wife doesn't want answered.

"I have to take care of this one thing." Blake grabbed his keys. "Settle something."

"Is it the case? The one you're worried about?" I asked indifferent.

"No, it's something more important. I promise. I'll be back. We need to talk."

His last four words stung my heart; fear and anger crawled over my skin. "Is that a bad we need to talk or a good we need to talk?" I asked, deceiving myself with our plans for Paris. I wouldn't let him answer. "No, Blake. I'm leaving." I snatched my jacket, biting my lip to keep from crying. "Do whatever you have to do. I told Megan I would go shopping with her. Strange, she said she needed to talk, too."

"Sophie, stay home tonight." Blake wasn't a beggar; it made me want to flee. "I'll make dinner. We'll talk about our plans for Paris. Everything's going to be all right. You'll see."

Paris—tickets in hand, tours of the countryside, the Louvre, pastries, drinking chocolate. Blake wanted desperately to break out of his slump and shouted to wake me from mine. "Sophie, we need to get away," he insisted.

"*Why? Everything will be here when we get back: your deadlines, my 'sickness.' Is that what you call it?*"

"*You're grieving. You lost your father. I get it. You have regrets about your dad, questions. We need Paris. You need Paris.*"

"*Are we kidding ourselves?*" I searched for my keys now. "*Something's been missing for a long time. I haven't been myself since Dad died I know. I thought you understood.*"

"*I can't do this now. I told you . . .*" His cell dinged a text; he hid it from me.

"*Right,*" I said, praying he would drop his keys on the table, close the door, and come into my arms.

Silence.

Frozen silence.

The squeal of tires in the museum's parking lot brought me back to the lavender sky. The drizzle stopped. I opened my journal and scribbled a few thoughts to fill a page:

I wonder if Blake ever thought about silence, the silence he left me with when he slammed our front door, his silence at my question: "Do you want to stay married?" The silence of me standing at the window, waiting for him to come home.

"I can't do this," I said, slamming the journal shut, closing my eyes at this memory. One I wished, after all this time, would dissolve away like a wisp of a cloud in the falling rain.

"*Do whatever you have to do,*" I said, walking away from my husband, wishing I had the courage to face him, face it all. "*Go.*"

"*Sophie, couldn't you trust me this once? Stay.*"

"*It's not fair. Whatever you're doing, it's not fair.*"

"*You don't make it easy. You don't.*"

"Neither do you," I said to no one. "But it doesn't matter now, does it?"

A glimmer of morning sun stretched behind the clouds longing to brighten this day. I opened my journal, splattering my heart onto the page.

Regret.

Brain bruises. Soul pain. Heartache.

Should haves. Maybe ifs.

"I wish."

15.

Camille

I raced downstairs to the shop. Papa's sign read *Open at 10:00 today*. "He fetches Cousin." I scooped up Raphael and peeked outside. Three artists gathered at Monsieur Belrose's haberdashery: Monsieurs Monet, Bazille, and Renoir, a blond, pink-faced charmer clutching his paintbox as if packed with gold coins. Renoir spotted me and rapped on the door, "Mademoiselle, we require your assistance," he called, flailing his arms, rattling his paintbox in the air.

I spun around hiding my snicker. "What should I do, Raphael?" My little dog pranced to my unfinished display, plopping on the rug inside the window. I spied on the men from behind the curtain. "You don't belong in there. Go find Geneviève for a treat." He scampered away. I grabbed a parasol armed to join the men's fray. At my hesitation, Claude Monet opened the door, its bell jingling his arrival. "Papa left it unlocked," I gasped, forgetting Raphael left.

"My fortune, I hope. Mademoiselle Doncieux." He tipped his hat, glancing at my parasol tucked to my side as a saber. He chuckled. "Monsieur Belrose doesn't recognize us today."

"He is too old for your games."

He inched toward me. "Your father suggested I return this afternoon. My manners betray me yet again; I had to see you." He fidgeted with his hat, quickly setting it on a chair.

I held my staggered breathing as he walked closer, searching past him to the street. "Is this what you fancy? Harassing the shopkeepers in our quiet village?"

He perused the shop, glancing at me as he did among Elise's flowers. "Careful with that parasol, mademoiselle; I know of your history with faulty umbrellas."

I twiddled the handle, watching him tour the shop and examine a table of handkerchiefs and satchels. He smiled, impressed at a show of pastel feathers and ribbons, and snubbed a display of black capes. He paused at our newest dress: billowy cream linen, a ruffled lace jacket, topaz bows, and lace trim. "This interests me," he said. "I must see it in the sunlight."

"Indeed," I said bothered, unmoved.

He studied the garment further, fanning out the skirt, thumbing a cuff on a sleeve. "The movement in the light, the way it skips across the sleeve there casting a shade of lemon and there a sliver of pink. That is what makes it interesting."

"That dress shows no pink, monsieur."

"Then you know not this dress."

"No fashion for a portrait; it is a morning dress for leisure in the privacy of one's home."

"All the more alluring—perhaps I shall paint . . . a lady in conversation with her maid, secrets whispered to a visiting friend."

"A mischievous smile to herself while reading on a lounger," I added intrigued.

"You are beginning to see. Barefoot in a garden . . ."

"Absurd."

"Is it, mademoiselle?" I held my tongue as he peered around a cabinet, snickering at the parasol teetering in my hand. "A woman caught in the rain in her garden." He sauntered behind me taking my parasol. "A beautiful woman tucked underneath a lilac tree, this buried in grass."

"Sitting alone at a white, wrought-iron table, a bowl of strawberries, and an empty chair next to her as the sun rises casting a splash of pink light upon her dress."

He leaned in close from behind me and whispered in my ear, "And now you see."

I caught my breath, snatched the parasol back, rushing away to put it with the others, and slipped past him hiding behind the counter. "We are closed, monsieur," I said, coming to myself. "You and your friends have riled my poor neighbor enough."

He swiped his fingertips across the countertop as a master checking for dust, cocking his head to view the fans in the cabinet behind me. "No other shop about the city has this shade of lavender on its walls. They are plastered with gold and velvet papers." He held his chin tapping his finger on his cheek as he studied me. "Bold, setting yourself apart from what is ordinary."

I shuffled hat stands on the counter. "Are you talking about our walls or your manner?"

"Your shop boasts much wealth, yet it is not on the rue de la Paix . . . respectfully."

"Perhaps not the rue de la Paix you expected?" I swirled the lick of hair on my cheek. He noticed. He noticed everything.

"I spent five francs on a carriage searching for you." He plucked a post-card from the counter and read, "The Elegance Shop, 37, rue de la Paix, *Batignolles*. India and French cashmeres, black and white lace, and fancy goods."

"You searched for me?"

He shifted to the cool manner I loathed, returning the card to its box. "For this shop, *oui*," he said with his airs. His eyes studied me again, admiring my hair, searching my eyes, my lips.

"Your five francs might have served you better ogling the statues at the Louvre." He smiled and turned away, staring into the linen dress he fancied earlier. "What are you thinking now . . . about that dress, monsieur?" I asked, lured into his imagining.

"You wearing it, mademoiselle."

I held his stare, smiling to myself, standing taller. *His model*, I imagined. *No, not his*, I resolved, gathering a bundle of packages and ribbons. "I have a window display to finish."

"May I see the fan with the sailboat?"

"I'm sorry, monsieur, that one is sold."

"The one with the landscape?"

"Reserved." I twisted my bows in knots around my packages, staring at him.

"The courtship?"

"I am sorry."

He slid a peach ribbon off the counter, taking the package from my hand. He gazed at me, tying a perfect bow around the package without looking. I smiled at his handiwork. "My friend Renoir has painted well a fan or two—perhaps, one of his."

"I'm sorry, monsieur. We do not accept payment by . . . picture." I hid my grin.

"You don't believe my arrangement with Madame Pontray. She supports us all in our cause." He gestured to his friends outside still arguing with Monsieur Belrose.

"Cause?"

Monsieur Monet leaned in close ready to share his secret, fondling the forget-me-knot bracelet on my wrist. "The new art," he whispered, spinning the flowers tickling my skin.

"Monet!" Renoir shouted, startling us. "Mademoiselle," he called, tapping the glass with the end of his paintbrush. "No time for love behind counters. The shopkeeper's gone mad!"

"Heavens, I will never have any peace." I left Monet in the shop; I could stay with him no longer. The men quieted as I stood before them. "The police might be a good lesson for you."

Frédéric Bazille offered his stately bow. "Mademoiselle Doncieux, may I introduce—"

Renoir pushed past him blurting his greeting, "Pierre-Auguste Renoir, a fine painter indeed." He tipped his bowler hat, tucked his paintbrush behind his ear, and despite a cough from Bazille, kissed my hand.

"Monsieur Belrose," I said, strolling toward him. "What is the trouble, my neighbor?" I cradled his hand and walked the old shopkeeper to his store.

"Child," Monsieur Belrose cried, coming back to himself. "I'm sorry," he whispered.

"Indeed, he should be," Renoir exclaimed, riling the beast.

"*En garde.*" Monsieur Belrose lunged toward him raising his cane as a sword. "They tried to rob me. I saw the red one steal a cravat."

Renoir raised his paintbox as a shield. "He fancies you," I whispered to him. "Please, put the cane down, Monsieur Belrose."

Monsieur Belrose pitched it into a bucket. "Where's the dandy?" he asked, wriggling his nose as if sniffing sour cheese. "They'll spoil my sale with their games."

Monet arrived grinning and adjusted Renoir's disheveled coat. "Kind monsieur, you know us," he sang. "Renoir fancies your cravats and Bazille purchased two pairs of opera gloves from you last week. He can't afford them," he whispered to me, his nose brushing my cheek.

Monsieur Belrose picked up a top hat from his sale table. "Claude Monet, the artist," he hissed, "made me believe it was an honor I should offer him a new hat without charge."

"Alas, Claude was born a lord, you see." Renoir swaggered in to save his friend, enjoying his mischief. "I fancy your English cravats, the truest blue. The French cravat is neither blue nor black but gray. Shall I a beach stone or blueberry around my neck—I heartily choose blueberry."

"The red one's daft. Lost your buttons, have you?" Monsieur Belrose came back to himself for a moment, turning to me with a great laugh. "His black eye proves he's a troubling sort. I warned the lad, colored cravats are prohibited at evening parties."

"All the more to wear one," I said, winking at Renoir.

"Our beautiful peacemaker," said Bazille. Frédéric's height and elegance rose above his friends. He sported a double-breasted vest and checkered trousers. Every time Monet whispered in my ear, Frédéric tugged at his beard as if signaling him to cease. Renoir reveled as a jester with his black eye. I hoped for the scandalous details on the brawl before Papa's return. Monet changed his jacket, tailored and black without a smear of paint. A cluster of violets in his buttonhole amused me. I missed his faint limp. Renoir brushed the injured leg making Monet wince. Standing before me, the young artists posed as Dumas's dashing three Musketeers.

"Your sale looks fine today, Monsieur Belrose," I said, taking his hand. His eyes glazed with tears as he searched his surroundings. "These men want to honor you with their patronage."

"Camille?" Monsieur Belrose said, at last recognizing me. His harsh demeanor melted before them, and they could see he was unwell.

"It's all right now," I said softly. "Monsieur Belrose, Papa will help you with your sale."

"You'll dress my window, child?" he asked, rubbing his round spectacles with his handkerchief. He ushered us inside his disorganized shop, shelves stacked with top hats, bowlers, racks of cravats, shirts and jackets strewn across tables. An unusual offering near the window caught my eye: a painter's easel and table displaying a rainbow of tube paints and paintbrushes.

Too clever for Monsieur Belrose, I thought. "And when did you start selling colors?" I asked him. "This is a haberdashery, is it not? You must specialize."

"My wife said they were cosmetics," he said, making us laugh. The old shopkeeper disappeared into his stockroom reappearing balancing a platter of orange cake. "Men must eat," he said, his eyes scanning us over the rim of his spectacles. "Perhaps you'll stay and indulge me in a game of whist?" The men enjoyed the cake. I caught Renoir pocketing two slices.

"I'm certain these artists find plenty of colors at Ottoz or Latouche," I said, turning to leave. "This appears sorted. Monsieur Belrose, you can trust them."

"Do you, child?"

I reveled, scrutinizing the men, smiling at Renoir, motioning for him to wipe the crumbs off his cheek. "Renoir's black eye indeed exudes ruffian," I said, "and Monet's limp—is he brute in similar brawl?" I turned to Bazille's impressed glance. "Monsieur Bazille, you could not end this fray? A cultured gentleman as you should know the music to play to calm a soul as this."

"She's as mad as the old shopkeeper," Renoir whispered. "I fancy her."

Monet led their laughter pacing eager to make his case. "You seem to have a penchant for judgment, mademoiselle. Renoir's ghastly injury is but an occupational hazard. He fought a tempest in the Fontainebleau forest. Shop girls—"

"Shop girls, indeed," I said.

Renoir struck a fighting pose. "By Blue, trolls and dragons stole my paints and palette."

"Harassing our comrade for his hideous blue smock," Monet said, pacing his imaginary stage. "The evil horde of shop girls and their gentlemen monsters accosted our poor, little man."

"How did you escape?" I asked, transfixed.

Renoir took the stage acting his tale. "The goliath, Master Diaz, arrived as my hero, fighting on a wooden leg no less. The famous artist thrashed my tormentors into the sky."

"Heavens," I declared, laughing at Renoir's swordplay.

"I stood in disbelief. At battle's end, I showed Diaz my painting. 'A fine drawing,' he said. 'But, Renoir, why the hell do you paint it so black?' Alas, my painting changed forever."

"We applaud Renoir's blasphemous blue trees and lilac grasses," Bazille cheered. Renoir bowed. "Monet also shines as a hero," Bazille continued. "In this forest, he saved three children by jumping in front of a flying metal discus." Monet bowed to his friends' applause and bravos.

"Monsieur Belrose," I said, "you cannot trust these men. They tell sordid fictions."

"Oh, but they do amuse." The old shopkeeper fell back onto his chair with laughter.

"You do not believe them," I insisted. "No one paints outdoors or in the forest."

"Certainly we do, mademoiselle," Bazille said. "We pride ourselves in our new school."

"What school is this?" I asked.

The men signaled for me to lean in close, searched the street for spies, and back to Monsieur Belrose who nodded off in the chair outside his door. "The school of nature!"

"Blazes, my heart is too old for this revelry." Monsieur Belrose retreated into his shop at our laughter. "Lads, when you finish boasting your tales to the lady, I'll show you the new tube paints and a red cravat for Renoir." He waved and kept his door open, retreating into his shop.

"*Merci*," I said to the men. "You have given Monsieur Belrose his pride today."

"Forgive us, mademoiselle," Bazille said. "We're celebrating."

"Celebrating?" I asked, rummaging through dress shirts on a sale table with Renoir.

"The Salon accepted our paintings," Renoir sighed, finding a red silk scarf. "The jury was into the champagne accepting my portrait. I'll burn it after the exhibition."

Bazille joined us. "With my unfinished painting this year I celebrate the Opéra."

Monet edged his way between us. "This player ponders painting, playing at plays." He caught a top hat from Renoir, tried it on, and tossed it to Bazille who placed it back on the table.

"Indeed, I saw Monet's *scandal* on Varnishing Day." I walked back to my shop window.

Monet and Renoir dashed in front of me. "What scandal?" Monet asked.

I stared at his reflection in the glass. "Papa regretted spending the twenty francs to see it."

"Manet," the men said in unison.

"Monet." I turned to him indignant. "I cannot imagine how one as you could paint such a horror. It does not fit your nature."

"How so?" Monet asked, studying my empty shop window with me.

"Monet unknown yesterday, became at once a reputation in this single painting," Renoir said. "Lacking study but oh, his taste in color. Monet conquers Paris with two seascapes."

"Mademoiselle, I cannot let you leave us thinking ill of our Monet," Bazille said. "The artist of the *horror* you so describe, *Olympia*, is my friend Édouard Manet, not Monet."

"Bazille now makes the case for his Manet's every creation," Renoir moaned, sketching two women scouring Monsieur Belrose's sidewalk sale.

"I am relieved Monsieur Monet is not the creator of such a painting," I said. "A nude prostitute reclining on a chaise longue—she stares right at us without apology."

"Without anything." Renoir snorted. "No—earrings and one shoe." Renoir's pastels swirled across his paper, captivated by his unsuspecting models. "The nude is the highest of art forms." Renoir squinted, hobbling to me for a closer look. I giggled as my sister.

"Wisdom from our old teacher Gleyre," Bazille explained.

"You studied together?" I asked. "At the Academy?"

"And quit together at Gleyre's school," Renoir said. "To the forest Monet proclaimed."

"Claude played at study more than any of us," said Bazille, darting his eyes from me to the two women at Monsieur Belrose's sale. "Monet rather dash off mittens for hands on his canvas."

"Monet will never paint a nude," Renoir said to me, laughing.

"I will do my best to keep you sorted." I glanced at Monet. His eyes never left me, even as I contemplated ideas for Papa's window. "Édouard Manet. Monet. Manet. Quite a puzzle."

"The confusion with this infamous Édouard Manet draws people to my pictures," said Monet, watching Renoir sketch the giddy women. The coquettes wiggled their fingers in a wave, fighting over Renoir's red silk scarf.

I grabbed a handful of colorful feathers from a box Papa left outside the window. "This Édouard Manet does his worst painting the vulgarity of his model—his Olympia needs a bath."

Monet smiled, impressed. "His painting shocks the public." He plucked a yellow feather from my hand stroking it across my palm. "Made them feel. Master Courbet claims he paints an occasional obscenity for rejection at the Salon. In their refusal, his paintings make money."

"What of us?" Renoir asked. "We hold not Courbet's purse, fame, nor stomach to placate our government's mandate for classical art. Paint a Venus—pale skin, blank expressions."

"What does Manet's *Olympia* do for our cause?" Bazille asked. "I'm ashamed my uncle holds a banquet in the man's honor. At best, Manet makes progress frustrating the Salon."

"But is it honest?" I asked. They paused at my question.

"Mademoiselle reminds us," Monet said, smiling. "Manet soils what we hold dear."

"What is that?" I asked, intrigued.

Monet plucked out the red feathers from my hand, leaving me with a bundle of violet and white. "Truth in art; if one desires to paint a scene or set scandal aflame, do so truthfully, not in charade or comedy as a dirty picture hidden in the back of Uncle's newspaper." Renoir lingered with his laugh. With a tug to his beard, a nervous Bazille stepped away.

"You must show them a different way," I said, my heart leaping into their hands. "Shall our government forever have the right to dictate what is and what is not art?"

"By Blue, our Joan of Arc." Renoir waved his hands for me to continue.

"The public roams the Salon's galleries as a herd of lost sheep," I said. "They follow in ignorance and taste what is force-fed. The Salon varies not this diet of shadowed mythology, Madonnas, and war. Have we not stared at battle scenes long enough?" I no longer hid my thoughts in the window display. "If we, in this time, never challenge what has always been, we will never gain anything new and worthy of change. We are worthy of change." Renoir applauded. Monet and Bazille said nothing. "Forgive me," I said, blushing. "I'm not often swept up in such conversations, but you men make it hard to resist."

"Must they be so cruel to Manet who paves the way for us?" Bazille asked. "They bemoan, 'killer of respect.'"

"Paint a nude, don't strip it," Renoir added. "A discussion better suited in our café." Renoir took on the role of my protector, escorting me back to the business of Papa's window.

"Claude will surely be the star among us," said Bazille.

"Tonight, a champagne dinner for Monet at his benefactor's—lobster with truffles and browned Bercy sauce," Renoir said, slapping Monet's back. "And four commissions besides."

Monet offered me a violet from his buttonhole. "A steep climb ahead," he said. I took the flower returning his smile.

In awe, Renoir and Bazille studied a quiet Monet. "For the Beauty that tames all manner of beasts has caused our decadent dandy to display a smidgen of humility," said Bazille.

Renoir swiped a feather from Monet, tickling Bazille's nose. "You could rise. Ever playing piano," he squealed. "Acting, writing—enchant us with your *Le Fils de Don César.*"

"Is this true?" I asked Bazille. "I had no idea you fancied the theater."

"Before my play finds a stage they judge," Bazille said, turning to leave.

"Paris has been made for judgment," I said, lost in Papa's window: a salon scene, a gilt armchair in pink velvet, a parlor table, floral rug, and violet paper lanterns.

"I hope you and Gabrielle still plan on attending the Mabille as our guests," Bazille said.

"Must we leave now?" Renoir asked. "I'm sketching her nose, slender with a slight upturn, the jaw difficult, but the downcast eyes, *magnifique.*"

I covered my face with a fan at his mention. "Gabrielle has yet to arrive in Paris," I said.

Monet's indifference returned. "And I leave for the Fontainebleau Forest for my studies."

"See how Monet turns with mad thoughts on his next triumph at the Salon," Bazille said, following Monet's gaze to the women outside Monsieur Belrose's shop. "Crazed seeking models for his great machine in the forest."

"What is a great machine?" I asked.

"A monstrosity of a canvas," Renoir moaned. "To drive an artist insane, in debt, nursing aches, and lamenting lack of paints. Never mind our madman intends to execute it *en plein air.*"

"Out-of-doors," I said. "Splendid. How will you accomplish this, Monsieur Monet?"

"We are all asking that same question." Bazille tipped his hat to leave.

"It has never been done," Monet said to himself, lost in the thought of his task.

"Cynicism only spurs him on," Renoir continued. "I tolerate Paris, as Monet. Claude longs for the sea, Frédéric aches for the country, and I'm content wherever I roam."

Monet froze, his finger in midair contemplating the women before him. He shook his head displeased and examined Bazille and me. "Secrets under forest shade . . . lovers—friends. Your height precisely—I must have her for my picture."

"No. Too young," Bazille insisted, shooing me to Papa's window. "Her chignon high."

"Modern," Renoir said. "By Jove, a brunette as all of Paris turns blonde as the Empress."

"Now you see." Monet grabbed Renoir's sketchbook, scribbling our forms in the middle of a primitive forest. "A modern scene—a forest picnic, the sunlight's effects before my eyes in nature, not imagined, softened by all manners of shaded colors. Our generation. Our time."

"Monet detests meager beginnings." Bazille said, jealousy sneaking into his voice. "Master Courbet warns Claude will never finish it in time."

"Courbet longs for his youth," Monet said, wringing his hands at the thought. "I will finish. Her beauty shall win Paris for us all. Mademoiselle?"

I tamed my thoughts at his smug smile. "I will never finish this window." But I had what I wished. I stood with artists, the subject of their study and enchantment. My ideas respected and explored between the men thrilled me, the business of Papa's shop less and less the more they spoke and tempted me with thoughts of painting and modeling in the forest.

"It's settled. Who will she be?" Monet asked. "A lady contemplating the latest *la mode*." Monet grabbed a scarf from Papa's box, flinging it around my neck.

"With an odd penchant for men's kerchiefs." Renoir placed one in my hand.

"And lace gloves," I said, slipping them on.

"Bonnets," Bazille said, topping my head with a purple hat.

"A parasol." Renoir placed it at my feet. "More feathers!"

"Ribbons," the men cheered to the disapproval of onlookers and Monsieur Belrose.

"You are all indeed mad," I said, casting off the garments with a twirl as my sister. Bits of ribbons and feathers flew about them. We cheered and laughed, the artists bending me as their model in poses, tossing flowers, ribbons, making a greater commotion than at the start of our morning. I curtsied as the men offered me a flower, bowing to their modern Parisian queen.

"Camille, a measure of respect," my mother's voice scolded from the window above. I whisked off the bonnet and hid the flower behind my back. "I assisted Monsieur Belrose ... as you requested," I said to her. "These gentlemen offered to help with my window display." I looked at the men, holding my laugh, their heads buried inside the empty box.

"You've wasted enough time this morning," Mamma said. "Come out from the street among these men—flirting about as a common courtesan."

Our muffled laughter ceased. The men parted as I walked to our shop's front door dropping the costume pieces back into the box. "We are sorry, mademoiselle," Monet said softly.

"I am forever her disgrace."

"Madame Doncieux!" Monsieur Belrose shouted. "A dressing gown is no respectable fashion for greeting my customers and is revealing to the men below as a mere ... *courtesan*." At the crowd's laughter, my mother closed the window and walked away.

"*Merci*, my neighbor," I said, kissing his cheek.

"I'll catch hellfire from your mother but what of it? Why, Madame Doncieux," he pretended. "I don't recall I said such a thing at all." He grinned, his cheeks flushed with rose.

"Will we see you at the night concert, mademoiselle?" Monsieur Bazille asked.

The shrunken shopkeeper sprouted as tall as Bazille, grabbing his arm, pulling him away. "Come, man," Monsieur Belrose ordered. "Do you not know the repercussions that will rain down upon you from the spurned mamma?" He led Bazille and Renoir to his shop leaving Monet behind. "Bazille, you owe me for the gloves. And you, Renoir, for the paints."

"Today the dandy wins at love," Renoir said, looking back at us as Monsieur Belrose corralled the men. "There's always tomorrow, my Joan of Arc. Tomorrow," Renoir called.

"The lad is surely daft," Monsieur Belrose said to the laughing crowd.

16.

Sophie

A party. I want you to remember me with laughter and sunflowers. "And lavender." I stared at Mom's darkened gallery across the street. *"Abstract, cubism, expressionism, impressionism—I don't know what ism I am, Mom, I just paint."*

"Bien. You don't need to know right now, feel . . . see, Sophia. I taught you."

"But it's your reputation. I'm not good enough."

"I believe in you." Two years ago, Mom's last exhibition was mine: a mother-daughter collaboration setting the art world abuzz. Paintings, offers, and motivation, disintegrated the summer Dad died, Blake, her. My ex-best friend, Megan, said this, *it*, wouldn't last long, this empty hole burning like a Vader lightsaber into my soul. My life mirrored Megan's except for one important detail: Megan moved on. Moving on was Megan's superpower.

"Visit the twenty-first century email, text," I yelled at my phone. "I bet she has a rotary."

"What's a rotary?" our receptionist Jacey asked, squinting at me through her rhinestone cat-eyes. "Oh, the dial thingy phone—candy apple red highly collectible." In her late twenties, Jacey was a quirky optimist who insisted she was born in the wrong era, so she wore them all: poodle skirts, leather jackets, June Cleaver dresses, and a fetish for Bakelite bangles and eighties neons. A favor to Mom, her former student, Jacey, hadn't a clue about the travel industry, but we counted on her social media magic and creative prowess to revive our struggling agency, we prayed wouldn't close next year.

"It's power," Joe said, shaking a bag of burnt popcorn above my head. "Mrs. Lemon's a sweet, elderly woman with nothing to do."

"Sweet?" I sifted through a stack of travel catalogs: *Alaska; The Essence of Europe; River Cruises: Switzerland to the North Sea.* "Why didn't I visit you on my vacation?"

"Couldn't stay away?" Joe asked, surprised to see me.

"Someone please buy this man a microwave with a popcorn setting." I buried my head in a closet searching for more brochures to amazing destinations I should have visited.

"Mrs. Lemon's a control freak." Jacey waved a vial of essential oil under my nose. "Lavender Rose." I closed my eyes breathing in peace. "She comes in here to spy on us."

"She does that from her condo window," Joe snickered, inhaling Jacey's wrist. She giggled and shooed him away.

Lovely, I'm stuck in a Jane Austen novel. I schlepped back to my desk avoiding my reflection in the antique mirror. Damn antique mirror. I never imagined myself as a gifted dancer, until after Mom became sick when she pushed Joe and me onto the dance floor to figure out the intricate steps. Joe and I had a history: a flirty friendship that remained a friendship. I skipped around the truth, glided past our feelings, and twirled away from my past to the tune of melancholy violins, sometimes a tango. Single again, it didn't occur to me to push the boundaries of our friendship until last week after Mom died—Joe kissed me, or I kissed him, but mostly because Jacey had a silent crush on Joe, and by all accounts, it appeared reciprocated.

"That Mid-Century Modern table is worth five hundred smackers. I paid thirty bucks," Jacey giggled. "My little brother wanted it." Joe and Jacey disappeared into the breakroom.

I turned on my radio, soft jazz ready to fill the silence. "Go home, Sophie." I stared out the window at the gray day. Memories as movie scenes skipped forward and backward in my mind, stuck in the static of emotion, suspense, and frustration. *Mom's Last Night* rewinds and replays; the pixilated image unfreezes. The permission of lingering privacy, I watch it play.

The snow fell horizontally, each flake drifting out of formation, bouncing where it will. Huge flakes covered my hair; Joe brushed them off. "She is not a name, Sophia, she is a spirit now." Joe, my guardian angel, stood outside my mother's room. How he held and rocked me when Blake should have been there and ushered me away before my mother's final breath. I made my peace, promised Mom I would be all right, and left the room. If I stayed, Mom would fight to stay with me. It was no longer noble or beautiful but heart wrenching.

Joe walked me to my car. His kiss, unexpected, welcomed. "I'm sorry, Joe. I shouldn't have done that," I said, lingering in his arms.

"I'm not. Let me take you home, *mpenzi wangu*."

"My love." I shimmied out from his arms pretending to search for my keys. "The families are waiting at the restaurant until the nurse calls. They'll reminisce in French; I'll sip tea."

"Let me come with you."

"I don't know half these people. French whispers, intrusive questions, I'm saving you."

"I wanted to save you tonight, Soph."

"You did." He opened my car door and handed me my keys, grinning. This time when Joe kissed me, it was more than our friendship kisses in the past. I wasn't sure what type of kiss it was; I absorbed his affection, his hands holding mine pulling me closer. I stepped away. "I'll take it." I left him standing there. "You did that to keep my mind off the call didn't you?"

He walked away to his car. *"Maybe. Maybe not."*

"I didn't call it Lavender Hose!" Jacey's outburst startled me back to the office. "Rose." she said, shoving Joe. I shut off my radio enjoying their laughter. Jacey slipped her fingers into his, retrieving her vial of oil. Joe held on. Her pinkie brushed his as he threw her a sexy smile. She caught it, keeping it to herself. "It's nice," Joe whispered to her. "Your scent—the oil's—"

"Fragrance," I blurted.

"I'll remember that," Jacey whispered to Joe, strutting into the breakroom, leaving me with his tender stare.

"You should go home, Soph." He sauntered toward me in imagined slow-mo kicking sand, slathered in oil.

"I didn't want to—way too many beach posters around here." I turned over my sketch of his hand interwoven with Jacey's. "Well, I had an interesting morning: Randall's retiring, the Monet exhibition ended, and I met a British grande dame in a bathroom at the art museum."

"You didn't."

"I did." We didn't need many words; that meant the world to me now.

He stroked my cheek. "You do whatever you need to do. I'm here."

"I know . . . your Denzel stare is working overtime."

Jacey returned with a cup of coffee and set it on my desk. "I'm here too."

"Thanks." The mug's warmth tamed my chills. "I'm glad Mom owns her gallery. Mrs. Lemon is buying up the whole town. Someone had to stop Mr. Potter."

"She's just sentimental," Jacey said, fluttering around the office filling vases with flowers. "Faraway Travel was her husband's agency."

"Take Mrs. Lemon, Joe," I said. "Fix it. You always do."

Joe and I were Krazy Glue friends in college. His given name, Ayotunde Kamau, but he never used it, and I never asked him why. That was the magic between us: a deep-rooted connection neither of us could peg. Joe's father, a surgeon, moved his family from Kenya to London when Joe was a child, and as if he followed Mom and me, from California to St. Louis. Joe saved a modest fortune from a software company he started after college but always spoke of travel. After his father died, his mom moved back to London. Joe and I were all each other had.

Joe's our seasoned adventurer: African safaris, Inca trails in Machu Picchu, diving in Fiji. When Faraway Travel was for sale, I stared in the window, a recent young widow on a mission. I dabbled in art and worked with Mom at the gallery, but after Blake died, I wanted something of my own. Joe towered behind me looking into the same storefront window. I thought I imagined him until he squeezed my hand, shining his Hollywood smile, carrying those capable shoulders and washboard abs from college. We took it as a sign. But as trips came across my desk; I shuffled them away. I longed to see the world, but suddenly I didn't want it to see me.

"I wish I could fix it all, Soph," he said, reading me.

"Some partner, huh? What are you doing here, Joe? You could work anywhere."

"I only let you partner with me because you saved me from Wanda Werewolf in college."

"Oh, she would've made a fangtastic wife." I gave him the pass for now.

"Fangtastic." Jacey snorted. "Mrs. Lemon's the cat's bananas. She likes my outfits."

"Cat's pajamas . . . that's because they're from her decade," Joe said, winking at me.

Jacey flipped her black bob his way. "OMG, I totally need to raid her closet."

"Only you could pull off a black and white poodle skirt, yellow hose, and red heels in the dead of winter." I dipped into Jacey's M&M jar and wandered back to my desk.

Joe's phone rang his rescue; he escaped into his office. "Do you like the new paint color, Sophie?" Jacey asked, powdering her nose. "Isn't it ziggity?"

"It's nice, the posters, retro furniture, everything." Jacey transformed our office from invigorating lime green to soothing mauve. Vases of lavender and sunflowers sat on windowsills and desks. *Lavender. Jacey remembered. I'm painting a new series, ma petit chère. Summer Lavender,* Mom whispered in my thoughts. *We'll go to Paris. Provence. Can you smell them, honey? Can you smell the lavender fields?* "Yes," I whispered, catching my breath.

"Do you like the flowers, Sophie?"

Violet stretches across the meadow, piped rows of amethyst buttercream shells. I smell a hint of lavender. I do. "Why didn't we go?" I asked myself.

"Sophie?" I thwarted my tears searching through my desk drawer for nothing. "I know lavender . . . was your mom's favorite. I was going to bring fresh flowers . . ." Jacey stopped herself from crying, "but the silk ones look so real. I didn't want them to . . ."

"Die?" Silence dropped a thick wall between us. I suddenly loathed my mom's favorite scent, lavender, muddled with burnt popcorn and ugly wall paint. With a tap on her desk, Jacey hid her vial of lavender oil behind a family photo. Our office sat away from the hub of noisy traffic, but the howl of a siren whizzed past covering my whisper, "I'm sorry."

"It's okay, Soph." Jacey stared out the window, wiping her tears. "I miss her. She believed in me."

Quiet, my tears spoke for me. *Sophie isn't rude. I don't know what Sophie is anymore.* Jacey and I continued staring out at the empty, frozen street. "I can't keep it together for . . .'"

"Soph." Joe's handkerchief landed on my nose. I imagined after Mom died, he bought dozens. "You just had the funeral. You shouldn't be here." He held me tight.

I offered him a slight smile. "I have no edit button right now. It's no excuse." I wanted to thank Jacey for the weeks of trying: trying to get closer, trying to get me to trust her, discerning my heartache as a real friend, but genuine compassion tore me to pieces. "Thanks, Jace."

"Jace. Love it, Soph! *Merci*." With a warm smile, her big brown eyes welled up as if she helped my Grinch heart grow two sizes that minute. *Jace.* I crossed into best friend territory as the christener of a nickname. *Great, an informal contract with witnesses.* I wasn't ready for a new BFF. I rather enjoyed my text-free cell, rare French relative shout-out, and Joe's faux work-related sentiments. Joe had access. I wasn't hypersensitive to Joe. Joe was my antidote—words in action—real, everything inside me craved real.

Jacey finished opening the curtains searching for the sun. "She's back?" She gasped, rushing to close them. "That broad gives me the memees."

"Who?" I asked, rubbernecking.

"Nobody, nothing, zilch." Jacey zipped back to her desk. "You should work on Mrs. Lemon's trip." She bolted to a potted lemon tree, trying to push it in front of the window. "Crikey, it's an elephant. Hilarious Mrs. Lemon gave us a lemon tree for Christmas. Have you smelled this? Bananas and totally needs to sit near my desk . . . in front of this window."

"Jacey, if you don't tell me who's out there I'm coming over."

"You are seriously gifted at daggers, *Children of the Corn*, *Dracula* good. Coffee? Rum?" She sniffed a lemon blossom and peeked out the window. "She's out there again, the woman trolling your mom's gallery, the blonde bubblehead zombie stalking around yesterday."

"And the day before." I ducked under my desk. "Don't let her see you."

Jacey snatched a pair of opera glasses on her desk spying. "OMG. She's clutching a pink Louis Vuitton Alma bag—that thing's two thousand smackers."

"Magenta, twenty-eight hundred bucks; it's the big one. What's Zombie doing now?"

"Scratching her beehive."

"That's her." I avoided the window, staring at the photo on my desk of Mom and me in her sunflower garden. *Why now? Why her? Everyone in your life is a gift, Sophia Noel, even your enemies. It's up to you whether you receive them as a gift into your life or not.* "Some gifts are meant to be returned. I didn't ask for this. Is she still there?"

"Big announcement." Joe clapped his hands startling us, marching to the window to look.

"Did she leave?" I asked, fumbling a sheet of paper into an airplane.

"Mrs. Lemon's watching us. Wave." Jacey opened the curtains again waving at Mrs. Lemon. "The beehive with the pink purse drove off. What do you think she wants?"

"Everything." I buried my thoughts into the sunflowers on my desk.

We lost a bright light in our community. Loving mother, daughter, and friend. Josephine de Lue Gallery: closed until further notice. I had no idea what to write on the sign. I removed Mom's paintings; I didn't want anyone else to have them, for now. I wasn't doing what they did to my dad: box, sell, and trash every memory before I could think. All I had from him was a bomber jacket he gave me when I was eight and a cowboy hat he claimed was John Wayne's he won in a silent auction. "I didn't think you wanted to be bothered with 'stuff,'" my stepmother had said. "You barely knew him." *My father barely knew me. He barely knew us.* Mom's art gallery was free and clear, now it was mine. I didn't have the guts to tell the staff I hadn't the mind or heart to run it. Joe took over everything for me, including my finances. I trusted him. I trusted Joe with everything.

"Let's quit for lunch. Mrs. Lemon won't call you, Soph, until you leave your desk." Joe's voice, mellow and steady through the years; his hands covered my shoulders again. I needed his touch. I trembled at the thought of the woman trampling the sidewalk of Mom's gallery. A ghost.

I turned my thoughts back to my paper airplane, but they flew away from me, far away.

"Hold on, Soph. You holding on?" Dad asked as we soared through the clouds.

"We're so high, Daddy."

"My brave Sophia, I've got you."

"My tummy's doing flip-flops, Daddy. Is this what you fly at work?"

"No, honey. It's our Cessna. Mommy said we could fly with the angels today. Happy Birthday, Sophia. Are you holding on?"

I held my tears captive again. "Yes, Daddy. I'm trying to," I whispered.

"Mrs. Lemon," Joe said. Jacey shut the sheers. "Soph? Sophie, you shouldn't be here."

I'm holding on.

"It's cold. I'll close the curtains today." Jacey placed a cookie on my desk.

I'm holding on.

17.

Sophie

Merry-go-round. No circus tent, white bulbs, or soaring stallions with gold manes. No cherry sleighs, plum dragons, or pipe organ music. Up and down gliding past blurry faces; hair flies as a cape, cheeks in the air; nose savors popcorn, funnel cakes, and cotton candy.

But cold metal, mustard, minimalistic ponies bolted to a carnival pinwheel in primary colors. Peeling paint and shouts for turns, whizzing, spinning metal traded for an old-fashioned Parisian carousel. Hair whips across cheeks, face to the sun; nose savors mowed grass and honeysuckle. A ride that's hard to jump off, not the smooth, slow finish of a carousel.

"It feels a little better writing in that journal, doesn't it?" Jacey asked, waking me.

"A little." I tucked away the journal and stared at an email requesting one of Mom's favorite paintings, *Carousel*. I deleted it. "I can't. Not that one," I whispered. Joe caught my words as he roamed the office chatting on his cell.

"You're so bad, Brad. So bad." He chuckled. "Let me get back to my desk. I'll see what I can do." Joe's cool voice faded to imagined carousel music.

Forgotten childhood memories played fast and often now without her.

"Sophia, he came all the way from London to see you," Mom said. "Please ride the carousel for your father."

"He forgot I was thirteen, not nine. It's for babies," I whined.

"She's still afraid of it," I heard my dad whisper, so I ran to a white horse with a slick gold mane, but another girl with blond curls and squinty blue eyes grabbed it.

"Sorry, little girl, this horse is for my daughter. It's her favorite," the girl's mother insisted. "You'll like that brown one."

"It's plain like you." The girl giggled and offered me a stick of Juicy Fruit like

some mafia payoff to stay mum. "I'm Megan," she said. "We'll be best friends. I'm sure of it."

"I'm Sophie and you're weird."

"See, best friends talk to each other like that. The ride's starting. Hold on."

I walked away from pretty in pink Megan wishing I had worn my new yellow sweater and paint-splashed leggings instead of the crummy jeans and flannel cowboy shirt I thought my dad would like. I climbed onto a cream horse with a pink mane. It was the best-looking one there. I never liked carousel music, but I loved the ride, most of the time.

"Windsurfing?" Joe's laugh brought me back to our office. "Time to nix the toupee and grow a goatee, mate. Nobody's listening." He smiled and roamed past me, his ear stuck to his cell. Every day Joe entertained us with his roaming. After a year and half, it was clear: Faraway Travel wasn't for us. We shared a passion to support our community, embraced the routine, but Joe never settled. After Mom died, he held on longer than he should, for me.

"Joe, we can't handle the clanking of your oxfords today," Jacey said, waving him away.

I found the email regarding Mom's painting and moved it back into my inbox. "I'll think about it." When Joe's massive frame moved past the window, I walked to it staring outside at the snow-dusted day. The steady traffic signaled lunch. A group of women buzzed by, carrying matching lilac dresses ready for a fitting at the bridal shop next door. A bundled jogger flew past Mom's empty gallery and our favorite café across the street.

A woman in a fitted red coat stood outside the café sipping a steamy drink. She touched up her makeup, fluffed her blond waves, and searched down the sidewalk. I wanted that back, the thrilling desire to look beautiful and sexy for someone, for myself. An older woman stepped out of the café and rushed to the blonde, tossing her shawl over her shoulder, tousling her silver hair. "Annabel? The British woman at the museum." I grabbed Jacey's opera glasses. "That is her."

A cordial exchange, laughter, the blonde shook her head *yes*. Annabel opened the woman's red coat a few buttons and as a magician produced a white chiffon scarf and tied it around the blonde's neck. She powdered the woman's nose, pinned back her hair, and handed her a lipstick as she did me at the art museum a few days ago. Annabel finished her sidewalk makeover pinning a yellow flower on the woman's coat, leaving her with an approving nod and wave. The woman laughed, adjusting her scarf. A man soon greeted her with his passionate kiss. He unbuttoned her coat and slipped in for a tighter embrace. They disappeared inside their café.

I stared into the café's entrance trying to find them, live through the handsome, giddy couple until I caught the corner of a magenta purse headed for our front door. I grabbed my cell and flew into the breakroom. I peeked around the doorframe to see if the hot pink purse passed. Jacey sorted mail. Joe continued roaming the office talking on his cell.

She slithered in like a snake searching for something to devour—me.

I froze.

At our door's tinkling bell, sweat pooled under my sweater. Tension gripped the back of my neck, and as she scanned the office, anger rose inside my chest. I swallowed to tamper it down. A flush burned my cheeks; tears were next. The childhood bully she always was, I hated the thought of Megan making me cry at my age. I had more than enough anger to suffer through it, facing her. She didn't deserve it; not today, not ever. Joe knew what to do.

"Excuse me," she whispered, acting demure when she usually entered a room like a hyena.

Jacey stared at Megan's purse first and snapped around to my desk. She searched the hallway next catching me shaking my head. I gave her the hitchhiker's thumb to throw out Megan. Joe spotted Megan next. He ended his call and shot me a text: **Stay put.**

I texted back: **Get rid of her!** *Why didn't I move back to California?* I had friends there who offered to help if I picked up my paintbrush again. I missed our artist family, their electric creativity, permission to remain child-like, the competitive edge, rebellion, and obsession. I knew Joe spoke to his former partner, Brad, in New York. Miles apart, but I never assumed Joe would live here forever—not for me, and I wasn't sure he'd stay for Jacey.

My left hand trembled, the jitters that resurfaced after Mom's diagnosis. A tingling sensation pierced my shoulder blades. The ache spun around back into my chest like a golf ball dropping into its hole. *Thud.* I inhaled; my breath shuddered on the way out, a gulp of water—useless. My heartbeat flittered and fluttered against my chest as a hummingbird trapped inside my ribcage. "Why am I the one hiding? Is this what it felt like when you were on the run?"

"I know how you feel, lass," Monet said. "How many times I escaped debtor's prison."

"I've done nothing wrong." I paced, mashing a silk sunflower into abstract art.

"Face the unpleasant business straight on. You stop a charging bull by—"

"Never going onto the bull's path to begin with, that's not my solution here."

"I see. *Oui*, one's better off alone, to work and live."

"Obviously your chosen path, I'm beginning to agree with you. She's not worth it."

"What's worth? In desperation, ten francs bought you a Monet. Madame, I never quit."

"When you don't see something you like . . . repaint it. I don't have a big enough brush at the moment." I spied around the corner ducking in time as Megan searched my way. "Megan's lying about me. Her damn fake lashes are twitching."

"Hang their words. If I heeded the slanderous fictions printed about Claude Monet, I would have thrown my paints and brushes into the sea."

"You threw yourself into the Seine."

"A mere slip, madame. My battle raged within, not with the lot of them, nameless lot."

"Geniuses never care about what people think."

"What is of the utmost importance is not allowing the corrupt barbarians dictate our existence, our purpose; one should choose to rise above and prove such mongrels wrong."

"I have never cared what people think of me. But I care what people say."

"That is the battle, *oui*? Indeed, you will not have a moment's peace to live. I dare say you won't have time to grow or attempt anything beyond the weightless rulings of others."

I snagged the argument swimming in my head, but it slipped through my fingers and swam away from me. My chest loosened its grip.

"I'll take care of her, Jacey," Joe said, glaring. "Finish your project in the *breakroom*."

"Sure thing, Joe." Jacey rushed in and by my daggers left me alone drifting to the back of the room. I glued myself to the doorframe spying on them. "You all right, Soph?"

The envy from my childhood rose as goose bumps on my arms. Amazing how beautiful Megan looked after all this time. I don't know why I was surprised. She worked at it. I thought with the year we had she would look awful, weighed down with stress and guilt, as I. Megan never carried guilt. That was her gift. In the face of guilt, Megan was the Queen's Guard.

Her petite lips matched her purse in hot pink. An overdone spray tan hid the constellation of freckles across her nose and cheeks. Her hair, piled high as usual with a myriad of highlights: copper, platinum, honey. I always wanted to snip the curled linguine stuck to her left cheekbone. Since I've known her, this was the hairstyle Megan clung to for power: a soda can beehive. A royal blue peacoat hugged her slim figure, put together with an ivory silk blouse, black leggings, and pink Jimmy Choo stilettos.

"You shouldn't be here," Joe growled. He was the most compassionate man I knew, but when injustice, insensitivity, or intolerance smacked him in the face, you were better off playing tetherball with a beehive.

Megan slithered closer to him eyeing his fitted black sweater, nodded, and smiled flashing her bleached fangs. "You're looking fit, Joe." She polished his chest; he moved away. "Solid. Ignoring a meaningful social life for 24/7 at the gym? I bet you still drink those awful protein shakes in the morning. That was one wild night. I remember it, do you?"

Jacey snuck beside me for a peek. "It's a lie, Jacey," I whispered.

"What'd she say?"

"What do you want, Megan?" Joe asked, ignoring her while he sifted through the mail. He caught himself realizing he shouldn't take his eyes off Megan for a second.

Megan scrutinized the nook in the foyer Jacey created, snickering at the travel posters and retro loungers. Megan was a gold Renaissance type, overdone and gaudy. She rolled her eyes at the vintage décor. "The office looks . . . homey. May I have a cookie? I know who made these. I could never resist them, you?" Her cackle smothered smooth jazz playing from my desk.

"That's it." Jacey rushed past me before I could stop her.

"Hello again." Megan fluttered her fingers in a happy wave to stop a charging Jacey. "Is your skirt Gucci?"

"Close. Alice Poochie can sew anything. Wow, killer heels . . . in the snow—sounds like a horror movie. Your heart—feet must be cold."

"And you are?" Megan asked annoyed.

"You're Megan?" Jacey said, surprised, bothered. "Nice scare—hair, and your bags—the bag's bananas."

"Oh, this ancient thing," Megan said, impressed with Jacey's digs. "I'll give you last year's if you want it." Megan never missed a beat to buy a new friend.

"Seriously?" By Joe's scowl, Jacey realized she almost made a deal with the devil.

"Sure. You're a thrift store fashonista. I'll save you the trip."

Jacey ignored the jab, surrendering to her desk. "Just split. Joe, we done here?"

"Yes. Megan's leaving." If my glare was award-winning, Joe's scored Olympic gold.

"I can't come in here for advice from the best *independent* travel specialists in town?"

Joe held his breath, trying to stay calm. "When are you going to learn enough is enough?"

"You'd be more than enough," Megan said, slithering closer to Joe.

Jacey slammed down the phone. "I can't work with your blueberry ass in my face."

"Cool it, Laverne."

"Laverne? Laverne."

"I'm extending a freakin' olive branch," Megan snapped. "Sophie keeps throwing it back in my face. She won't even take calls from Blake's mom. I deserve a conversation."

"There's a time and a place, it's not here." If Joe held his phone any tighter it would bust.

"Oh please, is that her desk? I can see the Monet coaster from here. Tell me Sophie's not obsessed with the whole Monet thing again. She's still talking to walls, isn't she?"

Joe pocketed his cell. "Sophie's been through hell. You know that."

"Thanks, Joe," I whispered.

"It's all for attention." Megan held her ground. "She pulled that in high school. I bet she never told you. On our field trip to the art museum, she went berserk at a Monet painting insisting she was related to the woman in it, the woman with the parasol. The whole class laughed at her. Sophie went nuts. We all called her nuts considering how she was acting."

"That's enough," Joe warned.

"They had to kick her out," Megan continued, reveling in her story. "She sat on the bus while we finished our tour. I would have hoped she grew out of that by now, found help. I heard her mom hired a shrink for her, but it didn't work from what I hear."

"Is that why you came in here?" Joe asked. "To blather one of your stories for attention? I don't have time for this. Leave."

"Stories? She's riding that story about how her family is related to Monet, isn't she? Camille—that's Sophie's middle name—and the name of the woman in the painting. Maybe it's true, but who cares. She needs help, Joe. Blake's mom wants to help her. I feel bad for her."

"I've heard enough . . ."

"Forget all that. I saw the coaster and—"

"You have one minute to get the hell out."

"You don't want my business?" Megan whined. "I need to book a few trips."

"We'll manage without it," Joe answered.

"*Putain*," Jacey whispered, resuming her fake phone call.

"I know what *putain* means," Megan said with a snort. "I tolerated that stupid French word for twenty years. Come on, even you should know Sophie and I have a history."

"One she's working overtime to erase," Jacey said, fending her off with a letter opener.

Megan's fingernails rattled on her desk. "So you're both fighting her battles for her."

"She deserves to move on . . . from you." Joe escorted Megan to the door.

"It wasn't easy coming here," Megan said in a squeal ripe for a tantrum.

"I'm sure it wasn't, but it would be easier for you to leave. We have clients coming."

"Riiight. She's here, isn't she? I see her ratty brown purse. She's had that thing forever."

"Megan." Joe's anger rose. "I'm asking you one last time, don't embarrass yourself. Leave, now." Joe opened the front door. I relished the frosty breeze cooling my flushed face.

"All right." Megan turned to leave. "You don't have to get all tribal on me."

"What's that supposed to mean?" Jacey jumped from her chair and pounced next to Joe.

"I'm not the enemy." Megan stood her ground using her purse as a shield. "I have important issues to discuss with Sophie. Things her mother—"

"Not now, not ever," Joe said, holding the door.

Megan only laughed inspecting a fingernail. "I might not be able to growl as loud, but I can bite. Just remember who owns this building. You might think twice about throwing me out."

"You've said enough." Joe opened the front door wider.

"You're sweating, Joe. Where are those cute hankies you carry around?" He didn't budge. "I thought you'd have a little compassion considering we know each other ..." Megan noticed Jacey clinging to him. "Intimately." She snuck in and pecked Joe's cheek.

"Seriously?" Jacey crumpled the sides of her skirt puffing out steam. "You're a joke," Jacey said, looking behind her shoulder at me. "I take it you've always been desperate the way you've carried on, but to come here .. . now. You don't deserve to be Sophie's best friend. You've proven you never deserved her friendship. Joe, I'm taking a break."

Megan smiled watching Jacey fumble to gather her coat and purse.

"Jacey, don't," Joe said. "This is what Megan does. She lies."

Jacey punctuated her departure slamming the front door.

"Sit," Joe told Megan. She obliged. "I know what you're doing. Do you really believe you're in any position to make threats?"

"I know you have that crush of yours on overdrive. Does Jacey know? Does Jacey know about you two? Oh, I see, she doesn't."

"Astounding how much venom you carry."

"Yes, let's not forget that." Megan lost her edge nibbling her fingernail.

"Let's play nice," she hissed. "I need to make things right. I don't hate her like she hates me."

"Sophie just buried her mother."

"Cremation is not actually a burial. I'm surprised Sophie held a funeral. She didn't have the guts to go to her husband's grave, so I had to do it."

Joe's anger rose without his careful control. "You're heartless," he shouted. "Get out."

"I'm not heartless." She slipped her sunglasses on. "You think I want to barge back into her life like this. You think I would bother her if it wasn't important? I told you, her mother—"

"You want something from her. Haven't you taken enough?"

"Don't do that," she whispered, voice trembling. "You don't know what you're doing."

"We're done."

"Megan Hilly, get the hell out of here before I call the police," I said, storming into the room. "Don't you ever talk about my mom like that you heartless bitch. You don't even get to say her name. If you ever threaten my friends again, you won't have enough money to bail yourself out of the hell I'll put you through. Make your threats. Mine aren't threats, they're promises." I never saw Joe manhandle anyone before, but he picked up Megan Hilly like a pick-up stick and tossed her out the door before she could say a word. I stood in the center of our office gasping, crying. "Why would she say that? How could she?"

"She's not worth it, Soph." Joe tucked me into his arms and rocked me. I stared at the tender portrait in our window: a man cradling a woman. I knew I shouldn't. It wasn't fair to Joe or Jacey. But I dropped my body into his and closed my eyes to my mother's smile.

18.

Camille

"You must leave," I told Monsieur Monet, rushing into the shop.

"My hat, mademoiselle," he said, following me inside. He swiped it off the chair. I sighed at the door's bell chiming his departure. He remained, tossing his hat back onto the chair as a game of horseshoes with a perfect landing. My smile his reward. "Meet me this afternoon," he said, coming to me. "Did Elise deliver my message?"

I struggled with a dress form fitted with a violet silk gown. He took it from me and placed it inside my display. "A garland of lilies of the valley—for the festival." I handed him the flowers as he fit himself inside the window, draping them on an armchair. "Go now. Please."

"We have a window display to finish." He grabbed the store cards.

"Not those. You've done it all wrong." I joined him inside the display to arrange the sale cards. "The fashion plates for spring," I mumbled. "Hand me the vase of peach roses."

He reached beyond the display to a nearby table, quickly coming back to my side, roses in hand. "The lilac bonnets, glorious, but might I suggest—"

"No. My mother will come down any minute." I set ice-blue pumps and roses on a table.

"Good, we keep our word I assist with the window." He offered lace handkerchiefs and a mother-of-pearl fan. "Mademoiselle, I have a better idea, if you—"

"I will finish from here. It's too cramped, both of us in this window. The crowd at Monsieur Belrose's sale, under the direction of your Renoir, believes we are a sort of . . . entertainment." I twisted out from under his arms as he reached to straighten a crooked sales card. Losing my footing, he caught me as a dip in our dance and held me. "You can let me go now," I said, staring up at him.

"Perhaps we should stay as we are," he said, holding me, his hand firm upon my back. I rested at his chest. "Monsieur Belrose's crowd looks to gather at your window now." He laughed setting me upright. I scooted away masking my smile, tugging my dress. He took his bow, I, my curtsey to the crowds' cheers. I waved to Monsieur Belrose shooing away our audience to his table of toppers. Monsieur Monet examined our progress, me, waiting for my next command.

"Tie the curtains with peach sashes." He winced at the task. "I'm well aware orange and purple are disagreeable together in a display." I pointed to a book on the counter.

"Have our sunsets over the Seine so been instructed?"

Our eyes smiled in laughter. "I find when I am ordered not to, I fancy it more."

"Meet me. Elise will send her carriage." He tied the last curtain. "I've arranged everything." He blocked my exit out the window folding his arms as a Roman guard awaiting my answer. Disheveled as I was, he tucked a strand of my wandering hair back into place behind the rosebud he fixed earlier. My unbridled excitement was on full display. He knew, snickering to himself while he at last released me, scattering his touch of rose petals on the table and rug.

"You will share more about your great machine—your painting in the forest?" I asked. He caressed my hand helping me out of the display, lingering in the shop, eyeing our work on the window. "I am intrigued, but I do not see how I could ever sneak away to Fontainebleau." *Sneak away.* A rush of warmth covered my body at the thought. He closed our distance.

"You said yourself, 'If we, in this time, never challenge what has always been, we will never gain anything new and worthy of change. *We—you—*are worthy of change.'"

I laughed at us, pleased with our finished display. "You use my words against me."

"I have watched you stuck inside this shop day after day, longing to live outside these windows." I turned to him surprised he noticed me before as I did him. "Bazille insists you have talent. Let me paint you."

"I told you—I am not, nor will I ever be an Olympia."

"Why I must paint you. You are unlike any model. I'm unlike any artist you presume."

"Your friends are right . . . you will not let go of this idea?"

"No, mademoiselle. If not in the forest, let me paint studies of you with Bazille. This would bring you comfort as you know him. We share a studio but blocks away."

"Will Renoir be there?"

"*Oui.*" He squinted at me puzzled. "It is easy being captivated by Renoir."

"Not how you presume. It is not all love and intrigue for a young woman. I know him little, yet, he offers a comfort I cannot explain."

"Because he knows no airs as we do."

"My heart is refreshed by him—as a brother I wished I had known."

"Renoir has little, but what he has is yours. I envy his simple life. He will seek more from his art, but waking up to the sunrise is enough for him." He admired the carvings on a silver purse, tracing his finger over the flowers, trying to figure its clasp to open. "Women deserved to be showered upon with splendor," he said to himself.

I came to him; with a press of the button, the purse opened. "My world, monsieur, is stifling. I am suffocating under complicated obligations and expectations." I closed the purse, placing it back with the others.

"We all long to escape the mandates of our parents."

"You men are allowed."

"We in my group are not much different than you. We ache to have our voices heard. We left our homes, families, and wiser professions for what most declare foolish artistic pursuits. I left everything to come to Paris. Yet, once I tasted it—progress—I could not imagine going back to a life of business, confinements, and customs."

"That's what I'm afraid of, monsieur. You have Renoir and Bazille. I'm alone."

"You will never be alone." He stood before me awaiting my answer. "You can trust us."

"Can I, monsieur?" I walked away, admiring the linen gown he studied for his painting. I peeked outside the window; the crowd at Monsieur Belrose's thinned with no sight of Bazille or Renoir. I noticed Papa's sign on the door reminding me the reality of business at the shop will soon begin. "I confess . . . I long for more," I whispered, coming back to him. "I have always longed for more."

"Meet me," he said, thumbing through a book on the counter. He set it down and joined me at the window. "I will tell you of my plans—you shall be my triumph at next year's Salon."

"I am not sure I am ready for such a triumph."

"You will come?" he asked, adding a blue, beaded bag on the salon table in our display.

"*Oui.*" I reached in and removed it. "It is too crowded."

He walked to the counter, looking toward our private salon, disappearing into it. Out he came carrying our best corset snug on its form. "Your window," he said, placing the corset before me. "Though fine, needs a bit of—"

"Scandal! I dare not." Monsieur Monet redirected his gaze as I admired the silk corset covered in ecru lace and embroidered with shimmering pink and peach roses.

"A fine window must sell goods otherwise it is just a fine window. I read it in your book on the counter," he said, waving the manual in the air.

"The sign shall read, *Spring Amour.* Papa will be furious." I fondled the corset's gold buttons running a finger along the silk trim.

"If you don't experiment, how will you ever know what works beyond what is usual."

I gestured for him to place the corset inside the window. He positioned it in a corner of the display nearest our front door. "I will pin a card on it; 'Inquire within our private salon.'"

He turned to me surprised, pleased. "You stand on your own genius." I walked him out of the shop. He nodded with approval at our window display. "Perhaps a few more feathers," he said, turning to me, raising my hand as a delicate piece of lace, leaving it with his gentle kiss.

I saw myself in the glass wearing the violet gown elegantly displayed. "A lady adorns herself for a secret rendezvous in the forest of Fontainebleau . . . against her heart's warning," I whispered to myself.

The window display would indeed be a fantasy topping all others, for, before my eyes, it cast its spell transforming me from amiable daughter to model—Claude Monet's model.

19.

Sophie

Streams of tinsel across a jeweled sky. "People say before you die your entire life flashes before your eyes. It's not true, *mon trésor*," Mom said. "All I see flashing before my eyes are the silver streams of Heaven's light and my daughter's beautiful smile."

"Mom, I discovered something, too," I whispered, shivering behind my desk. "When someone you love dies, your entire life with them flashes before your eyes." My problem: the memories weren't flashes, but drawn-out epics now showing live and in person. I didn't need a cameo appearance from Megan to stir my last memories of Blake or Mom. Though I tried to put those images behind me, the memories with unanswered questions were the ones that wouldn't fade to black. They never do.

I finally understood Mom's "even your enemies are a gift," saying. Megan's visit made me realize I have to find what's missing so I can move beyond those memories, find what they stole from me, what I lost. Maybe that's why it's called loss.

Megan scurried down the street. The gray, misty clouds on the night Blake died, blue and red siren swirls, and tears washed over my eyes. Joe whispered explanations to Jacey. I wasn't at the office anymore. I sat in the seat of my husband's wrecked car headed for Megan's house. Megan, who should have been there to comfort me when Blake died, Megan, who should have had my back.

I was there for them all—there, when Megan's marriage fell apart, her sister ran away, when her parents divorced. There for Blake, enduring his trips away, the tedious office hours, his father's underhanded remarks, and his mother's third degrees. Maybe Blake and I should have parted ways years ago. He didn't have to run to someone else.

"You're not even certain, Sophia. Confront him," Mom said, handing me a slice of pound cake as if her vanilla pound cake made everything better. It did.

I stared at its top savoring bits of powdered sugar and the white chocolate swirl. "Life's too short to waste living a lie. I'm not made that way." I nibbled at my thumbnail next.

She smiled, sat next to me, and gently took my thumb in her hand. "And you think I was, don't you? It wasn't easy leaving your father. It was both our decisions. I thought you knew that. You're too old for this. You're too old for questions."

"I am not. Not when everything around me has turned into one big question, one big lie."

"This life we live, walking along our petaled paths, dreaming in fluffs and sunshine, all the while a storm creeps over the horizon, with it, rain, hail, and violent gusts. Storms shape us."

"They destroy."

"My Sophia, Blake's gone. There's nothing you can do now. He's gone."

"So are you." I weighed escaping to Mom's house—her journals waited there. *Read them, ma fille. It's time.* I closed my eyes to her imagined wisdom.

"Are you all right?" Joe's warm hands held mine while Jacey answered the phones.

"I'm glad Jacey came back. I bet she loved watching you toss out Megan." I looked down at our hands threaded together. "I'm fine now. Megan hit a nerve. Since we were kids, she's known which buttons to push, and I let her. It's so stupid."

"Give yourself credit. You've battled through a war, Soph. More loss than anyone . . ."

"I know," I snipped, slipping my hands from his, rising to leave. He followed me to the door. "It's supposed to hit seventy today, the end of January. I'm ready to look at something other than gray clouds, and no offense, these mauve walls."

"I don't like them either," he whispered. "Have you gone to your mom's house yet?"

"There you go again," I said, smiling at him, craving his affection.

"What?" He caught my stare. We looked away from each other, around the office.

"Blake was jealous you could read my thoughts. No, I haven't been to

Mom's since her family left. I've told myself I haven't had time. I bet your father didn't leave you a few loaded journals to decipher after he died?"

"No, but I wish he did."

"I'm sorry." He sighed with me. "It's too much. I can't absorb this. Maybe I'm afraid to."

"Do you want me to go with you?"

"To the gardens? You're playing golf with Steve."

"You're changing the subject again."

"Yep, as fickle as the weather." I clicked off my radio and buried the Monet coasters in my desk drawer. He noticed and saved one, *Poppies at Argenteuil*, and set it back on my desk.

"We're all worried about you, Sophie. I'm doing my best to give you space."

"Really? Don't think I haven't caught glimpses of you at Hardware Haven . . . the art museum?" I folded my arms giving him my best third-degree glare.

"I don't know what you're talking about."

"Several people are showing up lately. I think you might know something about that."

"I didn't think Megan would come here. If I did, I would have handled it days ago."

"Did you know she was in town?"

"No, I would have warned you."

"I know, Joe. You fix it. You always do." I kissed his cheek and paused in front of the window staring at Mom's empty gallery. "Remember Mom's Christmas sale? She made us wear those goofy Santa hats. What am I going to do about her gallery?"

Joe strolled to the window and drew a smiley face over the foggy glass. "You don't have to think about that now. Take your vacation, Soph. Maybe it's time you think about Paris."

"I'm thinking about a lot of things, Joe. My trip to Paris isn't one of them."

"Faraway Travel. What's buzzin', cousin?"

"Jacey needs a script." Joe adjusted my collar. "Watch out, Jace. Your cologne is—"

"Sexy?" He wiggled his eyebrows waiting for my smile as my eyes searched past him out the window again. I decided if I spotted Annabel at the café, this time I would join her.

"Girly." I chuckled, adjusting his scarf.

Joe gave me his Hollywood smile. "Sophia Noel, if I wasn't in like with you-know-who," he whispered, "I would sweep you off your feet."

"You have, twice. And you broke my heart."

"Oh no, you broke mine. But here you are."

"Here I am." I was thankful for our moment alone until we questioned Jacey's muffled chatter. "When are you going to ask her out?" I asked, anxious to leave. "I never took you for a sunny-side up girl."

"There's more to her, you know. She's—"

"Complicated. Interesting. You seem to like that." I sighed. "I haven't gotten to know her much, anyone lately."

"Come to Charlie's with us for lunch. No, it's not a date."

"With me or her?"

"There you go again."

"We're easy, Joe. We've always played this game."

"It's not such a bad game, is it?"

"Maybe it's dangerous, too."

"Sophie?" Jacey offered me the phone.

"Mrs. Lemon," Joe and I said snickering.

"It'll wait." Joe blew a kiss out the window to a spying Mrs. Lemon.

"You're horrible." I laughed with him.

"But it's good to see you laugh." His hands dropped on my shoulders. They lingered fondling my collar again, a few buttons. I savored a morsel of joy tossing Mrs. Lemon a salute.

"It's not Mrs. Lemon," Jacey whispered. "It's . . . Mrs. Wilton."

Blake's mom. My joy evaporated and floated out the open window. A warm breeze teased with a taste of faraway spring. Joe watched me drift to one of Jacey's Boho loungers. I swiped a cookie and closed my eyes to the sweet, creamy burst of a butterscotch chip.

I sunk in the chair, losing myself in the invitation of an Art Nouveau travel poster: Australia. Jacey's whispers to Blake's mom turned into the whirl from a seashell at my ear. The static of the tide splashed the shoreline;

its rhythm stilled my heart. I inhaled the sea. "I can't face her." *You blame yourself, ma fille. Blake wouldn't want your life covered in guilt.* "So what if I smash through that roadblock, there's you, Dad. Life's loaded with guilt; talking to Blake's mom won't change that." *Sophia, find your way back home.* "I was home until everyone left."

"Soph?" Jacey cupped the phone waiting for my answer.

I spotted another stroke of lime paint near the windowsill. The mauve sucked. I missed the green. "What does she want?" I asked. "I can't. Everyone's coming out of the woodwork."

"What do I say?" Jacey whispered.

I spied out the window at Mrs. Lemon mocking me now. She held her cotton ball cat and waved at me with his paw. "Doesn't she have anything better to do?" I hoped Blake's mom heard me. Maybe if I acted rude enough, she'd leave me alone. Stop inviting me to dinners and movie nights with "the girls." "Why can't people leave me alone?"

"Why? Are you closed?" A handsome man stood in front of me shaking the slush off his shoes onto Jacey's *aloha* welcome mat. He stared at me, smiled, and closed the door. "The silver bell on your door, *très magnifique*," he said. "Old-fashioned, *oui*? So . . . you book trips *and* give wings to angels." He laughed.

We didn't. "Wings?" we asked dazed.

The man hit the bell making it ring. "Clarence," he said. "Every time a bell rings, an angel gets his—"

"Or her," I insisted.

"Wings," the man finished, chuckling. "*It's a Wonderful Life.* Isn't it?"

I hadn't counted on my husband's mother calling me at work. I had no idea I would have to acclimate to a mauve office when I loved the lime green. I hadn't thought about tender moments with Joe, meeting a British woman in an art museum bathroom, or facing Megan Hilly . . . my past. In fact, with the afternoon sun, I planned a walk at the botanical garden to escape them all.

I was supposed to be on vacation. A winter break, everyone called it, a prescription from Dr. Arnold so I wouldn't have to stare at Mom's empty gallery across the street. And I certainly didn't count on this strange man sauntering into Faraway Travel, looking like someone out of *The Godfather*, briefcase in hand, slick black hair, boring his green eyes into mine with a smug grin talking about bells and angel wings.

And I didn't count on him being hot . . . extremely hot. Nobody would expect that.

~

"*Putain.*" I stared down at my half-eaten cookie and tossed it.

"You know that isn't a cuss word, right?" Joe asked oblivious to our guest. "It means—"

"Prostitute," the stranger said, smiling at me. Not a pity smile. Why would he? A Joe sexy smile at Jacey smile.

"You could say wonkers if you're trying to squelch, in my opinion, your uncoolio, vulgar cussing phase," Jacey said with a *West Side Story* skip and a snap.

"Wonkers?" I asked, plotting my escape into the breakroom. "What the hell is that?"

"*Merde* or *scheisse* works equally well," the stranger added with another one of his smiles. I wanted to see basil in his teeth. They were perfect. Damn, they were perfect.

"Huh?" we grunted, hobbling toward him like a mob of zombies.

"Right, if Americans swear in another language it's not really cussing. Wait a minute . . . you're French?" Jacey asked the man, intrigued.

"On my mother's side," he answered. "German on my father's but I'm uncertain. A bastard you see. Is that an everyday noun or a cuss word in America?"

"Love that about the French." Jacey raced to her cookie tray. "You're so kablooey with everything."

"Kablooey?" he asked us. Joe and I shrugged and pointed at Jacey for his answer.

"*Out there* with everything," she explained. "Straight. Square. Sophie's like that. She's sort of French, aren't ya, Soph?"

"An orphan," I answered.

"I am sorry, mademoiselle."

"Madame," I said, glaring at the man. "Technically, I'm half French and half I-have-no-idea-because-my-father-didn't-stick-around-to-tell-me."

"My mom used to say bastage. Sophie, you could say bastage," Jacey said, pleased. "Or son of a bench, my little brother's favorite."

"Who are you?" I asked, eyeing the man.

"Sorry for that stare of hers," Joe said on the sidelines enjoying the show.

"Feral, isn't it?" Jacey asked.

"I don't know," the man said, studying me. "It's rather . . . sexy."

"OMG, I thought that too. I didn't want to say." Oblivious, Jacey offered him a cookie. "Sophie made these," she said, winking at me. "She's a *grrrreat* cook, well, baker. I don't know if she can cook. She's never invited me over to her house for dinner. How come?"

"*Délicieux*, mademoiselle," the man said, interrupting for me. "*Très excellan.*"

"How may we assist you?" Joe asked, coming to my rescue.

"Monsieur?" The man looked confused. "Ah, *oui*." He sauntered toward me in a foggy haze. He knew he was hot. "Can you help with tickets . . . a few trips," he said to me, tossing his bangs—his nervous twitch. *There's the imperfection.* "Several trips."

"Did you hear that, Joe?" Jacey gushed while I stood there an arms-folded skeptic.

"I'm sorry," the man said, staring at me with his tortured grassy eyes. His back and shoulders bragged expensive sessions with a trainer, his abs, much cardio. Shoes, Gucci, covered in slush. We stared at the water trail into the shop. "*Excusez-moi*," he said, noticing. He wasn't shy about staring at me, cocking his head to one side and the other ending in approval. I couldn't help staring back with a strange feeling we've met before. He walked through the door and his cologne overtook the office: cedar, eucalyptus, sandalwood. I caught myself breathing it in.

"He smells like freakin' violets. OMG," Jacey whispered.

"How may we help you?" Joe ignored my scowl and ushered the man to my desk.

"*Bien*," he said under his breath.

"Kooky, let's make tracks, Soph." Jacey pulled me along. "Lunchtime. Joe can handle Monsieur Hunk."

"I agree." Joe corralled us to the front door and whispered, "I'm going to get our nice French friend some hot coffee and book what I hope are some expensive trips. And Sophie . . . stay home tomorrow. Stay home this week. You're on . . ."

"Vacation. You don't need my help?" The man nosed around my desk. He picked up my Monet coaster, squinted at it, and grinned. "I won't forgive myself if you get whacked."

"Are we in business, monsieur?" the man asked, joining us. "If that vintage Australian travel poster is an original, it's worth a small fortune."

"OMG, he's dreamy." Jacey floated to him handing him the cookie tray. "Help yourself, Monsieur . . .?"

"Moiner. Philip Moiner."

Philip? Lily's Philip! Did he say Monet? "Do you work at the art museum?" I dared to ask. "Do you know me?"

"Now . . . that's a bit complicated," he said with a wink.

"That you know me?"

"I know *of* you."

"From Lily?"

"Perhaps, mademoiselle . . . madame," he said, snickering to himself.

"I think if I knew you I would remember."

"*Oui*. You will, *Petite Fille du Jardin*."

My stomach dropped at his words. "Joe, Jacey, I'm officially on vacation. I've had enough surprises for one day."

"What did he say?" Jacey opened the curtains; sunlight filled our office. "It's going to reach seventy today. It's winter," Jacey said, following me. "What did he say?"

"Thank you, sun," I said to myself, staring back at Philip. A flutter happened in my lightsaber hole that wasn't meant for a stranger, no matter how handsome he was, who exuded citrus and cedar and abused low growls and halfway sexy smirks. *It's adrenaline,* I told myself.

Philip smiled again.

I got the heck out.

~

If you're not up for winter coats and gloves in the morning and shorts and tees by dinner, don't come to Missouri. This winter was strangely void of ice and snow with tennis courts and golf courses overflowing. What we can count on is rain, hail, and tornadoes. The center of the Midwest sat prime for wild things.

I gave Jacey the excuse I needed to skip lunch, nix my sweater and wool skirt. "Yeah, your cheeks look like I beaned you with two snowballs. One day, you'll see what an awesome lunch date I really am," Jacey said, working her plum pout.

"Jace, I'm hot."

"So is that guy. Come to think of it—he called."

"Who called? Philip?"

"Sophie Nooeelll, you remembered his name."

Great, more singing. "I'm leaving."

"You don't want to know?" Despite the slush, the usual business crowd bounced off each other scurrying to lunch. We wandered past Jacey's favorite resale shop and the Sugar Shack breathing in cotton candy. "I love being an adult and eating my dessert first. You game, Soph? Be right back."

I wandered to the street corner inhaling crisp air. Baked pizza crust and oregano overtook spun sugar. I closed my eyes to the rhythm of an American flag flapping overhead and opened them to a bell at the nearby train station. "An angel gets his wings." I laughed to myself. "Mom, what are you up to?" My shadow stared back at me, a globular form with gray stick legs. "Who are you?" Two giggling teenage girls ran past me. Gangly, self-conscious, they plopped on a bench together showing off lipsticks, bedazzled cell phones, and candy necklaces. I'm shocked, twenty years ago, that was Megan and me.

A row of 1920s two-story brick buildings with picture windows and old-fashioned awnings interspersed with modernity. Mom and I loved this historic town in an eclectic suburb outside St. Louis. Half of Main Street preserved its rustic charm, our half, the other offered trendy eateries, wine bars, a farmers' market, and lofts. "It's changing so fast, Mom."

Fashionable boutiques, an indie bookstore, mom-and-pop pizza joint, candy shop and bakery, staples of any tourist town, and an art gallery— Mom's gallery, a fixture in the neighborhood for over fifteen years. Artists from all over the country came to visit my mother, some to intern and learn about her artistic style: modern impressionism combined with an occasional abstract. *It has nothing to do with how you paint; it has everything to do with how you see.* "Maybe that's my problem; I need glasses. Right now I can't see a thing."

"If I tell you Philip called because Lily gave him our number would you freak?" Jacey snuck up behind me with an extra stick of pink cotton candy. "It's not lunch, but it's a start," she said, unfazed by her molting faux fur wrap.

"What?" I looked back at the travel agency feeling their eyes on us.

"Give Philip a chance. Lily gushed he's sweet." Pink fluffs and blue fur stuck to her glossed lips. "Never eat cotton candy in a blue faux fur wrap in sixty degree weather."

"I haven't had cotton candy since . . ." I dove in. Melted crystals crackled over my lips. We traded pink-stained smiles giddy at the sugar rush of childhood and comfort of vanilla. "Thank you for this, Jace. We'll do lunch soon. I promise."

"Monsieur Hunk totally came to see you. So his style screams *Mad Men*. He needs to cool it on the gel and eighty-six that awful eighties skinny tie." Jacey eyed a woman leaving the resale shop with four stuffed shopping bags. "So, he acted a little nutty."

"Hiiii, Jaaceeey," the woman with the shopping bags sang.

"I've had this nightmare," I said. "I'm in an awful musical, nobody can sing in tune, and I can't remember my lines." I waved to Joe watching us at the window; he gave me a thumbs-up.

"*Putain*," Jacey shouted. "That chick's hoarding all the good stuff. Hoarder! Come on, Soph. Go into the resale shop with me. I'll doll you up in some pink tights, blue velvet ankle boots, and a floral chemise . . . for your daaate with Phiilllip. He's delicious."

"Another time . . . and, Jace, can you please stop singing words."

"Sophie Noel, you'll find your song again I promise." With her Aesop bomb, Jacey flew into the resale shop lost in the fifties.

"Is it time to go to Paris?" I asked myself as monotone as a one-note organ.

20.

Camille

A long walk to the Louvre might have offered the levelheadedness I needed to decline his invitation, but I would have looked ridiculous carrying Monsieur Monet's hat. It teetered in the seat next to mine. The soft rhythm of the horse's trot made my heart beat even faster.

I couldn't wait to tell him the scandal of our window proved sensation. The Elegance Shop crowded with ladies pleading for luxurious corsets and a peek inside our private salon. Purple silk and black lace, brazen magenta, red bows and silver buttons, flew out the door in discreet packages. Mamma happily served in the shop for the first time in years. I assured her Mademoiselle Rousseau would deliver the extra corsets I fled the shop to obtain—my thrilling excuse to leave for Elise's carriage arrived to sneak me away as Monsieur Monet promised.

The driver stopped at Ninette Rousseau's. "You sell more than I, Camille," she snickered.

I leaned in close and whispered, "I hear a good shock in Paris has a resounding effect." I offered Ninette a bouquet of lily of the valley.

"Careful, deary, your shop boasts a fine clientele, whereas I know the types that visit me—actresses and courtesans." We clucked together as gossiping hens. "The festival! You gift me good fortune." She breathed in the flowers.

In Ninette's boutique, one turned spellbound under the amber glow of glass lamps and candlelight. Enveloped in pink and gold, the romance of her salon mimicked a woman's fantasy boudoir in Oriental décor. A stage displayed Japanese kimonos, lingerie, and lace petticoats. Ladies giggled behind exotic dressing screens and gossiped on tufted loungers. Corsets seduced enraptured patrons; tempting gold bracelets, garters, and colored stockings nearby. Rose perfume took one's blush away, flowering vines dressed crimson velvet swags.

In this city of secrets, Ninette Rousseau disclosed little about her family or arrival in Paris. In her late twenties and unmarried, whispers swirled she herself was at one time a courtesan. I never believed them. An English-woman with a head of red curls down with a twist and a fluff in the oddest arrangement; Ninette proved gifted at designing corsets and catching the choicest gossip floating about Paris. Too scandalous for Papa, I relished my time away and the solitude of a carriage ride. "You have a fine shop," I said, stuffing a lily of the valley in her hair. "All women deserve a chance to feel, shall we say, tastefully mischievous."

"Smart little bird. Your consignment idea has profited us all."

"Luck and timing kissed our success today. While husbands shopped at Monsieur Belrose's sale, their tired wives flocked to Papa's window."

"What would he do without you?" She managed the last of my order, arranging the packages on the counter. "But people are whispering, Camille."

"As you can see the Elegance Shop is thriving." I searched outside at the cab, anxious to leave. "I plotted an invitation-only sale around this next order."

"Why, you're delightfully delicious. If it wasn't for you, love, I don't believe the other merchants would part with their goods. Perhaps someday you'll own the shop."

I shuddered at the thought. *Stuck inside this shop longing to live outside these windows*, Monet's words covered my mind. Yesterday, I might have bubbled at the thought of owning a dress shop, now, talk among promising artists seduced me onto a different path without giving my heart permission to wander upon it. "I love The Elegance Shop," I told myself as Ninette walked me to the door. "But I will not work there forever."

"Right, love, you will soon marry and cannot work."

"Why I have no interest in marriage." I offered my hug and kiss. "Ninette, my good friend, we whisper our secrets. I can trust you."

"Do not trust a lot as me so freely. Keep a few scandalous secrets close to the breast." She giggled. "Work doesn't keep you warm at night, my love. My prospects are scarce without a dowry; therefore, I lose myself in this shop. It brings me satisfaction."

"As Madame Pontray."

"The sublime Madame Pontray. My uncle deems her deliciously

inappropriate. The ladies cannot wait until our next meeting. Will she have a potion to soften my hair? I too suffer a visiting cousin. The trollop claims my updo is a dried willow in need of a spring deluge."

"I can always count on you for a laugh. I must go." I failed to hide my blush.

She put a hand to her hip and scratched the lily out of her hair, searching me for my secret. "Yeessss," she sang. "I wanted to ask why you came in carrying a man's hat; your blush offers my answer. Cheeky girl, my smart bird knows well how to leave the nest, eh."

I hadn't a notion how Monsieur Monet's hat fell into my hands; I had no excuse to offer. "Until our next visit."

"Pleasure, mademoiselle. Perhaps a corset in lemon satin trimmed in lace . . . for *amour?*"

"Incorrigible." I left her giggles, rushing outside into the cab.

"Where to, mademoiselle?" the driver asked.

Back to the shop, I thought. "You have caused me enough trouble," I said to Claude Monet's hat. "And Mamma . . ." I laughed imagining her covered in ribbons and sale's tickets.

"Mademoiselle?" the driver asked again.

"To the Louvre."

∽

The horse walked on, the hat now in my lap. I brushed its rim; nerves hit my stomach in a winding blow. "I have toured Paris on my own." But it was the first time Papa knew nothing of my excursion. I set the hat onto the seat, tempted to curl its rim. The coach arrived at the Louvre.

"Mademoiselle, does she require an escort?" the driver asked.

"I will not be long." The door opened. Before my foot touched the pavement, a hand reached inside to assist me. Monsieur Monet.

"I knew you would come," he said.

"I had not planned to, monsieur, but as you see . . . you forgot your hat." I handed it to him, plucked the wilted violets from his buttonhole, and added a sprig of lily of the valley.

He stood bewildered, intrigued, drawing me closer, his hand sliding around my waist. He crossed his eyes admiring the flowers making me chuckle. "Sweet lass," he said, squeezing my hand. "Come, I will tell you about my painting."

Upon our entrance into Louvre, a familiar scent made me pause. The musty smell of antiquity mingled with the lingering scent of new construction. Fleeting memories of family outings skipped across my mind. As Paris and this museum, my family's landscape transformed, ever moving away from our treasured past.

Monsieur Monet whisked us through a maze of galleries, secluded halls, and up the Grand Staircase into one of the most opulent rooms in the palace: the Galerie d'Apollon. The sweetness of rose petals and orange blossoms of the imagined aristocracy permeated the golden hall. They say gold possesses the power to hold scents, and so, a magical potpourri of oil paint, varnish, flowers, and perfumes of the court swirled inside my imagination.

Sunlight gleamed across a wall of gilded moldings and carvings of flowers, leaves, and fleurs-de-lys. White light shimmered and danced atop my skin, skipping across crystal cups and royal crowns under glass cases as bits of ancient dust floated among the tapestries opposite the windows overlooking the Seine. Celebrated French artists depicted in rich Gobelins tapestries watched over crown jewels, artists plotting triumphs, and lovers sharing secrets.

Monsieur Monet walked to a window; its view overlooked the Pont Neuf toward Notre Dame. "Napoleon's builder may enforce the law of unity among the treetops, squares, rooftops and gaslights of Paris, but never art," he said to himself.

I took in the great frescos and gilded ceiling above. "When you live in Paris, you forget such beauty exists outside your door." I lost myself in Delacroix's ceiling-painting *Apollo Slaying a Python*, remembering my tiny hand clinging to Papa's as his frightened little girl. "The monsters overwhelmed me as a child. 'But look,' my father would say, 'splendor decorates every corner. How the goddesses' tunics float with clouds and the fire's glow halos the chariot."

"Apollo purges the earth of monsters," Monet said, joining me. "He shoots numerous arrows from his golden chariot with his sister Diana. The sea monster breathes his last fire."

"But is the monster vanquished or alive?"

"The genius of Delacroix . . . his translation leaves it up to you."

We searched the painting together and turned back to the other. "Light," we said together. I smiled, nodding for him to continue. "Succeeds shadow," he finished, searching me again, but this time his eyes held not intrigue but surprise. I captured him with my admiration of Delacroix, my questions, meeting him here. I looked up at the painting no longer afraid.

"What monsters must you slay, monsieur?" I asked, sitting at his window.

"I dare not fight as many as Apollo. I confess one: self-doubt."

"Monsters abound in this world. Your Renoir can attest to that."

"Perhaps, if we all played a part instead of leaving it up to imagined gods and goddesses, we might make progress." He glanced at the balcony and strolled back to his window loosing himself in the streets below. "They labeled Delacroix a painter with an intoxicated broom because he saw everything in color. But what else could he see?"

I rose from my seat to share his view. "What do you see, Monsieur Monet?"

"Everything," he whispered, mesmerized by the city before him. "They paint in there," he said with disdain, pointing to a nearby gallery. "I shall set my easel here and paint Paris."

He offered his arm and led us into the Salon Carré; its walls covered with ornate gilded frames boasting the most precious masterpieces in the Louvre. The gallery dotted with easels and artists copying the endless Italian pictures.

"You are not fond of historical painting, yet it pleases you to be among them," I said, marveling at the works.

He paused at Raphael's *Royal Family*. "I admire tradition yet long to destroy it." He laughed at himself. "I recognize it as great and strong, and so attack it."

"Have you always desired to be an artist?"

"My mother said I was born in Paris on the rue Laffitte, the picture dealer's quarter, naturally an artist I would be."

"Why not study?"

"I study always, but what have I in common with Venus or a cherub?" He led us to a bench in front of one of the largest paintings in the Louvre, Veronese's *Marriage at Cana*.

"Except for a round belly and knowing of love?" I asked, unable to hide my blush.

He gestured to the monumental masterpiece before us. "Twenty-two feet high by thirty-two feet long, mademoiselle. Can you imagine a modern work near as large at the next Salon?" he asked wide-eyed, turning to me for my answer.

"Can it be done by an artist so new to success?" I held my breath at the thought I might play a part in his endeavor.

"All the more to achieve it—not a feast in a palace . . . a luncheon on the grass—the trees of the forest: columns of their temple, a blanket: the table of bourgeois kings and queens."

"Monumental," I said, losing myself in the scene. "Will they accept your vision?"

"I strive to create new art intoxicated with vibrant colors and the light. The Emperor has ordered the rebirth of Paris, tearing down the ancient for his modern city, yet he excludes advancement in art and so bans us. His jury at the Salon, the only entrance for an artist before this public, keeps art stuck in the past despite the progress all around us."

We admired the grand painting, listening to the chatter of the visitors. "Every painting in the Louvre hangs with precision and order, antique in shadows, motif, and technique. What of those men who declare rules and order ensure excellence in art?" I asked.

"The standards by which critics judge art have not changed in two hundred years," he said, sitting at the edge of his seat. "If I wish to paint you, mademoiselle, in a sunlit forest, is this not as worthy as Courbet's peasants, Raphael's Madonnas, or Rubens' Venus? To paint you . . . well, your upturned nose they would cry, 'Paint it straight, Monsieur Monet.'"

I covered my nose embarrassed; he took my hands away from it, tracing the outline of my palm with his finger. "Your able, strong hands," he said, gently turning one over. "They would scold, 'Paint them thin and weak.' They would insist the mole on your cheek 'Should vanish forthwith' and this would indeed ignite my great rebellion."

I took my hand from his, hiding it under my shawl. "We both suffer a presumption by those who believe they have the power to rip away sight; they cannot unless we ourselves look the other way."

"Year after year the Salon refuses paintings void of the antique and pro-claims depictions of nature as base," he continued, his passion kindled. "The Academy condemns artists to paint falsehoods, not the truth before them, only images of the past, the antiquated depiction of the perfect human form. 'Drawing is paramount,' he mocked. "'Brushstrokes must be invisible . . . experimentation with colors, heretic.'"

I searched the gallery noticing the dark portraits and allegories exuded no joy but solemn reverence, past remembrances, imaginings of our origins and the heavens, but never the curiosity of the future, that dangerous stir, or nature's splendor: timeless, imperfect, without rules.

"My school is nature," Monet declared. "Thus, they label us modern painters because we do not wish to paint the past? Study, mademoiselle? We study simplicity most of all."

His fire frightened me setting a spark within. Thoughts of a forced mar-riage, inequality, and Papa's tradition twisted inside my heart. I honored tradition, yet yearned for what lie beyond it. "You long for more," I said to myself. "You purpose to lead the way to incite real change."

He stared into the massive wedding feast plotting a vision of his own. "I wish to record our time, nature as it happens before my eyes. Not as a day—in moments, with feeling in the vibrant palette God provides, they refuse. These men paint to instruct, we paint to inspire."

A mother shuffled her two girls along. She paused, petting the locks of one, straightening the collar of another. "Will the public accept you?"

"It makes no difference if the public understands. I must understand my art. The light changes so shall I. How can we evolve when our art does not evolve with us?"

"Yet, the artists copying these paintings stay hidden within these walls, why?" I marveled at a woman navigating a contraption of stairs and plat-forms to paint her large canvas.

"An artist gains fame by the art of imitation or originality. I will never waste away in this museum copying when I could stand out there with the model of nature before me." He gazed at me as if seeing me for the first time, adjusting again the wilted rosebud in my hair.

"You are fond of this rosebud, but I am afraid it is past saving." I offered it to him.

"I must have flowers, always, and always," he said, tucking it into my hair.

I wanted to know everything about him now. Amidst opulence and old masters, I listened as he recounted his own history: as a boy in love with the sea in Le Havre, studying in Paris and his early mentors Boudin and Jongkind. "Visionary artists," he said, "inspiring me to paint landscapes outdoors." His laughter unnerved the artists engrossed in sketching and painting. "They barricade themselves in here for months copying paintings instead of creating their own. You see, mademoiselle, unless one is ready to wield the tools of modern thought, plan, demolish and reconstruct as our Emperor—the new shall never rise."

"You seek to be art's Haussmann, our master builder?"

"I only wish to paint what I see, not what I'm told."

We circled the great hall eyeing the old masterpieces and the artists copying portraits, flowers, and nudes. Claude Monet battled the tradition under its roof, but the Louvre housed his motivation. Everything he saw on the walls inspired him to best them—the artists he passed, the masterpieces of old. Back at our bench before the *Marriage at Cana*, this dichotomy within his person, his bold pursuit and helplessness at its origin, this longing for something modern yet clinging to tradition, began to draw me closer for I understood it.

"You think I'm bold," he said, grimacing at a student's poor copy of the *Mona Lisa*.

"Monsieur, your ideas demand boldness. Enacting change in Paris takes courage."

"No emerging artist has attempted the scope of my new painting. Beyond the gimmicks of Manet's nudes—decency, modernity, in the light of the nature they shun."

"Your great machine." Our bodies huddled together as he whispered his plans.

"I have committed it will be nearly as large as this marriage feast."

"Life-size figures?" I asked, breathless. "It will take you months. In the forest no less?"

"I hoped to win you with my aim." I offered him my hand in solidarity, my heart leaping at my bold, brave yes. His lips touched my ear, my cheek.

"To Watteau," he said. "In this master's painting lies my design." We stood together, my hand in his, and for the first time since our arrival, Monet cast off indifference and distraction ignoring the palace, the people, and pictures about him. He held my hand claiming me as his. I tossed pretense, nodding at a woman painting her picture. One by one, the artists and students Monet knew greeted us.

"There's the lad," a hearty voice thundered across the gallery. A broad-shouldered pirate with a round belly and black beard barreled toward us. "Who is this handsome couple beguiling us all?" he asked. "With their elegant fashion, raven hair, dark eyes, and royal manner. You are all but missing a trail of little princes and princesses." His howl echoed in the chamber.

"Dash it, that's Master Courbet," Monet said under his breath. "Though he's harmless, mademoiselle, forgive the man. He's brash, big-hearted, and balmy."

"The Master of Ornans bids good day." Courbet attacked Monet with his embrace.

"Gustave Courbet, Camille Doncieux," Monet made introductions.

This beast of a man quieted; his twinkling black eyes admired me sincerely. He turned to Monet in envy and back to me stroking his fan-shaped beard. "Exquisite." He tipped his hat.

"I'm beginning to believe, mademoiselle," Monet whispered to me, "you indeed tame all manners of beasts for this is the softest I have seen Courbet in weeks."

"Balderdash!" Courbet came alive, gathering us as his children. He smelled of beer, tangerines, and tobacco. I slipped from his grip. A celebrated artist of Paris, Gustave Courbet, overpowered the splendor and sacred masterpieces of the Louvre. Intoxicated with himself, students and artists acknowledge Courbet's noble presence. He puffed his cheeks as if swishing a gulp of beer and said, "Have you seen our little Fantin? He labors at the flowers." He tossed his hat on the bench, shaking out his thick, black curls as a wet dog after a bath. "Our little Fantin fills his Friday with the frivolity of flowers." Courbet wheezed with excitement, settling himself after his belly laugh. I chuckled as his faint lisp added a delicacy to his manly airs.

"You wake the ghosts with your carrying on," a timid voice joined us. A young man with an auburn beard eyed me, juggling his paintbox and easel, searching for his choice location.

"Henri Fantin-Latour, Camille Doncieux," Monet moaned, annoyed by their intrusion.

"Mademoiselle," Fantin said aloof, buttoning his smock. "Is she your new model, Claude?" he asked, scrutinizing the other artists, me.

"This magnificent lass is our Monet's greatest find," Courbet said, laughing. "I was thin and handsome once," he whispered to me. "But I rather enjoy my port and pâté."

"I am no one's model, monsieur," I said, eager to leave. The game I carelessly played with artists ended with innuendo and rudeness. *Papa was right*, I thought. *A woman seen alone with an artist soils her reputation. I must slay the monster of my own folly.*

Catching my offense, Courbet rushed to my side tenderly taking my hand, sitting with me on the bench. "Mademoiselle, forgive me," he said. I welcomed his soft gaze. "I'm old and brash, and when I'm among my comrades . . . thilly . . . sss-illy." He snickered to himself and his fellows, taking his handkerchief dabbing his spray of rain off my cheek.

"That is the beer we smell upon you," I said, tendering my smile of forgiveness.

"Stupendous. Oh, I love this lass," Courbet bellowed, rising with a grand gesture to the hall. "Ah, striking. I don't blame you for denying us the privilege of painting you."

Monet scooped me off the bench. "Gustave Courbet is the most arrogant man in Paris."

"And proud of that honor," Courbet said, eyeing the work of a female artist. "I'm warned Monet plots to conquer me with his colossal rigmarole in the forest. He'll vanquish us all at next year's Salon." He cleared his throat, wiggling his fingers at the tart waving her paintbrush.

"Master Courbet is our outspoken radical," Fantin said, dropping his paintbox and easel.

"My clumsy lad speaks the truth. This museum would prove more decadent with my portrait of *Mère Grégoire*." I joined the men's laughter, but the crowd of disloyal artists hushed the man, enlivening Courbet. "Philistines!

The asses believe quiet improves their copies. Rubbish all. Schools have no right to exist. There are only painters!"

Fantin set up his easel. "They're used to Courbet's howling. He's royalty in these halls."

"Fantin copies his flowers and Veronese's *Marriage at Cana* for the twentieth time," Courbet groaned, deflating from his high. He puffed his chest. "Twenty years of suffering, then I gained my fortune. My dandy prides himself in colors and scarcity of technique."

"Monsieur Monet has valiant ambitions," I said, clinging to his side. He squeezed my hand and led us on.

"Marry her, lad! Heaven's blessing, finding a beautiful lass who supports our madness."

"Master Courbet," Monet said, "I utilize technique and abandon it all in the same." I took his arm. He nodded to his fellows and ushered me into the Grande Galerie.

"Damn your riddles," Courbet howled, sketching with Fantin the female artist in her tight blue dress and bosom she proudly displayed.

We promenaded down the Grande Galerie. Monet returned to intriguing stories of his youth—the highlife with one Count Théophile Beguin Billecocq, officer of the Legion of Honor, as my grandfather. The count was a wealthy family friend of his mother, where in her celebrated salon; notable guests applauded her singing and poetry. "Théophile is like a father to me," he said. "After my mother died, my father did not indulge my artistic leanings. His favor fell on my older brother Léon talented in business. I traveled the countryside with my sketchbook."

"Your father let you leave?"

We paused and looked up at the skylights, the light cascading down the marble columns and vases, streaming over the paintings of Dutch, Spanish, and Flemish masters. We stretched our chins to the light, breathing in imaginary fresh air saturating the clouds. "I recall spending more summers and holidays as a boy with this kind family, than my own," he sighed.

"Perhaps they recognized the artistic gifts within you, the ones your mother loved?"

He paused again, eyeing gilt decorations on a nearby panel. "They paint everything new now." Surprised at his tenderness, he turned to me with a look of great pain. "I was sixteen, mademoiselle . . . and lost without her."

I slipped my hand inside his arm as our stroll continued. "Camille," I insisted, fixing my gaze forward as he composed himself.

"Claude." He smiled at his victory of familiarity. "I was heartbroken, rebellious. Théophile whisked me away on extravagant excursions: horseback riding and picnics in the forest, trips to Paris, seaside resorts, and country cottages. I fell in love with nature as a boy."

"Théophile is your benefactor?"

He stared ahead. "You will find many artists, even my comrades, hold the particulars of such supporters dear. You will meet him soon."

My heart embraced his willingness to include me in his world, without care or thought to the place that it would lead me. "Why keep such secrets from each other?"

"If I reveal my generous patron, the next dinner, my friend arrives with a seat at his table. We help each other with commissions but have unspoken rules and rivalries deep within us all."

"It sounds like a game, Claude." I turned cold. "I don't have the aptitude for."

He looked at me with a hint of rage that frightened. "This is no game for me, Camille." He caught himself, laughing off his manner. "I am sorry."

"I am frank with you," I said taken aback. "You make promises and invite me to join you, but I will not deceive my father for mere vanity. I will not betray myself."

"Master Courbet shames me," he said to himself. "His naysaying works me into frenzy, he knows. Forgive me." Displaying a glimpse of humility, he offered his arm.

Claude handed me the excuse I needed to flee his bold idea, this treason, but his ambition gripped my heart. "It appears we both struggle with our temper." He welcomed my laugh. "I was not so kind to you this morning." I caressed his arm walking by his side.

"I have made my living as an artist since I was fifteen, as a caricaturist. I earned my own way to Paris. After my first success at the Salon, my father and aunt now support my endeavors."

"I cannot recall what dreams I plotted at fifteen. I know a lady with an enormous head that would make a suitable model for your caricatures."

"I made the most money painting the heads of giants."

We strolled through the French galleries where I shared a bit of scandal about my grandfather, a duel, and a portrait of a wounded knight in the Louvre I claimed was he. Claude touched on the painting by Watteau that inspired him, *The Pilgrimage to Cythera*. "The island of love?" I asked, surprised. "I would not have taken you for a romantic."

"Watteau was the first to catch the sunlight. If I could steal but one masterpiece from this magnificent temple, this would be the one. Come, our lovesick Watteau is for another time."

We walked to the exit. I shared about my life in Lyon and Papa's dress shop, but I craved more stories about Claude. I dared to ask, "Would your mother be pleased with your painting?"

"*Oui*," he said simply, leading us out of the museum.

We savored the fresh air. Madame Pontray's driver waited where we left him. Claude acted reluctant to leave me, eager to learn more about my life. "Another day, perhaps," I said.

"Of course." He handed me off to the driver.

"And your father?" I asked, coming back to him.

Forgetting himself, he stroked my hand tucked inside his arm as we walked to the shade of a nearby tree. The swirl of his fingertips to my skin sent a surge of warmth inside my body. My ruse before him, his professional model, disintegrated as I relished his handsome looks and caring manner. I could not help wanting to know everything about him now, and decided, however it would be, I would see myself in the forest in Claude's painting.

"I studied as my father required until the walls of a haggard workshop pressed in around me," Claude confided. "And the need to breathe outweighed the will of my father and the lure to see something other than base models and cracking plaster under the dimness of a studio drove me mad. The many deceptions to my aunt who supports me are great, Camille, and the approval of my father, delicate. I will not lie. For I have taken up my tools—"

"To demolish and rebuild."

"I cannot turn back now."

Nor I, I wanted to say. I teetered on the edge of rebellion with him now sharing the breath he spoke of, the warmth of his body into mine. Every step closer to him, I invited his recklessness into my heart to topple my own fear and attachment to tradition.

He helped me into the carriage. "Camille, you will come to my studio on the rue de Furstenberg? I leave in a few days."

"I will try."

He left me with his tender kiss to my hand. I offered him my rose. "Driver wait," I said out the window. "Claude," I called.

He turned back. "Camille," he said, relishing my name.

"Is it true you have never painted a single nude? Why?" I asked over his laughter.

"I never dared," he said, tipping his hat as the driver moved on.

21.

Sophie

A flower called rain lily brought me stillness. It wasn't Monet's garden, but on a winter afternoon alone, it was my own. The botanical gardens offered a sanctuary I needed.

Flowers don't ask questions.

Flowers don't force you to do anything but admire.

"How did Philip know about *Petite Fille du Jardin?*"

Petite Fille du Jardin: Little Girl of the Garden, a twenty-four-year-old French newspaper headline followed me to St. Louis and Philip carried it here. "It's all garbage," my mother insisted. "A fabrication to sell papers." The "fabrication"—a story about a ten-year-old American girl abandoned by her parents at a garden in Giverny, France: Claude Monet's garden.

Authorities questioned two Americans, a mother and father, in the incident involving their daughter on Friday evening in which they claim they lost Petite Fille du Jardin at the garden until closing. A sunhat thrown into the water lily pond by the little girl had authorities fearing the worst until they found Petite Fille du Jardin safely under an Empress tree playing and crying inside our beloved Giverny garden with her imaginary friend, Claude Monet.

"A misunderstanding," my parents insisted throughout my childhood. Blurry images I barely wanted to recall, a lifetime of unanswered questions. I buried their version of the past, the pain, as children are often convinced to do, deep within wondering when this weed might drift apart as a wish flower scattered by the wind.

"Maybe it is time I go back to Paris." I studied the rain lilies, a flower shining on its own. My heart fluttered at the thought. With a measured breath, I closed my eyes to the wind skipping through the trees. "Alone?"

"One's better off alone," Monet said. "And yet, it is a horrible business, madame. The patch of flowers, a fine subject; the white and yellow against the myrtle interests me."

I walked along the path of sleeping roses. "I have the tickets, but how do I step on the plane without you?" I felt as fragile as the delicate rain lilies, but for the first time in months, I absorbed the quiet. The urge to paint nudged my soul awake. Among the flowers, a tossed-away dream stretched to grow. "How will I keep up with your garden, Mom . . . my life?"

"Madame, the only way to garden is to plunge yourself heart and soul into the matter," Monet said. "You're not planting flowers but colors. How Renoir and I painted the flowers."

"I thought Renoir favored portraits of busty maidens."

"Stuff and nonsense. Renoir was born to paint and love women, tempted by calf's eyes."

"Calf's eyes?"

"Spanish maidens with their sad, black eyes; one woman nagged Renoir incessantly, 'Paint me,' she said. 'In the moonlight on the rocks; I shall pose nude gazing at the ocean.'"

"Did he paint her? Was she lovely?"

"*Non*. Renoir spied her breasts to the floor and said, 'Mademoiselle, I have no rocks. I have no ocean.'"

I laughed at myself at the thought. "I dream of Paris in the moonlight and the Normandy coast. I think I'm going," I told myself.

"Madame, there is nothing like the sea or a sunrise on the Seine. One never runs out of subjects to paint in France."

"I don't remember Paris. I was a child."

"I had no interest in coming to America. A man said, 'Monsieur Monet, paint our bridges and landmarks as London.' I told him, 'I only paint what I know, and I barely know France.'"

I turned my thoughts back on the flowers picturing my new name as Rain Lily, a brief bio attached: "Original to St. Louis, found in Paris."

A gust of wind, I rushed inside the orangery. Fragrant olive and Meyer lemon trees kissed my nose. Jacey was right; the perfume of a lemon blossom is otherworldly: honey, white roses, a hint of ocean air. The pings and trickles of the small fountain settled my thoughts. I found a secluded bench, savoring warm citrus air. "It's not Australia, but it will do."

For the next few minutes, the orangery was mine. The vibrant oranges, lemons, and limes against the red brick walls inspired me to paint them. The sun tucked itself behind the clouds; the windows dripped with mist. "Silver beads and streams of tinsel." I smiled to myself.

A visiting French family, an elderly couple, and a group of college students scribbling in notebooks rushed through the picturesque Victorian greenhouse and out the door. "In a haggard world, so many rush past real beauty. They skipped the kumquats, tangors, and limes, missed the stained glass, the Parisian walkway and the pink camellias. *C'est la vie.*"

I glanced at the lavender journal inside my tote and the tattered teal one beside it remembering Mom's plea. *"The journals are my gift to you, Sophia."*

"Why save the teal one? That was mine as a teen; it was torture. I threw it away."

"It's time we faced the words in them . . . together."

"Why now?"

"You heard what Dr. Arnold said. Sometimes we have to revisit the past to find what we lost along the way to move forward. We need to do this. I'm ready. Are you?"

"No, Mom. I never was."

Mom's journals sat at the bottom of her hope chest waiting for me to read them. Thoughtfully ordered with her special notes and ribbons, buried under vintage silk scarves and crocheted blankets. "You win." I opened my lavender journal, turned to the next blank page, and started writing:

January 22, 2014

Lemons, limes, and oranges . . . it smells like Paris. The musty brick walls, fountain, camellias, and potted earth stir happy childhood memories. I'm thinking about you, Mom. Mulling little girl thoughts like, can you see me? Since no more tears exist in Heaven, does God only let you watch me when I'm happy? Does He ever let you see me? And has He given my mom the assignment of painting sunsets over St. Louis? I think so because the other night it feathered across the sky with a brush of lavender.

I match the misty windowpanes in the greenhouse as my tears drip on the page. I remember as a kid during a spring rain I said, "Look, Mommy, the windows are crying." You said, "Come, look closer. See, Sophia." We watched raindrops bouncing and jumping on the glass in an effortless dance. "That one twirled," I said. "This one hops," you cheered. You turned a rainy day into a dance with raindrops.

That's what you did. You helped me see and dance my own way. What I miss most. I won't ever have anyone in my life who embraces the way I see as you did. Journals are supposed to be about me, but I find myself writing a letter to you I wish you could read. Words I wish I said when you needed to hear them the most.

I met a man today I wondered if I knew, a hot guy who visited me at the office. Philip. We locked eyes in a strange, wonderful tease. I'm scared because he made me feel something I hadn't felt in years. He made me feel like a woman. OMG. Why am I writing that?

I closed my journal and tucked it away. "So many people rush by without seeing." I said, watching pink camellia petals float across the water in the fountain.

"I'm standing here, madame . . . seeing . . . taking in this fragrant olive tree and you."

"I'm not talking to you today. I'm learning to savor the quiet. It's not as easy as it looks."

"But we spoke a few hours ago. Well, you didn't speak, madame, you stared." A hand brushed my shoulder as he leaned on my bench. "*Bonjour.*" I turned around to the French accent staring again into Philip's green eyes.

"Mr. Moiner," I said, blushing at the words in my journal. "Or is it Clarence?"

He smiled, slid his hand across my shoulder, and sat next to me. "Philip. I'm no angel."

I ran for the exit. "Great, you're a stalker." I fled the orangery and ducked behind a wall in an herb garden. Philip raced out, searching for me. "Jacey, what did you do?"

"I didn't do anything," she squealed out of nowhere.

"Son of bench!" I pulled her down behind the wall. "You scared the crap out of me."

"I'm so proud of you for not swearing. Why are we whispering?"

"Are you following me? Joe, you can come out now."

"Joe's not here." Jacey dragged me into the open. "Monsieur Hunk split."

"Why are you here? Is Joe all right?"

"I decided to go power walking since you dumped me at lunch. Joe took the afternoon off. Philip booked some stellar trips."

I eyed her outfit: a purple romper, Olivia Newton-John headband, off the shoulder sweatshirt and a stack of rubber bracelets. "You're power walking in kitten heels?"

"I brought my kicks." She flung her high-tops over her shoulder and sat under a gazebo.

"Joe sent you, didn't he?" I sat admiring the private nook. "What's Philip doing here?"

"I promise total kismet." She stretched her rainbow of rubber bracelets to the sky and watched them hula-hoop around her wrist. "Cool."

"Jacey, let's pretend it's the twenty-first century and you use words I understand."

"A coincidence. It's sooo romantic Philip's perusing you." She kicked off her heels and slipped on her sneakers.

"Pursuing. Good, you'll be my witness on the police report for the restraining order."

"Kooky. At least you're wearing a smile. Now, *passeggiata*. Enjoy the sunshine. *Ciao bella*," she said, pumping arms toward the Victorian garden.

"When did you learn Italian?" I asked, walking in the opposite direction.

"You're missing out when you skip Charlie's for lunch. Enjoy the Japanese Garden. It's so tranquil this time of year. And don't be mad. Give Philip a chance! And peace. *Innamorarsi*."

"What?"

"*Innamorarsi*. Fall in love!"

"*Innamorarsi*," I whispered to myself trying Italian. One Italian word reminded me I was missing so much in my life by staying alone. Alone wasn't as precious as I thought.

～

I trudged up the Japanese footbridge's steep climb to its overlook of the lake and Japanese Garden. "Oxygen," I wheezed. "So out of shape; I needed this." The rippling reflection of a bare cherry blossom tree floated atop the water below. Gray clouds bordered smudges of aqua. Purple shadows stretched to keep pace. I lost myself in the pond's gentle waves pushing the sky to my feet. "I see you, Philip," I said surprised. "And I smell your cologne." He kept his distance on the other side of the bridge rustling in a bamboo grove. "You shouldn't be in there."

"You can?" He sat on a slanted rock resembling a tortoise's head. "It's peaceful here."

The wind carried Philip to me. "Okay, what's that smell?" I stared into the water. His footsteps inched closer.

"Me, I'm afraid." He scooted next to me on the bridge. "You don't like it?"

"Familiar." I leaned over the railing, watching reflections of clouds drift across the water.

Philip leaned beside me. "Lemon blossoms, cedar . . . a concoction of my mother's."

"You wear your mother's perfume?" I couldn't stop staring at him. His profile familiar, his smirk after he said his jokes, sexy, the ringing of his finger to settle his nerves; he made me feel at ease and I hadn't a notion why. My body lingered closer to his.

"It's awful, isn't it?" He pitched a rock across the lake. "It's the last time."

"No . . . it's nice."

"Really? I was going for sexy."

"Then you shouldn't say it's your mother's perfume."

"Oh no, my mother . . . she creates perfumes, a hobby of sorts."

When our eyes connected, that strange, wonderful, warm spark shot me off the bridge like a bottle rocket. "Enjoy the sunshine," I shouted giddy as Jacey leaving the sizzle behind me.

"It's cloudy. You don't like me," he called, power walking after me.

"I don't know you," I yelled behind my shoulder.

"Mademoiselle—"

"Madame!"

"You're fast," he shouted, trying to catch up.

"It's your Guccis." A cramp hit my love handle. I plopped on a bench overlooking the lake. "That's it." I caught myself fluffing my auburn waves as the blonde at the café. *I could use an Annabel makeover, silk scarf, lipstick. Sophie Noel, what are you doing?* "I'm going back to the gym tomorrow." Philip pushed his way onto my bench suited for one. "No, please. Join me," I said sarcastically, scooting to the edge. He followed me. We sat in silence. Gray clouds overtook the sky bringing a wind chilling my ears and nose.

"You're shivering." He took off his jacket and dropped it over my shoulders. "Where's your coat?"

I snuggled under it. "I thought I wouldn't need one." He stared now. I finally smiled.

"It's the dead of winter. I hear if you don't like the weather in St. Louis . . ."

"Wait five minutes, it will change." In our laughter, we scooted closer together.

"You don't remember me do you, *Petite Fille du Jardin?*"

I felt his eyes on me as I gazed at the lake. "No, but I wish you wouldn't call me that. Wait—how do you know about that?" I spun around to him, my hip bouncing into his. I tugged at my sweater, nervous at his reply. Quiet, he readjusted his tousled jacket over my shoulders.

"Do you have the time?" a woman asked, startling us.

Philip revealed a gold pocket watch from his pants pocket. A darling antique engraved with filigrees and stars Jacey would admire. "Exquisite," I whispered, clinging to Philip's jacket, inhaling his cologne. He smiled. *A man with a pocket watch how charming. Crap, he's charming!*

"It's three o'clock, madame," Philip said.

"Madame." The woman giggled. "That's so cute. We're getting four inches of snow tomorrow. In the Japanese Garden, snow is considered a flower. I'm coming back."

"Sounds wonderful," I said. Philip's leg brushed closer. "Enjoy your walk."

"Thank you." The woman paused admiring the lake. She turned back to me smiling and said, "I took my time today to see it all. Sometimes, we need to do that, give ourselves time."

"Thank you." I swallowed my tears. "My mom used to tell me that."

"We were supposed to meet. I'm Gracie. Enjoy. Lovers are so romantic at the gardens."

"Oh, we're not lovers," I said, noticing how close Philip and I sat now.

"Not yet," he whispered in my ear as Gracie left.

If he sat any closer, he'd be in my lap. Oh. My. Gosh. Patches of aqua filled the sky pushing out the gray making way for the sun. "It's getting colder. I have to go," I said.

"More shoes are coming." We turned and listened to two young couples, one explaining *Lord of the Rings* to their nonbeliever friends. "Do you think they'll ask us if we're lovers?" Philip whispered as they passed.

"What do you want from me? Who are you?"

"Philip—"

"Philip Moiner I know. Is that supposed to mean something to me? And how do you know about *Little Girl of the Garden.* Do you collect vintage French newspapers or something?"

"I'm sorry if I bothered you." His hand brushed mine, a few of his fingernails dotted with yellow and blue paint.

"You're an artist?" I searched across the lake, spotting a magenta purse swinging past the trees. "Jacey, you're cruisin' for a brusin'." It headed in the other direction.

"Sophie, what's wrong?"

"I have to go. The garden closes at four today." I rose to leave, but my hip stuck to Philip's leg. He stood with me making me turn into him. "My sweater's hooked on something—we're stuck. Let me go. For the record—you shouldn't smell this good. It's irresponsible."

He held me close, searching for the trouble. "It's my pocket watch. Give me a minute or you'll rip your sweater."

"I don't care. Let go of me."

"*And* my watch."

"Oh, I see. I'm sorry."

"I love this watch."

"Yes, it's nice."

"It's dear to me, priceless."

"You did this on purpose."

"Madame, do you truly believe I came here to find you and devise this plan to snag your lovely pink sweater into the delicate chain of my great-grandfather's pocket watch?"

"Just . . . get it off. Megan's probably headed over here now. Damn it. *Putain.*" I dropped my head; his chin rested on my forehead. "Let me try. Your fingers are too fat."

"They are not. It's cute you saying *putain.*" He breathed in my hair, his lips grazing my cheek. "You smell like coconut."

"It's not really a coconut day, lilac," I said, indifferent how long we stayed together now.

"I love lilac," he whispered, staring again, no longer working the chain from my sweater. "It means first love, doesn't it?"

"I give up." I closed my eyes absorbing the heat of his body into mine.

"I almost have it. It's in the loop."

"Rip it. I don't care about this sweater. It's raining now."

"Sprinkling." He stood closer. Forgetting the watch, he let me try. My hand brushing his, feeling the gold chain entangled in the fibers. Every twist and turn our bodies moved together. "I think . . ." I caught myself staring. *I am not this person.* He lifted my fingers off the chain, staring back at me with his perfect smile. His dark bangs covering one of his green eyes studying me. The chain released. We stood breathless, closer, as chilly sprinkles of rain dotted our skin.

"Your eyes are so sad, Sophia. I never liked seeing you cry." His finger swiped a raindrop from my cheek; he leaned in and kissed me.

I let a stranger kiss me in a garden.

"I don't do this," I said softly, closing my eyes to his affection.

"What?"

Unaware he still held me, I snapped to my senses leaving his arms. "This! Kiss a stranger in a garden."

"I'm not a stranger. We met—"

"How do you know about *Little Girl of the Garden*? Please, Philip, tell me." I let him hold me close again, afraid of his answer.

He backed away and swiped my tears with his thumb. "You're shaking. Come on." We ran off the path, through the trees, searching for shelter. I should have run all the way to my car. "In here." We tucked ourselves inside the Climatron, a domed-shaped greenhouse with a glass ceiling covered in tropical palms.

"Is this real?" I asked, clutching his hand. "I'm running with you into a rain forest."

"Come, *mon amie*, here." He led me to a bench in front of a banana tree. The tropical heat tingled my skin. "You don't remember me?" he asked. "See, Sophia."

I stared into his eyes again, a comforting place, trying to picture them in my life: warm, inviting, sexy . . . safe. He wiped the water off my chin, my cheek. He tugged at his finger again and looked at me as a nervous boy hoping for his answer. I remembered.

"Philip?"

"I've changed, but you haven't." He slipped his hand into mine. "I still remember that day . . . in Monet's garden. It was so long ago, Sophie."

"I can't do this." My mind wanted to leave him, my body kept me in place.

"You sat on a bench in Monet's garden," he said carefully. "Your mother dried your tears and introduced me. I was as frightened as you were, Sophia, and counted the days when I would see you someday in America. And I did."

"Philip . . . the little boy. How did you . . ." A flash of him as a boy with a mop of brown hair skipped across my mind; his small hand clung to my mother's and mine.

"I thought you were an angel. I said so to your mother. She rescued me, you see. She hadn't planned on bringing me there, but my parents were friends of hers and in a bind shall we say. It is a hazy memory. Parents have a way of helping their children forget their sins."

"You're Philip?"

"The name—you kept calling me Philip Tommy. Thomas is my middle name. In high school, you insisted I was a Tommy. Remember now? We actually kissed a few times."

I covered my face at the thought, the pixilated memory coming into focus. "In Monet's garden—you kissed me on the cheeks. I never had a boy kiss me on the cheeks before."

"*Oui.*"

"And high school—I can't believe this. Tommy? Is it really you? You look—"

"Twenty years older." This time his insecure smirk churned up a rush of memories. "Not you, Sophia. I hit the gym, longer hair . . . a nose job."

"Seriously?" He showed me his profile laughing. "Always joking . . . is this real?"

"Young love, at least it was for me, no matter how brief."

"You moved away? But you stayed in touch with my mom. I hardly remember."

"Why would you? We moved on, Sophie, went to college. I'm more art historian than artist, a curator of Impressionist art. I travel and lend a hand at any museum that wants me."

"And you're here now."

"When your mother came to Paris she mentored me. She never told you?"

"No. Mom never told me a lot of things." I slipped on his jacket settled in the safety of our memories binding us together now.

"She never told you about her fling with my father?"

"Please tell me I did not just kiss my brother."

"No! *Oh, la vache.* Sophia, you haven't changed—you and your imagination."

"Dot, dot, dot. You said my mom had a fling with your dad?"

"It happened when we were children when you lived in Paris . . . and last year."

I choked on my breath. Philip held me close until it settled. "Last year?" I backed away. "When Mom used my tickets to Paris. Blake and I were supposed to go."

"I know." Philip let me think, examining his pocket watch, me.

"So . . . Mom had a fling with your dad in Paris. I suppose that's in her journal."

"I heard about Josephine, Sophie. It broke my heart. You didn't notice me at the funeral."

"That's why I thought I knew you when you came into the office."

"When I saw Josephine in Paris, I hoped you came with her to see my show. She was so excited for me, you. I've seen your paintings. They're good."

"She planned this? *Us?*"

He shifted, admiring the greenhouse. "Not exactly, but she knew. Josephine wrote to me. Do you know what she wanted for you?"

"I can only imagine." I found my laugh. "Mom was a little out there like that."

"I can't believe I'm telling you this—it simply happened. I hadn't planned on kissing you. Your mother kept a bucket list of sorts."

"A bucket list? I don't know, Philip. This is all too much. I'm feeling dizzy."

"I understand. Let me walk you to your car." He stood and offered me his hand as boy eager to walk me home. I stayed; he sat beside me. I turned to him and smiled. We inhaled the moist earth and minty evergreens listening to the rush of a waterfall over the rocks.

"Tell me," I said, looking down at our hands threaded together. I thought of Joe, slipping my hand from his. "What was on Mom's bucket list?"

He laughed at himself swiping a blush off his cheeks. "A bucket list . . . for you; she wanted you to be kissed in a garden. She said it would start a new memory for you, and—she wanted me to do it."

I hid my face in my hands laughing. "That sounds like Mom."

"You're not angry?" he asked surprised.

"Are you sure you're real?" I snuggled next to him. "This feels so easy, why?"

"Because you know me, I told you."

"You never married?"

"That's the problem with artists." He stood admiring an orchid overhead. "I'm one of those obsessed ones. No. I had my heart broken a few times."

"Are you sure it wasn't the other way around?"

"Your mother hoped you would go to Paris." He sat beside me. "Will you?"

It was my turn to rise, walk away, search for orchids, and take in the smell of the rain forest. "I love this place." I sighed. "A rain forest in my back yard." I sat beside him.

"It's beautiful."

"Philip, do you remember that day in Giverny? Do you remember what happened?"

He lowered his head unable to look at me. "Only what I read. I see flashes sometimes, but I had my own parents to deal with. Your mother and I never spoke of it."

"Mom never mentioned she kept in touch with you."

"Why would she? You were married. I'm sorry about your husband, Sophia." His hand stroked mine. "I hope you hold your second exhibition. I promised Josephine—"

"Another headline? What is this, Philip? A play for Mom's gallery?" My anger erupted unchecked. I scrambled to gather my things, rushing away from Philip and these feelings. "Who does this? This isn't me. I don't kiss strangers. We're not teenagers." I fled from him, this time running outside in the rain, running from promises given to my mother from strangers, promises to myself, finding secret nooks I knew to lose him. I sprinted across a rock path and hid inside an English box garden. I passed the woman, Gracie, from moments before. She waved under her umbrella, I, to her. She looked back at Philip chasing me.

"Let me explain," he shouted. "Sophia!"

"I don't know how to *innamorarsi!*"

"What?"

"Fall in love!"

I sat in my car flushed with anger, embarrassment, and excitement. Philip quit searching for me. I opened my journal to Mom's imagined laugh, picturing her shaking her head smiling, thumbs-up shouting, *I told you so. Go for it.*

I looked back for Philip, a second chance. My pen skipped across the page:

Surprise.

Blue, pink, and yellow confetti fall in a swirl of fog.

A kiss with a stranger in a garden.

A taste of spring during winter.

A resurrected crush.

No memory flashes. Now playing live and in person: his sweet kiss. A woman's tender blessing, or was she an angel?

It was all confusing, but at least they were real.

22.

Camille

~

May 1865

"Did you see the look on Tilly's face when Papa introduced me and I walked in without my crinoline?" My sister burst into my bedroom in her dressing gown watching me ready for the night concert. She tricked me with her kiss, dusting powder on my cheek. "Now you are perfect."

"All that fuss. You were queen of your party." I added a ribbon to my hair.

"I fancy being queen." Genèvieve danced about my room kicking and hopping making us laugh. "I won the toy I wanted from the fairy bag. Thomas Maywheel tricked me with a trade."

I shooed her away from spying through the letters on my desk, grabbing my shawl for the evening. "You did not complain until you broke it."

"I wish I could have a party every day," she whined, plopping on my bed. "Can I sleep in your room tonight? It's fancier—you're forever in love with purple and freesia and violets."

"Lilac."

"Lavender drapes, violet pillows, plum curtains—where you hide your secret novels."

"You will sleep in your own room with such talk."

"Is it your turn? Will they crown you queen of the Mabille?"

I opened my fan, the one I loved with the sailboat, and covered my face revealing a coy glance making her giggle. "I listen to music with my friends tonight. That is all." I slipped the fan into its holder draping it over my wrist.

"And sip champagne. I heard you whisper with Madame Pontray."

"Sneaky mouse. Elise was in the shop but a moment."

"I didn't mean to. I was playing with Raphael. Sister, read to me before you go? I'll let you wear my violet comb." Her hand tugged mine, pulling me to my dressing table.

I took my seat. "Tuck it in my hair. Set it right, mind you."

"You smell of roses. When may I wear rose and lily waters when I fall in love like you?" She pressed her cheek to mine, holding my posy of pink rosebuds, a gift from Claude.

I savored their sweetness. "Claude Monet is but a friend."

She traced the black lace on my shoulders. "Mamma said the blue dress is *la mode*."

"Why I chose cream."

"A champagne silk bodice, black tassels holding tiny gold balls spinning as you dance."

"My, such a description, shall my little sister replace me in the shop?"

She waltzed around my room breathing in rosebuds, gossiping about Mamma's day at the races and Papa's indifference at her outing alone. My thoughts drifted, replaying my days with Claude: visits to his studio, his first sketch of me, his lingering in the shop after hours, and our secret meetings at the Louvre. *Was it a game for him? A scheme to mold his models?*

Posing for Claude provided an escape. I offered more than ploys for marriage; Claude was not in search of a wife. We served each other's purpose: Claude, my opportunity, I, his model. Every visit, Claude's touch grew less measured, his manner vulnerable, and gaze inviting as he painted me. Alone, I saw his purpose—what resided within him was larger than any artist's quest roaming the Louvre. It terrified me. This force shone all about him commanding attention, igniting intrigue and an attraction tempting me from all I held close and safe.

"Camille and Claude. Claude and Camille." My sister's childish song woke me.

"Who said I was in love?" I opened the window savoring the cool breeze. The streets below would soon glow with gaslight; a sapphire sky dressed in creamy moonlight and silver clouds would crown our evening, the crisp air perfect for dancing.

"I catch you dreaming with smiles, and you're upset if I interrupt them."

"Stuff and nonsense." I tossed her a rosebud. She snatched it off the ground.

"Now you sound like Papa, and your face burns red."

"It does not."

"Diamonds and toads. Toads and diamonds."

"Shall you be the disagreeable sister now? I abhor that story."

"Because it's about two sisters: one sweet and one sour tricked by a fairy."

"One humble and one prideful. Honestly, I will not allow you in my room if you insult me. Time for bed—in your room." Disappointed, Genèvieve led our march down the hall into her bedroom. Papa had lit a small fire. "I could cuddle you. It is a fine night for a fire," I said.

"And dancing. I didn't say you were the sour sister." She crawled into bed.

"I do not fancy that story."

"You don't like any story other than ones about Claude Monet." She snuggled under her covers. "Will Thomas ever look at me the way Claude Monet looks at you?"

"More spying in the shop?" I stroked her hair. She watched the fire's glow; we listened to it spark and crackle. "Genèvieve . . . how does Claude look at me?"

She hugged me goodnight. "He visits you on the hour, drawing and studying costumes and bonnets, all the while spying on you. When you catch him, he looks away to the ceiling and strokes his chin forgetting he wears no beard." She tucked herself in. "He makes messes of the ribbons spying on you. Papa complains and knows you sneak off to the Louvre to see him."

"He does? Papa said all this?"

"No."

"Now who is the sour sister with the toads hopping out of her mouth?" I tickled her.

"I am not. When I speak, diamonds and pearls come forth."

"Not if you gossip as Mamma."

Her eyelids heavy, she thought on my words with a final stretch and yawn. "Why do you speak of Mamma so?" she whispered. "I wish I had a bite of lemon cake."

I stopped her from rubbing her eyes and tucked her hands inside the blankets. "You will learn when you are older it is the nature of mothers and daughters to squabble."

Her tiny fingers swirled atop my arm. I kissed them and tucked her back into her covers. "Tell me more about Claude. He is a beautiful man."

"Honestly, such talk for a child."

"I'm no longer a child. I'm nearly ten."

"I forgot. My sister is nine and a week."

"Mamma says I'm mature for my age."

"I wish you to never grow up. Come now, you will make me late for the ball."

"Can't I go? The Lily Feast will make the garden as a fairyland."

"The Fête du Muguet! I noticed a fresh vase of lilies of the valley on her windowsill. Heavens, do you mean I celebrated on the wrong day all this time?" I asked.

"Papa said we shouldn't speak on it because it will upset you. But no one visiting the shop complained they received a lily of the valley early."

"I gave Claude a bouquet. He said nothing."

"So you do see him?"

"In the shop."

"Frogs and toads!"

"Stop with that dreadful story." I rose to leave.

"Papa said it was because you worked so hard on my party. But it was Claude stuffing your brain with love clouds. Papa said when Cousin Gabrielle visits he will buy another cake."

"You have not said how I look tonight."

"Too many feathers—the bonnet might fly off your head when you twirl."

"You are learning. The great art of a lady's toilette is the bonnet, however in Paris a greater joy is to go without." I took off my bonnet and placed it on her head.

"If Claude doesn't fall in love with you tonight, perhaps Monsieur Bazille will. Mamma fancies him best." She giggled, sitting up again, relishing the bonnet.

I sat in the chair next to her, taking the bonnet and calming her once again. "You are a wiggly fish tonight, and I cannot imagine where you heard such gossip. But I saw a few diamonds drop upon the floor when you spoke your compliment."

"Then I am the good sister."

"Enough of *Diamonds and Toads*. I shall tell you a new story, my own. Come, into your blanket." She turned sleepy-eyed and giggled again. We traded yawns.

"Camille, you cannot dance if you're sleepy."

"Hush now." I bundled her under her covers, but her tiny hand found mine. "There were two beautiful sisters, their very persons rich with jewels," I said softly. "Each held shiny onyx hair braided to perfection, porcelain skin shimmering as diamonds and sparkling topaz eyes."

"And lips as garnets."

"And lips as garnets. These beautiful sisters promised to love each other until the end of time. Both were loving and kind. So kind, fairies would flit to earth to watch them tell such stories, play, and love. The sisters spoke their secrets to one another, and a thousand flowers dressed the paths they walked. When they kissed, the heavens filled with diamonds. So much so, they say these two beautiful sisters gave birth to a million stars with one loving kiss."

"I will never want to hear *Diamonds and Toads* again, but your tale, *Two Beautiful Sisters*." The way my little sister looked at me fulfilled a thousand dreams.

Genèvieve closed her eyes as I kissed her forehead. "The sky fills with diamonds.

23.

Camille

Elise's coach arrived without her. *You will find me sitting at a café table in sight of the dance floor—to spy on you, my dear*, she wrote, her note sweetened with imagined sarcasm.

A lemon and rose sunset intertwined with gaslight beginning to flicker across the cobblestone below. Elise's descriptions of the Mabille twirled inside my imagination. *A spectacle of a thousand lights—waltzes among millionaires, nobility, diplomats.* All gather under the glow of gaslights, a gemstone of colors, and the fragrant gardens amidst lively music at the Mabille.

Elise's carriage ushered in the evening's magic. Yellow and pink rose petals curled across the seats. I relished the plush surroundings, sky-blue silk, and her violet perfume laced with roses. "What intrigue have you left me for, Elise?" A blush tingled my cheeks at the prospects of my own tonight. I pressed my locket cool against my skin. I wore no pearls or diamonds, but Papa's locket made me feel like a queen. I did not need the Mabille for that.

At the carriage's every turn, my stomach fluttered with excitement. A small box wrapped in violet paper teetered on the seat before me. I opened the card: *Camille will enrapture us all. Fly free, little bird. Your friend, Elise Pontray.* A hummingbird brooch with diamond-encrusted wings flickered inside the box. "How marvelous," I cried, pinning it on. I inhaled the flowers, the crisp evening air, laughing to myself, dreaming of the grandeur beyond the hill.

The carriage stopped. I searched out the window elated at the driver's detour: the home of my dearest friend, a young actress Marie Samary. Her aunts, Augustine and Madeleine Brohan, were stars of the Comédie-Française. "Silly Camille," Marie squealed, bouncing into the carriage. "Exquisite." She clapped her hands over her cheeks. "Must I cower in the shadow of your beauty tonight?"

Marie's presence illuminated the carriage reminding me she would light up the Mabille with her smile and coquetry. "Will you ever cease in jesting about my height?" I asked.

"No, I'm jealous of it." Marie fluffed her green satin gown about her. Thin black stripes complemented her short, raven ringlets. With a forced grin, she scratched at the ribbons in her hair as a puppy pawing its ear.

"Forever making faces." I laughed, admiring her.

"How I won first prize in comedy." She fluttered her lashes, her blue eyes twinkling mischief.

"You should brag." I stared at her lip's wandering rouge.

"Darling, one must boast to be known in Paris." Marie handed me a gold box and snatched it back, tearing it open with a jolly laugh. We shared the chocolates inside.

"I've missed you. You are winning awards, a two-year engagement at the Gymnasium—all at seventeen, an old maid to me now." *Stuck behind the walls of my father's shop.* I never regretted working in the shop with Papa. I never regretted anything about my life until now.

"Shall we fall in love tonight?"

"You fall in love. I wish to dance." We swayed our clasped hands, humming a stanza of the latest quadrille, our notes souring together as broken chimes in a clock tower.

"Will you sip champagne or are you stuck on a stick of apple sugar?"

"Marie, I am older than you, yet you act as if you are thirty."

She dotted a puff of powder on her nose and mine. "The handsome Frédéric Bazille shows off tonight. He was a bore at Madame Lejosne's salon talking only of this Wagner music."

"His eye favors my cousin." Marie leaned in gobbling my morsel of gossip. "Frédéric had me pose playing at the piano in a pink dress. The dress is dreadful and he is not a focused painter as Claude—but the way he looked at me . . . Renoir plans to paint me with Raphael."

"Camille wins with the scandalous new artists. Careful, darling." She rummaged in her chocolate box offering me a piece. I declined. She closed her eyes savoring the sweet. "I don't believe Frédéric will make a great artist," she said. "He falls in love little they say. How can an artist paint without passion?" Marie fell back into her seat awaiting my answer. "Édouard Manet claims Renoir is but a boy who loves to paint, not much skill at all."

"I don't trust a degenerate who disparages a tenderhearted soul as Renoir," I said, rising. "I fancy Auguste . . . the way he speaks of colors and the soul."

"Could your affections lie with this ruffian Renoir?" Marie sang. "No, I don't see it. Auguste Renoir is a scandal to be sure and loves all women. You're forewarned."

I snubbed her. "I love them all. My father promises his spies tonight."

"Shall you ever gain your freedom, poor Camille? I hear your dandy tolerates his own spy, an artist, Amand Gautier. Monet's wealthy Aunt Lecadre watches Claude's spending—so they say. Claude intrigues Paris and lives beyond his means."

"As all our friends."

She raised her imaginary toast eyeing me with a mischievous grin. "Debt chases Claude. Monet croons a gifted song to his creditors and bailiffs. Perhaps he should sing instead of paint."

"Careful, darling," I said with indifference at her words. "Your gluttony of gossip will sicken you faster than your indulgence in bonbons."

She patted my hand and smiled. "Monet comes from a good family surrounded by impressive celebrity: an influential diplomat with the French ministry of foreign affairs, the famous artist Gustave Courbet, and even Édouard Manet whispers compliments about him. One wonders who this Claude Monet is wherever he goes. He appears at the most notable salons."

I straightened the crooked ribbons in her hair. "Your artistic, carefree parents are gifts. You have the funds and freedom to play about."

"My aunt longed to adopt you years ago. 'Camiillle is the most elllegant among us,'" she said. "'What an actress she shalll be.'" Marie winnowed her fan reveling in her charade. "Darling, your mother made such a scene at Aunt Madeleine's confessing your father's troubles and her . . . shall we say sordid taste in soldiers."

As if the carriage jolted to a stop, so did my heart. "Your gossip goes too far, Marie."

The rustle of her gown signaled her misstep. "All in jest, darling." She tugged at my skirt. "Poorly played sketches and too much wine." I turned to her unamused. "You, my darling, have a first-place scowl."

I tossed a handful of rose petals at her; she took her bow. "The trouble with having actresses for friends—I never know when you are straight."

Her soft hand brushed mine. I recognized its pale, fragile form as a model chiseled in marble Claude would reject. I smiled at my imagined victory; my solid, strong hand covering hers. "A gossiping game your mother played well." Marie brightened, feigning interest out the window. "We'll arrive at the Mabille as old maids at this pace. Driver, crack on."

"What of your Aunt Madeleine?" I lightened my manner. "The whispers about her trysts with Napoleon III? The papers swirl with talk of her lovers."

"Camille," she gasped. "The word tryst sounds delightful, does it not?" She tugged at my dress revealing my shoulders and dusted my cheeks with rouge. "You must transform gossip into intrigue. Paris detests the ring of truth in gossip, yet places intrigue on a pedestal."

"Paris turns mad." *Has Paris discovered the secrets I held in since I was a child?* The chocolate I devoured in friendship soured my stomach. *Was I their joke tonight?* Marie sat worlds away from me now. Her elegant air, the way she used her delicate finger to brush her bangs into place, the perfect bisque hand of a sculptor's statue I now desired.

"I made you melancholy," she said. "Don't worry, *mon amie*." She stroked my cheek to calm its blush. "I don't believe what they say."

She presumed her words would warm me, but at their sound, my heart chilled. I longed to be home with my sister now, whose innocence cleansed me every night from this indulgent Paris, sharing fairy fantasies that only existed in dreams. "It is the fashion to be a mistress nowadays . . . glamorous." I barely heard Marie snip the words, as an intricate maker of lace, she trimmed and cut to the quick her false pattern of elegance, of dirtying grace.

"I don't feel like going to the ball," I said. "Perhaps it was the chocolate."

"Forgive me at once, or I will make such a clamor at your house, your family will ring in the papers." She rustled my dress until I laughed, shaking the darkness from our midst.

"We shall dance, sip champagne, and I'll not let you feel guilty one bit."

"But will it be enough . . . a taste?" I asked, searching the sunset sky.

"It must, darling, until next time." She pinched my cheeks curing my drawn complexion. "You'll never want to go back into the shop again."

Our carriage paused in a long procession of coaches, the lights of the Mabille ahead. "Driver," Marie called. "Let us out here. A walk will do us good." She grabbed my hand gliding us toward the garden glow and the faint strings of the orchestra. The way she walked, musical and staccato; we were already dancing. "Did Genèvieve whine as my sister, Jeanne, tonight?" Marie scrutinized a woman with a tornado of auburn hair. Her waist painted into a red, satin dress, her face a canvas of makeup. The woman in red cackled, adjusted her cleavage, and fluttered her fan at a group of men. "The hussies will be everywhere tonight. She is quite kept."

"A courtesan," I whispered.

"That one calls herself Camellia after Dumas' famous play."

"The courtesan who wears a red camellia when unavailable and white when ready for her lovers . . . but she wears no flower tonight."

"I didn't say she was *the* Camellia. I hear her boudoir is decorated as an African safari." We clapped our hands over our mouths muffling our giggles. "Palm trees, bear rugs, and tigers." The woman captured us. "And now Camille's cheeks bloom red rosebuds."

"You pinched them." I gave her a playful shove. The woman glanced at us unamused back to her audience; her porcelain neck stretched to the sky, a cigarette replaced her fan.

Marie batted her lashes at the courtesan. "They are pretty creatures."

I stood transfixed by the painted woman as she posed before the men in her red dress dripping with black lace and tassels. "A new fashion, so slim."

Marie pulled me along. "Jeanne longs to follow me on the stage. Aunt Madeleine warns two sisters in the theater make for brawling cats, scratching at the other for bravos and awards."

"We do not need the stage for that. You were born for the stage."

She patted my arm at the envy in my voice. "You will discover your purpose, sweet sister. Oh, I wish we were sisters."

"Paris glows." Revelers lined the streets, celebrations bubbling outside the Mabille. Sellers pushed carts past the parade of fashionable Parisians shouting, "Pansies, chocolate, ices." We neared the entrance; glittering stars covered the grass. The whole quarter was aglow from the rue du Juillet, past the Tuileries garden, along the Place de la Concorde and the Champs-Elysees.

"My aunts cannot wait to see you tonight," Marie said. "How they wish you would act."

"Papa has plans for me you see." I looked back at the woman in red standing in the middle of the circle of men vying for her affection.

Marie followed my gaze. "It is a hard life despite what you see. I'm forever criticized. A production depends on you, your performance, and charm. You must topple your best and be held to account for empty seats. The business makes you grow old."

It was my turn to cheer her. "You shall never grow old. And we shall never marry."

Her crescendo of laughter filled the boulevard. We nodded to a crowd of men offering a unison raise of their hats. Marie grabbed my arm and waved to a man hiding behind a tree. She found her someone: a debonair young man in the crowd leaning against a chestnut tree, puffing a cigarette. He had a head of blond hair and wore well the finest black suit. He opened his gold watch and pointed to it. Marie nodded understanding his secret signal. She turned to me with a bashful grin, hiding herself behind my tall frame, sneaking a peek at the young man she knew. He reveled in her bold coquetry. "He's as handsome as Michelangelo's David," she said.

Marie stared ahead, leaving her admirer behind. I looked back. He conferred with his arriving fellows, trailing behind us. She no longer acknowledged him knowing wherever she sat at the Mabille; he would soon sit beside her. She remained quiet sighing at the sunset's last blaze. "What love stirs your heart, Camille? I hear a certain handsome couple grace the Louvre. He wins at the Salon, this new artist and his . . . muse?" Her gossip set a tingle to my skin. "'Thoughts are but dreams till their effects are tried.' And so, she dreams."

"My place is a demure station behind Papa's shop counter, not here among stars."

Marie hooked her arm in mine adding a bounce to our steps. "Look how they stare. Is it any wonder when you stray from your father's shop you capture Paris?"

"I capture Paris . . . or will it capture me?"

Marie searched for her suitor. I spotted the young man before her, hidden behind a tree. He signaled for me to keep his secret. I smiled to myself, loving the Mabille before we entered. "*Oui*, the Mabille overflows with Romeos and Juliets," Marie said, wise to our ruse. "Now, we must find Camille's Romeo."

"I have," I said to myself over the clamor of music and revelry.

24.

Sophie

Innamorarsi. I considered the word all night as a teen with a first crush. "Fall in love," I mumbled to myself. Friendship love, spiritual love, soul love, lightning bolt love . . . lust. "Lightning bolt love, what's that in Italian?"

I sat in my car in the parking lot at the botanical gardens waiting for snowflakes to fall. The snow had yet to blanket the garden. "What are you doing here again? Looking for *him*?" I heard from Joe, something about Philip's jacket and Philip coming by the office to get it back.

I opened my lavender journal, the one I told Mom I didn't need.

January 23, 2014

Yesterday, I kissed a stranger in a garden, that hot guy from the office. I know, it's not me. I'm still replaying it, wondering if Philip is, too. Turns out, you don't have to go back to the past to find something you lost along the way; the past can come to you.

A soft peck turned into his storybook-perfect kiss. My life is anything but storybook perfect. I don't know who that woman was, but she wasn't me. Or was she? Could she be me?

My cell buzzed. Joe: Coming by the office? No. You're on vacay :)

Silence. I'm learning to hold it again. The quiet of a first snowflake and another . . . drifting, twirling, warming my heart.

Buzz. Jacey: OMG, Philip asked me to tell you he's in town "for a while" & to keep his jacket—for now. What happened between you two? Enjoy your vacay! :D

I let my cell buzz and ring without an answer. Jacey: Innamorarsi <3

I buried my phone in my purse, studying a naked oak across the way. "You're lonely, too. I know, Mom . . . see." Gold and copper leaves float to the ground fighting against a gust of wind. Holding on, giving in, letting go to spend winter blanketing the cool earth from frost and snow. One and thousands until strands of grass and its mossy trunk remain. Throughout winter, the few golden leaves refusing to fall, revel in their singular show.

"Independent, brave—I'm not there yet, Mom, but I see it now; it's on the horizon: color and light . . . change." A wash of pink drifted above the tips of the trees. The old oak's branches glistened with silver. A woman raised her hands to the sky catching snowflakes as if she was five years old. "I'm painting this," I promised myself. "*Snowy Morning*." I took photos, sketched watching the woman twirl as a girl under the falling snow, my hibernating gift stirring with each stroke. *That's my Sophia.* "One isn't better off alone." I sketched furiously now. "And lonely is a horrible business," I told myself, ready to leap out of my car and catch snowflakes, too. I did.

"*Innamorarsi!*" I shouted, snowflakes melting on my skin. "*Innamorarsi*," I shouted again enjoying the sound, swirling thoughts and feelings with every syllable. "*In-na-mor—*"

"Noel?"

"*Putain*," I said, bumping into my neighbor, Mr. Elders. "I was . . ."

"Catching snowflakes," he said surprising me, lifting his chin letting them land on his ruddy cheeks and nose. I closed my eyes and joined him.

We opened our eyes to a flurry of white. His wife Maudie watched the sky with us. "We're going to take pictures of the garden draped in snow," she said. "Do you want to come?"

"Thanks, but I'm leaving," I said. "Maybe I'll stop by this weekend."

We watched the woman catching snowflakes finish with a Mary Tyler Moore spin and walk inside. "She should have tossed her hat," Mr. Elders said making me laugh. "We'd enjoy that visit, Noel," he added, bundling Maudie into his puffy parka.

"I'll show you where I placed your mother's painting, the one with the balloons," Maudie said. "We love it. Come on, chubby." She rubbed her husband's stomach like Aladdin's lamp.

"It's the coat." Mr. Elders winked at me. "You're gonna make it, Noel. I know about these things, kiddo." He bundled his wife to his side as they strolled to the garden's entrance.

"*Innamorarsi*," I whispered, dusting myself off, getting back into my car. I checked my cell one last time. It lit up with Joe's text: Who's Annabel? She gave you a scarf. Said you left it at the art museum? She brought us hot tea & scones. Sweet. I smiled at Joe's selfie of them all wearing silk scarves, even Joe. *Buzz.* Joe: I can bring it over later—at your house— the scarf, not the scones. *Buzz.* Joe: If you need me to, want me to.

I turned off my cell. "You never make it easy, Joe." I slipped my journal into my tote. "Everyone in my life is a gift, huh, Mom? Who's Annabel? What are you up to?" I searched my memories for Annabel's kind eyes. "Georgie," I whispered, thinking of my stepbrother. "You did this to me on purpose, Mom. I know you." Something about Annabel reminded me of my mom, her gray-blue eyes, unapologetic strength, and joy for living. I wasn't prepared for missing Mom this much. I wasn't prepared to be this alone.

Today, snowflakes and a laugh with Mr. Elders kept me going, the thought of painting again and Philip's kiss. What about tomorrow? I knew the steps to this dance: spin away, ignore it. Disregard the pain, focus on everything else, let time pass, forget missing people you love because it hurts too bad . . . move on. "How do you move on when you're hurting so bad?"

The snow stopped leaving a dusting of powdered sugar on the grass and trees. With nowhere to go, I checked my cell again. Jacey: Annabel invited you for a cup of tea at the bookstore on Sunshine Street. Funny, huh? Sunshine. Hope you go. Happy Vacay! :0)

My heart started opening to Jacey, but I missed the wisdom of an older friend. Someone who listened without checking their phone, who let you talk until you were done, and didn't split when life got messy, compassion, empathy, and tough love. Most of all, I missed someone telling me I can.

I found myself driving to the bookstore to meet Annabel, skipping the art museum. I took Joe's advice and considered myself on vacation—indefinitely. Yesterday, he discussed his conversation with Brad, his former business partner in New York. "Plans are in motion, Soph. We should talk." Neither of our hearts settled in the travel industry. We wanted to rescue another mom-and-pop-business in our Mayberry town, inevitable to change, rescue ourselves. "A crazy chance to work together," Joe said. "I failed you, Soph. I can't make this work."

"You have never failed me, Joe, and you never will." That was that. Mrs. Lemon could have Faraway Travel back and turn it into a School of Rock, cupcakery, or millennial lofts. We just had to tell Jacey. Joe was leaving us.

25.

Sophie

I entered the bookstore. The scent of paperbacks, vanilla cake, and chocolate made me close my eyes and breathe. The café looked empty. I headed for the travel section. A woman in a blue hat, beautiful in a *Hello Dolly* way, spied on me from behind a carousel of cookbooks. She sighed when I picked up Greece, snorted at Tanzania, and hummed when I opted for Paris.

I peeked around a bookcase, her arms carrying the world: Spain, Japan, Italy. In her sixties and living life with no regrets, I wanted that. "Annabel?" I greeted her with my paltry, lonely book: *Fodor's France.*

She eyed it and handed me her stack of adventure. "You need these too. I can tell. Sophie, I've been waiting for you. Shall I bring us some tea?"

I juggled the travel books and hugged them as she led us to a café table beautifully prepared for an English tea. "You did all this . . . for me?" I asked. A pink, floral tablecloth trimmed in lace, a nosegay of pink peonies and lavender, flow blue china, and a silver tower of treats: scones, chocolate shortbread, white chocolate truffles, and mini vanilla pound cakes.

"Of course," Annabel sang. "I knew you would visit sooner or later. Why not today?"

I stared at the pound cakes the dusting of powdered sugar on top and a swirl of white chocolate. "It's beautiful," I sighed.

"They let me have the run of the joint." She chuckled. "After all, it's mine. We're not open yet, so we'll have the place to ourselves. It's not a gallery, but it is my own in a way."

"A gallery?"

"Yes, well . . . we'll have plenty of time to chat about that."

I placed the books down on the seat next to me. "I'm underdressed."

"Oh, this." She took off her wide blue hat teeming with lemon ribbons and feathers. "The hat rack over there, see." She pointed to an antique stand dotted with Victorian hats and scarves.

"That's where you get the beautiful scarves."

"I have a vast collection, why not share them. Those books are on the house." Annabel produced a red silk scarf with white polka dots out of thin air and draped it around my neck. The magician stepped back pleased with her trick: making my frown disappear. "That's better, dear."

I touched the cool silk against my skin, loving the splash of magic about me.

"I have a few changes in mind, English tea for one. You Americans have no idea how to enjoy or make a proper cup of tea. I met a delightful, artistic young woman, Jacey, who led me to Victorian décor. Did you know you can find oodles of treasures in a thrift store?"

"A tearoom. How lovely." I imagined Jacey's romantic bouquets and Victorian splendor.

"'You can never get a cup of tea large enough or a book long enough to suit me.'"

"C.S. Lewis, a perfect motto for your place."

"My place. I like that. I have yet to think of a proper name. We have plenty of time."

"Wait . . . you've been waiting for me?" My hands fussed with the tablecloth's hem. I caught myself, fixing my hair, smoothing my simple silk blouse. At least it was silk.

"We're testing recipes today. It's a good day for a guest." A young couple emerged, the blonde at the café in the red coat I saw days ago and her handsome gentleman friend. They smiled, waved, and disappeared into their trays of cakes and sandwiches.

"It smells scrummy in here," I said, surveying and envying Annabel's new beginnings.

"Scrummy." She smiled. "I always fancied that word. Now, let's get you comfortable." Annabel took my hat and gloves. I clung to my jacket. A young man appeared and traded my things for a bouquet of violets. "Perhaps we'll offer a few classes: tea selection, flower arranging. My nephew insists I hire a coffeehouse band on the weekend, whatever that means."

"No. Old-fashioned; you don't have to have a band if you don't want to."

"We could all do with a bit of old-fashioned these days—a string quartet."

"Annabel . . ." I shifted my focus on the travel books embarrassed by my life, of it all. "At the art museum I . . . I wasn't myself."

"Finding your way, are you?" She took her seat, loading my plate with sweets, searching me with her sympathetic gaze.

"I think so. I'm starting to." I tried a bite of pound cake. My eyes closed without my permission as I savored the bits of powdered sugar and creamy swirl of white chocolate on top. "It's warm." I said, looking at her grinning, tears pooling in my eyes.

She handed me a tissue. "That's all over now, dear. I'm thrilled we have the chance to talk about something other than toilet paper and an ugly brown loo. The bright side: the museum is considering my Oriental pink cherry blossom theme. Did you ever meet your fellow?"

"Uh, well . . . maybe." I clutched my jacket—Philip's jacket, a checkered gray blazer.

"Well, dear, either you're making a sort of Diane Keaton statement with that men's jacket, which isn't dreadful, or you found yourself a sweetheart."

"I can't seem to part with it. I'm sure he'll come for his jacket sooner or later."

"Isn't that the idea? Sounds scrummy."

Flustered, a piece of scone crumbled in my hands. I gushed at the thought of him, our kiss and blurted, "Philip. He's a swaggering bouquet of lemon blossoms and cedar, and he kissed me in a garden. I don't know what I'm doing." A flush warmed my cheeks.

"Why aren't you with him now?"

I smiled and gestured my mind was blown. Annabel stared at me, scratching her silver pixie hair into place trying to guess my charade. "You young folks speak in code, swag, and such. I'm a simple woman not keen on the lingo OMG, TMI, LMNOP, and all that rubbish."

"Oh, my mind is blown. *Poomb.*" I repeated the gesture. "*Kapow.*"

"You sit here, dear." She patted my hand stuck midair. "I'll bring us some tea. The scones need jam and clotted cream. It's an English cream tea after all. Try the shortbread."

I looked around the empty bookstore, noticing the sign now switched to 'closed' and a second sign at the café's entrance that read "Closed for renovations." Yet, Annabel let me in. How I longed to do the same.

Annabel returned and poured her steamy brew. The whiff of spearmint carried a welcomed childhood memory: tea with my mom. "Tea before milk," I whispered, losing myself as I swirled a drop of milk into my tea. Annabel let me drift, going back behind the counter for the jam and cream. *"Sleepy tea,"* Mom whispered in my thoughts. I closed my eyes breathing in spearmint vapors; they rose to warm my lips and tickle my lashes.

"What's in this tea, Mommy? It smells like Christmas."

"I could say spearmint and chamomile, blackberry leaves and lemongrass, but I rather whisper: special golden berries grown by sleepy fairies make this brew."

"Sleepy fairies?"

"Oh, yes. They know the right berries to use to invite sweet dreams: a pinch of rosebuds, silver herbs, sparkling sugar buds, and a smidgen of secret spices. Spices so secret, they place them in a jeweled box in the top of the tallest tree and guard it."

"Who guards the box? What happens when it's opened?"

I wouldn't have heard her answers. A muffled giggle, her soft kiss to my cheek; I drifted to the sight of a purple forest with flashes of green sparks from flying fairies with crystal wings. They brought me tea, kept my face cool and my toes warm, and silenced the forest for slumber.

"A sprinkle of fairy spices. You made everything better," I said, embracing this memory.

"Sophie?" Annabel said, waking me with a gentle nudge.

"Thank you." I savored my tea. "You brought me a special memory today."

"I've always believed tea holds a magic all on its own." She took her seat. "Now, tell me about yourself." Quiet, I looked at her over my teacup breathing in minty vapors. She waited, patiently sipping her tea. Annabel raised an eyebrow. "A dull chat if I do all the talking, dear."

"I wish you asked me that question five years ago," I said. "Life was thriving."

"Why, because you were young and pretty? You still are. Spoon on the saucer, dear." I corrected my faux pas. Frozen, I stared at my scone, her, and the jam and cream. She smiled and gave me one of her tender pats to the top of my hand. "The proper way to eat a scone, jam first, clotted cream second. Oh, there's a whole school of thought on which goes first jam or cream."

I copied Annabel, feeling her eyes on me, waiting for my answer. "Divine." I savored the tender scone slathered with strawberry jam and cream. "May I close my eyes while I eat this?"

"Of course. I promise to give you the full lesson, but as to my question."

"I know. I'm changing the subject." F in etiquette on all accounts as I shoved in another bite of loaded scone. "Not sure how the jam would spread on top of cream. Yep, jam first."

"Right."

"I'm doing it again?"

"You have a talent, Sophie."

"I might start painting again. I'm . . . was an artist."

"Gifted at changing the subject." She signaled for me to wipe the glop of jam sticking to my lip. "I gather it worked for you as a child not now." Annabel's eyes wouldn't leave mine. "How old are you?"

"I just turned thirty-five."

"*Just* turned, you see? You're holding on to thirty-four."

"I am?"

"Do you know why young people obsess with aging? Fear."

"Fear of what? Death?"

"Regret. Death is too easy. It's deeper than that."

Regret. I devoured my scone ignoring the word. I could take the others: Annabel's jab on changing the subject, the proper way to hold a saucer and eat a scone. The English cream tea was sublime, but my soul craved sweetened conversation served with it. "You think I'm another spoiled American girl, huh?" I asked, acting like a spoiled American girl.

"You're a woman who's missing something. I know, because I used to be her."

"I've enjoyed this, Annabel, but . . ." I wanted to rise, find a bathroom, hide. It was her turn to offer a halting gesture. I honored it and sat back down to listen.

She poured another serving of tea and lightened the moment with her friendly smile. "A dear friend shared this with me years ago," she began.

"It's something you need to hear. I used to think the main killer of geezers my age was uselessness. Believing the bloody lie: you're done. Your life is rubbish and you have nothing anyone wants anymore. You sit outside on your porch, sleep, and dream about past glories, tragedies you endured until that's all you see. Sad really."

"My mom challenged me to see differently than anyone else, but lately, it's all a blur."

"Bollocks, there's more life to live! It's a gift, Sophie. When you realize that, you stop worrying about wrinkles, tight jeans, risks, and regret—you're thankful to have something."

"What?"

"A chance."

Chance. The quiet fell as tender snowflakes. I soaked it in, letting the word settle in my heart. I scanned the bookstore, sitting areas, shelves of books waiting for a home, for someone in need of an adventure. "I love being among books. They feel like old friends."

"And new ones." Annabel extended her hand. I took it.

"Why does the word chance sound hopeful yet look dark and frightening?"

"Chance is not a word to toss in the air. It's a word to take in, a word to give yourself."

I spotted a crocheted throw over a sofa, a few novels strewn across an antique armchair. "I should have told you, Annabel . . . I'm grieving. I lost my mom."

"I'm so sorry, dear."

"It doesn't get easier no matter how many times I say it."

"Losing one's mother is traumatic. A daughter's heart never expects it. Our children expect us to live forever."

"Last year, I lost my dad and my husband . . . myself." I held up a hand to any pity, though I hadn't figured pity was a word Annabel ever uttered. "I'm sure you'll say that it's time to move on as most people do."

Annabel sat up at my statement keeping her eyes on me. "I am not most people," she said, bothered. "I would never dare say such an insensitive thing."

"It's just . . . everyone else does," I said surprised.

She pushed her scones to the side indignant. "We Brits have stiff upper lips, but we're not stupid. Americans—always in a rush to sweep things under the rug and act tough and strong like John Wayne. It's not normal."

"It's not?"

Annabel stood pacing in circles having a fit for me. She caught herself and with a sigh sat back down. "Bloody hell, move on. Who invented this nonsensical idiocy as it pertains to grief? We move on in traffic. We move on past an expensive dress in a department store we can't afford. My dear, we do not move on from grief; we move through it." She finished with a swift sip of tea and daintily set her cup and saucer down on the table.

I sipped on her words, unable to swallow them. "Annabel, please . . . say that again."

"What?" She poured us more tea. "Moving on from an expensive dress?"

"No," I said, flustered. "You know what I mean."

She held up my travel book on France, thumbed through it, and said, "I do. But, Sophie, are you sure you're ready to hear it?"

"Yes." I stared into her warm eyes, my tears already falling, skipping across my cheeks like the snowflakes on the windows.

Annabel set the travel book in front of me and opened it to Paris. She firmly took my hands and held them as if she had known me for years. I looked into her fiery eyes, the wisdom and joy hidden inside, the secrets of a life fulfilled, a self, found. She waited and with a smile stroking my hand said, "Sophia, we do not move on from grief; we move through it."

"We move through it." I swallowed a gulp of tea but my tears fell. She held my hands and cried with me. "Through it," I whispered absorbing her wisdom into my unsettled heart.

"We want loved ones to live forever, dear." Annabel never took her loving gaze off me.

"Not forever . . . a little longer."

The blond woman walked to our table and whispered her name, "I'm Sal," she said, handing me a handkerchief I didn't want to soil. "I knew your mom. I was one of her students."

I looked at her and smiled. *Was everyone in this place an angel?*

～

"It's your eyes," I said, taking hold of myself. "Georgie's not coming is he?" I asked, catching Annabel with my question.

"Who's Georgie, dear?" she mumbled, her voice quivering. "We need more tea." She stood and wiped her eyes searching for someone else to look at but me.

"Aunt Annabel." My gaze bore into hers waiting for her reply.

She sighed and picked up the bouquet of peonies and lavender inhaling its calming scent. "I planned on asking you that next."

"Is this place really yours? You're moving here from London?"

Annabel offered me the flowers. "We'll need a few more teas to catch up on each other's life. You were a teenager the last time I saw you."

"I knew I remembered your eyes."

"But you don't remember me, do you?"

"Not precisely." I wasn't used to seeing this Annabel, twiddling her thumbs, looking for backup. "I remember a few flights. A stewardess held my hand to deliver me to Dad in London for the summer. A boy with pale skin, apple-red cheeks, and blond curls looked as frightened as me when we met. Georgie bowed and shook my hand. He was ten."

"Georgie's cheeks are still red. He turned into an odd young man. Odd."

"How's Pauline?" *The mistress that wrecked my childhood.*

Annabel swallowed and sucked in a breath of courage to face me. She smoothed the tablecloth, fussed with her yellow scarf. "Your stepmother . . . it's been difficult for me all these years. Pauline was the baby sister I failed. Your mother was my best friend."

"My last summer with Georgie in London, Dad 'suddenly away,' you invited Georgie and me to stay at your cottage in the country. It was the best summer I ever had."

"Thank you for that, Sophie. What gave me away?"

"The pound cake." My tears returned. We looked at our cake and savored a bite. "A dusting of powdered sugar, swirl of white chocolate, dash of almond extract . . . Mom's secret."

"It took me thirty years to pry that recipe out of your mother. She loved keeping secrets."

"Too many secrets. And the scarves, the one you gave me at the museum. Mom has one like it, a bunch of scarves in fact."

"I loved Josephine, Sophie. I don't know where to start, but I'm here. I'm sorry for my nephew. Georgie doesn't do well with this sort of thing . . . since his dad—your dad died."

"I know. He's a mess. He called when Mom got sick. I hardly know them, Annabel." I lost myself in the flow blue china, tracing flowers, smiling at the English cottage scene.

"Maybe it's time you open your heart to Georgie again . . . to me."

"It's time for many things, the truth for one." I searched Annabel for the answers I've waited a lifetime to hear. She leaned back in her chair, arms folded—I wouldn't get them today.

"There's a great deal you'll want to know about me," she said sternly. "But I think it's best you hear that from your mother first. Have you read them?"

"The journals? I can't."

"Then I can't help you." Annabel's tough love returned as she rose to clear the table.

I stopped her. "You promised Mom something. What was it?"

"I'm not here to interfere with Josephine's wishes."

"But you are here for her."

"For you. For myself. Change was a word she helped me face after I lost my Henry." She sighed and sat next to me.

"When did you see Mom?"

"Last year."

"Her trip to Paris. Aunt Annabel . . . did Mom know she was sick?"

Annabel stared at the travel book on the table opened to Paris. I closed it. "Yes," she said, taking it in hand. "She couldn't tell you, dear. Not yet. She didn't want to lose you. She fought for you, you know." I nodded. "You're surprised we kept in touch. Josephine never blamed me for what happened with Lewis. There's much I don't know, so if you want answers—I promised your mother I would encourage you to read her journal . . . and your own."

"Was my dad happy with your sister? I rarely saw him happy."

"Your father's life was weighed down with regret. But you know that."

"I'll never understand him. He had everything. He had us and his son Georgie."

"Lewis didn't see it that way." We rose together as I gathered my things, stuffing my tote with books I promised her I would read. "Paris?" she whispered her invitation.

I gave her my hug. "You had a greenhouse . . . lemon trees."

"You do remember. Georgie recalls fondly the stories you told him while you played in there—fairies, giants and magical flowers. Oh, how he cried when you left. We both did."

"But you're here now. Thank you."

"Would you like me to go with you to your mother's house?"

"No, but I promise I will tomorrow. I just remembered a friend had counted on me today, and as much as I'm thankful for you, I hope I have time to make it up to him."

"Of course, dear." She noticed I left the travel book on France on the table and offered it to me once more. I took it. She walked me to the door.

"Annabel?"

"Yes, love."

We stood at the door the snow falling steadily. She took my hand and we breathed in a fresh beginning together. "Would you like to go with me to Paris?" I whispered, falling into her.

She held me as my mother letting me cry until I was finished, and I held her, our tears and love for Mom reconnecting a treasured bond. She placed my wool cap on my head and handed me my gloves and the posy of flowers. "I hoped you would ask me," she said, revealing an envelope from Faraway Travel plucked from her pocket. "I met a wonderful travel agent today, Joe, who happened to be saving these tickets for you. Wouldn't it be lovely seeing Monet's garden in the spring, not imagined at the museum, but before our eyes?"

I nodded. "Maybe tomorrow you can come by Mom's for dinner; teach me more about a proper way to host an English cream tea. I have something she would have wanted you to have."

"I'll be there . . . here, always."

"It's good to have family again," I said to her, to myself as I moved through it all under white streams of snow.

26.

Camille

The scent of lilacs and orange trees from the Tuileries danced with roses and mums at the Mabille. Marie and I strolled under a grand archway lighted with the wonder of colored globes, the garden emblazoned with light. A steady stream of visitors paraded in their opulent fashions twittering about the orchestra and anticipated fireworks at midnight. This was no subdued night concert, but one of the grandest and notorious outdoor balls in Paris.

Marie found her beau sitting on a bench, holding a bouquet of roses. Before their love set flame, Marie's aunts called. Augustine's fan flapped while Madeleine cajoled her sister walking her to a café table far from the pagoda bandstand where the orchestra trumpeted a waltz.

I stood in a garden of gold, an enchantment framed in gilded leaves adorning golden archways. Ribbons flew in the air; the twirling ladies in pastel silks and satins created a picture surely the artists pondered. Couples dipped and tiptoed in light, happy dances. When the music blared a frenzied tempo, the bold jumped and cheered with abandonment. One man tossed himself to the floor in a somersault as the couple's spectators cheered. A woman shook the front of her dress at the crowd with a kick and a hop, shocking and delighting her audience.

"Heaven forbid I should do such a dance," I said under my breath.

Marie rushed past her aunts to her sweetheart. "I'll visit my aunts after this dance," she shouted. Her aunts settled at a table swaying to the music, examining Marie's folly, and inviting me over.

Mesmerized, I beheld the spectacle. Artificial palm trees dropped glowing bulbs as magical jackfruit; gaslights encircled the dance floor. A stage trick, giant lily bells held red flames, tiny colored globes lighted walkways and tree trunks. Hues as spring flowers shimmered from thousands of gas jars. "Sister," I gasped, "the Mabille is a fairy tale."

Sparkling fountains trickled over marble dolphins and Venuses. Blossoms sweetened the air tinged with tobacco, beer, and fried batter. A blue and red glow emanated from shadowy coves and grottoes offering private settees for lovers. Secluded paths invited the bold on a secret rendezvous. Indulgence was the dance, excess and extravagance night's song.

The main stage for the guests' vibrato was the dance floor, the liveliest spot in the garden. A makeshift circle of soft sand swirled underfoot the elegant and buffoon. The orchestra leader displayed a plaque announcing waltz, polka, or quadrille. Professional dancers led couples in the newest steps, most to their doom. Crazed, men left women, women their men, to dance with others skilled and jolly. The courage of champagne convinced all to dance with strangers.

"A shame Marie left you alone." I sighed at Claude's soothing voice, his tender kiss to my cheek. I relished it, thinking of the mysterious paths I glanced upon our entrance.

"Where's Cousin Gabrielle?" Monsieur Bazille pushed his way to me and bowed.

"I am sorry, monsieur. Gabrielle is delayed at my uncle's cottage near Fontainebleau."

Bazille examined Claude welcoming my news. "Claude visits Fontaine-bleau in days."

Claude smirked, fondling my hummingbird brooch. "Do you plan to visit cousin, little bird?" he whispered. His lips grazed my ear; his warm hand cupped my back claiming me now.

"By Blue, banish proprieties; we're old friends." Renoir burst in between us handing me a glass of champagne. "Camille, please call him Frédéric, me, Auguste or Renoir—I fancy both."

"We fancy other names." Claude plucked the glass from my hand giving it back to Renoir who, after a sip, studied a group of coquettes waving him over. He swallowed his drink and raced away engaging in wild dancing as the band played a polka.

"The poor bastard has no rhythm, but what a sight he is for us." Claude laughed, offering me a seat at their table.

Frédéric held out my chair. "We only come to watch Renoir dance. Bravo, man."

"I could hardly sit now," I said, bouncing to the tune. "Gabrielle looks forward to seeing you, Frédéric, should you return to Paris this summer."

"Darling, no one stays in Paris for the summer." Marie reappeared. "Look who I found."

"I see by your blush, Camille, you're having fun." Elise winnowed my face with her fan.

"Our goddess of the flowers." Claude tossed his hat and twirled Elise giddy as a girl.

"Heavens, I'll not be the old maid who ruins your fun. I spy from over there." Elise winked, motioning to a table under a shade tree. A man in a red scarf sat waiting. "When you tire of dancing, dear, I have news," she whispered, as if the ball had not intrigued me enough.

I rushed her with my hug. "My hummingbird, *merci beaucoup*, but it's too extravagant."

"Made for you." She eyed the champagne on the table, the artists, nodding to the dance floor. Renoir vanished into the crowd. The man at Elise's table browsed the carnival games. He caught me spying and tipped his hat, passing a pistol gallery swarming with ladies.

"Our goddess lassos a god?" Renoir sprouted in the center of us winded and disheveled.

"It pains me to leave you with this scoundrel, child." Elise shot her warning at Renoir sneaking me a wink, gliding back to her table.

"Hercules, indeed," Renoir snickered, waving to Elise watching us as a mother hen from her roost. "Help us all if that's Master Courbet sitting next to her."

"The braggart with the wandering hands? I hope not," I said, eyeing the champagne.

"Ah, Joan of Arc casts her demure ruse aside," Renoir said, toasting me.

The music stopped. A chorus of laughter and chatter swelled. "It is beyond what I imagined." I stood alone with the artists, a crowd spying at me as Elise.

"Camille already captivates Paris," Claude bragged.

Elise disappeared under the shadow of her tree. Her companion smoked his small pipe. Marie lost, I relaxed under Elise's eye, gazing at the carousel behind me. Reserved for children, tonight billowing gowns and men's top-pers rode horses and sleighs.

"Shall we dance?" The timbre of Frédéric's voice startled my spying. At his invitation, a flock of ladies rushed us. In a flurry of pink, blue, and yellow silks, the elegant women turned feral sweeping Claude and Frédéric away in a flood of revelry for a dance. Claude raised his arms in protest, but he failed his escape. Frédéric's charm lost as he tossed his hat to Renoir, reveling in his capture. Claude shrugged his shoulders at me as a dainty blonde in a gold dress tugged him to the dance floor. I waved him off with a forced grin. Claude was not mine to claim.

"Don't be cross with them. This is how it goes at the Mabille," Renoir said, waving to Elise. "It appears we shall dance." Renoir extended his hand.

"Oh, I am not ready to throw in with that lot."

"The Reinhold sisters are nothing to fear," Renoir assured, jealous at his fellow's capture. "We should have warned you about the onslaught of our patron's daughters."

"Why this ball is so grand."

"May I be frank, Camille?" We watched Claude and Frédéric fail at dancing with the frenzied women losing their ribbons and feathers spinning.

"I wish you always to be plain with me," I said aloof, eyeing my cham-pagne.

"Indifference won't win Claude," he shouted over the music's crescendo. "That's his weapon of choice. Come, we'll show them." Eager to join the dancers, as Renoir snatched my hand, Marie's aunts bombarded us with their greetings.

"Shallll you make us wait forever, darling Camilllle?" The trill of her l's and resounding timbre of her voice was unmistakable. I happily greeted Marie's aunts, Paris's beloved actresses, Augustine and Madeleine Brohan. "Fetching and fitting, your champagne dress for a champagne evening," Augustine said, slathering my cheeks with kisses.

"A tiara for your slim waist, my darling," Madeleine said, smashing her cheek to mine.

Marie reappeared, dancing up to us with her beau. "*Bonsoirrrr*, dear aunties."

"Oh, child," Madeleine said with all grace and poise for no syllable uttered by her was insignificant in tone or diction. "We shall work on that squeal. Elocution, child. Elocution."

"May I introduce Monsieur Albert Devian," Marie said, clinging to his arm.

"My honor," Monsieur Devian said, kissing their arched hands. "I apologize. I seem to have lost my hat in the crowd." He tousled his blond hair grinning.

"As most men have," Madeleine said, making a grand gesture toward the dancers. "Marie, we highly approve for Albert dresses like a prince and has sparkling white teeth."

"Madeleine, I dare say you're right," Augustine quipped. "For the man you were with, what ailed him so he could not smile?" she asked, egging on her sister.

Madeleine obliged wiggling her eyebrows at me. "Such horrible teeth to be sure; I could not bear another minute of his smile." We snickered at the sisters' impromptu performance.

"Oh, but he was a handsome lad," Augustine encouraged, an elbow to Madeleine's ribs.

"With a smile resembling a small burning village," Madeleine finished.

We laughed and applauded the actresses waving to their crowd of admirers.

I spotted Claude alone on the dance floor soon dragged away by a woman in pink ruffles. His previous partner, the coquette in the gold dress, rushed to Augustine. "Augustine, we mourn your retirement," she wailed, intruding. "Let me tell you some stupid thing to make you laugh."

"You have only to open your mouth, child," Augustine snipped, the crowd honoring their star with guffaws. "That rude child was fired from Dumas' new play. I don't recall her name."

"Why she was fired," Madeleine said, reigniting our laughter.

"I should like to finish our dance, Marie," Albert said, love-struck. Marie's aunts rolled their eyes as if rehearsed shooing the couple away.

"We'll miss you on the stage," Renoir said, toasting Augustine with his never-ending supply of champagne. "But look forward to your jests as you grace the salons about Paris."

Marie returned out of breath, her ribbons lost. She walked Augustine back to their table. "A lover's quarrel so soon, Marie?" Augustine asked, brushing the spangle of diamonds on her ear. "Young love makes one young; I long to be in the presence of it."

"He'll learn his lesson when Karin bludgeons his feet during their waltz," Marie said.

Madeleine shimmered in teal, diamonds draping her neck. "May our girls find the best men." I sipped the champagne Marie offered. Its sweet, sharp liquid tickled my tongue. The warmth of another gulp calmed my nerves as curious eyes ogled me standing with stars.

"Slow down, darling," Marie whispered. "Feigned courage; you don't need it."

"The highest compliment I ever received was from Arsène Houssaye." Augustine roused my interest. "'Wit and cleverness lit up the heart.' Camille is certainly a constellation."

I leaned into her with my hug. "*Merci*, dear Augustine."

She brushed my cheek as my mother. "Now, I rest my ancient bones on that bench, for my feet will not see the dance floor tonight with my bunions the size of a brioche."

"Come, sister," Madeleine said. "We let youth shine tonight."

"He's learned his lesson. See, Albert sits rubbing his feet searching for me." Marie hugged my shoulders. "I soothe him now." She rushed to her abused Albert Devian.

～

"Heaven help all men," Renoir said, studying me. I took his arm, and we strolled to our table. He offered me my second glass of champagne. "We have bottles to enjoy."

I took a measured sip and out of the corner of my eye, spotted the woman in red, the courtesan. Her auburn hair, a twist of black feathers, her neck bedazzled with emeralds. Four men trailed her as pups as the woman in red flit her fan, her signal for their bidding. She cared not the lace train of her seductive red dressed dragged along the dirt, her sleeves falling off her shoulders catching the attention of the men she passed. She would not dance, but stood as Venus of the Mabille.

Unsatisfied with her company, she caught the eye of an older gentleman staring her into his arms. He twirled his cane as a dandy strutting before her, dismissing the boys in her presence. When they fled, he held her and swept her up in a loving kiss as the band played on. He twirled her, her dress spinning in the wind brushing up clouds of dirt, her arms covered in primrose gloves. She fit into him perfectly, her hand stroking his hair, his cheek, as he spun her. She floated about the dance floor as a dancing, breathing sunset swirling in pinks and red. The older man flashed a burst of youth as she rushed him off to a secluded grotto.

"You'll see all sorts here." I laughed at Renoir's manner, impatient to dance, stuck as chaperon to me—Virgin of the Mabille. "No bother the hussies ignore me and my haggard coat."

I straightened his tie and jacket. "The cravat is no mere ornament. It serves as a letter of introduction, and you introduce yourself well tonight in blue with white polka dots. You are the most beautiful man here, if they could see your heart." I pecked his cheek.

He swirled his hand across my back and whispered, "I don't know how to take this adulation. I wear a fine coat tailored by my father."

I enjoyed our play. "You love the dances, Renoir?" I asked, laughing.

"My poor father no longer threads a needle. He suffers his dance twisted up as an oak's gnarly limbs with affliction. I fear someday my bones will wither as his."

"I forbid it. I believe that if you speak it, it must be so. I shall pray for him."

"A virgin and a churchgoer—I fear you have no chance with us. Flee, we'll corrupt you."

"Intolerable." I fancied our toast and the elixir in my glass. I swayed into him. He rocked us to the waltz.

"The bubbles speak their truth." He backed away tempering temptation.

I laughed at his genuine way. "I am but lightheaded not foolish," I said, eager to skip and hop with the others.

"Don't blame Claude. He's afraid of you and yet certainly needs you."

"I'm but a model of clay. Claude Monet sees nothing but his work."

"Why are you not dancing?" Marie fluttered in. "Camille, I'll not let your melancholy ways ruin your first ball. Come, dance with Albert. He's a fine dancer."

"Are you not afraid of her beauty?" Renoir called, trying to keep me.

Albert escorted me to the dance floor for an amiable waltz. He was not Claude, but the music swept me up as the courtesan in red, the breeze skimming my cheeks, wisps of hair falling across my neck. "You're a divine dancer," Albert whispered. I held him tight. He was beautiful, and all watched us glide in circles under the lights.

I scarcely heard the music stop, catching Renoir's hand pulling me back to our table. Claude and Frédéric still lost. I finished my last sip of champagne. "Claude doesn't make mischief with those women," Renoir said, refilling his glass.

"*Mon ami*, you have spent the better part of my first ball explaining away Claude."

"Look." Claude sat drawing Frédéric leaning against a tree. "Claude won't bend for anyone, Camille." Renoir searched the dance floor longing to be in the midst of its party.

"This is how it goes with artists?" I asked. "Even your friends are a study."

"Your beauty is worthy of a portrait, but what of this sadness?" The champagne did not move him, but his genuine concern at my answer. He looked through me so intently I slid away.

"Sadness?" I looked for Claude past the dancers coming and going.

"In your eyes." He studied me brushing his finger across my chin. "Monet sees skies and seas—I observe eyes. I don't paint as the others. They tolerate me; I embrace tradition. I don't daub as Monet or paint on a whim as Bazille. Nothing disconcerts so much as the simple thing."

"What of this revolution you proclaim?"

He scratched his beard thinking. "I embrace a soft touch, my own technique, and not that of the past. I rather paint a pretty picture and one I enjoy or none at all."

"You fancy painting women." It was my turn to see through him.

"*Oui*, I love often. Enough horror exists in life. I need not paint it."

Marie and Albert spun as a carousel. I chuckled as she held a sugared apple, toasting me from afar. "You are not as the others," I said, smiling.

"Before you judge, nobility runs in my blood. Here we can be whomever we wish. But you, mademoiselle, belong in a salon surrounded by suitors fighting for your hand."

"Proprieties?" I scooted closer. "Tonight, I'm right where I wish to be."

His cheeks warmed to peach. "I've seen what the Salon does to fine artists. Obsession, madness . . ." He shook his head. "Poverty." He mimed a frown revealing his empty pockets.

"I am not afraid."

He sighed. "Claude wins your heart hastily. I will break and bend, but I shall never paint as Monet. I could never see what he sees."

"What is that?"

"He strives to see everything new as if for the first time. His obsession, the light."

"Besting France?"

"You will never find him stuck in a studio or painting portraits staged in a parlor—nor obsessing to win the hand of anyone."

"What intrigues me most," I whispered.

He grinned. "And this is what will rile the Salon," he whispered back. "Claude holds no training," Renoir shouted. "No teacher, and yet astonishes—for now." He toasted a fellow with his glass, gazing into me. I declined his toast, sensing his protection turning from me onto his friend, hardly the first conversation he indulged on the subject of Claude and Camille.

"He sees beyond art," Renoir said, snickering. "Walks a path at any cost; he will not quit. We'll cower. Monet, never." He shifted on his heels, closing his eyes to the music and laughter. I stood out of place, scanning the crowd, regretting I trapped this eager soul. I turned to leave; he stopped me. "Alas, I've spent the night in dire warnings when we should be dancing."

"Auguste . . . I do not know if I can walk this path, but I am not afraid." I admired the crowd, dances, and toasts in midair. The bright lights had yet to dim for the evening, the moon beginning to glow, and the crowd warming up its fever pitch. "Of what *they* think."

"The answer I've been waiting for, but you'll be tested mixing with us."

The champagne bubbles from my second glass buzzed about my nose, its warmth surged within my chest. I no longer cared about Papa's spies, the imagined threat of an intruding Mamma and forced suitor. I closed my eyes dizzy with delight of the evening, listening to the orchestra's muffled music and crowd's glee. The colored lights blurred into a wet canvas. Renoir steadied my steps. "The dance," the crowd cheered. "The dance!"

"Now she's ready," Renoir said to our onlookers. "The quadrille cancan! Now we get to it," Renoir shouted, pulling me to the dance floor. The brisk quadrille introduced itself with blaring trumpets, fifes, and flutes. The tuba's steady oompah guided the rhythm along, and a cymbal crash denoted the next sequence for the dancers.

To the lighthearted march, a hop, shuffle, bow, a fling of one arm to each other. A couple joined us in a promenade tossing one partner to the next. Renoir left the group—I was suddenly twirling with Claude. Renoir hopped back in, pushing a laughing Claude aside, and I followed Renoir's steps with a kick and another, ending with a windmill whirl of our arms.

With each step, my heart pounded faster, savoring the freedom of the music under the stars. Out of the corner of my eye, I saw the woman in red, the demimonde, Camellia, watching me amused, and during a second of a respite, she nodded at me and smiled.

The dance continued. I left to catch my breath, feeling Claude's hand slip into mine. Marie's dignified Albert turned acrobatic, performing a handstand amazing the crowd with a hop, legs in the air. Marie absorbed the applause for her beau as the two returned center stage sharing high kicks and chassés.

The Brohan sisters and Elise cheered us on clapping and laughing as girls before us. I searched for Renoir; he stood in his own circle, dancing his own way with a crowd of onlookers cheering him on. Noticing me, he offered a salute and nod of approval at Claude. "Marry her!"

Claude searched my eyes as we stopped dancing, the crowd bouncing around us. I looked toward the forbidden trails dressed in lily bells and red light. We left the music and revelers, tradition and expectation—my hand in his to walk our own path.

27.

Camille

"Daughter!" Mamma hovered at the Mabille's exit, clinging to a man I only knew from shaded memories. "Daughter?" Her wave hung in the air; her fan masked her face. "Take me away, Claude." I covered my shame with laughter. We skipped through a grove. Mamma disappeared.

"Who was she?" Claude asked, chasing me.

"A drunken mother searching for her lost daughter." I faded into the shadows. Claude found me. Far from the ball's gleaming lights, I held him. "I will pose for you in the forest . . . in Fontainebleau. I am yours." We hid inside a secluded grotto. I lost myself as his hand caressed the nape of my neck. His fingers traced the curve of my bare shoulder and brushed across my lips. He pulled me to himself; his passionate kiss quivered inside as his body caressed mine.

Footsteps.

We stayed quiet. Claude hushed my laugh, fondling the rosebud in my hair. "You are so beautiful." Blue lights flickered across our faces. He smiled, trying to brush the sapphire glimmer from my cheek. "The music stopped." I kissed him with the passion I held in as we danced. We lingered in the garden. Smoke from the fireworks drifted in the night sky. In a flurry of departures, Mamma vanished. We lost Marie, the Brohan sisters, Frédéric and Renoir. All scattered to their homes and secret spaces. "This is how it goes," he said, kissing my neck.

"At the Mabille." He tucked my hand in his as we walked toward the exit. "More champagne." I showed off my cancan steps. A crowd of stranglers cheered for another kick.

"Oh, no." Claude waved them off. "I promised Elise I would return you home with both glass slippers." He wrapped me in my shawl stopping my twirl and opened my coach's door.

"Elise's carriage arrives again without Elise," I giggled.

"Shall I see you home?"

"Rescue Joan of Arc from Monet," Renoir shouted, Courbet on his arm.

"Escape them now or suffer their manner, the repercussions of copious libations. And I shall never let you go home," Claude whispered.

I tossed a shower of rose petals at a frowning Renoir, but the shame of my mother intruded our play. The thing I feared dropped onto my shoulders as a soft, warm cloak: I tasted freedom as Marie promised and would never be the same again. "Driver, to Madame Pontray's."

~

The carriage arrived at Elise's dim flower shop. She stood in the doorway surprised. "Why are you not home, child?" Elise asked, nervous. Her firm hand guided me inside. She bundled herself in a chocolate dressing robe, a swag of pearls still draped her neck.

Roses, violet perfume, coffee. "At this hour—a nip of brandy, *oui*?" I giggled, sniffing the air. The shadowed shop had only the moonlight casting on the greenery and flowers as the secret coves at the Mabille. "Lovers should steal away here amid gilded ivy and peonies."

Elise rushed to close the curtains. "No hour for visiting. Stop dancing."

Her breath sweetened with brandy. "Madeleine Brohan, the most famous actress in Paris, invited me to her salon. Imagine, me, at her soirée." Elise searched toward the stairway to her apartment. I plopped on a settee sprinkled with rose petals. "You kept Henri Valentine away."

Her hand swept her pearls. She removed them contemplating me, draping them on the counter. "The bubbles speak. Rest. I must get you home."

I sprawled across the settee closing my eyes. "His arrogance tests me . . . his tender words and ambition draws me back."

"Who?"

"Claude Monet, the artists. I will not waste away behind shop windows."

"The dandy? No, child. You're silly with champagne. But my news . . . your papa softens regarding Henri Valentine." She plucked wilted flowers from my hair.

"Valentine's a bore, darling. Strange, I don't love a man called Valentine."

"Love is disruptive and often makes no sense at all." Elise surrendered, sitting beside me.

"It is in a convent . . . in—"

"Inconvenient, quite."

"A rebellion raging inside my heart I cannot stop." My mind raced. "Oh, his kiss."

"Silly with exhaustion and revelry; come, you'll stay with me tonight."

"Balzac claims great love affairs start with champagne and end with . . . chamomile— Camellia? Shhh, the red courtesan." I rested my head on her shoulder. "End with tea, disdain?"

"Tisane." My father walked out from the shadows. My warm, giddy feeling turned instantly straight. He tugged at his red scarf loose around his neck and pocketed his small pipe.

"I knew that was you at the Mabille," I said, rising. "You sat at Elise's table the entire evening." I did my best to straighten my manner. My ruse failed; I crumpled onto the settee.

"I left. Madame Pontray insisted."

"Are you angry, Papa? I had an evening enchanting."

"Hmm. Enchanting evening. I'm reminded we all stumble a time or two with the drink."

"I cannot close my eyes without seeing flashes of light." I studied Elise's ceiling covered in flying cherubs and cotton fluffs, tracing pudgy cupids with my finger.

"My daughter found notoriety among the Mabille's artists and actresses. Mamma will be none the wiser." Papa bundled me in his jacket smelling of brandy, tobacco, and violet perfume.

"*Oui*, Papa." I imagined floating in Claude's arms but landed with a thud in Papa's. "I danced the cancan, Papa. You are not the only one doing scandalous things in the dark."

Papa cleared his throat and glanced at Elise, leaving her with an awkward grin, rubbing his guilt away with the swipe of his mustache. "Well . . ."

The sting of my childhood surfaced at Elise's expression. The champagne's numb, giddy influence vanished as she frowned and left me without the rise and fall of her laughter or kiss goodnight from a trusted friend. "Papa, will our house ever be rid of secrets? I fancy I shall have another one of my own now." If he answered, I heard nothing, falling asleep on his shoulder during our ride home.

28.

Sophie

"Sophia Noel, you are no good friend." I thought of my tea with Annabel, my aunt's loving commitment to my mother, me. I used to know how to love people like that, but something in me years ago closed the door to trust. Maybe Dr. Arnold was right, or maybe it had to do with the fact everyone in my life left when things got messy. It's easy being a friend when it doesn't cost much, but what kind of friend was I? Randall didn't deserve a slammed door. I scribbled in my journal, the one I started to need: *What's good about goodbyes?*

I usually rushed into the art museum, this time I entered cautious, scanning Sculpture Hall for Megan's intrusive pink purse and Randall. He stood in the middle of his staff balancing boxes and gift bags. He caught me, unable to wave, and slowly turned back to his friends. "Look who failed whom."

"Madame, it's easy to wake and take notice. What is difficult is standing and taking action," Monet said. "Alas, the quote is not my own but Balzac's."

"I don't have time for you now," I mumbled, dodging a security guard.

The paper skinny kid with the banana peel hair threw me a half wave. "What up, Sophieee. We think you're slamming when you space," he said, breezing past.

"Hey . . . you. Thanks for waking me."

"Jimmy." He winked and shot me with his fingers, highly inappropriate for a security guard. "Randall asked about you. Man, the icing on his cake— thick as Cézanne's impasto."

He wiggled his brows awaiting kudos at his art joke. I smirked. "Did he seem mad?"

His Joker cackle made me jump. "Randall's never mad unless you hide his cowboy boots." Jimmy left me with his wink and shooting finger again;

someone mean told him that was sexy. He flirted with Lily who looked thrilled as a kid drinking prune juice.

I ducked behind a statue. When Lily left, I sat on a bench waiting for Randall. He strolled to me as cautious as I did upon my entrance. "Randall, I'm so sorry."

"Sparrow, I decided you're taking me to dinner." He offered his hand; I accepted.

"It's three o'clock." I checked my cell for an excuse to leave, shoving it into my purse.

"I'll take that as a yes. I'm hungry. We seniors eat dinner around three or four." He winked. "You like dark chocolate?" He handed me a box. "Hurts my teeth."

I snatched the chocolate as a greedy child making him laugh. "I'm sorry I missed your retirement party." I avoided his eyes. "I missed it all."

"You missed a good ten minutes. Everyone vamoosed after Lily cut the cake. They know I won't stay away long." He nodded to a group of tourists. "I promised a lady friend I'd take a trip," he said, raising an eyebrow. "About damn time too. I haven't had a vacation in years."

"Sounds intriguing. No more Monet exhibition?"

Randall's twinkling blues put me at ease, any offense regarding missing his retirement party forgotten and forgiven without a word. "Maybe that's a good thing, Sophie. Maybe you'll be too busy off seeing Monet in Paris. Your red scarf looks pretty with your red—auburn hair."

I wanted to tell him about my trip with Annabel, but I was still telling myself. We looked around the hall, the crowds thinning. "This was the best part of my day."

"I bet your schedule is packed with younger friends." He swiped his mustache.

I squeezed my brain trying to think of one. "Mom called me her old soul. I've always had older friends. I know the secret: who wouldn't want a retiree as a bestie? If you were a treasure hunter, wouldn't you want to be friends with the folks who owned the map?"

"I like that, Sparrow."

"Good, Cowboy." We strolled through European art to a trendy restaurant overlooking Forest Park and Art Hill. Randall devoured a steak. I picked at my fifteen-dollar burger. We talked John Wayne movies and his puppy Cole ignoring deep subjects until he mentioned Mom.

I dove into my pomme frites.

"Josephine," he sighed. "The most beautiful woman I had ever seen. Her long black hair, blue eyes, tenacity; she knew exactly where life would take her, and if it wasn't going in the right direction, she took life by the collar and turned it right, not the other way around."

"That's Mom, except for the long hair."

"Yep, forgot she cut it."

"Yeah. She knew how to turn heads."

"I always regretted not asking her out."

"Mom?" My eyes popped open. "You, afraid to ask Mom out?"

"Oh, she kept us all on our toes."

"Marge's exhibition; Mom was afraid of 'getting too big.' It happened for her once."

"I know . . . in Paris."

"Yes." At his mention, the flutter in my heart returned. I took in a deep breath to calm it and a sip of water I now wished was a glass of wine.

"She told me about it." He searched out the window. "She used to sit at the Monet as you." He looked at me fondly. "Not the exhibition but our center panel *Water Lilies*."

"You never told me that."

"On Thursdays. She came in the morning and sat for a few hours writing in a pink journal. Sometimes she would sit out there." He pointed to an empty bench under a tree outside our window. "I wondered how she filled all those pages."

"Really?" I sipped my water swallowing my tears.

"We had a good talk that day. She's something else. Josephine spoke about herself for ten minutes and an hour about you."

I stared at the empty bench outside, wishing to sit in it now to feel Mom again. Her view: magnolia trees, a pond and fountain, forest glen and lawn for picnickers, dreamers, lovers. "She painted out there, didn't she?"

"*Oui, mon amie.*" He grinned surprising me. "She taught me a few French words, too."

A flush of shame washed over my face as I imagined the words Mom thoughtfully left me in her journal. I hadn't read them because I was afraid, not of her words, but that I could possibly miss her more. "It's the hardest thing Mom not being here." I turned away from the empty bench outside our window. "She listened and believed in me more than anyone."

"Are you going . . . to Paris? It's all she wanted for you."

My tender look turned harsh. I wanted it to be Mom and me in Paris, our new beginning, facing the past together, dreaming of brighter days for our future. I felt my heart pulling away from Annabel's offer, tempted to stay home, stay hidden.

Randall took the last swig of his coffee. "I'm sorry, Sophie. It's none of my business."

"I think so," I answered, unable to hold his stare. "A lot has happened. I can't keep up."

"Staying busy is great medicine." We left the restaurant lingering in the hallway. Randall looked at his watch. "Closing time. I'm glad we met, Sparrow. It's a good thing, reaching out to people. Life's too damn short to live it alone."

"I'm beginning to see that."

"Sophie, there's always someone who'll listen. You just have to give 'em a try."

"Mom says everyone in our life is a gift."

"Oh, I heard that one years ago. Never forgot it."

"She had that effect on me, too."

"Your mother loved you, Sophie. She wanted everything good for her daughter. I wiped her tears a few times, too, and it was my honor. She is a special woman."

"Randall, thank you for telling me, and thank you for saying . . . she is."

His giant paw gingerly swiped a tear off my cheek. "Remember," he said his voice breaking, "those sweet tears of yours are a testament to the special relationship you had with her. Not many people have that." I looked into his eyes embracing the warmth behind them clutching his words. He stuck out his hand for his manly handshake; I rushed him with my hug. "I lied," he said, overcome. "I'm retiring next week. We can do this all over again."

I smiled and gave him his handshake, mustering my best Katherine Hepburn. "You're a credit to the male sex and I'm thankful you're my friend."

"Not bad. We need a shot of whiskey now, don't we?"

"Next time."

"You never know about things until you have to say goodbye." He masked a sniffle with a cough. "Should've worn my coat shoveling that walkway this morning."

"See ya around? I'm not good at goodbyes, Cowboy."

"No one is, Sparrow. No one is."

He watched me stroll away. I came back to him. "Hey, why do you call me Sparrow?"

Randall flashed a mischievous grin. "Wondering when you'd ask. When we first met, you reminded me of a sparrow flitting around from place to place, nervous, afraid, but you had a song. You just hadn't found it yet."

"That's nice."

"A song my wife sang in church: His eye is on the sparrow. He watches over you."

"I need watching over?"

"We all do."

"Thank you. I'm working on it . . . singing."

"Singing's strange that way; it only works if you try it. No matter how out of tune, a soul singing sounds beautiful to me. See ya around?"

Being with Randall was so easy. I wanted to stay with him, let his deep, rich voice tell me more stories about Mom, his life. *Not a bad vacation*, I thought contemplating ways to see him again. "You're retired."

"Time I admire a Monet." He tipped his imaginary cowboy hat making me smile.

29.

Sophie

I meandered through the parking lot watching the sledders on Art Hill. The boisterous crowd frolicking in the snow was a stark contrast from the quiet observation of the past taking place inside the art museum a stone's throw away. I sat on a bench under the trees taking in winter's canvas. Everywhere I looked, scenes presented themselves worthy of painting: a line of maple trees hugging a snowy trail dusted with pink and periwinkle; a cardinal tucked inside a holly bush, glistening red berries frosted with snow; a bundled little girl impresses Mommy with a twirl; sweethearts make snow angels on a snowy bank. Life all around me; I was missing it.

I looked down at my lap, my journal open, waiting for my impression of the day:

We do not move on from grief; we move through it.

I'm writing this on Post-its and sticking them everywhere, especially on my heart. I don't own loss, but it's followed me my whole life. I'm tired of it defining me.

Change. A word I'm learning to embrace. It won't happen overnight. Why did I ever tell myself it had to? The lie of moving on. You thought it made us stronger, Mom, but it weakened the fabric of us because as the years wore on, strings of that pattern frayed, now they've broken.

Annabel's right, we can't all be John Wayne. I know why Dad loved those movies. He tried to be as fearless, but he couldn't live up to it, no one can. It's not real. I didn't understand that as a kid. All I saw were my parents sweeping things under the rug. That's what I do. Eventually, you'll see the lump in the rug where you've swept the ugly debris. The longer I wait, the uglier it becomes. I'm scared to lift it, see what's under there, but no one else can do it for me. Though John Wayne says, "Trying ain't gettin' it done." I'm going to try because trying is better than walking away.

I closed my journal. Residual snowflakes took flight off the tree branches above. A chill hit my body. Gray clouds fought against a golden horizon. "I'm painting this, painting . . . again." *Again.* My heartbeat skipped at the thought of unfinished dreams; this time it settled at the promise: I wouldn't have to do this alone. "How did you leave painting once and embrace it again?" I stared into the patches of sunlit bark at the base of a tree.

"No Bodmer oak; I'll see what I can do." Monet dipped his brush in yellow. "When the gift of art grips your soul enabling you to see like no other, you can never give it up, madame."

"You did."

"When an artist no longer sees, how can he paint? My quest is a torture: to see such beauty, strive to capture the light, believe you have, and doubt you haven't."

My eyes caught the flicker of sunlight on a snow bank. "Why am I so afraid? I gave up art when I got married. I couldn't measure up to Mom's works. I've run out of excuses."

"You cannot run away from destiny. It will pursue you until you pursue it."

I turned to the sky searching for answers. "I see what this is. I'm freaking out about change." I inhaled chilly air, overwhelmed at Mom's empty gallery, my future.

"I have never found any use for quitting," Monet insisted.

"Haven't you? Is that what you think I'm doing, giving up? You never gave up on your work, but you gave up on people. I don't have time for this. I'm moving through ready to share my heart. It's no gift being alone, no matter how you paint it."

Sunset. I sat on my bench embracing the quiet. "Sledding, snowball fights, drinking hot chocolate—snow scenes, a perfect start. And I'm going to France, Monet's garden, to repaint blurry images into something beautiful." *Spring.* I closed my eyes imagining the scene: a water garden in vibrant water lilies, a bed of plum irises, and an Empress tree in lavender blooms.

Laughter and shouts rang out as dusk covered the sledders; their snowy hillside now shaded in Cookie Monster blue. An unexpected warm breeze mingled with winter air. *Buzz.* I searched through my tote grabbing my cell. "Time to leave you at home." I stared at the text from Joe: I'm coming over. You home?

No. Maybe tomorrow.

Joe: Right, you're on vacay. You sure?

Yep. I took in the wintry scene one last time. On cue, my cell lit up with Jacey's text: Did you drink tea on Sunshine Street with Annabel?

Yes, fab.

Jacey: Movie? I'll bring my homemade chocolate cake & Chocolat so apropope.

Apropos. Maybe tomorrow.

Jacey: Really?

Yes! My heart warmed to Jacey and chilled toward Joe. "Sophie Noel, you're as fickle as the weather. You need to figure this out."

"Figure what out, Sophia? This scene makes a stunning picture. You must paint it."

His cologne hovered behind me: cedar, jasmine, tangerine. *Philip!* I shoved my journal into my tote, my hands flailing fluffing my hair. "I was going to the office and—I got nothing."

He eyed his jacket on me. "Not bad, but that won't keep you warm."

"It's wool . . . and I shouldn't be wearing it." I reluctantly handed it over.

He rushed to drape it back over my shoulders helping me put my arms into the silk-lined sleeves. "I wouldn't want you to catch a cold."

"How did you find me?"

"Annabel serves a wonderful English tea and wanted to know all about us."

"Us?"

"*Oui.*"

"You must have had a short visit." My hummingbird flew back, this time flitting in my stomach. Tingles shot down my arms, giddy, not frightened. "Is there an *us* to talk about?"

He led me back to the bench, bundling me close, his grassy eyes inviting me in. "It's up to you."

"This is all going too fast. It's been a long day. I'm tired, Philip." *And scared.*

"I understand." He walked me to my car as the sun set behind us. "Missouri is an interesting place," he said. "One minute it's winter, the next it's spring. I can't keep up."

"That's the Midwest; you never know what's going to happen."

"You never know." He opened my car door; I slid inside. "Keep my jacket so I can see you again. *Bonsoir.*"

"Philip, I'm awful at this, but I was thinking of having friends over at Mom's house, but it could just be . . . us. Dinner Saturday? I'd love to hear more of your stories about Mom, you."

"I would like that, but what about your friends?"

"They'll understand. I'm on vacation." I wrote Mom's address on a piece of paper.

"I remember where it is. I want to get to know you. Would that be all right, Sophie?"

"I thought you said we already knew each other."

"Our younger selves do. Do you remember bringing me here?"

I stepped out of the car and put on my coat. "I think so." Faded memories washed with color as Philip stood before me, his tender eyes and handsome smile popped up in cherished remembrances I made my heart forget. Me as a lanky teen in a blue wool coat, Mom's crocheted mittens clinging to Philip's hand. Flashes of young love throughout my adolescence, a kiss from a boy in Monet's garden, a long-distance boyfriend in junior high, sweet sixteen kisses and Romeo and Juliet vows at seventeen, plans for college— giving away my heart, until fear prompted me to take it back, and never saying goodbye when Philip moved back to France.

Philip didn't know I had a horrible history with goodbyes. Forgotten memories buried under life's moving on. Memories now playing before my eyes, churning up feelings I thought vanished, the wind carrying second chances.

"That's our bench." He tossed his bangs, rocking on his heels, waiting for me to follow.

"I don't believe you." I walked with him. "It's new."

"Art Hill." We sat on my bench watching sledders crisscross the hillside. "I was eighteen, headed for college. Your mother and my off-again, on-again parents were busy in the museum."

"I had a set of those too. I was seventeen. You broke my heart."

We watched a couple cling to each other as they sled down the hill ending in a puff of snow. "No, our parents did, Sophia." He brushed my hair behind my ear. "My father took me back to Paris, but I begged him to see you again."

"Winter break. You and your father spent Christmas at Mom's; your mother arrived for New Year's. You stayed a month. Mom had a show at the museum that year. Your father . . ."

"Worked with Josephine for years; my parents' last trip. The last time I saw you."

I sighed, my body falling into his. "Teens feel love and loss ten times more."

"And you forget as fast. I never did." He chuckled at three boys sledding down the hill, his hand stroking mine.

I gently pulled it away. "I haven't forgotten as much as you think, but it's all a bit fuzzy."

"I know." We let the quiet fall and like magic, the park's holiday twinkle lights flickered in the trees above us; fountains threw amber streams in the pond below. "You lectured me on the color of shaded snow at dusk," Philip said with a smirk. "Cookie Monster blue."

"How do you remember that?" I laughed. "I wanted to impress you, the artist."

"You held a sled working your honey wheat eyes daring me to go down that hill."

"Honey wheat." I covered my face, embarrassed. "You remember everything."

He stared at the sledders with a mischievous smile. "You game?"

I waved him away. "Oh, no. I'm too old for that."

"I'm not." He stood defiant waiting for my hand.

"We don't have a sled." My heart raced at the thought of flight, his playful smile and invitation to try something new, try us. His pensive green eyes willed my yes. "You never quit."

"A sled. *Un moment.*" Philip raced over to a dad and his kids whispering something in the dad's ear. They looked at me and laughed. Philip pointed, shrugged his shoulders, the dad patted him on his back and handed him his sled.

"Ready?" Philip asked eager to go.

"I'm crazy, but you're nuts." Philip grabbed my hand and found a steep drop. He sat on the sled waiting for me to join him. "Do you know what you're doing?" I asked.

"*Non.* That's the best part."

"Okay . . . I trust you." I plopped down behind him, holding on.

"*Un, deux, trois,*" we counted together, the French from my past bubbled inside of me.

"Phiillllippp," I yelled as we glided across the snow. He steered the sled from side to side. I squeezed him tight, resting my head across his shoulder remembering what it felt like to fall in love. "*Innamorarsi,*" I whispered, the frigid air bouncing off my skin.

"*Bien.* I'm glad." We sat at the bottom of the hill, gasping, laughing, contemplating another ride.

"You game?" I asked.

"It might cost me a knee, but you're worth it."

"At least I didn't ruin your jacket. It's safe in my car."

"And you're safe with me, Sophia. Come on."

I soaked in Philip's promise taking this chance. I didn't want the night to end, but I was tired. Tired of a year of guilt at the slightest bit of happiness, the thought of trusting another man, giving myself so easily now, and the guilt that screamed I didn't deserve it: love and a second chance. *Moving through*, I reminded myself, *as a sled ride through the snow, thrilling, new.*

He grabbed my hand and led us back up the hill. By the time we walked to the top we abandoned the sled to its owner, shared a dozen more memories and though I wanted to kiss him again as that teenage girl in high school, he let me go with two soft kisses to my cheeks. "Are you sure you're real?" I asked.

"Always pretending. It's what I loved about you."

Loved? "Philip . . . I don't know what's ahead, but I'm glad you found me."

"I'm glad you let me," he said, coming back to me with his tender embrace. This time he looked at me as if asking permission and the giddy feelings of a teenage crush covered me as I soaked in his goodnight kiss.

≈

I slipped into my house with a quick wave to Mr. Elders salting his driveway.

I laughed at myself—Philip—sledding down Art Hill as teenagers again. It felt so good; it all did.

I turned off my cell ignoring the world. Hope warmed me. After a hot shower and a search through old photos, I found it: Halloween. Philip and I dressed as French painters, black-and-white-striped shirts, brushes, palettes in hand, matching berets and handlebar mustaches.

I wandered into the basement searching for my easel, buried and forgotten for years—until Mom dusted it off again. A whiff of a honeysuckle candle to cover the must; I walked into the storage room, the unapologetic room of unfinished walls, mazes of wiring and ductwork, packed with years of forgotten hobbies and endeavors.

I stared at the empty cement wall before me and noticed the hidden gift basket packed with Mom's favorite sweets and art supplies in the corner, a handwritten coupon crowned the top: my promise to paint with her this year. I eyed the empty view: a foundation wall—the small basement window, a glimpse of grass.

A blank cement wall the size of a Monet masterpiece.

"The size of a panel, a center panel of water lilies."

I stared into the basket of Mom's paints and tore open the cellophane of her unused birthday gift, spreading its contents on my old dining room table covered in protective pads in the center of the room. I grabbed a palette, a large brush, and squeezed out the expensive colors.

I ran into the exercise room, grabbing the framed poster of Monet's *Water Lilies*, a gift from Mom when I went off to college. I set it on the easel and studied it. My eyes caught the basket again thrown to the floor now empty of the prizes thoughtfully chosen for my mom: a box of truffles, French macaroons and tea, perfumed lotions, the art supplies now strewn across the table, and my birthday card for her. I read it.

A mother's love comes close to touching God, as I will ever know here on earth. Thank you for being my angel. Thank you for holding and taking care of my heart.

We did our best, Mom, and it was more than enough. Thank you for being my hero. Happy Birthday. Now, let's paint. Love, your Sophia.

I crushed the card in my hand, with steady tears swiped the large paintbrush from the table, and slapped it in cobalt. I struck the wall with angry swirls and desperate globs. The cement was so porous I threw the brush down, blue splattering on a lounge chair, me. I poured a bottle of water into a bucket, grabbed a sponge, and spotted a can of the blue paint meant for the master bath. "Peace. I knew I bought you."

I pried the lid open, stirred, dabbed it with a wet sponge and swirled the paint on the concrete wall to create my mass of water. Angry punches turned soft. I grabbed a sock from the floor, rubbing the blue paint into the pores of the cement. I filled a shoebox with rags, socks, and sponges, spotting a pyramid of mini paint cans next to a box of floor tile. Guy's rainbow of paint samples would not go to waste: blue, lavender, lime, pink skies, white clouds, and yellow water lilies with red bellies. Wasted pro acrylics mixed with latex wall paint. I followed the shape of the marsh, reflection of sky and willows, one layer with hundreds of brushstrokes to follow.

A start.

I faintly heard my mom laughing, the massive wall before me, and her tickled pleasure I had at last thrown my heart and soul into painting. I switched on my old boom box, my heart resting at Ella singing a lazy jazz classic, "The Nearness of You." "How apropope," I snickered.

Swipes of blue, dabs of pink, mostly an empty wall yet to be touched, splatters over my favorite T-shirt and lounge pants, my nose. I stood before the massive wall applying colors until my shoulder and wrist begged for rest. And in a steady rhythm, I now applied the paint in smooth, focused waves. "I'm painting, *Maman*. I'm painting."

30.

Camille

∼

August 1865

Make him see. Show him you are unafraid, mature, and patient. Reveal the subtle control of your smile from your lips, inside your eyes; he will observe you command your talent. A genuine expression or none at all—if you hold the pose—he must paint it.

We began with sketches in his studio, but Claude was more at ease painting in nature. A folded easel, paint box, and the new tube paints offered him his open-air studio in a garden, park, or forest. Mounds of color squeezed onto his palette: flake white, cadmium yellow, vermillion, deep madder, cobalt blue, and emerald green. Enveloped in silence, he freed his brush to paint what he saw. What Claude Monet saw proved his ultimate gift.

A scene brushed with tiny dabs of luminescent color, thin and thick strokes rough and unrefined—an impression. The opposite of what masters mandated as worthy French art built up into an effect; hundreds of hues and shadows played tricks to the beholder, of movement, shimmer, the feeling of a moment: a rippling sunset across the sea, sunrise in a garden, a sunlit path in the forest. Claude sometimes doubted his brush but never his eye.

Painting his obsession; besting the Salon his aim. "Black shadows no more," he declared, exploring his own technique as a composer of a new sound in music. He detested the unoriginality and conformity taught at the premier French School of Fine Arts. The Emperor's new Palais de l'Industrie was a monument to French art, agriculture, and progress. Inside its galleries, known as the Salon, the annual art exhibition invited the best artists to compete. When they insisted on darker tones and classical poses, Claude painted vigorous pastel dabs, natural poses, and figures wearing modern fashions in nature. "Objects enveloped with sunlight and the blue dome of Heaven reflected in the shadows," he said. Claude painted anything but angels, but I watched as he painted with them.

Summer brought the slow season as throngs of Parisians abandoned Paris for seaside resorts and country cottages. Claude painted studies in the Fontainebleau Forest. Despite Renoir's warnings, we fell in love. Lofty ambitions failed to impress my father. Papa planned a summer in Lyon, striving to erase Claude Monet from the landscape of his daughter's life, to no avail. Marie, Albert, Gabrielle, me, and Courbet formed a merry troupe of actors for Claude's staging of his *Luncheon on the Grass*. Frédéric's delay as Claude's main model sullied all.

"*Would Frédéric sabotage Claude's progress?*" I asked Marie.

"*Darling, you have much to learn about artists, rivals, and love. Frédéric lives at the theater. I hear whispers regarding his affections—toward all things in besting Claude Monet.*"

"*I will ensure he wins in art and love.*"

"*Who, darling?*"

The rain postponed an outing with Marie to the Parc Monceau with our sisters. "Raphael, life as Claude's model satisfies me." I hung Claude's pastel on the wall behind the counter, a forest trail a blink before sunrise. I inhaled his imagined pines, cedar, and rain on the horizon drifting to drench Claude's afternoon. Raphael yapped for my attention. I tickled his belly and with a stretch, my little Bichon snuggled on his bed. "Papa closes the shop again, few customers with this rain. Claude requires sunlight and flowers—always and always."

"My daughter dreams inside a pastel by her Monet. Today, frowns cease." Papa waved a letter with his handsome smile I missed. "*Oui, ma fille.* Read while I sigh over the ledger."

I squeezed Papa, snatched the letter, and escaped into the stockroom. Raphael followed, snuggling in my lap. "Do not tell me you are jealous, too." Pressed leaves and wildflowers fell onto my dress. "Claude sends me the forest."

Dear Camille,

I miss my little bird. Frédéric postpones his arrival again, bent on

my ruin. Next week I return to Paris to take you to Fontainebleau. A
glorious beechwood grove offers shade and a shower of sunlight through
a canopy of trees for my picnic scene. Everyone praises what I'm doing so
I best do it well.

I count on you, ma chéri, and your friends as you promised. Gather
the summer dresses and bonnets. The outlandish Courbet awaits your
arrival. He fancies your whimsical pink cravat; so do I. He begs you wear
the angel water he so loves. I boxed his ear on your behalf for his tone. He
suffers my nerves with his drunken harmonica playing that drives even
the feral cats away. Renoir distracts Bazille inviting him to the regattas
in Bougival, your spy Marie informs. Bazille promises a week of posing
to which I replied, 'It will do me no good to wait until winter.'

Love, Claude.

I slipped his letter in a drawer for later and returned to Papa unable to
hide my blush.

"Let's abandon your mother's weak coffee and visit Madame Lucinda's
for a sip of chocolate," Papa said. "I'll even take you to Renoldi's for a slice
of gingerbread."

"Am I a little girl today? Shall we ride the carousel too?"

"By the saints you're nineteen, but still my child. Today you fancy your
hair in braids as my girl, but why the gray dress? Wear the white with green
stripes to brighten my day."

"You know I save that dress for Claude's painting in the forest."

Papa shook his head at the mention, scribbling in his book. "Your sister
begs for a day at the park to float the toy boat from your Frédéric Bazille."

"How could Frédéric refuse when you allow Genèvieve in the shop to
beg customers for toys for bargains on ribbons?" I hid my embarrassment in
the messy ribbon display.

Papa watched me fiddle, somber back into his figures. "On that miscalculation we both suffer your mother's wrath." He waved Raphael away in
no mood for play. Papa carried a weight when we were alone. I counted on
Raphael as our distraction, not today.

A tap on our window and wave from Monsieur Belrose lightened my
heart. I missed him. His jig reminded me of the people I abandoned in
the trade for new friends. I applauded his performance. He waddled under

his umbrella into his shop. I wished I invited him inside to interrupt the storm brewing between Papa and me. I missed Elise, too. None of us spoke regarding the night I caught her with Papa. This summer, she escaped to a cottage in Sèvres accompanied by her companion from the ball—I believed was Papa. Perhaps it was . . . still is.

I thought I found something of my own, but I lost myself more each day. Love swept me away faster than a flood. Standing before Papa, I shivered as his child in Lyon. Afraid I could not hold my head above the water to breathe. My independence lost, for I saw nothing but Claude.

I waited for Papa to speak while he rearranged hats on the counter for the third time. He avoided my eyes; his shoulders slumped, catching himself downcast, he stood taller. "I canceled the preposterous lingerie sale you arranged," he said, eyeing me. He hoisted corsets and Kimonos out of our display. "I'm beginning to miss selling curtains to nuns."

"As you wish, my father. Marie and her aunts invited me to dinner again at Maison Dorée. Her chef promises a chiffon pudding with an orange sabayon."

"My father?" he said hurt. "*Oui*, delights I no longer give my daughter who was once elated with a sip of chocolate and a cab ride with her papa." Raphael tugged at Papa's trousers.

Papa sighed. I sat beside him. "You will not frown when I bring you home a slice of marshmallow cake with strawberry jelly and whipped cream."

He removed his spectacles, squinting at a page of numbers. His hands trembled; he caught me noticing and stuffed them into his pockets. "I knew Paris would steal you away from me someday; I didn't believe it would happen so soon."

"No one has stolen me away from you."

"Not even the brazen Claude Monet? I now need these spectacles but I'm not blind."

Mamma burst in discerning our awkwardness. I rushed into the stockroom, reappearing modeling a sunhat to cheer Papa. It might have thawed the frostiness between us save Mamma's presence. "Madame Durant's gold dress arrived," I said. "She fancied one at the Mabille."

"Child, it's summer. Haven't we heard enough of this vulgar ball," Mamma said, curious at Papa's quiet demeanor. She swirled a row of lace handkerchiefs on a table. "Include these in your sale. They're poor quality, plain—dirty."

"As you wish," Papa said, glancing at me.

I winnowed a Japanese fan at him. "Red for the window, Papa, summer love?"

"No need for a grand display," said Papa. "The masses leave Paris for the country."

"As your daughter," Mamma said, gliding in a dress with pink roses and teal ribbons too fine for a rainy day. She admired a pink bonnet. "You intend on allowing this foolishness in the forest?" I traded the hat in her hands for a black veil to Papa's snicker.

"Camille's in the company of respectable friends and Cousin Gabrielle," Papa said. "My brother promises her safety. She takes the train and comes home. That's the end of it."

"Your beloved Madame Durant appears concerned. She whispers, Camille and these—"

Papa banged his fist on the counter startling us. "Léonie, not today."

Mamma bristled, her nails rattling on the counter mimicking the ping of raindrops on the windowpanes. "People are talking, spying those sordid artists lingering here. You should no longer rent out the dirty costumes . . . nor our daughter."

"Léonie," Papa shouted.

"I model the character of the dress for Papa," I insisted. "I have a talent, so the artists wish to paint me. Keep to your rendezvous at the races, Mamma. Do not lecture us on selling."

"Camille Léonie Doncieux, you shall not turn into a rude thing. You shall not." She stomped her heel as a child nearly crushing Raphael.

I scooped him up to calm him; my little Bichon settled my heart instead. "Speaking one's mind is not rude. I refuse to sit in a corner flapping a fan."

"Perhaps your mother is right, Camille. You hardly work in the shop now . . . next year."

"Next year?" Mamma snipped. "Charles, you gave me your word on retiring."

Papa dismissed her, burying his head into his figures. "Despite what you insist as my decrepit nature, I wish to work. If Camille joins me that's her choice. I denied her quest for the stage. I tolerate a bit of posing as is proper. I've seen the work. It's respectable."

Mamma scuttled to a lilac gown inspecting its lace sleeves. "What's changed?" she asked, claiming a pair of long lavender gloves. Despite Papa's glare, she tucked them under her arm. "An evening as a coquette at an outdoor ball? Our daughter . . . a star among actresses and painters who will dismiss her once she is . . . used."

"Léonie!" My father pounded his fist again frightening Raphael.

I set Raphael down, watching him scamper away. "Where does my mother go at night?"

Papa slowly walked to the front door and flipped our sign to *Closed*. "Daughter."

Mamma threw the gloves on the counter. "I advance us among those who matter."

"And neglect those who truly do," I said.

She rang her fingers through a row of crystals dangling from a lamp. The shop hadn't a sound other than the tinkling glass. "I see," she said, shifting her gaze between Papa and me. "In one month, my daughter, the coquette, and my husband plot against me."

"Enough," Papa said. "You'll not use that word regarding our daughter."

"Especially when my mother knows precisely what it means."

Mamma stood defiant watching Papa snuff out the lights in the shop. He closed the curtains glancing at me ashamed of my manner. Despite the ruse of a sparkling appearance at a notorious ball, introductions in the salons of Paris, and a quaint dress shop selling fineries in the Batignolles, the Doncieux family frayed apart in need of a talented mender of things of the soul.

"All right," Mamma said. "If Camille wishes to parade in the shop inviting artists to dote on her as harlot to sell a gown so be it. No respectable man will want her."

"I wish to work," I insisted. "Have something of my own."

"You have always turned against me."

"I'm not the one who cast her daughter aside . . . for what?" I asked.

"Camille, hold your tongue," said Papa. "Or you will spend your days alone in Lyon."

"A dream compared to the war between you two."

Papa remained quiet spying at us from behind the counter. Mamma wandered to the empty window display peering out at the gray day. I unfurled my fists, caressing the lavender gloves she threw on the counter, turning to Claude's pastel dreaming of a walk in the forest.

"Why do you hate me?" she asked me, walking back to us.

I swallowed my tears. "I wondered that about you my entire childhood." Papa hurried from behind the counter, locking our door, staring outside as a boy unable to play in the rain.

"*Oui*, lessons must be learned," said Mamma. Her dead blue eyes hardened my heart. "I'm sorry, Camille, for you will learn them at a tremendous cost." She ran upstairs, and at the slam of a door, Raphael's tail spun in circles at my feet. I shooed him into Papa's arms.

Papa held my hands, Raphael bouncing between us. "I adamantly disagree."

"Why does Mamma hate me so?"

Papa set Raphael onto his bed, burying his thoughts in scribbles. "Your mother loves you. Her youth is past, *ma fille*. A beauty, but her disposition sours her among the circles she clings to for prominence. I go against my wife because I desire more for my daughter. Will I regret this?"

I slid his book away, covering his hand with mine. "You do not accept Claude regardless of my happiness?"

He gazed out the window at Monsieur Belrose's shop. "The morning rain ruins both our sales today. Summer storms plague us."

"Papa?"

He waved me away, turning back to his window. "It is for men to shame themselves, to rise or fall in vanity. Do you want to be alone and suffer shame on this house?"

"Claude is not like the other artists. He portrays respectability, a new art."

"Ah, what he whispers to my daughter while he disrespects her alone in the moonlight filling her with champagne. You've wasted my morning." He fought with a dress on its form.

"You will not face what is real. Even after the night of the ball . . . at Madame Pontray's."

Papa's skin flushed, disappointment washed over his face. He shook his head, staring at me in disbelief. I held no shame but anger at the life of my parents judging my own. "Your sharp tongue slashes your own father. Don't test me, or I will send you away as your mother insists, and that will be the end of this talk of something *new*."

"I need the truth."

Papa's sigh deflated his posture. His fingers fumbled tying a green sash around a yellow dress, only to tug it off and toss it aside. "You know why we moved to Paris. Some things must remain unspoken."

My anger failed to stop my tears. I whisked them away with a swipe of the modest handkerchief my mother disdained. "But my sister—"

"No!" Papa held his breath and let his grief out with a gasp, slinking behind the counter back into his ledger. "In a few weeks' time, I lost my daughter, for the daughter I know would never humiliate her father so."

"Papa." The familiar dread and caution stuck to me throughout my childhood. I longed to rid myself of it now.

"Enough," he whispered, tempering his anger. "You gave your word to pose for a painting, that's the end of it. Force this, I will send you away to Lyon. I must protect you."

"You may send me away, but you will still have to live with what is coming. You cannot halt this storm, nor is it fair I should bear the force of it."

At the clap of Papa's book, I gazed out the window. "When I met your mother, she wasn't hiding in corners at the ball; she led the dances. You need more than my shop provides." I placed my coins on the counter for the lavender gloves for Mamma. My mind demanded crude resolutions, my heart longed for peace. Papa faintly smiled at the gesture. "I see a daughter filled with a wonder I cannot hold, a wonder bigger than my shop can hold, and this frightens me." Papa emerged from behind the counter tucking his ledger under his arm. "I also see a world that will not welcome her, a cold city of gossip and cruelty."

Among the vibrant summer ball gowns and day dresses, sadness hung in the shop clouded by a storm. I wrapped the gloves in a box, tying it with ribbon. Papa stayed quiet, fussing at a stand of umbrellas. "Papa . . . when will you realize I am not her?"

He searched my eyes. "Now . . . until you give me cause not to."

"Mamma...left me to drown." Papa ran to me, taking the package from my hand, cradling me as his little girl afraid of the dark water. "She loves Genèvieve more."

"Because she loved him," he whispered. His clinging hands slid away in shame. He swiped his mustache, cleared his throat filling the quiet. "This is what you wanted? Truth. My wife will not love nor leave. How can I look into my daughter's eyes with pride I'm her papa?"

"I am tired of secrets." I cried alone.

"I fear someday you will learn some secrets are meant to stay hidden in the dark. The unfairness and true sin: a man may withstand his immorality, a woman cannot."

"I have not disgraced myself. I carry no shame loving Claude."

"Yet, you judge me. Now, I go mourn the loss of my daughter for I know now she will leave me. Perhaps in her heart she already has."

"With Elise?" I said to his back as the shameful daughter I now was. "I will always love you, Papa," I whispered. My heart tore from his as he hung his head and quietly closed the door knowing this would be our last conversation regarding life and love. I watched him suffer the rain, struggling to open his umbrella and walk our route to the flower shop and his mistress.

"You will have no happy ending today, sister?" Genèvieve's tiny voice whispered behind me, quivering with tears. "I know a secret . . . frogs and toads fill the shop floor, but I will not look at them. I will wonder at the diamonds. Can you see them, my sister? Can you see them?"

"I can now."

31.

Sophie

Reality knocked on my chest as I pulled into Mom's driveway alone. "This is your house, Mom. I can't fill it without you." *Ma fille, it's all arranged*, she whispered in my thoughts. I inhaled the crisp air, the fresh scent of evergreen and snow-dusted grass. Cottage style luxury covered in stone. Nantucket blue shutters, white Tuscan columns on river stone bases; her front porch lined with potted bulbs to surprise me in spring. *This was our dream house, Sophia.* I want you to enjoy it. Manicured lawns, uniformed hedges and cedar fences, magazine homes and far-off neighbors would take getting used to. A lawn service, carpenter, security—I never imagined living in Mom's house required instructions. "Change is a loaded word, a hard one."

Mr. Elders volunteered to finish projects around my house. "Pay me by letting me do the work," he said. "Maudie's trying to sign us up for some ballroom dance crap. Says it'll be good exercise. So is raising a hammer and painting a house, Noel." I wondered who would inherit my kind neighbors, the Monet copy I painted on my basement wall, and a Cinnamon Squares orange front door. I couldn't imagine living in Mom's house alone, nor could I picture anyone else in it.

A few acres to ensure distance, her neglected English garden, I hoped Maudie could help me manage, and a backyard deck where Mom entertained friends. "You gave me more than a house, Mom. It's you." I grabbed the groceries and headed inside, catching a glimpse of a man's pant leg kneeling behind Mom's favorite oak. "Are you going to help or pull weeds?" I asked.

"Sophie!" His middle finger set to action pushing up his glasses. "I hoped I'd catch you."

"Can you catch one of these bags, Dr. Arnold? They're heavy."

"Good to see you. I knew you would come." He grabbed the bags and followed me inside. "It smells delicious. Are you baking?" He sat at the counter watching me put food away.

"How long have you been waiting for me?" I asked, unamused.

He laughed and grabbed an apple. "May I?" I nodded. He looked bundled for a jog, grew a short beard. He grinned, stroking his whiskers, raising a brow for my opinion. I folded my arms happily making him squirm and smiled. "Don't be angry," he said. "I drove by the past few Thursdays to see if you'd show, for Josephine."

"It's Saturday morning." I tossed him peanut butter. "Sorry I missed you at the funeral."

"Understood." He removed his glasses, avoiding a plethora of middle fingers. "I recognize that smell. Your mom fattened me up on her vanilla pound cake."

His visit appeared harmless; I let him linger. "It doesn't taste like hers. I miss it, Dr. Arnold, her. I'd offer you some, but I'm waiting for . . . it's not ready."

He peered into the dining room noticing my set table and smiled. "Anyone interesting?"

"You mean real? Someone special from my past; I'm giving life a try."

In our familiar places, Dr. Arnold sunk into Mom's couch engulfed in purple pillows, I, her chinoiserie sofa. "Good to hear. You look great, Sophie."

I played Donna Reed this morning shopping in a pale yellow dress and floral heels. "Dr. Arnold, can I call you Brian? This will be easier if I view it as a chat."

"Of course."

I kicked off my heels and bundled under the Beast. "I know you've been following me."

"Excuse me?" He settled in.

"Brian, I know you promised her. Apparently, Mom made several people promise a bunch of things. Jacey's working on the friendship. Joe's clingy. Even Mrs. Lemon asked me about my plans for the gallery. People are coming out of the woodwork. Sure, they don't know I know, and maybe it's nothing, but I know Mom."

He smashed his praying hands to his lips. "That's a lot of knows . . . and the girl Megan that killed Gimbletook?"

"*And* my husband." Brian shifted in his seat his eyes glued on me. "That's one monster I haven't had the guts to face. I've done a noble job slaying a few dragons this week."

"You need someone to talk to, I'm here."

"I know. Mom did all this to help me, prove I'm not alone and alone isn't as tranquil as I imagined." I wandered to the fireplace searching the photos of our past. "I can't remember."

"Remember?"

"Who this girl is." I showed him the picture of me a gangly teen needing braces.

"Young Sophie? We all change."

I stared into the young, happy image of Mom, Dad and me in front of the Eiffel Tower. "It's something else. Even before I lost Blake and Mom . . . I lost me." We turned our attention to her pink journal on the coffee table, its red rhinestone heart sparkling in the morning sun. I grabbed my lavender journal. "I'm writing in this now." I showed him my scribbled pages. "I'm drawing again, too." I waved Mom's journal. "I read this . . . a few answers. She wanted to keep me busy. Mom's orchestrating my life and she's not even here."

"She loves you." Quiet, Brian watched me as he teetered on the edge of intrusion and tough love. The tough love Mom would have offered.

"Thank you for not saying loved."

"She wanted to make sure you'd be all right."

I crumbled onto the couch. "I'm not." The glee from the past few days dissolved. I held my breath calming my rattling heartbeat. The aroma of pound cake shifted my thoughts, hopes. I sat up resolved hugging our journals together. "They once taught artists lavender and pink were offensive, never use them together, violet and blue injure the other. Yet, pink, lavender, violet, and blue create the most stunning Monet masterpieces. I'm glad they didn't listen."

"Who?"

"The Impressionists. They fought for a greater purpose: inclusion, free-thinking, modern art beyond the dictates of their time, government, or peers. They abandoned usual. I'm not giving up, Brian. Saying I'm not all right, doesn't mean I won't be."

"I know." He smiled and held up a pillow covered in violet and blue ribbon roses Mom and I made. "We were waiting for you to say it."

I stared at him fondly. "'Craft a life, Sophia,' Mom said as we sewed that pillow. So many people lose themselves alone crafting art when they miss the thing that gives their art life."

"What's that?"

"Their own. You can't fully experience life alone; it's only half a life, isn't it?"

"I might have to write that on my business card." He stroked a blue rose on the pillow and set it down treating it worthy of its own display.

"I'm sorry you and Mom broke up."

"Josephine didn't want to burden me. I wanted to be with her through it all."

"It meant everything. Most friends disappeared. Mom's so forgiving. I can't be like her."

"Sometimes we need to remind ourselves in the darkest times, light shines."

"That's worth all our Thursdays put together. I saw you at the art museum, the paint store, my office, and I assume you saw her."

"Who?" He tossed his apple in the trash.

I followed him into the kitchen, poured him a glass of milk, and handed him the Oreos. "You tell me. I'm sure Mom arranged that, too."

"Sophie, I don't know anything you're talking about but naturally all this is coming to a head." He dunked a cookie. I grabbed one and joined him. "Are you still having panic attacks?"

"I lost my mom. I didn't expect it, Brian. I didn't expect this quiet house, or the quiet when I drive down the street, the quiet at my office looking at her empty gallery, and the quiet at my house unable to call her. I survived losing Dad, Blake . . . but I don't know what to do now."

"I'll share what she told me: open your heart to the people around you. The first step."

"The second, third, and fourth?"

"One step, Sophie. If you can take that first step, I'd feel better about not keeping tabs on you. And the journals, I can help you navigate those."

I walked away from his offer, burying myself under the Beast on the couch. "Writing in the journal is helping me remember the good, not anything else. That's a start."

"A great step," he said keys in hand.

"I'm painting again. Tonight's step three."

"And those pills?"

I grabbed my tote, searched through it revealing the empty amber bottle, placing it in his hands. "I called my doctor and told him I'll never need them again." Brian jingled his keys, winked, and headed toward the front door. "Where are you going?"

"That's all I wanted to hear. You're expecting company."

"Next Thursday? I owe you a slice of pound cake. Brian . . . I'm going to Paris."

He shrugged his shoulders and left me with his charming smile. "I know."

"Mom was so sure about everything wasn't she?"

"She'd never bet against you."

"I still can't remember. Maybe I never will. I thought she'd leave me more."

"Memories are funny that way, especially those that have wounded us deeply. It's as if our mind and spirit protect us until we're ready."

"For what?"

"Forgiveness." I hadn't realized he was holding my hand until I felt its warmth. We noticed Mom's gardening tools, abandoned seed packets, and pots on the front porch. My stomach dropped at the sight. "Give yourself time, Sophie," he whispered, kissing my cheek. "The good thing about stages, they're temporary . . . if you want them to be."

"But I have to walk through them."

"We all do, but never alone. Remember that, Sophie."

"That's what she wanted you to tell me. Thank you." I watched him drive off.

32.

Camille

Genèvieve showed off reciting *Diamonds and Toads* during our carriage ride to the Parc Monceau. I stared at the Seine imagining its silver-blue ribbon winding through valleys and villages to Claude in Fontainebleau. I pictured the landscapes he might paint as we traipsed the countryside cloistered in cottages by the river, the river that carried Claude to me in Paris and away to his family in Le Havre—his lifeblood and my reminder of a common station in Lyon, drifting through the twists and unforgiving swells of a fickle existence in Paris.

The city that once brought hope to Papa now offered despair. In a household of anger and secrets, I pondered leaving Paris for a life on my own.

"Look how my sister dreams inside her love bubbles," Genèvieve giggled.

"I was marveling how fairy magic changed us all into birds," I said. "Marie and I crow gossip while our sisters chirp as chickadees about little Thomas Maywheel."

"Chickadees don't chirp, sister, they trill," Genèvieve said, spraying us with her attempt.

"Whistle," Jeanne added. "Like this." She puckered and blew a long two-note whistle.

"The Parc Monceau invites imagining." Marie laughed, scooting the girls onward. Roses and lavender replaced spring pansies, reminding me of my last stroll here with Papa. "Albert and his fetching brother, Dax, wait at the pond to preside over our sisters' boat race," Marie whispered to me. "Albert brings kites for the girls. We have an hour to ourselves."

"With our promenade on the Champs-Élysées, the marionettes and gingerbread this morning, I do not feel guilty. I welcome a quiet hour with my dearest friend."

"I wear pink; Jeanne wears blue," Genèvieve shouted. "We're a bed of hydrangeas."

Marie and I sat on a bench watching our sisters twirl. "*Bonjour,*" Albert called, waving the girls over. He stood near the pond; a mock ruin of Greek columns skirted its bank. "The boat races started." Dax reared his head from behind a kite and waved.

"Claude made Genèvieve promise not to disturb the water lilies," I said, watching the girls run off. "He said it would be like smearing an artist's wet canvas."

"Genèvieve is taken with Claude as Jeanne is with Albert. How easy they fall in love."

"Marie finds no Romeo in Albert?"

"Too close to the water, Jeanne," Marie shouted, ignoring my question.

"I loved the curiosities in this park as a child. A Dutch windmill, Egyptian pyramid. A peacock chased Papa once and a lemonade man magically appeared at every corner."

"Look, the author Gustave Flaubert's home, the most famous dinner table in Paris. I hear no admittance for mutes or bores." Marie laughed, flapping her fan, fluttering her lashes. "Perhaps we'll be invited. You swim in the right circles. You do swim, Camille?"

I stole her fan hiding my face. "No, darling, I dance." I sprang up, keeping her fan away from her as Albert and the girls shouted, "Higher, higher."

"We're not impressing Flaubert," Marie said, chasing me around the bench, winning back her fan. "Now we're eleven."

A passing vendor looked on us with delight carrying a contraption on his back. "'Tis sweet today, mademoiselles," he called.

"But is it cold?" Marie asked the lemonade seller.

He winked and tipped his cap. "As a cup of snow." He squinted at me; his burly red mustache covered his grin; he poured us two glasses.

"Hurry along. Do not ring your bell," Marie said, paying the man. "At present, our baby sisters don't need another ounce of sugar, but do come around again in a while."

He nodded thrilled at her plan. "Mademoiselles, the flowers have competition with you blossoming in the park today. *Merci.*" He hobbled off to a cluster of parasols.

Marie closed her eyes to a breeze. I nudged her awake. "Look how Albert plays," she said. "He wants many children."

"Oh, Marie, has Albert proposed?"

"I haven't said yes." She closed her parasol, watching the lemonade seller serve a gathering of women and children. "Are we fashioned from a different cloth than our mothers?"

"Albert is a good man. What does your heart say?"

"It turns mute, poor company for Flaubert."

We laughed at our sisters hopping a victory dance as the brothers set kites soaring. "Should I ever meet the author," I said. "I will tell him I cared not for his scandalous *Madame Bovary*." Marie turned to me elated. "His story rings as the diary of my mother. A diary I wish I never saw . . . things I must now keep secret for Papa."

Marie grabbed my hand, sweeping us away into a private nook. "*Oui, mon amie*, daughters should never uncover their mother's secrets."

"Mamma longs for someone else." A flicker of light danced upon my skin, a glow of lemon and gold. "Her love is as fickle as this light. I do not know what cloth I am fashioned from, Marie, but I will never love as my mother." The flash of light shimmered and rolled in my palm until it vanished. "I see why Claude chases the light. I see many things now."

Marie found her shimmer, wiggling her fingers in the light as it rained on her through the trees. Her handkerchief brushed my face; her smile outshone the sun. "You confess your heart to comfort mine," she said. We walked to the pond admiring the water lilies. Marie blew a kiss to Albert as he guided the girls' small hands, running off with the flight of paper butterflies.

Liquid silver rippled to an open water lily dressed in lavender and lemon. "I envy your stillness," I whispered to it. Marie grew lost in Albert's tender way with Jeanne. I studied the water lilies, their scalloped pads holding drops of water as doilies on a table.

Marie's fan fluttered as the kites skimming the air. "Elise misses you," she said. "Mend your friendship. She loves you as her daughter. What contract does Claude offer with his debt?"

"His inclusion keeps me. You fear giving your heart to Albert. I dread stealing mine away from Claude's."

"I have the answer—Albert and Claude must marry."

"Always making jokes."

"Claude Monet sees water lilies aglow, never wilted or struggling. How will you live?"

I wandered to the pond's edge. Marie's boots shuffled in the grass after me. I froze at the ripple of my cream dress, a ruffle floating past as my mother's in my dream. "This is the closest I have stood to water in years. I cannot swim."

"Then don't attempt it."

"I'm shipwrecked, *mon amie*. I boast independence tossing it now for infatuation."

"Love. Elise quips love is messy, complicated—when you know it's real."

I hid my tears finding joy as our sisters danced as sprites among the flowers. "Papa struggles to concentrate on basic tasks. He grows weaker. The quiet of the country lures my heart." Marie held her breath ready to burst. "Crow your snip of gossip, my magpie."

"Claude will never paint what they tell him, so he cannot support a wife. His wealthy circles may soon abandon him." Her eyes widened, discovering my secret. "Heavens, a taste isn't enough—Camille . . . you're leaving?"

"Twenty-five is a lifetime away to marry without Papa's consent."

"No official will marry you without threat of jail. You're no Juliet. Do not give into this."

"We prepared a feast, sisters," Geneviève called. "I won the boat race."

"I flew my kite higher," Jeanne shouted.

Marie and I waved back, shaking off our mood. "A moment," Marie called.

"Leave your storm clouds behind." Albert conducted his symphony of giggles.

"You fear for nothing, Marie. Claude has not indicated marriage, yet."

"Nor will he." She examined me with concern. I looked away. "Camille, when will you learn, secrets don't keep you safe they keep you lonely."

My charade shattered. Geneviève frantically waved us over. Dax appeased her impatience with a show of shadows across the lawn. "What else?" I asked. "Our sisters wait."

"Frédéric's company is worthy, Renoir's is not. Jules Le Coeur, a premier cabinetmaker in Paris, introduced Renoir to a model, Lise Tréhot. He is smitten with his new mistress-muse."

"Renoir is harmless. This Lise must be an amiable model for Renoir to paint her."

"Frédéric ponders Lise for a painting—she's quite gifted."

"I've warned you. You're trying to rile me with Frédéric. I am no mistress-muse." I gathered my things ready to race to my sister. "Claude will win in art. He will make us all see."

"But who will make Claude Monet see?"

"Camille's too serious again," my sister called. "She's slouchy like the Hunchback of Notre Dame." Geneviève smashed me with her hug.

"You are a sweaty beastie," I said, holding her.

"I'm not a beastie. I'm a fairy."

"We have a surprise for you," Marie cheered. "The lemonade man rings his bell."

I took in my sister's sweet promise and joy radiating as a blazing sunset to our day. But I could not help catching Marie's anguish. She handed a parasol to her sister watching her twirl under the canopy of linen shade. *Marie is right. I should run home to Papa*, I thought. *Embrace a life of comfort and predictability.* I watched the tranquil water lily unmoved, unchanged, settling my mind. *I will not travel with Claude to Fontainebleau*, I decided.

A loving voice thwarted my heart's treason. "There's my little bird." Claude sauntered out from behind the shrubs surprising us all.

Geneviève ran to him with a hug. "Camille dreams of you," she giggled.

Marie snickered. "The lemonade man will make his fortune today," she whispered, her fluttering lashes and fan brushing my cheek.

33.

Sophie

Buzz. Annabel: What's for dinner?
   Light tomato basil pasta—keeping it chill.
   Annabel: LAU
   LOL?
   Annabel: Laughing @ you! At least you know Philip like likes you.
   CRZ
   Annabel: Czar?
   Crazy!
   Annabel: TTYL
   Text dictionary?
   Annabel: Of course. I own a bookstore :)

Hope bubbled inside as I buzzed about Mom's kitchen her spirit cooking with me. The smell of warm vanilla pound cake permeated the house. I dusted the top with powdered sugar; tiny snowballs formed and melted making me think of Philip's embrace under the falling snow.

I lounged on the sofa and opened my journal to write:

February 1, 2014

I missed a week thinking it was January. That's what happens when you miss someone. You miss days, weeks, months, and if I'm not careful, I'll miss my life.

Life isn't as ordered as we wish. Mom, you used to say the hardest bit about gardening was the weeds; toil's reward arrives in spring when the colors and fragrance of nature surprises you. When you open your heart to surprises, to things outside the strict boundaries of your ordered life—something unexpected and beautiful can blossom. Maybe I'll start looking for surprises. I know, Mom, it wouldn't be much of a surprise if I found it first.

I closed my journal placing it on the window seat for later soaking in the sunny afternoon. The warm air and sunshine melted most of the snow. I grabbed Philip's jacket and wandered outside, sweeping leaves off the deck.

By late afternoon, I battled with my cell, itching to text Joe for Philip's number. But I didn't want to cancel or let Joe know I invited Philip for dinner. My heart was doing that thing, closing to people who are about to leave, when anger and distance protect the fragile bits left of me. The chasm between Joe and me kept my heart from crumbling if he moved to New York. But isn't this life—people leaving? I didn't count on everyone doing it all at once. My feelings for Joe tripped through an obstacle course, with Philip, a glide down a snowy hill warmed by the thoughts of new beginnings and second chances.

I shut off my cell tossing it in a drawer. "I'll live without you today." I perfected touches to the dining room table. "Sophia, you're acting like a teenager. Good for me." I loved Mom's elegant style. A round walnut table, white chairs upholstered in dark blue leather, a patch of flow blue flowers studded on the backs. The Japanese mural she painted on the dining room wall: white cherry blossom trees on a stormy-blue background, colorful birds in mossy grass, and the view of her garden through French doors.

I took in this room, picturing the glossy table covered in board games and puzzles, losing ourselves for hours in mother-daughter conversation and competition. "Za, the slang word for pizza, sixty-two points your ultimate Scrabble win." I laughed imagining Mom's goofy victory dance. "You always picked the *z*."

I fluttered around the kitchen unable to settle my thoughts, concocting a pitcher of sangria. "I'm so not good at this. *Putain*. Why did I ask him?"

"Who?" His voice made me jump. "You forgot to close your front door."

I dropped an orange watching it roll into the hall to his shoe. "That doesn't mean you should barge in. You scared the crap out of me."

"Sorry, Soph. You haven't answered my texts." Joe stood in the entryway holding a bouquet of magenta peonies.

"I'm on vacation. I needed time alone, okay. Are those for me?"

"I don't know." He hid the flowers behind his back.

"Don't pout. Quit the Denzel stare. You're too big and strong to pout. It makes you look silly." I stormed away from him back into the kitchen.

"Don't be mad. I thought . . ."

"Joe, I know what you thought. I love you, but I'm unfair to you. *This* is unfair, whatever *this* is." Tossing the thought of our kiss behind me now, I threw my hands in the air escaping into the pantry to find a vase. "Give me those you big jerk." I planted a kiss on his cheek.

"We have loads to discuss." He watched me arrange the flowers.

"We made a decision about Faraway Travel. Good for us. Magenta?"

"Fuchsia." I raised an eyebrow at his correction. "My friend's an artist who taught me to recognize the difference between fuchsia and magenta."

"*Touché. Merci.* They're beautiful."

"You're welcome." He tugged his collar. I never made Joe nervous, and we never did awkward silences. "You set up your easel again." He scanned the house eyeing the snacks on the countertop, dim lights in the living room. "Awesome, Soph."

"I'm attempting Mom's oak tree. This fickle weather isn't helping much. One day it's covered in snow, the next warm sunlight."

"Tonight's one of those warm nights. Crazy, huh?"

Fuchsia peonies dazzled, petals trimmed in silver. "I'm painting these."

"I know." He stuffed his hands into his pockets proud of his pick.

We wandered into the living room. "I'm glad you stopped by."

"Stopped by," he said, disappointed. "That means you want me to leave."

"I have a gift for you. Let me get it." I ignored his hint to stay. I waddled back into the living room hugging the heavy box and set it on the table. "A microwave with a popcorn setting."

"Movie theater butter." He waved the box of popcorn. "Thanks, Soph." Joe admired the house ready to leave. "I should let you get back to your—"

"Vacation. Yeah." *Silence filled with noise.* "Joe, I know we have things to work out."

"I'm not going anywhere, at least not yet."

"My life is moving in a fresh direction. It feels good, right."

"You have several big decisions to make."

"Not regarding Mom's gallery . . . me. Why have you stuck with me all these years?"

"I love you."

I backed away from his words. We said them to each other a hundred times. Tonight they sounded different. "I love you too, Joe, but—"

"Soph, I didn't say I was in love with you."

"Really?" I gnawed my thumbnail. "Huh. I doubt I ever felt true love."

"Don't. You loved Blake. He loved you." We plopped on the couch.

"Enough to have an affair . . . ugh, I feel so cliché. I've moved on from that." *Moved on. Another pile of dirt swept under my lumpy rug.*

"Have you?" he asked, reading me.

I rushed into the kitchen for a task. "Joe, this isn't us. We don't do *this*."

"What?"

"This!" I waggled a finger between us. "Loaded glances, sexy touches, and awkward silences—we work together, go to dinner, complain about awful dates, and pressure each other to date other people, not each other."

"What?"

"I don't know! I don't know what to do with *this*."

"I haven't asked you to do anything with this."

"You have. Confusion, that's what *this* is." I chugged skunk sangria to stop myself from hyperventilating. "This sucks. Confusion at first sight."

He eyed me and sat at the counter contemplating a sip of my toxic brew; he opted for a pear. "I'm here for you because that's where I want to be."

"We use each other. You run into my arms and you're home. You don't have to face the hurdle of committing to a serious relationship when you know I'm here."

He slowly set down his pear. "The truth hurts worse than I imagined."

"We've always had the truth." I stood by him. "There's much to say, but I'm not ready."

He spotted me looking toward the dining room, at the clock. "Philip."

"You know?"

"I saw it all over your face when he entered the office that first day."

We walked into the dining room looking out at Mom's garden. "Snowdrops and Christmas roses, I bet they're beautiful. I haven't gone in there yet." I walked away from it, him. We stood admiring Mom's Japanese mural.

"White cherry blossoms drifting against a steel-blue sky." Joe laughed. "You two used to argue about that blue."

"Mom shouldn't have died like that." I swallowed. "No one should."

"*Mpenzi wangu.*" He slid behind me; his warm breath kissed my cheek.

"My love." I focused on the petals in Mom's painting. "Did she remember what we talked about at the end? How I told her to quit, give up.

"No. Your whisper, go home. Be at peace. I will—"

"Be all right. Mom said my sight and memory are gifts. Erase them."

"You know how to repaint those memories."

"You sound like her." Tears rose in my throat.

He held me. "Don't do this, Sophie."

"A drug shortage, chemo that cost dollars to make. No one knew what the hell was going on. No one cared about people dying, children."

"I wish I had answers and could erase it all."

"You always save me. Maybe it's time I save myself."

"Come here." He planted his strong hands on my shoulders demanding I listen. "Remember our first week of college, when we 'ran into' each other?"

"Memories play hazy these days." I took in Mom's garden view.

Joe sat in a corner near the French door. "I never forgot that day. You looked past this." He pointed to the long, thick scar across his cheek curling near his chin most people couldn't get past. "To this day you've never asked me about it. You weren't afraid of me."

I sat trapped in this corner of Mom's spacious home. "Why would I be?"

"You introduced yourself and—"

"Asked you a ton of questions rambling on and on—"

"Before I could answer," he snickered. "We couldn't stop laughing." Joe paced at his memories. "What's your next class?" he asked, remembering.

"Psychology. We were laughing at the joke eighty percent of students who take a psychology class need to see a psychologist. Great, I'm a stat."

"I still remember what you wore."

I stood next to him admiring Mom's mural again. We never avoided each other's eyes. "An ice-blue dress, black sweater and ballerina flats," I said.

We wandered back to the French doors flooded in sunlight. "I told my mom I met an Audrey Hepburn with long, red hair."

"It was the sunglasses . . . pearls, Mom's present I wore every day." He lifted the strand around my neck, the sexy touch from his fingertips, warm, inviting. "I don't know what—"

Joe stopped me from saying the words. "Meeting you, my first day of college was perfect." He walked to the window. "We neared our building and this quarterback and his mates charged us. Set a laser focus on my path."

"Freddy. He hated everybody."

"I've been pushed before; this was different. 'Hey, Kenyan,' he shouted."

Joe noticed his waded fists shaking the past out of them with a snicker. "You stayed quiet, Soph, but as Freddy spun around to see what I'd do, you held my hand and gave that jackass the biggest grin."

"I hated that feeling. I never wanted to feel it again."

Joe towered above me, his protective presence stronger than ever, my hands nestled safely inside his. "When he left, you didn't let go of my hand. We just met, and you walked with me to our first class, and everyone thought you were my girlfriend. It was awesome."

"It was."

"I'm holding your hand, Soph. I won't let go."

His handkerchief appeared to wipe my tears. "I'd let you blow my nose, but you'll ruin my makeup . . . what's left of it."

"After that, we met at that same spot and walked the long way to class."

"It was as if I knew you forever. I felt safe with you, Joe."

"I hope you still do."

I handed him his hankie; he tucked it back into my hand. "But Joe, you don't owe me anything. I met Blake, you, Judy. Life moved on. I wondered what happened with you two."

"Work. You said I was a cosmopolitan man not a Mr. Cunningham. I never knew what that meant until Jacey made me binge watch *Happy Days*."

"When did this happen?" A bite of jealousy nipped my skin.

"Last week. I almost settled down with Judy, but I was building my career, supporting my mom. Judy couldn't wait. You married Blake."

"You married work. Losing Mom changed me. I'm not sure how to get me back yet, and you don't deserve that again." We let each other go. "I should finish getting ready."

"Sure," he said softly, following me into the kitchen.

"Joe, I know why you're worried. I'm not that woman—the one who locked herself in a bathroom after her husband died. Life's a gift. I plan on giving my passion—myself—a chance."

"You deserve it." Our eyes connected the way they should. He held my gaze catching himself, offering a peck to my cheek and his exit.

I held on. "Why does this happen with us?"

His nose nuzzled my cheek, his final goodbye. "I'm willing to try us . . . but no man wants to be confusion at first sight."

"It's the wrong time," I whispered, resolved. "We had our chance. We chose a different path. There's nothing wrong that."

"Yeah." He dropped his head tossing me a half smile. "I have a microwave to try. Have a good night with Philip. What'd you say? A fresh direction?"

"It's confusing, isn't it?"

He scooped up his microwave like a football and spun around avoiding my tackle. "The box says don't use popcorn button. Microwave popcorn doesn't work with a popcorn button?"

"Now look who's changing the subject."

"Soph, without looking, what color are my eyes?"

"What? I said I was confused." I played his game keeping my focus on the peonies as Joe waited for my answer. "I don't remember."

"What color are Philip's?"

"Green," I whispered. "The color of baby grass in spring."

"You're not confused. Have a good time tonight. Dinner next week?"

"Here, bring Jace." I waved to his silly grin watching him drive away. "Mocha, gold flecks swimming around your pupils. Sophia, what are you doing?" *Oui, having two men fall in love with you isn't so wonderful,* Mom chuckled in my thoughts. "It isn't? No, it isn't."

"Sophie?" I smiled at Jacey's timid whisper. "You shouldn't leave your front door open. Is Joe all right? Are you? Awesome microwave; he can't wait to use it."

"Hey, Jacey. He was just checking in on me."

"Me too. My chocolate cake's in the car. You order pizza. I made Joe skedaddle. He said ignore instructions, rules, it's worth the risk—even if you get burned. What's he talking about?"

"Microwave popcorn—and friendships with friendship buttons."

"Okaaay. OMG, it smells delish in here."

"You didn't get my text did you?" I eyed the clock.

"No." She noticed the snacks, romantic vibe. "OMG! This is for Philip, isn't it?" she squealed. "Blazes, we need to fix your hair." She checked her cell. "Crikey, there's your text."

"I'm sorry."

"No prob. Lunch at Charlie's tomorrow, and you're not saying no. Come on, I'll Frenchy your hair. OMG. I really am a beauty school dropout. How apropope."

"Apropos."

Jacey pulled me into the bedroom. "Your hair's a hot mess. Pomade is for pros." She examined the strands near my ears: waxy stickpins. "I'm no fairy godmother, but I'll try some magic. I'll get my makeup kit." She clapped her hands as my amiable cheerleader.

"You drive around with a makeup kit?"

"Of course, don't you?"

My heart began its usual tricks: flutters, kabooms, and drum rolls. Jacey flipped me her Fonzie thumbs-up working fairy godmother magic. "That lavender dress looks nutty with your complexion. Soph, you're stunning." Jacey turned me to the mirror as a makeover reveal, waving a comb as her magic wand. "Ta-da."

"I have lips! How did you do that?" I surprised her with my hug.

"It's called lip liner and gloss. Stop biting that thumbnail and it might last an hour."

I hid my hands behind my back before she slathered them in glitter polish. "Thanks, Jace." I tossed a curl and stroked my pearls, spotting a glimpse of young Sophie in the mirror.

"It's not the makeup, Soph. You're beautiful in a smile."

The sunset cast a purple glow in the room telling me Philip would arrive any minute.

"My Cinderella's ready for the ball. Don't worry. When the clock strikes midnight, you'll still sparkle." We froze at the slam of a car door. Jacey rushed to the window. "Philip's here! I'll split out the back door." Jacey grabbed her stuff. "Later, gator. *Innamorarsi*," she whispered our newfound sisterhood word, punctuating it with a fist bump.

"*Innamorarsi*." I spotted my journal on the bed. "Jacey." I inhaled netting my butterflies and wrote: *I watched Philip rush to my front door. Confusion wasn't necessarily a bad thing, but it wasn't love either. And I didn't have to figure it all out in one evening.*

34.

Camille

Plumes of steam signaled our departure. "I have never done this before," I whispered to Claude as the train set off. A howling whistle, I searched for Papa; Paris vanished in a hazy mist.

Claude tucked my hand in his. "You've never visited the Fontainebleau Forest?"

Marie spun around at our snickers. "We're off. Journeys end in lovers meeting."

"Aghast," Albert moaned. "Cease your quotations, and I'll buy you a box of chocolates."

"Aghast." Marie and I chuckled with the sparse passengers on the morning train.

Claude's kiss lingered on my cheek. "Roses, myrtle, orange." He breathed in my skin surprising me with pink rosebuds.

"I wore the angel water for Courbet." I savored the bouquet twirling its lavender ribbon.

"I'll tell him. But the way you study her roses . . . you still haven't spoken with Elise?"

I gazed out the window following the Seine as our train left the city. "No."

"We leave the noise of Paris now." He tucked a rosebud in my hair. "Your father will see his daughter portrayed in the splendor of nature unlike any painting he's admired." For the next half hour, Claude settled my nerves sharing summer stories. "Wait until you see Renoir." He laughed. "He shaved hoping to look younger. Don't tell him I replace him with Courbet."

"We'll make a grand scene," Marie squealed, resting on Albert's shoulder.

"She could hear a feather land in the forest." I gazed at the landscape I missed, romantic villa gardens, thatched cottages draped in wisteria, and wildflower hills. A girl wearing a navy cape and sailor hat at each train stop waved a sign of the road we passed. "She looks like Geneviève."

I lost Claude to the countryside. He stared out the window as a boy traveling for the first time enraptured by the view. "How can one merely glimpse landscape from a railway train? I long to paint them the nature they wish to see, the nature they fail to see."

The sight of the valley of the Seine and forest ahead, the train pulled into a splendid viaduct of thirty arches at the Fontainebleau station. Albert bargained the price of our carriages. "We shall meet you in the wood we know not where," he said.

"Your driver knows the route," Claude said. "We take the path of Margaret, past the Monte Cristo, a right at Crystal Cave, past a grove of hundred-year-old oaks."

"To Robin Hood's lair." I blew Marie a kiss as she waved out her window as the queen.

"Our coachman, Pierre, is the best guide in Fontainebleau," Claude assured. "Ready?"

"Marie and Albert will grow lost for hours touring the palace." My heart skipped at time alone with Claude. *Fairy magic turns bold little bird into a jellyfish.*

Claude squeezed my hand as I watched Marie's coach drive away. "It will be fine." He laughed, whisking me into our carriage. Claude's tender kiss calmed me. "Here you are."

"I have not ventured into a forest since I was a child." A narrow hunting road started our journey into the woods. Dirt trails crisscrossed around ancient oaks and pines. We passed two carriages. Claude waved to a man riding a donkey. Women waded in a stream, their parasols strewn across the grass as billowing, giant orchids. An open carriage of well-to-do Parisians navigated an alley in the forest; the ladies' plumes blew in the air the colors of autumn leaves.

"It is a rite of passage, painting in this wood." Claude smiled at my skittish manner. "Look, the blue arrows on the trees mark our way, a map by Monsieur Denecourt."

"A magic resides here, noble knights, fair maidens. I am not afraid." I nestled into him. "Pines and lavender." I sighed. "I do not miss Paris. A man spied on us at the station. He sneered at Papa."

Claude snickered loosening his collar. "You'll grow accustomed to Amand Gautier. He means me no harm. My aunt suspects a certain person wishes to destroy my reputation."

"I, ruin you? Why, Marie's gossip could make me run from you this instant."

"It's a long walk back to town, *ma chéri*. You might encounter a bear or wolf."

"It appears I already have—and no bears stalk this wood."

The rattle of our carriage filled the quiet for a mile. Claude tried to win me with a caricature of me wearing a floral headdress. "Shall I open an umbrella for the coming storm in this carriage?" He pulled me close, finishing his drawing, scribbling a broken parasol at my feet.

I snatched his sketch. "Tiny ears? Wise adding Raphael in my arms; he calms me."

"Ten francs, mademoiselle—no, twenty; I charge double for giant heads."

We ventured deep into the forest; the sight of visitors and carriages dwindled. We passed the hut of a seller of brandy and keepsakes. I tasted a sip and bought a spinning top for my sister. Our ride ended at a footpath brushed with heather and yellow broom. "A fairyland," I said.

Pierre waited at the entrance for our friends' arrival. We reached a winding trail where the trees grew dense and hills strewn with rocks. He led me to his picnic scene: a grove canopied in lemon and lime leaves, shaded glen in the background, a green lawn strewn with fallen leaves and violets. Two beech trees sprouted from one, patches of turquoise through the branches. We stretched across the blanket. "I hear you do not sleep. Will you finish?" I dared to ask.

His body slipped away from mine. "Every leaf on this tree is as important as the features of your face. I don't strive to capture Courbet's realism or Manet's fantasy, but this moment." He brushed a blade of grass across my nose. "To invite one to see something they have never seen."

"Backstage in a forest." I spotted his table of props; a cloak piled on the grass behind a tree, blankets, and bonnets left in a hurry. Three parasols, two canes, and a jacket rested on a branch. I toured his forest stage spying his sketches. "Men stand here," I said, posing. "At the old beech flirting with Flora who soaks in the sun dressed in light, resting as a fallen leaf." Claude smiled, amused. I raced behind a tree. "A spy, your father, hides behind this trunk. I arrive with Frédéric, primping my ill-fitting hat. In love or parting?" Claude scrunched his nose. "Love; in this glen no sorrow grows. Watteau invents an island of love, Monet, a forest of friends."

"And now you see."

I inspected a table of hats. "You softened Papa sketching our portrait. He speaks without words, paranoid glances. Elise . . . I do not know what to think; I sensed his loneliness for years."

Claude invited me back to our blanket, fluffing a pillow under my head, positioning his model to paint. "My father believes I know nothing of his mistress and illegitimate child," he said. "Mother died, Father fell in love with her maid—a damn Dumas novel."

I closed my eyes at his confession, my heart resting inside his hands. "I wish I could confess my secrets." I fell back onto the pillow. He kissed me, but my thoughts clouded with shame. I gazed at the leaves dipped in gold as his fingers caressed mine. Claude smiled, wrapping a wild violet around my pinkie. "I used to know where I belong. I don't any longer." Claude watched me, always. "I am not muse, mistress, betrothed, or wife. What am I, Claude?"

"Come." We walked to a beech tree a heart carved in its trunk. "What do you see?"

"A man who has not answered my question."

"Do you not see the trunk's gold necklace, emerald flickering, and square sapphire?"

I squinted to see his colors, but all I could do was look into his eyes. "Tell me."

In awe of the scene, his eyes darted to the sky, me. "Amber and lemon halos encircle the branches sunrise and sunset; a tapestry of rust and crimson leaves decorate the forest floor. Raspberry squares at the trunk's base, strands of moss wiggling down its side." He clasped our hands and held them in the sun. "A little square of cobalt, an oblong of pink, a streak of yellow."

"I see."

"Now, a cast of blue hangs overhead," he continued wide-eyed, "bits of white and cream between the branches. A sheet of white light turns the bark gray as if withered, yet it is more alive than ever. My brush rushes to capture all on my canvas before the light fades and turns everything into a purple and cobalt formless wonder. This is how I see."

"A breathtaking lesson, but can you so dissect love?"

Claude laughed at himself, his spell broken. "I was trying to impress you. I don't look deep into myself or others as Renoir, nor obsess with the Opera as Bazille. I absorb nature, perhaps because it appears to me ignored. I'm not doting as Frédéric, but someday I will grow a garden to surround you in flowers, but, *ma chéri*, when I'm home I will ponder my pictures."

"I have always been impressed. But your comrades never cease their warnings."

"Then heed them." He closed our distance. I breathed him in now.

"What of your father? I might walk another path. Marie's roles could be mine."

"No. Do not blame another for what you yourself do not take up arms to defend nor attempt."

"Claude Monet will never placate pity and offers little to those who need it."

"My aunt is no aunt by blood. My father's parents abandoned him as a child to a wealthy family. As a boy, I suffered torment and shame missing my mother; I spoke as if she were still alive. My passion for art grips me, for all shout I will not and cannot and so I must. Love confounds me, but you capture my heart. Secrets I confessed to no other soul."

"You know, as all of Paris, Elise is Papa's mistress. But Mamma—this man, a soldier, keeps a secret apartment . . ." Tears glided over my lips; his kiss washed them away. "I caught Mamma going inside," I whispered. "Exposure means my ruin. Wealth so possesses her, Papa is no man in our house. In my loneliest night—I wonder if I am even his." I fell into Claude's arms.

The forest enveloped us in silence. I heard nothing but my heart and Claude's pounding together, my soft sob, his sigh and kiss to comfort me. He brushed the hummingbird brooch on my dress, making me look at it now. How it sparkled in the light as Elise's flowers in the sun. "Don't abandon Elise, true friends. Many times they prove more worthy than blood."

I shuddered at his words. A chill racked my body in the hot sun, the worry my family was not falling apart but had fallen, and I was too pigheaded to save it. "I want to be with you now."

He pulled me to the blanket in a tender embrace soon whisking me away into a shaded cove, his makeshift theater. We hid backstage in a private room, cool and dark. His hands caressed my body, his fell into mine warm and stirring. His love made me forget my home, its secrets.

"Next spring, I rent a cottage," he whispered. "Live with me. My next work is you alone, *Women in the Garden*. The country does not judge as Paris. My friends will not spurn us."

"What of mine?" I walked deeper into the cove, the heat from his body still racing through mine. I stilled at the sight of blue poppies by a pond. "Mistress. Olympia? You paint this light; I wish to live in it." My love blurred into a stream of tears. I slipped away at his touch.

"Frédéric is a horrendous actor who fails to hide his affections for you. He's not so inclined to this path and would take you to Montpellier. You could live a comfortable life amidst wineries and mountain villages while he happily paints your portrait for his own viewing."

"When you do not reap what you want, you turn a fool." He grabbed me, claiming me as his as he did at the Mabille. We ran back into our sordid cover, lingering in our embrace. "Triumph," I said, giving into him. "So we can flee Paris."

"Romeo? Juliet?" We froze at Marie's faint call. "What am I, Claude?" I asked.

He held my shaking hands. Marie's giggle echoed in the distance. "Mine. I will not fail."

I caught my breath at the emerald ring he slipped on my finger, a painted pansy and inscription: *think of me*. I took in his kiss. "If loving you is wrong the world is upside down."

"*Bonjour*," Marie called. "Pierre showed us beguiling wildflowers on our promenade. By your blush, a wondrous flower blossoms here." She spotted my ring; her eyes crinkled with glee.

"Incorrigible," I said, smashing a sunhat into her hands.

"Beauty, tame this beast," Renoir said. "Courbet snarled our entire journey."

Courbet rustled Renoir's jacket. "You daft fool; you said nothing about riding a played-out donkey and a sleepy nag." Courbet's sigh rattled the trees. "Ah, lass," he said, savoring the air as a hot apple pie. "Roses, myrtle, orange—you caress your skin with angel water."

"My jesters. You curled your mustache," I said. "I detect lemon, orange, and jasmine."

Courbet's chortle echoed in the grove as in the halls at the Louvre. "My Eau de Cologne . . . tangerine, lime, rosemary, tobacco—I missed one," he said, inspecting Claude's sketches.

"You need another?" Renoir asked, holding his nose. Renoir smoothed over his missing beard, eyeing me if I noticed.

"Now who appears as a boy with his smooth face," I said, straightening his cravat.

"The loss of my beard jinxes me. I paint nothing but sad flowers in this wood."

"Cousin," Gabrielle squealed, prancing to me as a doe escaping the hunt. Her red hair hung as a fur around shoulders. "You look stunning . . . and messy?" she snorted, hugging me.

"I missed you." I straightened my blouse, wishing to style her hair to hide my blush. She looked older, plump in a fetching white dress with black dots sheer at the neck and arms.

"You must be Claude," Gabrielle purred. "Camille, your letters declare Claude's handsome, deliciously handsome he is . . . an artist who blushes, strange."

"Darling, we're in the forest but we're not savages," said Marie, eyeing my cousin now flirting with Albert. "This David belongs to me." She pulled Albert from Gabrielle's grip.

"Come, my wildflowers, strike your poses," Claude announced, reviewing his sketches. "I have an hour before the light changes. You may chatter once you take your places."

Giggles and reunions continued as we juggled straw hats, ribbons, and flowers. "Friends, have you forgotten? I brought a most anticipated guest," Albert announced. Frédéric jumped out from behind a bush. Our grove echoed with applause.

"Don't faint, Monet. Your Bazille appears," Courbet cheered.

"Wine from Bazille's vineyard lures Monet's friends to pose," Renoir said, toasting us.

"So Bazille arrives—without fanfare, my light fades," Claude said, indifferent. Frédéric bombarded Claude with his embrace.

I stood surprised, smiling at Frédéric, Claude. Our friends expelled a unison laugh. "Ah, but an Arctic blast chills our outing with Monet's icy greeting," Courbet said.

"Bah," Claude mumbled, stationed at his easel, yielding his brush in dashes and dabs.

Renoir tripped about our forest scene as Claude's stagehand. Frédéric took me in, offering his hand to me to join him in the shade. "Fetching silver gown," he said, grinning.

"Come, women," Courbet said. "We chased the spiders and spies eager to best our Monet." He sat on the blanket near my shoe, raising his glass. "Cheers to Claude Monet, our painter of nature."

"Places," Claude shouted. "My canvas is ready and daylight burns away."

"Mesdemoiselles et Messieurs," Frédéric announced. "Monet's *Luncheon on the Grass.*"

I imagined at the opening of our curtain, the audience's gasp. Marie's body hugged Albert; her green-and-white striped dress billowed across the blanket. Gabrielle slouched out of place; a plate teetered in her hand. Frédéric leaned against a tree, lounged on the grass, and posed as my aloof suitor whispering as I adjusted my hat, and again admiring my gold dress. Courbet sat in front of the turkey and wine, his hand in need of a glass, wandering into Gabrielle's lap.

Claude's play of light marked his masterpiece. It shimmered through the leaves, across our faces. Watteau's island of love visited Fontainebleau as Claude hoped. "Will he finish?" their whispers ended our day. "Camille poses for hours. What does she think on standing so still?" *Confessions, love in the forest, Claude's promise to take me away from the pain of Paris. What about now?* If they whispered, if they laughed, I heard not, until Frédéric touched my arm.

35.

Camille

Claude rented an open carriage for our last outing into the forest. Frédéric and I posed for Claude alone under the dome of gilded leaves. "Dash it." I fumbled with my buttons.

"Agreed," Frédéric shouted behind a tree. "A forest makes a poor dressing room."

"You fancy peeping through keyholes as Renoir?" I peered around the screen.

"Tree trunks, never keyholes. Come now, I spend my summers in a house with three female cousins decked in frills requiring assistance with misaligned hooks and buttons."

"Help me before Claude shouts us into submission." Frédéric playfully walked his fingers down my back and fumbled with a hook on my skirt. I held in my stomach, pinched by a suffocating corset. "Too many deserts shared with Marie and Madeleine at the Grand Hotel."

"So, this is how you spend your summer . . . with delicious tarts. There." He smoothed out the folds of my skirt. His handsome eyes admired me. "Claude tortures himself."

Posing for Claude in the forest tested us all. Frédéric lost his aristocratic air, sulking about the glen at Claude's demands. His frame, thinner, and muttonchops replaced his manicured beard. I unbuttoned his jacket and tugged at his crisp, white cuffs. "You are in the country."

"I read a curiosity in the newspaper," he said. "A Frenchman wears his best clothes for an excursion in the country, an Englishman his worst. Claude's fashion plate comes to life."

"I need your cheer, Frédéric." I sighed. "Claude paints the light and sulks in shadows."

"Posing in the forest has not been as glamorous as you imagined?"

"Not this week." I switched his black bowler for blue. "Modeling for

Claude varies as a sunrise." We watched Claude ready his palette. "A horizon of sunlight and pastels greet me when he revels in his progress—gray clouds and thunder during his fits of doubt."

"My painter of lights loses his way." He traded my plumes for a single-feathered cap.

"Frédéric, you caused his delay and undoing if he fails." I tugged at my knotted ribbon.

He loosened it, tying the bow. "No, Camille. If Monet fails he does so alone."

"Places." By Claude's cold, swift manner, I imagined he overheard Frédéric's warning. The end of summer, Claude acted less as an artist in love and one of desperation. "Stand in the clearing in front of the bushes and thin trees. Bazille speaks with Camille. Camille turns to me."

Frédéric yawned. "Édouard Manet bares all; Claude Monet is unwilling to reveal his model—clever. You're curious, Camille. I knew you would make a fine model but not—"

"Claude Monet's model?" I asked. "I have heard this speech before. He needed you."

"Camille, fix the old man's necktie; it drives me mad," Claude ordered. "Hurry now."

To Frédéric's delight, I retied his cravat. He wiggled his brows as my fingertips grazed his skin. "Now Camille's cheeks are kissed . . . by me." Frédéric's whisper tickled my ear.

"You act a lovesick fool as Gabrielle."

"I play my part." He laughed. I snubbed his joke and turned away hiding my smile.

"That is the pose," Claude shouted.

"I have my own paintings to finish." Frédéric blew across my cheek making me smile. "I fancy the silver dress and black cording best. Claude even belabors your fashion. I do not miss his fits. When I'm with my family in Montpellier, I do not miss Paris."

Claude crawled behind us fluffing my train across the grass adorning the hem with leaves. I stood still, letting him perfect and move me as my eyes searched the nearby wood for blue poppies. "Are you painting a boat race with Renoir?" I asked Frédéric. Claude stood at his easel encapsulated in his own world, studying my garment, dabbing his canvas. "Perhaps you do not want Claude to succeed." I tugged at my skirt. "I cannot breathe."

"I won at the Bougival regatta. Our boat was the La Cagnotte. We made the papers."

"It does us no good if this painting is not completed in time for submission to the Salon."

"*Us?* Camille, you're beguiled by the best bits of our friend." Frédéric moved closer.

"Fine," Claude said. "I'll paint the foliage." His paintbrush danced as blades of grass.

"This is no place for you," Frédéric whispered. "I would paint you in Montpellier, my home; clear skies, vineyards, and olive trees on the hill. A horse-chestnut tree shades our terrace overlooking the village of Castelnau and the Lez river valley edged in white poplars. Wild thyme, oleander, and lavender sweeten the air, omelets and fresh bread for breakfast."

He inched closer as Claude focused on the trees. "Why return to Paris?" I asked.

"For the same reason you escape into this forest." He caressed my arm, tickling my skin. "Camille, I didn't come to Fontainebleau for Gabrielle. I came to see you."

"Back to your disdain," Claude shouted. He shook his head. "Indifference interests me."

"We once fought over you on the Quai du Louvre," Frédéric said. "You stood by a lamppost wearing a lemon gown, tucking your black hair into a pink hat. An artist that dare miss you has no business painting because he does not see."

"Bazille, keep your hand hidden in hers," Claude said, "one less mitten for me to paint."

"Come to Montpellier," he whispered. I battled attraction, loyalty—loneliness. *Respectability, comfort, Claude never promised. A love that tears your heart and heals it all at once.* I had suffered Claude's moods: frightening, obsessed, indifferent. "You lose yourself when you pose as Claude paints." Frédéric caressed my finger, its ring, waking me.

"When Claude paints me, I am someone else." I spotted the blue poppies near the pond. Frédéric followed my gaze, pleased. "I should like to see Montpellier . . . someday," I whispered.

He held my finger admiring the ring, smiling at me, turning back to Claude. "Let me see you home on the early train to Paris back in time for dinner. Claude works on his canvas into the night at the inn, a studio in a barn."

"My tight skirt demands a bowl of soup and not one spoonful of custard, maybe one." I noticed a flicker of pink light on the dirt and dipped my toe into it to Claude's groan.

"The clouds frustrate Claude's effects. Are we finished?" Claude nodded, waving us off.

"And Claude frustrates you." I searched Frédéric's eyes as Renoir often did mine. "You are a bold one. How do you and Claude share a studio with your endless competition?"

He grinned. "After this, I leave for Montpellier and will not return to Paris until winter."

"In time to attend Madeleine's holiday party, I hope. Madeleine means to introduce me."

"I would not miss it, and you will shine." Frédéric tossed his hat at an oblivious Claude.

"We are invisible." I boxed the bonnets and packed the dresses in my trunk. "Claude changes his affections as his light. Will I not be enough?" I whispered to myself.

"No. Claude will never live poor. It happens often with models. The endless hours, tempers." Frédéric gathered props tossing them into a basket. "This painting bests him."

I rushed behind the screen to change. "Frédéric, why paint if it is not your passion?"

"I leave the distractions of Paris to answer this very question. I admire Monet. He understands how to win." Frédéric found us two chairs.

"He needs rest. So do I . . . time away." *How fast you betray Claude's love and secret confessions.* "The fire inside him resides not in us. He must win." He handed me a glass of wine.

Frédéric poured his glass, savoring a sip. "Claude possesses something I'll never have."

"What is that?"

"A mandate—you." He toasted me, admiring Claude painting in the sun.

"No one possesses me." I held out my empty glass for more wine; Frédéric obliged.

"Reconsider Montpellier," he whispered. "As my guest."

I watched the plum wine cling to the glass, the light revealing streaks of pink. "Perhaps."

Frédéric's eyes widened at my answer. He jumped up, entertaining me, pantomiming an impromptu charade, rushing behind a tree, acting like our spy in the forest. He hunched his back and played a monster, found three apples, failed his juggling, and fell to the ground in a stage fall. "I muddied my best suit to make you smile, mademoiselle," he said out of breath.

"A worthy performance." I tossed him roses.

"The jokes you tell your fellows backstage at the theater are not fitting for Camille." Claude stood before us with his finished study and packed paintbox. "Frédéric, will you escort Camille home? I stay behind . . ."

"For the light," Frédéric and I said together.

36.

Sophie

Winter's promise of a kiss of spring warmed our evening. After an easy dinner and walk with Philip down memory lane, we bundled in a blanket on the patio swing watching sparks from the fire pit. "I remember this," he said, scanning the yard, me. "Your mother had a big Halloween party here."

"We dressed as French painters." I kept my gaze on the fire, breathing in the cool night air and smoky pine. "We were so in love."

"You do remember."

I sipped the warm apple cider Philip made. "Why you brought cider. What's the secret?"

"Tiny cinnamon candies. Your mother's secret." A final toast and he cleared our mugs, moving around the patio as if he visited a hundred times. "For the record, this is all I can make."

"Red Hots. It tastes like hers. The house smells like the holidays. Thank you for remembering this, Philip. Everyone knows Mom's secrets but me."

He shifted the logs stoking the fire. "You invited me over early that night remember?" he asked. "You said you had something very Halloween you wanted me to hear." I loved the way Philip's eyes grew wider when he spoke on passionate subjects, his smirk when he caught me admiring what he said. He bit his lip trying to look sexy. He did. The nervous boy I knew was long gone, but the boyish mannerisms I once fell in love with remained. "We sat on this swing after your lecture on the color of grass," he continued, tucking us into the blanket.

"I don't remember that." I caught myself twirling my hair. The nervous habits of my youth resurfaced. He calmed my fingers rattling against his leg covering my hand with his.

"'Have you ever seen a blade of grass?' you asked very serious, *ma chéri*."

"'Of course,' you said annoyed." I snickered, remembering with him. "Blades bundled together, soft carpet. Alone, one sharp edge can cut you."

"How a strip of emerald holds a dewdrop, curling to the ground, stretching for the sun."

"Crossing each other with hugs and handshakes."

"You're an artist, Sophia. You have always been an artist."

"I wanted to be."

"Like your mother. So did I." We sighed, thinking of her. "Josephine used to say, we may leave our gift, but it never leaves—"

"Us."

"She believed in you and your art, Sophia . . . so do I."

I pulled away from him at the mention of Mom, art, me. The years seemed wasted to me now, so many dreams as that young girl in love with Philip, unrealized. "Why did I invite you to Mom's Halloween party early?"

"*Oui*, I'll let you change the subject, for now. You asked me to close my eyes and listen."

"Chainsaws," I said over his laughter. "Mom was livid her neighbor cut down his oak tree, her favorite. She loved painting it. I thought she was going all hippie chaining herself to it."

"You said chainsaws sound like a mob of mummies on Halloween."

"And hungry Frankensteins."

"Is there any other kind?"

"I wanted to impress you, all your talk about originality."

"Oh, that was original, there's—"

"No one like me—I'm starting to take that as a warning. Mom's neighbor told her he planned to cut down another small oak. She paid a fortune to have that oak moved over here. Mom didn't chain herself to a tree; she provided a home."

We rocked the swing gently. His thumb lightly traced my nose, lips, staring as if readying to sketch the deepest part of me. "Claude Monet was fond of a little oak tree by a river," he said, tracing my chin again. "But a serious problem arose—*tu es si belle*, you are so beautiful."

"That was Monet's problem?" I smiled, the warmth of first love kindling in my heart.

"Monet featured the oak in a winter scene but left for Paris before he finished his painting. Upon returning to the oak tree in spring, a disheartened Monet stood before it frustrated his tree had the audacity to sprout green leaves. Declaring his picture ruined, he convinced the landowner to hire two men to pluck every leaf out of the tree so he could finish his painting."

"Okay, that might be a better tree story than mine."

"I have never met anyone as passionate about seeing the world in a different way as you."

"Aside from Monet?"

"Possessing the passion to capture those things we take for granted makes for a fine artist, Sophia. To help one pause is an amazing ability."

"I don't know where that woman went."

"You can find her again."

"And you want to help?" My spine stiffened. We watched the fire's flame burn lower. My body rested into his. "Winter is so quiet."

"Not a sound but us."

"Us. Spring during winter, drought during spring—a myriad of strange things are happening in my life right now." I walked away from him, poking at the fire, looking for another log to throw in. He did, retreating to the swing leaving me alone with my thoughts.

The flames blazed licking soft swirls of smoke. I shut my eyes to the crackle and snaps of burning wood letting the heat rise to warm my face, breathing in the festive scent of pine standing alone, afraid of this new beginning.

"Life's done a number on us all, Sophia," he said softly.

"I can handle most of it, Philip, but walking into rooms missing people I love. Please don't insist everything happens for a reason; the pieces coming together couldn't take the blow."

"Why, *ma chérie?*"

"Because if hell on earth happens for a reason that would make God cruel. I don't have Mom's faith; it's fraying as I speak, but in the end, she taught me, begged me to see life may be cruel at times, God never is." I drifted farther away from him like an untethered balloon, seeking solace in the night sky. "Mom used to say blaming God for the ugly, unfair things in life would be like saying He created weeds to watch them choke the flowers."

He rushed to my side forcing me to face him, folding my hands into his. "No one has the right to tell you how to feel. No one will ever know what you've walked through. It's not supposed to make sense. Perhaps the *reason* is beauty—"

"For ashes. Mom lived by those words when the unthinkable happened. Things made sense with her words; losing her the way I did will never make sense."

"Others know your pain. I know."

"There's a beautiful, sad family of us who have to deal with death in a cruel way. It's one thing to know you're going to die someday; it's another to receive a prescription for it."

He stood behind me, wrapping his arms around my body unwilling to let me go. I didn't want him to. Of all our memories, Philip's childhood was no greeting card. Secretive pain is the last thing you reveal as teens in the midst of blissful love, its antidote. "Time," he whispered.

"Thousands of minutes, days, and years of time."

"My life was a pile of ashes. Your mother helped me to find the beauty in it—you."

I held my breath searching Mom's back yard for happier memories: the fiery oak tree she painted a dozen times in fall; her garden bench, how many hours we sat contemplating paintings, life; her studio, radiant with light and color, imagination swirled in the ceiling, across the walls. "I don't remember how to be that happy girl."

"See, *mon ange*."

I turned into him my body fighting to be close to his. "My angel. I haven't heard that in years." We sat on the swing. "Everyone's storming back into my life forcing me to see things I've buried years ago. I'm sorry, Philip. I can't do this."

"What happened, *ma chérie*? What happened in Monet's garden?"

I hid back under the blanket. "Maybe some things are better left in the dark."

"A painter doesn't have much use for darkness. Your parents told you a different tale, a bedtime story, *oui*? At least I respected my father for never holding back the truth."

"You know things."

"I promised your mother I wouldn't interfere. She alone wanted to tell you things."

"But she's not here to tell me. She tried, Philip. I shut her down."

"I saw it on the table in the living room. Is it hers?"

"Everyone's fascinated with Mom's journal but me. I assumed it held the key; it doesn't."

"Are you going to Paris?"

"What's in Paris, Philip? More pain?"

"I thought all parents did what ours did: love, leave, and paint different versions of the truth."

"I ran from art because I didn't want a scattered life or Mom's impulsivity for the sake of art. It hurt people. She painted the bad away and I let her." The fire lost its glow simmering in a plume of smoke, but everything about us appeared brilliant in the moonlight. "I'm traveling the next few months, to get away, find myself again."

"Alone?"

"What did Mom think? You'd waltz into my life and we'd dance off into the sunset?"

"Not dance, *ma chérie*. I can't dance."

"I have no idea how she concluded her daughter has an ounce of the impulsivity she had."

"You kissed a stranger in a garden, and in a sexy, dark corner of a patio." He walked me to a shaded corner to the sofa he spotted. "I have to go back to Paris, but I'm not giving you up so easily this time." My heart raced at his touch, his fingers running across my neck. I soaked in his soft kiss swirling with passion as my hand stretched across his back. He held me, and with another kiss leaned me back on the sofa in our hideaway, our bodies moving over each other's swept up like teenagers in love. "*Innamorarsi*," he whispered.

I burst into laughter.

"*Qu'est-ce qui ne va pas*? I've never had a woman laugh at my kiss."

"I'm laughing at myself."

He pulled me back into his embrace, our bodies twisting together. "We don't need the fire, *mon ange*," he whispered, making me belly laugh again. "This isn't going how I planned."

"I'm sorry." I sat up, gathering myself. We moved out from the shadows, doused the fire, and headed inside cloaked in blankets. "I'm not ready for anything . . ."

"Past a cozy friendship." He held me from behind, kissing my ear. "I heard that once."

I kissed him without laughter, fear. He slipped my sleeves aside kissing the top of each shoulder. "Philip, I'm not running away."

"Shh, *mon ange*." He kissed me again, his fingers fondling the zipper across my back. He pulled it down to touch my skin.

"Stay," I said, surprising him. I wanted to caress his body again, entangle ourselves in the messiness of love. "A bit longer." I hid my blush, awkward, out of touch. "I suppose to a man like you old-fashioned is a corny joke but—"

He held his finger to my lips calming my fear with his soft kiss. "You see, Sophia, too much sometimes." We kissed in the moonlight until a chill made me shiver. He noticed. "*Mon ange*, I'm in no hurry. But unless you have pizza and a mummy movie, *bon voyage*."

"I think I can dig up *The Invisible Man*."

"*Non.* No more disappearing acts."

"Are you sure a sexy Frenchman like you can tolerate old-fashioned?"

"I never expected anything less." He attempted to twirl me in an awkward dance ending with his smooth kiss. "I'm not demanding anything other than to spend time with you."

"But that isn't reality . . . you know, fifty shades of purple or whatever that is."

"How much wine have you had?"

"A little more than usual."

"That explains it." We ran inside the house nixing the movie opting for jazz, mulled wine, and a bit of old-fashioned necking on the couch. "Mulled wine, heavy on the cinnamon. It's a wonderful life, isn't it, Sophie?"

"*Oui*."

37.

Camille

~

December 1865

A heather and silver sheen painted the frost on the streets of Paris. The boulevards flurried with shoppers for New Year's fetes and soirées. A rush of selling emptied our shop, but that did not cheer Papa. We tiptoed around each other in a quiet existence. Amidst my parents' estrangement, I favored losing myself in a pose under Claude's eye lingering longer into the night hardly wishing to return home.

"I rather the scent of a yule log than varnish," I said to myself, waiting for Claude in his dim studio. "Crackling cherry wood sprinkled with red wine." For months, I imagined the glow, its warmth, anticipating Madeleine's party. My introduction to Parisian society and Claude's secret world of wealth, culture, and his finest benefactors ensued tonight. I strolled his atelier, lighting candles as the sunset cast a crimson shadow across an easel. The vast space could serve as a ballroom and often did for Frédéric's indulgent entertaining. I paused at the picture window, studying Claude's view below of a snow-covered garden.

In Frédéric's three-month absence, Claude claimed their studio as his own. A lineup of decorative frames stood against a slice of pumpkin wall displaying Claude's works. A long table held pots of brushes, two bottles of wine, and wooden palettes smeared in pastels. Sketches and fashion plates covered his desk. Work on his monumental painting, *Luncheon on the Grass*, overtook the studio with platforms, ladders, and carts of tube colors, sponges, rags, and medicinal bottles. "Poppy oil? For paintings or knees?"

Frédéric's presence in the studio vanished, but for his prized green armchair near the stove; his paintbox and traveling easel rested in a corner by his chamber. A staging of wilted azaleas and geraniums awaited Frédéric's loosely sketched canvas. "Poor flowers past painting."

"That's the idea," Frédéric whispered. "*Oui*, my excuse not to work, my new painting, *Potted Flowers*, a gift for my mother's cousins." Frédéric appeared barefoot, shirt unbuttoned. "Claude hides in the dark behind his monstrosity of a canvas that serves as a barrier between us."

"And other things?" I fiddled with my locket. He grinned and wiped a dollop of shaving cream off his cheek motioning to his new mustache. "A musketeer's goatee suits you."

"And you look divine in lilac with silver ribbons. Clever, when most will flaunt Christmas red and green." He stepped toward his chamber and quickly looked back at me again. "Your hair is lovely down. I owe you a proper greeting when I finish readying for the party."

"I'm happy to see you again, Frédéric."

He admired my dress gesturing for me to spin. I heeded his command. "Likewise, Camille." His laugh echoed in the ceiling. Frédéric smiled, favoring the candlelight glow. "Meet me at the piano. Monet needs a polka." He offered his jester's bow and dashed into his chamber.

"Despite the evergreen boughs, your studio smells as the Louvre—varnish, musty wood, and Courbet's cigars," I said, happening upon the sad sight of Claude and his colossal canvas, unfinished. The life-size figures and his treatment of an illuminated forest impressed everyone who saw it, but in quiet hours, despite his progress, Claude resolved he would never finish.

He drifted to the window watching the sunset. "I meant to greet you."

I offered my comfort with a kiss. "You're not dressed for the party."

"I fell asleep on the sofa. A new year comes so soon. I have lost track of so much, *ma chéri*." Claude guided me in front of his monumental canvas. No matter its partial completion, I gasped at this wonder. His hand slid out from mine. A slave to his palette and brush, he half-heartedly picked them up and dabbed the bottom of his forest floor with ochre.

"The wonderful Courbet sent his coach for me. Where is he?" I asked.

"'Chocolate and champagne,' he wailed. I saw the cloud of smoke; he vanished as a genie." Claude focused on the center of his canvass: a jolly Courbet in his pink cravat slapping his knee. "Submit your picnic painting another year! Gustave Courbet deflates my confidence."

"You painted him younger." I laughed alone. "Indulging in wine before the party?"

"Not enough with the decision I make. I wrecked my knee; don't beg to dance tonight." He tossed his palette to the floor and his brush into the trash. He stopped me from saving them.

"Claude . . . not tonight." He rushed to a table flailing through sketches. His reckless side, no longer hidden, fueled his obsession with perfection and tempests at his shortcomings. "Leave this work tonight. You have not commented on my dress or asked about your New Year's gift."

"A parade of visitors as your Louvre," he shouted. "To what end? My friends spy the haggard artist wishing him failure." He lunged at the canvas with a knife slashing its middle.

"Claude, stop!" I cowered behind a platform.

"Why? It's of no use now." He saw me hiding, coming to himself, throwing the knife in a drawer. "I'm sorry," he whispered, picking up sketches off the floor. I handed him the last.

"Is it worth losing so much?" He caressed my neck, breathing in my fragrance. I slipped from his arms catching my breath. "Nine months ago, you discovered my temper . . . but this."

"Forgive me." He left me, staring into his cocky young portrait. "Where did he go?"

"Your career has started." I studied the finished portion of his canvas; the towering figure before me . . . Papa. "You painted me with Papa!" Claude held me, searching my eyes for answers. "A dream my parents with me at your picnic, but where are you, Claude?"

"You imagine many paintings with me, and I cannot finish what I started." He caressed my finger holding his ring, spinning the emeralds back to the top. He paused, noticing my sapphire ring gleaming in candlelight. His fingers slid down mine one at a time lost in their form.

"My ring from Mamma, wearing it makes me feel as if my family is not falling apart."

"Our doubts are traitors . . ." Claude plopped on a stool in front of his autumn landscape.

"Claude Monet, you repainted a stunning silver dress into a garish red outfit with a scarlet petticoat. You doubt your purpose to paint your own way, afraid of success, our future."

"Twenty feet to cover, *ma belle*," he sighed. "Twenty of my friends viewed this work—I should have handed them a paintbrush—a foot for every artist, then I would finish."

To my dread, the great machine that intrigued me into a forest, offered a diversion from my house of secrets, and made me fall in love, betrayed us. The massive canvas swallowed Claude's studio and my hopes. Claude's mentor Gustave Courbet's fickle criticism and suggestions plagued Claude worse than the approaching deadline for submission to the Salon.

The life-size figures resplendent with the glow of Heaven in a forest glen, required a steady hand and a limitless purse, none of which Claude possessed. His bold, experimental techniques now hesitant and heavy-handed, yet, I believed in his daring to create a new art. I prayed with all my heart, this fall would not destroy him. "An evening with friends will calm your nerves." I stood in front of a looking glass twiddling Papa's locket seeking my own answers. "It takes courage to start something new and fight for your independence."

"Father praised your posing and the gilded leaves," Claude whispered.

"I would have liked to meet him. When will you tell him about us?"

"Claude's father is an astringent gatekeeper of his son's allowance and company. I doubt he even likes me," Frédéric shouted.

"Where is the greeting you promised?" I asked, relieved at Frédéric's interruption and warm embrace. He posed before us in a striped gray suit, an orchid in his jacket's buttonhole. "Your new mustache—you perform your new play. You finished writing it."

"Camille, attend Madeleine's party with Frédéric tonight. He makes for better company." Claude wandered back to his canvas in contemplation.

Frédéric raced to his piano. "The daggers come out now. That poor canvas is ruined and so shall our hearts if we do not rescue our Monet with song. A new play, *oui*."

"I found it hardly the time discussing Camille—such matters with my father," Claude said. "He's not impressed with any of my friends. 'Serious study!'" Claude mocked. 'My boy bankrupts me playing about in Paris.' He and my aunt demand my return to Le Havre forthwith."

"And so, I am a matter and friend," I said. "This is my New Year's gift from you? "You soar with accolades and sink at a wisp of rejection."

"These lover's quarrels suffer my nerves more than Monet's brooding." Frédéric pounded the piano keys in a polka. "Beauty, has he threatened to throw himself into the Seine tonight?"

"No, but our beast complained of a sore knee and last month, pains in his eyes."

"I don't doubt the latter. Claude works late into the night. My own father declares me his lazy son boasting Monet's dedication." He hit a clunker howling over his miss.

"We have cats to wail at night, do not help them." Claude disappeared into his chamber.

"Paris is not made for houses but pianos," Frédéric called. "You rather a funeral march, old boy? Beethoven's Piano Sonata No. 12 in A-flat minor," he whispered. "This will rile him."

"I *rather* the quiet I relished three months alone," Claude said. "Upon your return, our studio resembles a melodrama accompanied by trills and minor clamors."

"And soon, I gift you an abundance of silence as my New Year's gift and chocolate pipes to make you smile. Please, Monet, smile—and trim your mustache." I snickered with Frédéric. He rolled his fingers on the keys; his serene playing settled my heart. He glanced back at me making faces, stretching to see if his tune lured Claude back to us.

The somber, soft trill of Beethoven's sonata cheered Claude. "That's not funny," Claude said, poking his head out of his chamber.

"Hilarious." Frédéric and I laughed as Claude vanished again.

I closed my eyes to Frédéric's playing, enjoying his talent. "This studio ached for music."

"A funeral march . . . whose side are you on?" Claude asked me, dressed and ready.

"Yours," I promised. "Always yours. It is rather peaceful for a funeral march."

Frédéric's fingers hopped on the keys in a staccato march. "I'll end before the minor bit."

Claude grunted. "And now Bazille digs at the death of my canvas."

"Why are you so insufferable tonight?" I asked Claude, tying his cravat. "I posed for hours watching the scoundrel Courbet whisper poison into your ear. Why doubt yourself now?"

"Take heart, lass." Courbet marched into the room, swiping his opera cape across his shoulder as Porthos. He kissed my cheeks in greeting. "Don't fault the lad. The greater the imaginative gift, the less commonplace are its conceptions." In no mood for the fray, Frédéric returned to his piano softly playing Chopin. "Lass," Courbet said, holding my hands. "There's nothing harder in the world than to do art, especially when no one understands it."

"Édouard Manet mocks me," Claude said. "For two years, Manet exhibits a painting titled, *The Bath*, his naked prostitutes bathing in a forest stream, hardly a picnic but now he changes the title to *Luncheon on the Grass*, knowing what I attempt."

"Ah, we need no yule log, our man lights himself on fire," Courbet said. I gathered my coat and hat listening to Frédéric play. "Manet reminds you of your place. You'll not be the first, nor the last, to rebel against what is past and what is future. Nor fail at a bold attempt." Courbet picked up a palette and brush and shoved them into Claude's hands. "You've entered this fray fight, my boy. Fight with your eye and brush." Courbet sauntered in front of Claude's massive forest painting. "*Oui*, you ensnare the light, throw it on canvas but have not captured enough."

"Édouard Manet paints to mock his class," Claude shouted. "I paint to better mine."

"Marie dazzles as a blossom in nature, but Camille will never pass for a seductress. You paint Gabrielle as Venus, Camille as Flora, yet ruffled to the neck in petals—wait, I spy a wrist."

Claude blew out candles retreating to the window. "My *Luncheon on the Grass* would have proven an astounding success, a larger painting than you ever submitted to the Salon."

Courbet puffed out his chest and glared into Claude as a stag fit for the challenge. "So, we get to it. Lad, you think little of my investment. Hold your anger at the Master of Ornans. D'Artagnan, I'm not your enemy, no Cardinal Richelieu, but ally I say as Porthos." Courbet wrestled Claude's shoulders turning him toward me. "Hail our sweet Camille as Constance Bonacieux. Oh, how clever . . . Camille Doncieux is our Bonacieux."

"I'm in no mood for jokes," Claude said, wriggling out from Courbet's embrace.

"My brave Camille, see how your Romeo rages when doubt takes hold," said Courbet. "An ugly show, but how sweet it is the lightened heart, the floating steps when the world is ours showered with praise. Our Monet drifts as a snowflake unknowing where he lands but no joy to watch. You sold a thousand francs worth of paintings. Your career begins."

"And so will Madeleine's party without us if we linger here," I insisted.

"An angel comes to earth to chastise us," Courbet said, kissing my wrist. "You second-guess yourself, lad; a poor place to reside. I concur I'm fat, your palette knife on me is as heavy."

"A party will do us all good tonight," I said, straightening Claude's jacket. He smiled and turned back to his mistress, *Luncheon on the Grass.*

"Camille bewitches in a lilac gown. Come, child." Courbet led me in a waltz to Frédéric's playing. "Ah, rosewater tonight. If we don't attend Madeleine's soirée, I paint milady's beauty."

"A grand showing, Monet, but Master Courbet is right." Frédéric slapped Claude's back fitting Claude's topper on his head. "Trim your mustache."

"Monet, don't give the Salon's jury the excuse of imperfections they will use as pretext for excluding you." Courbet gulped the rest of an abandoned glass of wine. "Never let anything leave your studio that isn't completely satisfying. Work on a modest canvas you can paint well."

"Madeleine promises a grand affair," I said, pulling Claude away from the canvas. He stared into my eyes as a dejected child, forgetting his friends awaited our departure.

"Come, Bazille," Courbet ordered. "Our Monet will snap to the jolly lad we count on. Let him lament with his sweet Camille. She sets him right."

"I've witnessed her tame all manners of beasts," Frédéric said, tipping his hat. "She requires an extra dose of magic tonight."

"I'll send my carriage back around to transport my Romeo and Juliet," Courbet said, leaving us. "Lad, you're close. Don't give up now. I won't let you." He grabbed a bottle of wine and handed us two small gifts. "Your aplomb will spur you on," he called, shutting the door.

"But for Courbet's support, I might believe he sabotages me. He sees his money wasted."

"You suffer at his opinions and you suffer without them. Who signs your paintings?"

"Do not attempt to lecture me on the failings of this work. I know I fail." Claude snuffed out the last flame, his face hidden in darkness. He stewed in silence lighting a lamp at his desk and rose to tie back the curtains he closed. Moonlight chased the shadows.

"I don't pretend to know what it will mean for you to quit this work," I said. "You don't need Courbet to tell you what you have known for months."

"This painting puts me deep in debt. Do you understand? And I now know I cannot work here with Frédéric's cool manner and endless disruptions. Our friendship suffers his jealousy."

"This is why you are upset. Why Frédéric's belongings are sparse."

"My father gifts me the money to rent my own studio. The landlord kicked us out. It appears Frédéric has held one too many masquerade balls at the rue de Furstenberg."

"Start a new work. I will show you something, but toss this madness, introduce me to your benefactor Théophile at Madeleine's party. I have waited to meet him and enjoy this night."

"Renoir and Frédéric are right—abandon me. When Courbet's carriage arrives, go without me, make pleasantries with Frédéric."

"Thirty artists wondered at your effect of the light through the trees. You show them another way: paint what you see, not what you are told. Paris is abuzz awaiting your next work."

"Am I Monsieur Belrose now, shouting in fits, lost . . . a beast to tame?"

"No. You are Claude Monet, the artist."

"Do you sell songbirds, mademoiselle Lucy Larkspur?"

"I no longer sell dresses. No, monsieur, I am an artist's model, Claude Monet's model. And he has promised me a triumph, and so I must see to it."

Claude left me at the table of gifts for him and after a few minutes, reappeared, mustache trimmed, hair combed, handsome in his best black suit. He smiled and jiggled his garish lace sleeves. "What have you brought me?" he asked as I presented his gifts.

"You needed gifts tonight, and you will be in Le Havre with your father on New Year's."

He tore into the box, laughing at the new shirt with white lace cuffs. "What is this dessert?" He swiped a taste of custard.

"The American treat, pumpkin pie. Monsieur Belrose gifted me a pumpkin from his garden. An exhaustive process to bake one, but I added plenty of sugar and cinnamon, and Madame Belrose suggested I serve it with whipped cream."

"You also bring chocolates?"

"In case we do not fancy this pie. Claude . . . how can one fail in trying? Perhaps the alternate plan will prove sweeter than the first." I pulled out the fashion plate hidden in my envelope. "A new fashion I ordered for the shop last month. Frédéric rented this green satin dress but he will not use it now. Why couldn't we?"

He pondered the print and placed it on his desk, motioning for me to wait. He ducked in his chamber returning with two large boxes. "You wondered if I had forgotten. *Oui, ma chéri*, I plan to paint your portrait with Raphael next year. You spied the sketch."

"I did." I opened the boxes revealing a black velvet jacket trimmed in fur and an Empire bonnet to match ornamented in peacock feathers and crystal beads. "Claude, they are too fine."

"Magnificent." He slipped on the jacket. I reveled in its snug fit, caressing the soft sleeves. Claude eyed the fashion plate again, me. "A woman in green—leaves for a party . . ."

"Or has she returned with her love . . . lingering, tempted."

"He, never wishing her to leave . . ."

"Will she stay?"

"*Oui*, his wife will stay. Madame Monet."

I stood at the mirror admiring the jacket. "They have yet to marry."

"No one but them shall know . . . Camille." He handed me a small package. I felt the tiny frame in hand through the paper, a pressed violet behind glass rested in my palm. "A memory from our first day in the forest," he said, "the moment I knew I would love you forever."

My Claude returned. I fell into his arms no longer caring for the company of strangers in an elegant salon. "How could you ever fail?" I whispered, taking in his sweet kiss.

38.

Camille

"What is everyone doing at the same time?" Madeleine asked unaware of our arrival. Claude and I hid behind a curtain watching the guests play riddles.

"Growing older," Albert and Marie shouted.

"I have one." Courbet raised his hand as a child, cleared his throat, and said, "In spring I make you sigh, decked in flowers for your eye. In summer more clothing I wear. As colder it grows, I throw off my clothes. And in winter quite naked appear." Tickled with himself, he watched his friends contort and squint searching for the answer in the ceiling. "A tree," Courbet blurted. He slapped his hand over his mouth as laughter filled the room.

"You gave us no chance to answer," Augustine moaned. Guests sat before her in a semicircle of elegant elbow chairs. She rolled her eyes as Courbet pranced to her to make amends kissing her hand. Augustine ruled Madeleine's drawing room atop a tufted sofa in magenta satin. The salon décor appeared as bold as Madeleine, decorated in pale lemon and magenta array. Gold filigree trimmed the doors and mirror above the fireplace. A marble goddess on the mantelpiece, resembling our hostess, smiled at us. Turquoise urns showered a waterfall of wisteria, lilacs, and pink roses onto marble pedestals and rosewood tables. Photographs of Madeleine and Augustine posing in theatrical costumes adorned the walls, and landscapes by the new artists including a painting by Claude of her rose garden at sunset.

"I have no riddle but a gossip," Frédéric said, sitting at the piano surrounded by ladies. "I hear it requires three generations to make a gentleman. Do we have one among us?"

Claude lit up and burst into the room. "*Oui*, I've arrived." He escorted me into Madeleine's salon, bowing at their applause, gesturing to me as I offered my curtsey.

"Monsieur and Madame Claude Monet." Claude and I chuckled at the servant's announcement. "See, we are already married," he whispered.

"Our lovebirds at last arrive. Gustave claims his New Year's present to you was a private carriage ride under the falling snow." Madeleine greeted us with her kiss in a red satin gown smelling of orange blossoms.

Marie rushed me with her embrace. "I say, secret whispers in the candle glow of an atelier delayed my dearest friend."

"Forgive us, child," Courbet bellowed. "We're in the throes of a guessing game. I'll bet ten francs Frédéric cannot answer my next riddle."

"I shall take that bet," Albert said. "For you shall surely answer it for him."

"I have missed the sound of laughter," I whispered to Marie.

"*Madame Monet*, did you forgot to tell me something?" Marie held up my sapphire ring.

I hid it before she made a scene. "A jest," I said. "Claude plans a new painting."

"Gabrielle jumped out of her chair at the announcement—conveniently into Albert's lap."

"Now that my cousin plays the coquette, has Albert at last become your Romeo?"

"Cousin Gabrielle is insufferable tonight. Beware."

Madeleine introduced me to her friends and Claude, his benefactor, Count Théophile Beguin Billecocq, a distinguished diplomat and old family friend. Théophile won me with his instant embrace. "Madame Monet?" he snickered. "Why, that is news. Do not explain; it is an evening of jests. Camille is ravishing, Claude." He led us to a quiet nook offering me the chair next to his.

"I'll leave you two to chat," Claude said, presenting me to Théophile. "He won't bite."

But it was as meeting Claude's father. I stood before him, twisting Claude's ring, catching myself biting my lip. "Do you play?" Théophile asked, gesturing to a harp beside me.

I sunk into the mahogany chair in lime silk, tracing gold paisleys on the arms. "My mother used to play," I said. "*Oui*, she taught me . . . but it has been years."

His blue eyes brightened at my mention. "Delightful. I hope you will grace us with a song." I gazed into a portrait of two girls, recounting the long-ago lessons with my mother. "You should see the velvet chairs in Madeleine's study," he said, admiring me.

"Is it that obvious?" I picked up a jeweled box, running my fingers over pearls and garnets, surprised by the sweets inside. "Peppermints in the shape of strawberries—how clever."

"Have you seen Monsieur Siraudin's creations in his window on the rue de la Paix? Hummingbirds flit above sugared flowers and chocolate houses, a trick of course."

"My baby sister would love to see such a sight. I confess I feel out of place amidst the elegance." I laughed at myself handing him a sweet; he joined me.

"Refreshing." He grinned. "Honesty in this house of players. Claude and Frédéric speak well of you and your family." I shifted in my seat at the mention. "Tell me about the young woman who steals my lad's heart. Never fear me. I am forever on the side of young, reckless love." Théophile's charm settled me. He listened intently to my descriptions of Lyon, Papa, and he knew of my grandfather's service to Napoleon. "Men of iron," he said, pounding a fist. "They say the French cuirassiers were descendants of medieval knights. Have you traced such a lineage?"

"No, but I fancy tales of knights and adventure."

"You must meet Dumas. I embrace my linage to the Duke of Sully, trusted minister to King Henry IV of France. But I do not intend on passing down his son's disgrace of debauchery to my newborn Lewis." He caught his hand on my leg and quickly removed it. His sweet nature, mischievous grin, and handsome, black mustache reminded me of Papa. "I too wish to partake in the modernization of Paris. Claude impresses me; he strives to make his mark despite the mob."

"It is fascinating how a purpose travels through time to parents, children . . . for most," I said. "I know little of my grandfather."

"You need not know, feel." Our eyes connected. "The bravery of a cuirassier travels in the blood to his children. A mandate from God that may be carried out in other ways . . . battle."

The flame of the fire flickered in the garnets on the jeweled box. "A mandate from God . . . as if deposited in a family and passed through the generations until it is accomplished."

"Most insightful; curses, too, but that is the power of a generation—to end them."

"You knew Claude's mother."

Théophile rose and poked at the fire. "*Oui*. A gentle lass as you." He offered me a peony, circled the harp, and plucked its strings. "Beautiful, cultured, the voice of an angel."

I savored the flower's sweetness. "You watch over Claude as an angel, don't you?"

"I do what I must." I was surprised to see Théophile moved by my question. "The loss of a mother follows a child throughout their lifetime."

"Many types of loss follow children," I mumbled as Théophile greeted a friend.

He breathed in the cigar the man offered and slipped it in his jacket pocket with a nod of thanks. "Look, Claude acts engrossed in a game of dominoes with my wife's brother Théodore. He worries I reveal too much. Those two were inseparable in their youth." He saluted the men.

"You must tell me every story you can remember, Count—"

"Théophile." He patted my hand; I welcomed his gesture. He chuckled to himself, quick to remove it and fidgeted with the gold fob in his vest. "I feel we are now old friends. My wife and I shall expect your stay with us at our villa in Trouville next summer. There proves nothing like the theatricals and balls with Trouville's society."

"I would be pleased."

"And of course we rent a château near Fontainebleau where my family has taken to Claude's drawing parties. We are very fond of him. Do not worry about Claude's father. His family views him as their Oscar Claude Monet, lost lamb. We know better." He winked.

"*Merci*, Théophile. You made me feel welcomed. I cannot wait to meet your family."

"Your conversation enlightened me, Madame Monet," he whispered with a sly smile. He kissed my hand. "Enjoy the party, Camille." Théophile was a man of wealth but one of modesty in his position, possessing the quiet strength others respected. I imagined this mysterious code breaker of France indeed graced the pages of an Alexandre Dumas novel.

Next, I met Arsène Houssaye, novelist, poet, and Madeleine's former manager of the Comédie-Française. "The Inspector General of Fine Art," Claude whispered.

"Arsène made stars at the Comédie-Française." Madeleine's musical laugh introduced us.

"And mischief, she'll say next. You're an actress," Arsène grumbled, smirking at Claude. "You project poise, presence." He appeared aloof, riveted on a game of chess with Albert. Dax waved to me, trapped in a corner by a chatty model in a Christmas green dress. Frédéric was right, green and red fashions floated in Madeleine's salon as a garland of holly in the breeze.

"My, a grand compliment," Marie said, stealing me away. "Arsène Houssaye knows all the celebrities and recognizes the best talent in Paris." Celebrities and politicians waltzed into Madeleine's home in a whirl of arrivals and departures. Even my awkward Cousin Gabrielle pried an invitation from Marie. "Never divulge a secret to an enemy no matter her crocodile tears," Marie explained, dazzling in a gold satin gown and rubies.

"I'm pleased to host my cousin in Paris again, and you dress for the opera."

"Darling, we're in an opera. Performances commence all around us." We cringed at Gabrielle's guffaw echoing in the foyer. "She drinks champagne as a goat guzzles water, throws herself at the writer, Émile Zola, and poses for that photographer Nadar. She's an absolute bore."

"She is as nervous and excited as I am." We watched her trip to Frédéric at the piano.

"Your cousin pesters Aunt Augustine. Augustine threatens to leave the party before it begins. So did I if you hadn't come." Claude, Frédéric, and Courbet invaded Madeleine's salon in old hat. "You needn't do another thing tonight. Even I gasped at my friend's entrance in her lilac gown." She lifted my finger holding my sapphire ring, eyeing me for the truth. "A jest?"

Marie whisked me away on a tour of Madeleine's home. "Exotic fabrics, Sèvres porcelain, and tokens from Aunt Madeleine's many suitors, all hold a romantic novella." We entered the refreshment room and shared a glass of champagne. Opulence overflowed the dining room table: floral centerpieces, pastries, roasted meats, towers of confections. "My aunts longed to impress you tonight." We laughed, sneaking a bite of cake. The cool buzz of champagne chilled my nerves. "I wish I could gift you a happier home," Marie said, admiring Papa's locket.

"The gift of an agreeable father—but tonight, I escape to nibble your gossip."

She pulled me into a pink and gold reception room bursting with lilacs. "Madeleine finds a secret love. She contemplates quitting the theater to run off with him this summer."

"Madeleine quit the theater, leave Paris? Rubbish. Where is Renoir tonight?"

"Is it? To be so overcome by love one might abandon everything—and everyone."

"Renoir laments no women to paint this winter only squirrels," Frédéric said, startling us.

"You sneaky beastie," I wailed. Marie shoved him; Frédéric laughed falling into a chair.

"Is there any gossip Marie does not catch?" Claude said, finding us. "Renoir visits his parents at Ville d'Avray." We walked back into the salon. Madeleine called Claude and Frédéric over to explain a question on the new art. I rather join them as my cousin scurried toward us.

"Camille, am I not charming enough to sneak off with your friends?" she whined.

"Gabrielle, you have never needed me to dance about a crowd." I embraced my cousin; she did not in return my affection. "Are you not having fun?" I asked.

"Of course—Camille shines tonight. Yet, the gentlemen over there proclaimed to the salon, that I, Gabrielle Levelle, have the fairest red hair resembling the Empress."

"Better than the gaslight yellow you wore last summer," Marie quipped. "What is the name of your coiffeur? No matter, Albert fancies my chocolate tresses kissed by the sun."

"That's not what he told me. Dry as the pine needles on the forest floor—*last summer*."

"Cousin, it is a night for celebration not claws and catfights," I said.

"Catfights, Camille? As your mother and father scratch and yowl? I hear your father—"

"And I hear my aunts have piled high the table with cakes and puddings, your favorite," Marie interrupted. "To absorb the champagne you guzzle making your manner ungracious."

"Is it not meant to be guzzled?" Gabrielle asked, decked in pearls and glittery ribbons. The pink fashion failed to shine clashing with her unruly behavior.

"Sipped, my darlings," Augustine said, breaking through. "To the dining room, allll."

"Come with me." Marie tugged me away leaving my dejected cousin behind.

I turned around spotting Gabrielle cling to a man I did not know. "Gabrielle always manages herself in a crowd," I said. "I don't know why she is so intolerable tonight."

"She invited herself to join Frédéric at his family's estate in Montpellier," Marie whispered. "Darling, how he spurned her before us all. She was certain of his affections."

"Frédéric spurned my cousin?" We nodded to a couple matching in green.

"I say, he's not himself either. Albert and Arsène are not the only chess players tonight."

"It is Claude. They no longer share a studio and Claude's work—Marie, I'm certain I love him," I whispered, "but Frédéric's advances confuse me."

"Darling, it's not love if it cannot be tested."

"I cannot tolerate this whispering when I am not privy to the conversation." Augustine huddled us onward. "Come, my ducklings."

Tinkling spoons inside cups and on saucers cheered our arrival. Madeleine lit up the room and sang, "Normandy butter for Monet, shellfish for Zola, caviar for Courbet—"

"Bordeaux for Bazille," Frédéric chimed in.

"And cake, which Gabrielle's fingers have already poked." Marie leaned into me snickering as Gabrielle hid behind a nude statue. "What is your pleasure, Camille?"

"Your company," I said.

"Monet's queen serves us a slice of humility," Augustine said, leading the buffet line.

We toasted and savored the evening's fare, wandering back to the drawing room for music and games. "Next, lumps of sugar in the brandy." Marie narrated events all evening.

Madeleine led me to the center of her salon. "Welcome to my home. A flower blossoms among us, friends. I am thrilled you have welcomed our Camille, a refreshing breeze in our stuffy Paris. A toast, to the daring, young artists who promise to topple what is old, dull, and uninspiring, and to their queen, who brings to us charm, elegance, and an abundance of grace."

"And bargains on an opera cloak and bonnet; you promised, dear," Augustine quipped.

"Though her beauty shouts my youth has passed," Madeleine continued. "Camille does not boast but looks upon me as if I still shine."

I raised my glass. "You do, as the stars. *Merci.* I am happy to be a part of something, a shout that wakes Paris and reminds her she is the birthplace of the new in fashion and art."

"Here, here."

Courbet pranced to me worse for wear and sat beside me. "Camille's gifted in comedy. Tell them your fable about the stubborn ass that eats a bale of gold hay to turn into a stallion."

"Why?" I asked. "When the stubborn ass has just told it for me."

Augustine's laughter swelled above us. "My cheeky girl brings her best to our party."

"Are you speaking of my wit or my cousin's derrière?" I asked.

"Honestly, Camille," Gabrielle huffed.

Courbet patted me on the back as his fellow. "I warned you. Camille is not one to cower."

I curtsied to their applause. "Bravo," Frédéric shouted. "Camille's tamed a beast or two."

"Or three," Claude said, slapping Courbet's belly.

"I warn you. Camille is not shy about her opinions on women's rights," Marie said.

Madeleine nodded in agreement. "Nor should she be. We do not have to bore to playing cards or bantering politics. I wish to hear what our new star has to say on a subject other than love or folly."

"I admit a soirée is more agreeable debating literature instead of politics." Augustine insisted. "A shame you could not meet our Alexandre Dumas."

"His companion, the actress Adah Isaacs Menken, enraptures Paris in a sold-out run of *Les Pirates de la Savanne*," Madeleine said, gliding across the room refilling champagne glasses.

"Happily in France no stigma attaches itself to women of talent and information," I said. "Frenchwomen contribute everything they know, think, and feel on subjects that may arise."

"I will interpret," Marie said. "We don't have to pretend to speak as idiots."

"I'm lost," Gabrielle said, falling into Frédéric. He handed her off to Dax and snuck behind me tickling my ear with a rose. The crowd distracted with a hum of subjects and whispers. My cousin snatched my flower. Her scowl warned she was not herself. My stomach quivered not at the guests, nor the importance of my impression on Théophile, but her glare. "More champagne will help me to see straighter." Gabrielle's giggling failed to put me at ease.

"Overindulgence in spirits blurs judgment and manners," Augustine snipped.

I said nothing.

Gabrielle awaited my defense. "And makes others see straight," she said, surprising Augustine. "Your father's right," she whispered in my ear. "You're no better than your mother."

I held my breath, my tears.

Claude distracted the room with his offer to sketch caricatures. Our friends erupted on who should pose first. Madeleine tapped my shoulder as I stared into the fire. "And what of your wisdom on women's rights, Camille?" she asked, quieting the room.

I gulped, absorbing their stares eager for my response. "When you spot an article on women's rights in the paper, you fold it to rid yourself of the sight," I began, my voice warbling. I found courage in Madeleine's smile. "If you spy salacious details of a woman's moral standing, gossip as to which monsieur she degraded herself with or some poor relation, you are engrossed. You cannot thwart women from advancing. Inferior, you say. If in need, would you not take the solution of a woman to that of a drunkard who imagines he is swimming in a pond?" I asked.

"Here, here," a few women cheered. A puff of smoke drifted in Théophile's quiet corner; he stood, nodded at me, and offered a light clap. He signaled to the harp making me smile.

"Camille, I had no idea you possessed such spirit," Augustine said pleased. She patted the empty seat next to her inviting me over. All watched as I sat beside her on her throne, a star of Paris. I scanned the room for my cousin; she scampered away with her eager gentleman friend.

"I admire a grisette," Albert said. "She works out of necessity and doesn't seek marriage as her means and end. She provides for herself and so she can stand by herself."

"She stands to stay warm from a cold bed," Courbet added.

Madeleine clapped for our attention. "Before our theatricals and guessing games, Claude Monet, the artist, has agreed to draw humorous cartoons of my friends."

"I sign with well-wishes for the New Year," Claude announced to a line already forming.

"It is not an unforgettable affair without an ass or two making fools of themselves," Madeleine said to cheer me. Gabrielle stumbled into the room and sat for her sketch with Claude.

"I am sorry," I said. "I do not know what has come over my cousin."

"Never be sorry for another's offenses, child," Augustine said. "For I own my offense of wearing black to my sister's party . . . alas, my busts busted my glorious red gown."

"You, Sister," Madeleine said, "look glorious with or without a gown."

"Indeed," Augustine said, dodging a mischievous Courbet.

"Augustine's feathers flap her flushed face," Courbet said, pecking her cheek.

"This dreaded artist painted me with a big mouth." Gabrielle snatched the sketch from Claude and ripped it as a child.

"Naturally, Claude's a painter of the new art and paints what he sees—truth." I did not welcome Marie's quip.

"Cousin," I said, "Claude draws a cartoon in jest. He made you fetching."

"I'm holding three glasses of champagne with three arms," she squealed.

"I will see her home," Frédéric said, taking Gabrielle's elbow.

"No." Gabrielle slapped Frédéric's hand away at last garnering the attention of the room she sought from the beginning of the evening. "*I have a riddle*," she shouted.

I cowered near the curtain at a doorway ready to flee.

"Lass," Courbet said, making Gabrielle sit down. "The game is played-out."

"What is another name for an artist's model?" she asked, rising. "*Madame Monet*, do you have the answer?" Gabrielle stood before me twirling her hair, laughing at the guests.

"Child, most unbecoming," Augustine warned. "If you continue this, I will see to it you never grace another salon in Paris. Grace—an unbefitting word for you now."

"Cousin, please do not shame me further," I said, their stares burning.

"I wish to contribute to the new art with my truth and state what you truly are." Gabrielle's face turned pink as her hair. She teetered and smiled, boring her eyes into mine.

Madeleine took her by the arm. "Enough."

Gabrielle broke away and continued, "What. Is. Another. Name . . . for an artist's model—and a daughter's mother? Mistress."

The salon's laughter ceased; their gasps choked my pride. Faces blurred as I stood before the stars I wished to impress, no longer dressed in a fairy-tale gown, silver ribbons glistening as frost, but naked. Théophile rushed to my side. Claude stood still, alone. I managed a whisper at Théophile's warm touch. "I am sorry." I ran into the reception room.

"A fine theatrical," Madeleine shouted to applause. "But where's the comedy? My dear dramatic children, we practice our sketch in the reception room. We can all agree the smell of the peroxide you so indulge, Gabrielle, makes us all queasy." Her salon broke out into laughter. I wanted to believe Madeleine's genius fooled her guests; my heart knew better. "I shall return."

Marie found me first. "*Mon amie* . . . sister." I glared at Gabrielle in Madeleine's grip.

"The moment Claude painted your form on his canvas, he told all of Paris what you are," Gabrielle said. "You shame your family with your ruse." Marie retrieved Gabrielle's coat.

"Horrid toad," Madeleine said. "I invited you as my guest, and now you humiliate my friend. I'll arrange a room at the Hotel du Rhône." She rushed to her desk scribbling the request.

"My uncle will not be pleased."

"You leave Paris in the morning. Jealous tricks. Do not despise Camille because she dares to do. I'll not waste another syllable on you." Madeleine passed her note to the coachman.

A rush of frosty air, Gabrielle came to herself. "Cousin . . ." The driver took her hand and guided her down the steps into the carriage.

Frédéric towered behind and held me as I watched her carriage drive away. "Is it sorted?" he asked. He followed me back into the reception room. "Claude has not abandoned you as you imagine. He entertains the guests with a poor playing of the harp. He's brutal at comedy."

"Leave us," Madeleine said quietly. I sat on the settee glancing at the blue moonlit night. They left in a swirl of whispers. Madeleine's red gown fell next to mine. "In Paris, important events have a week of echo, but I should hope this evening stays with you for other reasons."

"How can I walk in there now? I am no queen, but a celebration in the moment. I pose for an artist. No matter my own purpose; I hear their whispers and suffer judgment."

Madeleine drifted to a cabinet examining her trinket hoard. "You cry no tears, good. *Ma chère,* if you do not have the stomach to walk in there and sit next to your Claude you will hardly have the fortitude for what lies ahead. Oh, Camille, leave us while you can."

"Why is everyone telling me to flee the people I love most? Why must I choose?"

Madeleine slapped her fan on a table and sat beside me. "At my first salon showing, a woman entirely forgotten, save this moment, declared ladies never go on the stage in France. I smiled, unashamed, my mind racing for a precise quip. I had none, no tears. My silence won the moment. We know what we are when we stray from the boundaries forced upon us by ugly women. That would have been a fine reply."

"Claude desires to marry me."

"They all do, my darling. Never apologize for love—or freedom. Thank God for it."

"I cannot walk away from these men now."

"We scream for independence and yet long for men to need us. You found a new family."

"I placate the sobs with a performance." Augustine rushed to me, winded. "The slings and arrows of outrageous fortune to take arms against a sea of troubles—and all that crap."

"Dear Augustine," I said, thankful for her laugh. She smashed her cheek to mine.

"How can a striking girl as that copper-headed dragon act so abominably?" she asked.

"I believe Gabrielle answered this riddle," I said. "She is lost."

"Well, you, my dear, are found." Madeleine and Augustine hooked arms demanding I strut into the salon as confident as a leading lady during a second curtain call. "See, already forgotten," Madeleine whispered as her guests twirled in her salon in toasts and dancing.

Courbet marched to me with open arms. "Juliet vanquishes her foe. Claude fights France with his pastels and parasols, yet mourns his forest rigmarole. What title graces his new work?"

Claude held me tight. "Must we talk of my sorrow now?" He leaned in, kissed my cheek, and whispered, "No one here carries more grace than you."

Courbet quieted the crowd ringing his glass. "My bold artist would have astonished Paris at next year's Salon. Camille posed in modesty and modernity as Claude's woman in yellow, and gray and blue." Courbet nudged me into the center of the room. I took my sweeping bow.

"Woman in Champagne," Albert said, twirling me as at the Mabille.

"Woman in Lilac," Théophile cheered. "Rose," cried another.

Claude took me in his arms and said, "No, my friends—Camille . . . Woman in Green."

Frédéric hammered out the Mabille's notorious quadrille cancan on the piano. Dax and Albert cleared chairs and Madeleine's salon turned wild with kicks and shrills. "What was the color of the wind and waves in a storm?" Marie shouted.

"The wind blue, the waves rose," Courbet answered.

"When is an artist a thief?" I asked Claude.

"When he has stolen a heart; how I love you." He led our polka to cheers and laughter, and we stayed until the last spark of the yule log gave way to silhouettes by candlelight.

"Our delightful evening ends as it began in friendship and promise of a new year," Théophile said as guests departed and regulars remained. "Camille, play us a musical *au revoir*."

"You can play?" Claude asked surprised. "And so, my little bird sings in her own way."

Claude relinquished me to Théophile as he escorted me to the harp. I sat on the stool, shaking the nerves from my fingers. "I will play a snippet of a song my mother taught me, *La Fontaine*, the fountain." I closed my eyes hoping the memory of song might travel through my fingers, and as it did, I thought of the sweetness of those days with my mother, swallowing to hold back tears, for everyone watched as I found redemption in a cleansing tune.

39.

Sophie

When the clock struck midnight, my dress didn't turn into rags or my hair to tangles. Even if they did, with every touch Philip made me feel beautiful. We traded stories until the wee hours, ending the night contemplating a stack of pancakes. I wanted this bubbly feeling and new beginning with Philip to last, but this morning my fairytale-filled heart reminded me I must face a dragon. I stretched across the window seat turning the page in my journal, the one I learned to need.

Pancakes. Melted butter, maple syrup, caramel streams drip down golden stacks dumping sticky estuaries across my plate. Sweet, simple, homemade truth, too hot to absorb. Why in a crisis do we avoid people who love us the most? I thought I could do this at my own pace. You made other plans for me, Mom. I get your reasoning, but you're not making this easy. I found the courage to look under the rug, but I want to deal with the dirt my own way. I hate sweeping up messes, but this time, I'm doing it right.

Jacey texted she spotted Megan at Mom's gallery again. Stay home, she said, though it was Sunday. I grabbed Philip's jacket for courage, my new-found comfort in us, snatched my cell, and texted the old number hoping it still worked. **Meet me at the carousel—now!**

Fine, came the one-word text from Megan.

I drove to the park avoiding our old neighborhood. Like a hurricane churning up relics, forgotten childhood memories washed ashore in my mind. Megan Hilly made me dread the day we moved to St. Louis and strangely love it, too.

Junior high. We all grew up in the same middle-class suburb with parents who sat in cubicles crunching numbers—except Megan. "We moved to this cheap place so my mom stayed close to Grandma," she said. "Otherwise we'd live in our mansion in Chester. I'd go to private school." Megan's parents were in debt as the rest of ours. Chester was her cat.

"Mom never uses boxed pancake mix," Megan said, flicking blond ringlets.
"Then you're missing out on some damn good pancakes," I said.
"Dopey Sophie, there's no one like you. Isn't that fab? Mom says I'm special."
"So does mine."
"That's nice, but at least my mom means it."

Somehow, during my zero self-esteem teenage years, Megan Hilly was my best friend until issues surfaced in her home. Family squabbles morphed into shouting matches, cops at her door, two rough summers, a ruthless divorce, Megan moved away without a goodbye. The connection with family dysfunction and divorced parents brought us together and pulled us apart. We reconnected after college. I must have trusted Megan's frozen heart melted because as I drove into the park, I couldn't conceive why we became inseparable as adults until Blake died.

"I'm going to puke," I said, picturing a spinning carousel and Megan's never-ending excuses. "It still smells like mothballs in here." I walked into the carousel house; the pipe organ version of "Take Me Out to the Ball-game" reverberated with children's giggles. It wasn't Paris, but this place held its own magic. A 1920s carousel housed in a building with a snack counter, video games, and banquet rooms. Splendid and frightening, sixty hand carved horses, four deer, and a sleigh spun around offering flashbacks of childhood and an earful of oompah-pahs. The song, smell—I turned thir-teen again. I shook it off, snubbing the spinning horses, searching for her.

Megan stood in a corner, a finger in her ear, cringing at warbling flutes. She spotted me, tapping her glittery, pink nails on the cabinet of the carou-sel band organ. "Can you believe this crap?" she said to frowning parents. "There's a laptop playing iTunes behind the snare drum." She dropped her magenta purse on a chair. "Why'd you pick this creepy place, dopey Sophie?"

"I thought you'd feel at home."

She squinted at me, nodding at my dig. "Where it all began—you do want to remember us," she said, gesturing to the ride. "You used to make us all laugh doing the chicken dance to this song, remember? The boys played pitcher and catcher and swung imaginary baseball bats, dopey Sophie did the chicken dance, and you swung a bat at the 'Chicken Polka.' That's what I liked about you. Sophie never followed the crowd."

"Save it. This isn't a feel-good reunion. I came here to tell you there's no more us. Respect me enough to leave my friends and me alone. I know what you're trying to do." Megan bore her fake blues into me unwilling to hand me my happily ever after so easily. "I don't know why you have to wear contacts," I shot off. "Your eyes are the perfect shade of sky-blue without them. Now you look strangely . . . X-Men." I gnawed my thumbnail.

"You're nervous," she said, smug. "Me too."

The music stopped; giddy children spun past us. Megan clicked her fingernails on the edge of a chair at the whirl of the carousel helping to fill the quiet. I glared at the annoying habit I tolerated for twenty years. She caught herself, silencing her fingernails. "You used to pop gum." She stared into me while I watched a mom lift her little boy off my favorite horse. "I promised your mom," she said her voice shaking.

"What?" I recoiled from her touch.

"I would show you something." Megan revealed her rhinestone-covered cell phone and pulled up a text, her fingertip stroking the screen. "Blake." I turned away. She tapped my shoulder, begging me to look at the screen. It's Blake, Megan. I'm using my mom's phone. You need to leave me alone. I never wanted you. Not now, not ever.

Mrs. Wilton. I fled happy children and eerie carousel music; her staccato heels followed.

"Sophie, don't leave!" She chased me outside to a park bench facing the carousel house.

The year hit me.

I fell onto the bench depleted of courage, the smidgen of understanding I mustered to get me here. I wiped my tears, staring at a prancing horse on the building. I took in the park, its storybook trees, winding pathways to gardens, a nineteenth-century village resembling Laura Ingalls's Walnut Grove; the backdrop for festivals with twinkle lights, carnival games, and homemade goodness. "I missed this place." The rusty merry-go-round and teeter-totter, gone. Childhood memories flooded this park—a fuzzy memory at thirteen reuniting with my dad at the carousel and meeting a snotty girl who stole my horse, topped them all.

Megan kept her distance waiting for me to speak, the flash of her phone dropped into her purse. "You could've had anyone send you that text," I mumbled. "I came for myself, not you."

"Look at the phone number, dumb head. It's from Blake."

"No. You don't dictate this." A flush crawled over my skin as the whisper of my husband's name popped from her lips. "Don't you think I knew," I said, leaving. "So what!"

"I had dinner with Blake's mom, Joe, and Mrs. Lemon," she called, making me freeze. "You should thank me. I convinced Joe to stay; Mrs. Wilton will stop bothering you. Sophie, she never knew about the text. Blake must have deleted it. She's worried about you. They all are."

"I don't believe you." I gnawed my lips, tears stinging my eyes. For over a year, I kept my distance from the people that could have eased the pain. No amount of anguish I shouldered would bring Blake back. I closed my eyes at Megan's muffled concern.

They shot open at her first attack.

"That's your problem, Sophie," she said. "You rather believe imagined things than what's real. Those trees you're staring at are probably drenched in pastels and dancing as we speak." She pointed to a grove of knotty pines. "Even though they're ugly, but that's what Sophie does; she makes ugly things beautiful."

"I don't know why I thought I could do this." The words 'unsafe relationship' seared across my mind; the flashing red arrow pointed to Megan. I walked away from her.

"Sophie, wait," Megan called, chasing after me. "You're not giving me a chance."

She cornered me under a tree. "You don't get to say I should haves, Megan. You'll spin your manipulative magic and convince me *I'm* the one with the should haves. I'm carrying enough of a loaded backpack without you adding your rocks to it."

"You never let me explain."

"Shit, Megan. You don't get to explain! I didn't come here to give you that gift."

"Wow, you finally traded in that stupid French word *putain*." She flicked one of her frizzy curls; with a gust of wind, it flew across her nose sticking to her lip gloss.

"I'm not doing this." I shook my head unable to swallow this medicine.

"I was your best friend."

"That's what made it unimaginable." Megan let me walk away as far as a second park bench. I had parked my car in the opposite lot. *Trapped. Where are you going, Sophie?* I wiped my tears and sat, watching her march toward me wobbling in heels. Megan sat on a metal donkey ride jiggling on a spring, wheezing. "What happened to you?" I asked. "You used to be the first to hike a muddy trail, now you can't even walk in those heels."

"Yeah, you could use a makeover."

"I had one."

She worked her pathetic pout in ruby impasto. I couldn't remember the last time I saw Megan's blond curls frizzy and unkempt, her face devoid of a mask of makeup, the dark circles under her eyes missing her stroke of raccoon white. She caught my smirk as I scanned her hair, scratching the back of her head, fluffing it into submission. She contorted her face eyeing me, looking away, steadying herself on the bouncy ride wishing for a seat on my bench.

The rage I imagined I'd throw at her made me feel ugly. *Jacey, you should have warned me the next morning my carriage would turn back into a pumpkin.* Megan climbed off the donkey, eyeing the empty seat next to me. I stared at a knotty pine.

"Gross, a monster from *Snow White*, a haunted forest tree, or something," she mumbled, tugging at the collar of an oversized flannel shirt, brushing off her faux-painted jeans.

"What the hell are you wearing?" I asked. "You look like Carpenter Barbie."

"You would've owned that one."

"They would have named her Fixer-Upper Barbie or Rehab Barbie."

"Yeah, that last one sounds like the sort of Barbie I'd have."

I zoned on the knots on the tree, its sprawling limbs.

"I thought you'd be madder," she said, guarded.

"So did I, must be the eye of the storm. I thought you'd be bitchier."

"Wow, you really do swear now. Your mom—"

"Don't." I set my glare into her sad eyes. "I can turn all Hulk on you right now. It's easier than I'm pretending."

"I hoped you weren't pretending. I'm sorry, Sophie," she whispered, sitting next to me.

I turned my back to her, scooting to the edge of the bench. It was her turn to drop some tears; sadly, with Megan, I wasn't sure if they were real. "You wore a red mini dress to Blake's funeral. I can't believe you showed up at all."

"For you. Sophie, I'm trying to tell you—Blake picked you."

"You're damn right he did." Megan was right about the trees, but they weren't dancing; their limbs grew lanky fingers to grab her so I could run. "If I leave, you'll follow me again, won't you?" My heart pounded ready to burst out of my chest. "You'll hound me the rest of my life until you spit out the crap you think I need to hear. It's not for me, Megan. It's for you."

"I've been sober a year now."

"Now I'm the one without compassion. It's cold. I have to go."

She showed her cell again as if that text was her Get Out of Jail Free card. "Nothing happened! I've done everything to make you believe me."

"No! You don't get to make excuses, soul cleanse or whatever the hell this is. You live with it." I stood to leave; everything blurred as if spinning on the carousel, afraid to jump off.

"But Sophie . . ."

"You killed Blake. Live with that." I walked away from her wishing I had the arms of someone safe to run into. *Of course, Blake chose me. I was a loving wife, his best friend.* Megan hung her head without a whimper. I left her, as she did me, without a thought. But it wasn't me. It felt sickening, pathetic. I swept this under my rug, but it wouldn't fit. "I'm not wasting another breath," I said to no one. "It's over. There's nothing I can do." I tucked my head like a turtle into the collar of my coat. I wasn't prepared for the sudden icy wind. I thought of Megan. The things I said. I wasn't the same person, and I was glad for it. I was sick of never sticking up for myself, but I was out of kilter. It hit me. Her words, my words, hit me—cold, heartless, and true.

Everyone in your life is a gift, even your enemies. It's time to find out now, Sophia. I turned around to see Megan clutching the bench I abandoned, staring at me.

"I thought you'd come back," she said. "This is intense. Can we go inside, get a coffee?"

"I don't owe you anything. I want you to leave me alone. You can do that, can't you?"

"Not until you listen to what I have to say. I made a promise otherwise I'd screw it."

"That's what I thought."

"I didn't mean to say it like that. My life's crap now. I've always been jealous of you."

"You don't look like you're hurting much."

Her diamond and ruby charm bracelet jingled while she pawed at her hair again. "Stuff, that's about all I have at the moment, no husband, no kid . . . no sister."

"That's what this is all about. Payback for something my mom did twenty years ago?"

"Sophie, your mom talked my little sister into moving away with my dad."

"You knew Sally didn't have a chance living with you and your mom." I saw a welcome sight: Randall walking his puppy, Cole. *He got my text.* He didn't see me. I wanted to run to him.

"He's cute for an older dude," Megan said, following my gaze.

"He's far from your type; he's kind and selfless."

I left her fist bump hanging. "Still making friends with museum guards and baristas? Do you know why you do that, Sophie?"

"Why don't you go haunt someone else?"

"Because it doesn't cost you anything; you were never good at investing in a friendship."

"Cost? You've never paid for a thing in your life."

"I'm not the one talking to walls and old men at art museums."

"Mom's right, I have a wild imagination. I'm proud of it because she gave it to me, but I'm insane to imagine any ounce of you has changed. I saw you stalking around her gallery."

"Your mom asked me to look into something for her about the property."

I tuned out the rest of her speech, remembering my first day in this town. Mom strutted down Main Street, an outsider, but even at her age, a clique found her. Mrs. Lemon courted her first, a shrewd, wealthy businesswoman who owned most of the buildings in Grandville, the eclectic suburb where Mom opened her art gallery. Dropping on the Midwest like an F5 tornado, Megan and her mom twisted their way into our lives next, after college and into my marriage—Megan, with her "new money" from a second marriage on its way out for number three.

Mrs. Lemon became one of Mom's best patrons and closest friends—until Mom got sick. Megan's mom transformed from the Cruella de Vil as teens, to a successful realtor and Mom's close friend. In the end, Mom had the right to settle her friendships, but I knew she would never have anything to do with wanting Megan in her art gallery again.

A gust of icy wind shocked me back to the present. "It's over, Megan."

"I'm trying to make this right. I was confused, drunk, a drunk. It didn't mean anything. Blake was lonely, Sophie. He needed to talk to someone. We never did anything."

"You. Did. Everything. You didn't come here for forgiveness; you came to dig the knife in deeper and get a thrill watching me bleed. I'm done with this ride. I'm jumping off."

"I thought we could be friends again. Your mom's gallery—I could help. We could open it again . . . together." Randall noticed me and looked away, kicking a ball to his carefree puppy. I wanted to join him, forget this tornado twisting in front of my face. Megan's sad eyes morphed back to the calculated stare I knew so well. She licked her lips, examined her nails, burying her head into her phone waiting for my answer. "Well?"

Her last sting, her last blow. Her smirk melted into a frown. For a second, our stare connected back to the bonds of teenage BFFs: secret pacts, crushes, soul bearing—what I wanted to see. Megan was a broken soul, selfish, unwilling to face the smallest faults, forget the major ones dismantling everything in their path. "You will never step into Mom's gallery again."

"I won't reach out." She flipped her Prada's over her eyes, dragging her cherry heels in the gravel. "I deserve an apology from you. If you leave here all bitter that's not forgiveness."

"Forgiveness isn't for you, Megan Hilly . . . it's for me. I'm letting you go. I wish I confronted you years ago, but I didn't like myself very much, and you took advantage of that. I'm not going to let you hurt me anymore." I turned from her, searching for Randall.

"Is that what you think I did? Hurt you?"

"And that is why you don't get the privilege of having me in your life. I'm done."

"I feel sorry for you. You've turned into a bitter woman."

I found peace watching Randall and Cole, children waiting for a turn to pet Cole. "I used to wonder about people like you." Megan shifted on her heels, playing with her phone, anxious to leave. "I thought sooner or later people like you burn out. But you'll never burn out. Nothing will wake you: rock bottom, death, loss. Not even your sister."

"Don't use her to hurt me. You had a part to play in Sally leaving me. I forgave you."

"You still believe that lie, the lie you made me believe about myself. You blamed me for tearing apart your family because I wouldn't lie to the cops and say your dad hit you, that he stole your sister away! He was there that night trying to rescue you both."

"Mom had her problems, but someone had to stay and take care of her."

"Leaving was Sally's choice. You couldn't face it was your mother's drinking, yours."

"I reconnected with Sally. You missed out on a lot of good things happening in my life."

"You've missed out on mine. It took me twenty years to learn I'm worth something. That your life isn't more important because you say it is. Let it go. It's what we both need to do."

She said nothing. Megan had her heartaches growing up, we all did, but she was the worst thing that happened in my life, and I never wanted to see it. A titanic history existed in my heart I didn't have time to dissect as I waded through living without my husband and Mom. It wasn't in Megan's nature to apologize; she wasn't wired that way. She knew how to dispose of people, family, sticky situations. With a blink of her fake lashes, I was gone without a thought. I spent years thinking about Megan Hilly; she spent minutes thinking about me. *No more.* I took a step away from the edge of the planet back onto solid ground. "Enemies aren't gifts."

"I'm your enemy?"

"Enemies are for war. I don't want this war."

"I never thought of our friendship as a war."

"Haven't you? We have enough casualties on our battlefield. It's over. Winners don't exist in war." *Don't look back*, I told myself walking away.

Randall's chocolate Lab ran to me awkward and clumsy. It was good to feel his soft coat and sloppy kisses. "Thanks, boy."

"Lamb bites wolf," Randall said, squinting at me, back to Megan. "You solid, Soph?"

"It doesn't feel as stellar as I imagined. Megan said it's unforgiving to walk away."

"I've never been religious as my wife, but hang what other people think. You have enough people in your life who see your heart."

"What I keep telling myself." My anxious breathing settled at his words, his smile. The tightness in my chest disappeared. "Thanks for answering my text. Hope I didn't ruin your day."

Randall made me laugh as he spun around like the carousel unwinding his legs from Cole's leash. "We come here every Sunday."

"I know," I said softly, shoving his arm.

He winked. "That carousel scares Cole. Made the mistake thinking it would be good for him to be around kids. Damn, horrible idea."

"It's always scared me." Cole plopped on the grass at my feet rolling on his back snorting. "You were here this whole time?"

"I heard enough. You should go inside; you're shaking."

"I'm good. Actually, I'm hot all over." Megan's car drove way.

"She a problem?"

"Not anymore . . . in my head a little, but never again in my life."

"Good."

"Randall . . . I'm not good at walking away from people. That was the hardest thing I've ever done. I feel free, guilty, too. How is that possible?"

"Ripping off a band-aid stings, Sparrow. But the wound will never heal unless you do it."

"Right."

"Promise me you'll head home. Oh, this is for you. Hope it's still warm."

"Hot chocolate, it's perfect. Thanks, Randall, for everything." I breathed in the cool air again, savoring steamy cocoa. "I really love this time of year."

"My eye is on you, Sparrow," Randall said with a soft hug goodbye.

"That's not how the song goes, Cowboy."

"Are you sure?" A group of kids ran up to Randall and Cole, Cole happily pawing and kissing them all.

40.

Camille

〜

February 1866

"That is the look," he whispered. "Down and away. No . . . close your eyes."

"As if you said something forward to make me blush?" I asked.

"I imagine you look breathtaking in a rose petal bath."

"Frédéric, now I blush and laugh. And the way you look at me while you paint . . . Claude does not stare at me so."

"He sees only colored squares and flecks of light—and cannot draw a nose."

"When Renoir sketches my face he looks deep within. It frightens me."

"Hold still. Do you talk this much posing for Claude?"

"Naturally. What else am I supposed to do?"

"To 5 rue de Furstenberg," I told the coachman, my voice quivering.

January melted away without a word from Claude. *"I've never seen a Romeo and Juliet apart so much,"* Marie snickered. *"Indeed, Monet trades love songs for the silence of abandonment,"* Elise warned. Claude found distraction with his family's doting in Le Havre while I found myself oddly in the company of Courbet. Gustave picked me up from Papa's empty shop, and we traipsed the city as old friends. A stop at his picture dealer's gallery left me taking another carriage ride alone. I visited Ninette Rousseau's boutique for a scandalous chat on men and bought flowers from Elise—fighting to ignore his invitation.

Frédéric returned to Paris. This winter I received only his letters. He heard Claude started my portrait for the Salon but spoke of his idea for a painting. *Since Claude is away, I would welcome you as my model*, he wrote.

Since Claude is away. I dismissed the nerves tumbling in my stomach. "I have posed for Frédéric before, no different," I insisted to the empty seat across from me. A blush warmed my cheeks as I stepped out of the carriage.

I looked up at his window; the green curtains no longer filtered the light. I changed as he requested a simple dress without the trappings of a sash, corset, or jewels, dusted my skin with rose powder, and shined my lips with salve. *Let them paint you to the neck in garb and fashion; I paint you as you are*, Frédéric reminded me in my thoughts. "A low chignon, loose, as if tousled by the breeze," I whispered to myself, walking up the steps. The door open, the stove aflame. I hid my gifts for him on a small table by the door. "The landlord refreshes your walls with burgundy. Lace curtains are too extravagant for an artist."

"Claude hangs no lace curtains in his studio at the Place Pigalle?" Frédéric asked, surprised to see me. He kissed my cheeks and ushered me inside the vast, empty atelier.

"This was a grand studio. I will miss your piano playing. I hope you moved it to . . ."

"22 rue Godot de Mauroy," he said, his blue eyes sparkled at my presence. "Your lively letters made me feel as if I never left Paris, Camille. I suffer my landlord's patience slow to move, but Claude and I no longer need this massive space."

"And yet it grows wider between you. Have you heard from him?" I searched the room for traces of Claude, a few empty frames, a landscape, and his red velvet chair.

"At present, friends only hear from Claude when he needs something."

"And so, he needs nothing from me."

Frédéric watched as I removed my coat and hat and rushed to take them from me. "You left this," he said. The Persian shawl grazed my neck with a stroke of his fingers as he wrapped it around my shoulders. I missed a tender touch. His body hovered behind me; I slipped away. "I recognized it from Madeleine's soirée. How beautiful you looked that evening."

I hid myself inside my wrap. "My father shuns my cousin as long as it takes. I do not know why Gabrielle turned on me. With Claude's silence, I wonder if he has, too."

Frédéric winced at the mention. "If Monet is not wandering in nature, he grows lost in his family's accolades and feasts of honor. But I know him. He paints the sea, stocking inventory."

"Your beard is back." I walked the empty studio. "Claude fancies only a mustache now."

"I am not so handsome with chapped cheeks from my winter excursions in the Fontainebleau Forest with Renoir." Frédéric busied packing boxes. He held up a crooked bowler and set it on my head. "Monsieur Belrose sold me a used hat. I hadn't the heart to return it."

I smiled thinking of my neighbor, examining the crimped brim. "His trick for your visit."

"I am glad for yours." A finger pressed his lips, like my mother catching me biting mine.

"During our carriage ride, Gustave fancied me biting my lip. 'A trick to make them rosy,' he said. He offered to paint me." I raised a hand to Frédéric's scowl. "I declined. But Frédéric...you stare at me in a way Claude or Courbet never have." A breath fluttered inside me.

"Inexcusable." He ducked into his chamber and reappeared in a pair of dark eyeglasses.

I leaned back on a lounger enjoying his show. "I am glad I came."

"When did you take to carriage rides with Courbet?" he asked, removing the spectacles.

"I grew tired of Marie's gossip, and Courbet required my assistance buying a suit from Monsieur Belrose. He grows worse."

"Monsieur Belrose or Master Courbet?"

"Both." Trunks, frames, and boxes sat near the door; Frédéric's green armchair covered in a cloth. Clouds overtook the afternoon sun dimming the studio. A cavilier Frédéric glanced at me with his mischievous grin as he lit two lamps. "Do you work best apart from Claude?" I asked, handing him a forgotten paintbrush.

Frédéric ignored my question, removing a painting from the wall. "If I could carry that green armchair on my back I would haul it everywhere I paint in nature. That helps me work."

"Artists and their superstitions."

"No doubt you inspire Claude."

"His muse?" I laughed. "No. I suppose a woman may be delighted as an inspiration, but muse whispers expectation and connotation."

He stopped packing and sighed, folding his arms in amusement. "The original meaning of muse pertains to a goddess, a protector of the arts. Do you not wish to be a goddess?" My posture stiffened. Frédéric grunted, noticing me contemplating my hat and coat to leave. "You've made amends with Elise. Good," he said, aloof, thumbing through his sketchbook.

I left him alone, glancing out the window at the frozen garden. "A garden of glass. I have yet to hear from him. Claude is adept at leaving me, whereas I suffer his absence. Even Courbet has no excuse for him." I sat at the window seat. Claude dismantled his great painting, the ladders and platforms gone. In this vast space, it still felt as if clutter existed between us all.

Frédéric sat beside me. "Claude deceives his father and says nothing of you for fear of losing his allowance. Surely after meeting Théophile, Claude's aunt knows of you."

"She has a spy, Amand Gautier; he keeps her informed on matters. Claude explained all."

"Has he? Don't despise Amand. He secured Claude's new studio and placates his aunt."

"An odd spy who gifts kindness." I retrieved my things, pausing at a painting of a dog sleeping on a rug. "I love the tenderness in this painting. What is her name?"

"Rita, my pointer; my father spoils her." He motioned to the red chair and uncovered the green one arranging an impromptu sitting area as in Madeleine's salon. "I wish I could offer you tea, please . . ." He removed my shawl; I took my seat watching him stoke the fire.

"The green dress I wear in Claude's life-size portrait is stunning; he struggles with my face and form. I laugh at times he paints me much older like my mother. We soon return to work at his new studio. Courbet spreads a rumor Claude has painted my portrait in four days."

The hearty laugh I missed echoed across the room. "Four days? I hope it is a triumph. They will all long to see it now with Courbet's claim."

"Scandal and tricks to sell paintings."

Frédéric walked away and set up his easel; I recognized the unfinished canvas. He positioned his stool before it and an armchair in front of a gray backdrop. "Happy birthday." A silver box fit into my palm with his soft kiss on my lips. "I didn't think you would come."

"Frédéric." I looked down at the silver box embossed with flowers and birds. "We should start working. I don't have much time." My lips still moist from his.

"Please . . . open it. My regret at leaving this studio—I will not see you. I am glad Claude abandoned his picnic painting. I no longer have to hear his bemoaning my sabotage."

"He does not blame you." I stood before him. "You are still friends."

"By the intimacy in our letters, I share this now. The failure of Claude's *Luncheon on the Grass* affects him deeply. He avoids Paris for fear his creditors will rob him of his paintings. His spirit is broken. He's in debt. Do not judge my confession as treason. My concern is your care."

"Art is not a trade to him but a goal."

"But Claude must eat. He leans on his benefactors, not for support for painting, but folly."

"Folly? Name one friend who has not ignored a debt for a night at the opera. I worked in a dress shop in Paris since I was a child. We earned our living off the Parisian's appetite to appear rich to obtain riches. You said yourself this is a gambling game."

"One should never bet with an empty purse. Are you going to give me a lecture suited for Madame Pontray or open your gift?"

I clutched the silver box curious at its contents. "Frédéric, I love you both. That is my gift to you. Wait." I retrieved my hidden prizes: pots of geraniums and forget-me-nots. "I see now I should have given you the silver opera glasses, but now you can finish your flower painting."

"You give me the gift of no excuses. I will huddle them with me on the train to Montpellier and keep them safe in my mother's greenhouse."

"You leave Paris again?"

He studied me at the concern in my voice. "Camille . . ." He set the flowers down and took my hands tracing a circle around my bare wrist. "Why are you here?"

"You asked me to model." I drifted away. "I missed you . . . today I feel abandoned."

"And tomorrow?" He slipped his gift back into my hand. "Open it."

I lifted the lid. "Frédéric," I gasped, holding a gold chain link bracelet, a heart locket, dangling center. He raised my arm and fastened the trinket around my wrist. I stared at the bracelet enchanted. "I cannot accept this," I whispered. "A keepsake . . . for your future wife."

"And so, I hope she accepts it now." His words chilled my skin. I took it off and handed it back, rushing to leave. "Camille." He stopped me. "We played this game all summer. I hoped away from Claude you might . . ."

"Turn traitor now?" I found my shawl, flinging it over my shoulders.

"It is no sin two men fighting for your hand." He held open my coat. "I wish you to stay."

I dropped it, standing before him. He lifted my arm and draped the bracelet around my wrist soothing my skin. "Frédéric," I whispered. I sat down, staring at a forest landscape Claude left behind. "I sense he does not want to leave you, this studio; he needs to fetch many things."

"But Claude does leave."

The bracelet fell heavy upon my wrist; a tiny gold key fit inside the heart-shaped locket. "I wish I held a key to love." I opened it. "How do you love alone?"

"Claude fears not failure but loving . . . everyone."

"I hold secrets, Frédéric. Secrets a man as you could not withstand. You relish your attachment to society. I have only a flawed introduction in Madeleine's salon. Paris whispers about my cousin, my mother . . . I do not wish to be whispered about ever in that way."

Frédéric dismissed me returning to his packing. "You should leave."

"But I am confused." I raced to him, stopping his hands shuffling books into a box. "Claude made no attempt to defend my honor that night . . . you did." I saw the phantom of my face loosely drawn in black crayon on his canvas; his palette loaded with dollops of blush, white, peach, crimson. "Paint me now." My hand slid down his shoulder and for the first time I felt at ease with him. I sat on the chair in front of his canvas slowly removing my jacket. He looked away. I waited for him to look back, removed my blouse, and sat still for him in a loose chemise.

His chest rose and fell in heavy breathing as he came to me. I unbuttoned my top; his hand fit into my sleeve caressing my shoulder. "You deserve to know you are loved," he whispered. He knelt beside me, running his hand down my shoulder, my arm, warming my skin, breathing in its scent. His lips fell over mine, soft, tentative. Kisses brushed my shoulders chilling them now. He took the bracelet in hand and turned its dangling heart across my wrist. It felt cold and smooth. His hands slipped loosely inside the back of my chemise swirling over my bare skin. I relished his strong touch, noticing the heart as his kisses grew more reckless.

My body stiffened; he released me.

I sat still, closing my eyes in the pose he requested. "I am sorry," I said softly.

He lowered his head, his cheek against mine, sliding away; he walked back to his canvas taking a cool sip of wine. "Leave," he said, breathless.

I scurried to him unfaithful, unsure. "Must I leave my family, Paris? Must I give up everything?" I fell onto the red velvet chair, burying my face in my shawl without tears—shame. I needed Frédéric to erase this pain, so I reached for him. He came. I pressed my lips against his, caressing his body, proving myself a child swept up in this dangerous game.

"You don't love me," he whispered, handing me my clothes, walking away.

"Love grazes and chastises me." I stared at him melting as the snow. "Your parents would never accept me and mine walk this earth but they are not here. But I will not regret this."

"In Méric, the noise and indulgence of Paris disappears. There would be nothing but you." Frédéric stood alone at the window.

"I am not enough." I put on my coat, leaving the shawl. "Do you still wish to paint me?"

"*Oui*, but not today. Go now."

I tucked the bracelet into his hand with my soft kiss. "Your friendship is gift enough. Frédéric, whatever has happened between you two, Claude stands stubborn in his affection, but he counts you as dear—so do I."

He stuffed the bracelet into his pocket and fitted Monsieur Belrose's crooked bowler on my head. We traded a quiet smile as he replaced it for my bonnet. We walked down the steps to the street in silence, and as he opened the cab's door, he whispered, "You happened."

~

The last of my winter days turned colder from Claude's indifference. Secrets about my mother drifted as ghosts across cobblestone streets into the salons

I frequented. I missed my simple routine with Papa, our flurry readying the dress shop for spring, choosing fashions and fineries. The Elegance Shop, all but closed—so was Papa. "Your father suffers his health and us. He retires," Mamma demanded. "Could I not stay on at the shop?" I asked, knowing her answer and my heart's intentions on leaving Paris with Claude. "No," she said. "I will soon gain my inheritance and we are moving. Genèvieve's off to school." *And I will be alone.*

And so, March was a time of packing boxes. Papa and I once fancied our quiet walks along the rue de la Paix, conjuring ideas for our window display, bickering about Shakespeare, Balzac, and love. We scarcely spoke now, for most days and nights Papa disappeared—so did I. My dream of the flood in Lyon returned, but I no longer skipped in a meadow with Papa, I ran away, and he still cannot tell me why Mamma never came to my room when I cried, and why she turns away from me in my dream, why she has always turned her eyes from me. Now I know.

I have always known.

I used to long for spring's rebirth until I faced my own. Every day Claude stayed away from Paris, was a day I wanted to spend with Frédéric and the distraction of posing for a painting Claude would surely see. A seduction I had not felt with Claude, one I stopped myself from feeling again. With the coming spring, Claude again asked me to flee Paris; this time I agreed.

A warm breeze chased the chill away. I found comfort in a place where assertions and hope bloom year-round with flowers: Madame Pontray's. "Ironic," Elise said, rattling her pearls. "Frédéric craves you and Claude beams as a love-sick puppy, a puppy that strays."

"Claude has not strayed—that I know. He obsesses more with his work than women."

"Claude loves you to be sure, but does he need you?" She cooled her flushed cheeks with the flutter of a fan in pink silk flowers. "I hear Claude Monet needs no one yet demands support and loyalty as a prince—an odd sort for one who has yet to accomplish lofty things."

I strolled to a display of pink roses, plucking one to savor. "I came to you for answers."

Her fan waved me back to her small table, our cups steaming with tea, a tray of macaroons and lemon cake reminded me of my sister's last birthday. "You're a woman now and must discover them good or bad for yourself."

"Claude's intentions turn hot and cold." I plopped on my seat.

"Have you given yourself to him?" Elise boldly asked. Her mischievous smile erased offense as she flapped her fan to cool my blush.

"No." I looked inside my cup lost in the brew of bobbing bits of herbs and flowers.

"An oddity," she said, handing me a macaroon. "A scrupulous artist—oh, to be young and beautiful in a tug of war between two smitten artists."

"I believed I would gain Papa's blessing in time."

"Nothing your sad, brown eyes will charm him into." She squirmed in her seat. "If you were of age, would Claude marry you? Will it matter if he asks you not?"

"No. Frédéric mentioned the house Claude wishes to rent in Sèvres near the Ville d'Avray station, having no idea I might join Claude. Claude strives with another large work, a garden painting. I model for him as four women dressed in spring fashions, his Flora."

"*Women in the Garden. Oui*," she sighed. "He hired me, in the loosest sense of the word, to ready his garden. Claude has a keen sense about gardening. 'One must plant according to colors, not flowers,' he says. Heavens, it will not be ready, as he demands. I designed two bouquets to captivate you. I don't know how you sit still for the man."

I walked to a small fountain, swirling a fingertip, rippling the water. "I fancy a pond nearby as Claude. If not figures he would paint only water."

"And sunsets."

"*Oui*. I watch waves lap the shore, losing myself in the breeze ruffling the water. I spot flickering light before Claude, on a leaf, my dress, wondering if he sees them. When he calls me to view his progress, there they are flickering on his canvas illuminating his colors as if he paints with crushed gemstones. He captures me in a work that may last forever." I sat, sipping my tea.

"I see." She smiled, staring into me, twiddling her thumbs as Papa. "When a model draws upon an artist's love, he heeds her call, and she becomes a powerful inspiration. He will not lose her. He will not marry her.

He must keep her as the imagined fantasy of his paintings. The woman no one will ever intimately know but him."

"Claude paints a new vision." I posed among her flowers. "He brings Paris, us, into the country in modern fashions showered in sunlight." I stood in a stoic pose at her applause, peering over the brim of a bouquet. "A garden of flowering ladies in billowing skirts, floral headdresses."

"He ruined a rose tree digging a trench for a pulley contraption to paint his tall canvas outside. Well, Frédéric is no puppy in love and wishes to save your reputation."

"It is not his to save."

"Your answer." She held my hand spinning Claude's ring around my finger. "Is Claude worthy of all that you will lose?" She tucked a yellow rosebud in my hair. "Come, I'll show you a surprise to settle your mind." We savored the sun walking into a garden courtyard near her greenhouse. "My son's idea." Elise showed me to a table. Wooden chairs teetered on the stone walkway. We stood under an ivy-festooned, brick archway. In spring's splendor, lush foliage and tree blossoms would encase this sanctuary hiding her visitors.

I inhaled. "Your cherry blossoms flower early. Why two tables?"

"A dozen tables with dozens of guests when I'm finished. *Table Ouverte*."

"Open Table?"

"A place where my ladies can share their views away from the closed-mindedness of the city. The modern woman will advance whether France is ready for her not."

"A garden tearoom—Elise, how lovely. I have missed your lectures."

"You live them now. Camille . . ." Elise rarely turned shy. She sipped champagne from a hidden glass on a table, a second glass sat empty from a previous visitor. Rattling her pearls, she continued, "Charles—your father helped me with this and will continue. Do you understand?"

"No." I picked up a fallen cherry blossom off the table and tucked it into my sleeve.

"He closes the dress shop. Your mother wins the expensive new apartment with the coming loss of her Antoine de Pritelly." I snapped around to her at the name. "You will all move to 17 Boulevard des Batignolles come spring." Elise let me chew on her bitter bite of truth, straightening chairs as if expecting guests. "Heavens, a rental of 1,070 francs a year—your father will never divorce her; they have in their hearts. It is all sad, but the distraction of art, modeling, and love in a country cottage may prove your remedy. Your father will never agree outwardly, but perhaps in time you two will mend, and you will marry your Claude Monet."

"Mamma makes the decision for me with this scandal."

"My truth crushes you." Elise handed me three letters. "Your papa saved these for you."

His handwriting, the painted flower on the envelope. "Claude's letters—Mamma!"

"*Oui*, she hid his letters. Enough hatred festers in your house. Think of your sister. Claude arrives today and waits for you. Who do you think I had to tea before your visit?"

"Champagne." I moved with the breeze into her arms and relished falling cherry blossoms in our hair. Her handkerchief dotted my tears leaving behind a hint of violet. "Elise . . ." I tucked her hands into mine, gazing into her eyes brimming with tears. She kissed my cheek, I, hers. "I don't judge you and Papa, but I cannot be happy. Yet, you have been more of a mother to me than my own."

"And you, my daughter. Go, Claude waits. Child, he knows of Frédéric's betrayal. It will take time for their friendship to mend. Naive, *ma chère*, believing Courbet can keep a secret."

"Paris is a mad city; it makes one do mad things. I am glad to leave it."

"Never hate Paris, for it brought you to me. Trust in love, in your prayers, for I am certain God paints the ugly things as beautiful and in time will reveal His masterpiece."

"*Merci.*"

"Wait. Friends who visit *Table Ouverte* for the first time leave with a token." She pinned a small corsage of violets, almond blossoms, and lily of the valley on my collar.

"Almond blossoms represent hope . . . I am afraid," I whispered.

"You're in love. Do not waste a moment."

I rushed into the carriage thrilled to see Claude. "Driver, to 1 Place Pigalle on the corner of Rue Duperré," I said, waving to my cohort in folly.

41

Camille

I stood at the door watching Claude quietly dab at his canvas, pausing to fan the gown's skirt across the floor into the sunlight. New furniture, a floral rug and drapes graced his small studio. The tall canvas of my life-size portrait sat near the window on its easel, the green-and-black striped satin gown, hanging where I left it on its form. Unmoved by my presence, I slipped inside tucking myself behind another large canvas, the start of his *Women in the Garden.*

A row of walnut palettes slick with linseed oil dangled on strings from a beam as wind chimes on a tree. He carefully squeezed a tin tube of flake white onto his palette muddied in emerald and indigo, and perused a table, a lineup of tiny brushes he called pencils, varnishing brush, palette knife, and a badger brush for blending. On a stand, a delft pot held his custom brushes: flat and square-ended with long, flexible handles for his broad, sweeping strokes. Today, a wisp of a pencil teetered in his hand as he dotted my portrait's lips.

I modeled hours, months for Claude, learning more about keeping his studio than Papa's shop and imagined living with him, I would know well how to care for it.

He stores his tubes of color in a wooden box rather than tin to prevent drying; olive oil on the tips of his brushes keeps away the moths. He prefers the light come over his left shoulder when painting indoors at his easel, but the cool of a north light is preferable to any other because it is more uniform. He paints only on a smooth canvas prepared in white, never brown, and poppy oil protects the colors on his canvas from yellowing. Above all, dust is the enemy of art, so his new floral rug will suit our salon, wood floors his studio—never swept only mopped.

He painted the walls a soft yellow encasing himself in sunlight. Still, a studio without Frédéric made Claude eager to leave Paris for the country.

Japanese prints and fans covered a wall. A basket of pears and vase of colorful mums sat on a table. "You do not fancy painting still lifes," I said. "Pears and flowers?"

"You surprised me again, quiet bird." Claude failed to notice me, squinting at his work. I hoped today, he would not be so indifferent. "I'm hungry and the flowers are for you."

"You are always hungry and always have flowers." He offered no kiss or greeting but stood stuck to the floor in front of his canvas perfecting a row of crystal beads on the hat. "Red chrysanthemums signify love," I said, admiring the bouquet. "White, truth."

"Yellow—slighted love."

I ignored his manner, tiptoeing around the open jaws of this alligator, hoping he would not snap again. "A Chinese chrysanthemum—cheerfulness under adversity." I closed my eyes taking in a sweet bite of a pear happy to hear him laugh.

"*Oui*, you know your flowers. Come, bring me a pear, flutter your little wings, and look."

"Share mine." I laughed at him as he devoured it, turning me to his canvas. "Claude," I gasped, lost in my form painted with grace and thoughtfulness. "You finished." I hoped he would relinquish his paintbrush and submit the painting at once to the Salon's jury for the exhibition.

Claude focused on his canvas with the indifference I came to expect while he worked. "I touch-up the folds on the skirt. I should have made you wear the crinoline."

"Never," I snipped, sneaking a kiss to his cheek. "You talk of moving to the country, but you add new touches in your studio, the elegant rug, drapes. Where did you get them?"

"My brother Léon talked my father into sending me a few luxuries so I may paint my patron's wives in a salon scene and take them with us to the country house."

"Your patron's wives or the furniture?"

"*Oui*, comedy. Théophile invites us to another theatrical evening. You've beguiled him."

I sat on his red velvet chair from the studio he shared with Frédéric, casting off thoughts of Frédéric's kiss. "You paint seascapes and gardens not wives in salons as the other artists."

Claude grunted trading a small brush for wide loaded with taupe. "I fancy commissions that pay my rent." A sable brush tipped in blush froze in midair; he stepped back, studied my face, looked at his canvas resisting the temptation to dab my nose.

"Nonsense, Théophile pays your rent." I had not planned to cut him. I retreated to his Japanese prints: a white cat staring out a window. "The cat has everything she needs, a towel to snuggle, a bowl of milk, and yet, she wishes to be outside not stuck indoors behind glass."

"Does she remind you of anyone? She spies a monsieur who will open the world to her outside her window. You wear a new dress. Yellow has always suited you."

"A new loose style a sash and no corset all the rage. I miss working in Papa's shop."

"I found the Japanese prints at Boudin's stationary shop in Le Havre. He asks of you and hopes to paint you in his grouping of pretty ladies on the beach at Trouville this summer."

"And when did Claude and Camille act their melodrama of innuendo and small talk avoiding this truth you obsess with." He finally turned from his painting to notice me.

"I don't have time for your theatrics today. I had hoped you came to offer comfort. I wish to celebrate tonight." I stormed to the dress fixing a fold on the skirt to match his painting. "Madeleine invited us to dinner tempting us with poached truffles, broiled steak, wine sauce, and the banana ice cream my aunt makes for me on Christmas. Augustine sends us off to the country with a gift, blue Japanese porcelain on the condition you invite her for tea."

"Gifts? Are we married, Claude? You painted over the rug again, it was a lovely pattern."

He stomped his foot as a child. "The only pattern I desire is the light across the green and black stripes on that train. I have not titled it *Woman on a Carpet*."

"What will you name it?" I asked, laughing.

"*Camille*." He hushed me with his answer, enjoying my surprise.

"*Camille*? Papa will be furious. The jury must accept it. We will celebrate."

"I intend to list you as Madame Monet in the catalog. This pleases you?"

"Fictions." The clouds tucked themselves away to his disapproval. He rushed to the window commanding they part. They did, shining light on the green dress. "I packed my belongings to Genèvieve's endless questions. What news of your family, Le Havre?"

"Apparently you have yet to read my letters."

"I told you, Mamma kept them from me."

"Did she keep you from Frédéric's?"

I blocked his view of the dress. "If I had received your letters, the way you are now . . . You stay briefly in Paris and off back to Le Havre! Why? You will ruin that portrait. Submit it."

"If you continue in this way, I will paint without you."

"And you have not changed your pattern. You painted me as bloated as Courbet with your fussing. The coat is too big, my waist is lost, and I do not fancy having the ass of a bull."

He slammed his palette on a table nearly splashing his canvas. I stood my ground, for if not here, never in a country home. Claude dropped his brush into a tumbler of turpentine. "My only surprise in my return is you've spent so much time with Courbet you're as vulgar a he is."

"Vulgar? Indeed, we visit the Louvre to yell at students and smoke cigars."

"Courbet boasts you fancy posing for Frédéric now at his new studio? Is it grand?"

I twisted Claude's ring on my finger wanting to toss it as he did in a tantrum with his palette. "You do not own me. I am my own model and choose where I work."

"And love?"

I bit my lip in anger, plucked a yellow mum from his vase, and dropped it at his feet. "You who love no one." His eyes burned into my form on canvas. "Will you slash her, too?" I asked. "Frédéric never shamed me the way you do now—the way you did in Madeleine's salon."

"This is why you have turned cold." Claude tossed another paintbrush into the tumbler, wringing his hands into a rag, taking a seat on a stool to watch me.

I walked to him. "I am sorry I criticized your painting. Papa threatens to send me away."

"And Frédéric is your answer, this Dax, perhaps Courbet abandons his mistress for you."

"Now you are foolish. If you dare feel for me as you do your work—I have always understood, but not now . . . your promises."

"I told you to leave me," he shouted. "You hold a phantom of one Monsieur Valentine and my dearest friend's affections over me. A wonder I cannot finish this painting."

"Your silence turned me into a scandal among your friends. My family is broken, but I do not devalue myself so much I would abandon them for continued heartbreak and shame."

"I don't want to need you." He kicked the stool in one of his fits. "I'm better off alone."

His bloodshot eyes glowered at me as a drunk. I noticed no empty wine bottles or glasses. I walked to his overturned stool to set it right; he looked away in shame. "Claude, you paint and live in fictions. You strive to capture moments rather than live in them. Look at me. I offer you myself against everything I know to be true and proper—to rip myself away from my family."

He slumped over on his stool as if his high ceased. "Watteau was an expert draftsman who loved his drawings more than his paintings. I am no draftsman in art or life."

"Watteau," I shouted, lunging in front of him. "You have no condition to say you will not live and yet you choose not to. Living inside your paintings is not enough."

He looked at me in pity back to the escape out his window. "My sight is a gift and curse."

"I'm no woman to leave behind in a cottage without a voice or purpose, and yet, here in Paris, I have neither. In your quest to see this light, you fail to see the life in front of you." My stomach wracked with our brawl. I poured myself a glass of water as he stepped back in front of his painting. He shuffled the brushes on his table, the wooded ends clacking together as a string of beads. My frightened reflection in the mirror stared at me for pity. "I am pale. I will leave."

"No," he said, standing behind me, his rough fingertip outlining my lips. "You are pink and yellow with a touch of rose madder and the palest gray."

I could not help but smile. "My hair?" I asked, releasing it, letting it fall on my shoulders.

"Indigo." He handed me a paintbrush tipped in white and led me in front of his canvas. "I trust you." The brush shook between my fingers; he held my hand guiding it to the green border of a fold on the skirt. A gentle stroke left a thin stream of pearl along the edge.

I exhaled handing him the brush. "Do not ever ask me to do that again."

He stepped back admiring our final touch. "But now you are a part of this. All of it." I absorbed his embrace I desired at the start and let him sweep himself up in our kiss.

"Paint me as someone else," I whispered, my hands slipping inside his jacket. I stared into the breathtaking portrait. "This is how you see me?" He captured my heart: its love and torment, adorned in a green-and-black-striped gown, fur-trimmed jacket, my hand tugging a ribbon on my bonnet. "She stays or leaves? The hours you spent taking in the curves of my face." I was not ready to leave then or now. "You poured sunlight down the skirt making the black stripes shimmer with diamonds and the green illuminated as an emerald."

"I paint you as you are. You gave me this. I see more when you are with me. I wish to be more." He left his canvas for me, untying the sash around my waist. His kisses caressed my neck to my lips taking me away from all I hated in Paris.

"Paint me as someone else," I begged, giving to him all he desired.

"No."

"You must win." I finished undressing and stretched my body across the chaise longue.

"What have you done to me? Stay, always."

"I will when you do."

The clouds tucked themselves behind the sun. In the last bitter cold of winter, he held me to himself, into his world, stretching across the sofa warming each other. I tumbled and drifted with every kiss, every touch I grew less afraid of drowning. I gave myself to him amidst the scent of flowers, paint, and stone I was his.

42.

Sophie

Jacey picked a secluded booth at her favorite Italian restaurant, Charlie's.

"I can't believe you finally said yes to lunch," she exclaimed, rubbing her full stomach. "But if you let me eat one more slice of pizza—"

"You forgot the number one rule of a great friendship: *Mangia! Mangia!* And always say yes to dessert."

"*Magnifico!* But zest for life doesn't work on going to the gym, does it?"

"Don't remind me. Can you *innamorarsi* with carbs?"

"Definitely." We toasted our victory over pizza guilt laughing.

I settled in this peace, moving through deep, dark loss. Waking to the color, I missed in all its subtleties: the vibrant hues of trust, laughing, embracing joy, and opening my heart to love.

"Soooo." Jacey's blue eyes twinkled with mischief. She tamed excitement, powdering her nose, spying at me over her compact. Purple now tipped the ends of her black bob. She tousled it. I caught a strand of green. "Sophieeeee," she squealed, slamming her compact shut. "You haven't said a word about last night with Philip. Was it *Happy Days* or *Happy Hooker*?"

"You didn't!" I relished the flush washing over my skin, thinking of Philip and our evening. Tender conversation convincing me his interest in us was genuine, that this might be the start of a welcomed, new beginning.

Jacey and I giggled covering our faces as schoolgirls. "Inappropriate jokes, nicknames, lunch, deepest thoughts, wow, Soph, I think we're—"

"Friends."

"*Anche in paradiso non è bello essere soli.*" A burly man exuding Einstein greeted our table with a chortle. Jacey gave him the hug his outstretched arms expected. *Her Randall*, I imagined, watching the two speak Italian.

"Hold on," Jacey said, bouncing back into our booth. "Charlie, you're talking too fast. I'm only on level two of Charlie Montanari's Rosetta Stone."

"What did he say?" I asked, entertained by his charm.

Charlie offered me a rose. "Your mother . . . *molto bello*," he howled with a classic Italian kiss to his fingers. "*Molto bello*," he said softer.

"Thank you," I said as he welcomed his next table. "What did he say?"

"First, your mother is extremely beautiful."

"*Molto bello,* sweet. And before that?"

"He said, 'Even in paradise it is not good to be alone.'"

"*Sì*. Thank you for this . . . for everything, Jace." I savored Charlie's gift, the pale, pink rosebud its petals laced with white. "I'm so ready to paint."

"I can tell by the way you're studying that flower. I'm excited for you."

"It's not easy. I've been blind for a year and everything I see looks and feels intense."

"Loads of decisions, too."

"Yeah," I said, surprised Jacey read me.

"It won't be easy for a long time, and you're so fab at changing the subject. Um, Philip?"

Before I could speak, Charlie brought us two cappuccinos and a plate of chocolate-covered strawberries. "*Grazie*," I said, trying Italian. Charlie smiled and left us squeezing my shoulder. "It's so great here."

"He likes you. I told you, you were missing out at lunch. This place would make a perfect second date with Philip." She wiggled her eyebrows and leaned in waiting for my juicy details.

"Last night . . . was *Happy Days*, Jace, and happier days on the horizon."

"I'm glad. You deserve happier days."

We dove into the strawberries, shared more stories, avoiding talk of Joe. Jacey discerned more than I gave her credit. "It's complicated. I understand," she said, leaving it alone.

"Jace, I've known Joe for years. He's a mystery, but he's kind and loving. It's a confusing time, new lines being drawn I can't make out myself."

"You guys have a history. He cares for you. I'm a realist."

"I'm all Impressionist right now. It's all fuzzy at least it's taking shape."

"Colorful, the best part."

Charlie never let you leave without your promise to return. "We'll come back next week," Jacey said. We left the restaurant and walked down Main Street. "Winter's back," Jacey said, bundling up. "We can skip the walk."

"No, I won't feel so guilty for eating those strawberries."

"Charlie wants the recipe for my chocolate cake after I bragged it was better than his wife's. It's my dad's recipe." We passed Jacey's favorite thrift shop. She didn't give it a glance.

"Your dad bakes?" My question made me wonder if my dad ever did, but I never thought to ask him those feel-good questions.

"A so-so cook but he made wicked desserts." We walked a few steps in silence before she stopped me. "Soph, I know what you're struggling through, how hard this is."

"I'm not great at this right now, friendships, opening up."

"Trusting. I know."

"I need time to get me back. I'm so exhausted."

"I know." Jacey stopped me, put her hand on my shoulder, and turned me to the direction of the swings in a small park behind Mom's gallery.

"I forgot about that little park," I said, smiling, absorbing the thud in my stomach at the view of Mom's empty gallery. "I miss it." I stretched to look at the gallery's entrance watching a couple read the sign on the door and walk on. "I'll figure it out."

"You will when you're supposed to. Your mom and I used to swing here when she needed 'thinking' time. That's what she called it."

"I never knew that." We skipped the park bench and sat on the swings.

"You don't know much about me," Jacey said, her combat boots kicking the dirt while she clutched the chains. I sat rigid on mine, my thoughts churning about Megan, but with each passing hour, Jacey's genuine friendship washed over the pain of Megan's. "I've understood why," she timidly continued. "It hasn't been the best circumstances for us to be friends."

"We're friendly. I like you, Jace, it's . . . my marriage took up a chunk of me, Blake's circle of friends, that were never mine, caring for Mom. I have to learn to like me again and this—putting myself out there. I imagine you have younger, more adventurous friends."

"You're not old, Soph."

"Yeah, I had that talk with Annabel, but when you try to brush a hair off your forehead and it turns out to be a wrinkle that's when you realize you're getting older and it's okay."

Her giggle filled the park. "OMG. The forehead thing, hysterical. My mom said I was born old. A reservoir of depth is nonexistent in most of my friends, too many distractions. I never had time for distractions. I had to grow up fast."

"So did I. Mom called me her old soul, too."

"I never thought age differences between friends mattered. Listening topped my list."

"I haven't been great in that department, have I?"

"It's cool. You lost your dad when we met at your Mom's gallery. Josie was so kind to me. Your mom let me call her Josie. I wasn't her best student. Years before I met your mom, I returned here from New York where I gave up a spot at the American Ballet."

"Seriously?"

For the first time, Jacey sighed and turned inward, her cheer dissolved with her memory. "You didn't know. I'm a thick dancer, strong," she snickered, squeezing her biceps. "I met your mom through a friend; she needed interns, and I needed to stay here for my little brother."

"I'm sorry, Jace. I haven't been good at friendships, maybe I never was."

"I understand why. You're tired of being hurt and taken advantage of. And so what, you like being alone and you don't care. You have a right."

I turned my swing to her, astonished. Jacey kept her gaze on a sparkling rock at her feet. She picked it up, brushed it off, and put it in her coat pocket. "How do you know how I feel?"

"I know." She found a pink rock for me. I took it, searching her sudden, sad expression.

"Jacey, I appreciate what you're doing. Joe said you lost your dog last year . . ."

"Yeah, that sucked, too. Soph, loss is part of our story, it isn't *the* story. Neither is cancer." I bristled at the word. "Your mom wouldn't have ever wanted that written as her story."

"But she didn't have a choice, did she?" I held my breath at Jacey's words, ordering myself not to leave. *The roots of a budding friendship are delicate, let them set, ma fille,* I heard Mom's whisper. *Aren't you tired of running?* I asked myself. "Yes. I can't go there right now."

Jacey held her stare into mine. She hid her lips one into the other, and with a swallow boldly said, "Because you're mad, and you have a right."

"Losing a pet is not—"

"I lost my parents, Sophie . . . five years ago. It ruined everything, my life . . . my heart . . . my little brother." She dropped her head; our swings froze.

I took her in, compassion arresting my heart. "Jacey . . . I didn't know."

We cradled the silence; our tears and sniffles rose together.

"It's not fair to compare loss," she said. "I wanted you to know I understand. I understand it never goes away as most people say it should. It doesn't. I learned sadly most people don't have great relationships with their parents. I did. I felt guilty for that growing up because my family was perfect. We were like the *Partridge Family* and *Happy Days*. We did all that corny stuff: drive-in movies, milkshakes, homemade popcorn balls and candy apples on Halloween, visits to the mall Santa, stringing popcorn, drives to see Christmas lights, and nutty summer vacations. We did it all, except camping. My dad hated camping."

"How?"

Jacey avoided my stare, twisting her swing away testing the ride. "I'm too old and my butt's ginormous for this swing," she said, disappointed. She closed her eyes taking in deep breaths to quell her anger, her clenched fists fanning out clearing a bench of its leaves.

"I'm sorry, Jacey." I sat close to her. "Today's a day for quiet park benches, isn't it? We could just sit if you want. You don't have to—"

"A car accident." My tears fell without permission, one drop, twenty, steady streams onto my lap. Her hand slid into mine. "I was dancing in New York." Her voice quiet. "I couldn't believe it, dancing. Mom couldn't believe it either. She was so happy for me. I auditioned, got in, and never looked back until I received that phone call and became an instant parent to my teenage brother." I turned into her with my hug. We knew each other for years, but it wasn't until Jacey said the words our hearts bonded instantly together. I squeezed her tight, she rested her head on my shoulder calming herself; she wasn't needy for sure. She toughened up; I tried to do the same. She brushed a hair out of my eyes and smiled. "You can't use that pomade ever again. I order you to throw it out," she said, sniffling, making me laugh.

"You can't be my fairy godmother, you're too young." I handed tissues.

"And way too busy."

I didn't mind this silence as we studied her rocks like kids. "It resembles tiny diamonds in there, doesn't it?" she asked.

"Yes."

"I make jewelry out of rocks, too. Your mom tried to focus my creativity, thought I was a gifted sculptor. I didn't know what I was gifted at anymore." Jacey buried her lips again one into the other. She caught herself, rubbing her lipstick back into place. "A friggin' drunk driver," she said, startled as if the words popped out from her lips for the first time. "I could have said worse; he deserved worse. I blamed myself, but he drank the shots, rejected the cab, and I blamed myself. My parents were going to surprise me when I came home for a visit. They took these goofy ballroom classes. My parents were totally Richard Gere and J.Lo. They looked like them. You ever see that movie, *Shall We Dance*?"

"No," I whispered.

"Mr. Elders is wonkers I told his wife about those classes. I couldn't imagine watching my parents together like that. My brother had a short video of them dancing a waltz. I loved they tried, but Soph . . . I never told them . . . and that sucks the most. I never thanked them."

"Life's a dance, isn't it, Jacey? Tangos, waltzes, confusing steps for most, beautifully fluid for others, like you. You handle life with such grace. I bet you are a beautiful dancer."

"Thanks for saying are. I haven't danced in years. It sort of left me."

"It never left you. There's so much we have to dance through in life. I've never been a great dancer, and I don't have many answers these days, but I'm certain your parents knew how much you appreciated and loved them."

"I'm all over the map with work, but at least I'm here. Soph, I'm here."

"Will you ever dance again?"

"No. The deal with dancing—you get one shot. It's a numbers game, age, fitness, flexibility. Teach, maybe. Design clothes, run a thrift shop, bookstore . . . fall in love . . . right now, my brother's doing great and that means more to me than anything."

"They're proud of you. Parents like yours are so proud."

"I fell in love with the past because it reminds me of them, simple, good times. It keeps them with me. That's what I miss the most."

"*Happy Days*?"

"Exactamundo. Now, what are we going to do with these rocks? Throw them at that beehive chick with the magenta purse?"

"Wow, you're wicked-good at changing the subject."

Jacey fussed with her hair and mine, powdering our noses. "It's time we both turn the page. I know about Joe and Faraway Travel. I'm helping Annabel. But, Soph, I would be honored to help you with Josephine's gallery, whatever you decide. It was my favorite place to work. Her spirit—she hoped someday to fill it with your paintings."

"Thank you. Buuut . . ."

"OMG! Sophie Noel, you're singing. One note, but it's a start."

"I made one decision—I'm buying myself a Louis Vuitton Alma PM bag in magenta."

"The one the Wicked Witch of the West owns?"

"She's not a witch anymore."

"You dropped a house on her?"

"She dropped it on herself. But that's another fairy tale for another time."

"Yeah, we can't let Mega Godzilla ruin a perfect accessory." Jacey searched the website on her phone. "OMG. I pick Rose Ballerine. I've waited years to splurge."

"What are we waiting for?" We locked arms racing back to our cars.

"Let's order them online. That way I won't buy two when the woman at the counter gives me a snooty look like I couldn't possibly afford one. OMG, it's so irresponsible, thrilling, huh?"

"I can't believe how alike we are. Meet me at Mom's house. We need a movie."

"My mom used to say if a fairy tale doesn't have the happy ending you wish, imagine a different one."

"Mom used to say something like that regarding painting . . . life."

"You're gonna make it, Soph. We both are." Shopping therapy helped Jacey find her skip and as a winter chill set in; we rushed to the parking lot before the first snowflake fell. "Finally, snow," she sang. "Let it snow, let it snow . . ."

"Let it snow!" I sang out of key the corny refrain, but as Randall said, it sounded beautiful to me. "One more dragon to slay," I told myself, picturing Mom's gallery open and thriving again.

Paris.

43.

Camille

The Salon, May 1866

Chestnut blossoms floated in the air as carriages dotted the boulevards in a procession to the Salon. Throngs of Parisian society promenaded into its galleries to witness the birth of a new star at the world's preeminent art exhibition. Three thousand paintings covered the walls in sunlit rooms and darkened corridors. The Exhibition's sensation: Claude's portrait, *Camille*.

Artists strutted in ruffled shirts and colored cravats, stuffing buttonholes with roses. Old masters sported black coats and toppers while ladies flaunted the season's colors: aqua, lilac, pearl. High on a wall in a darkened corridor, visitors flocked to admire Claude's life-sized portrait of the woman in green. Even the critics repeated the fable Claude Monet finished the work in four days. "No matter where it hangs it draws a crowd," I said, clutching his arm.

"I gain more commissions than time." Claude smiled at one greeting after another. "A grand day for us—we leave for the country after Théophile's dinner tonight. And your father?"

I twisted my handkerchief failing to hide my nerves, losing myself in his portrait. He took it from me and tickled my nose. A couple approached. "Her face in profile, uncommon for a traditional portrait," the man whispered. "Marvelous, the play of light on her dress," the woman said. *A glow across my hand, on my nose.* "You trimmed my waist," I said as they left.

"Daubs of brown on the backdrop, *voilà*. I finished your portrait with Raphael. His fluffy, white coat in the sunlight inspired the quick, broken brushstrokes I have wanted to explore."

"Your new technique," I whispered, thrilled. "But my dog as your muse?"

His fellows called. Claude signaled a moment. "You once growled you were no one's muse. And you didn't answer my question." He pulled me close, seeking answers in my eyes.

"I have not told Papa or my sister. Mamma ignores me busy moving into their new apartment . . . and with the funeral. I cannot take her looks, nor she mine. Papa sneaks visits to see your *Camille*. I hope it soothes the sting of losing his daughter, knowing inside he is proud."

"He hasn't lost you. It will all work out in the end. I'm sure of it." He fiddled, anxious to join his friends. I hadn't counted on Claude understanding the depth of my confession. This was his day. But as he greeted an admirer, my morning events burdened me and played inside mind.

Papa's shop closed. Bidding farewell to friends felt as a final punishment from Mamma. Despite Marie's warnings, I befriended the rumored once courtesan, Ninette Rousseau, relishing my visits to her lingerie shop. At the bell's chime, Ninette bounced into her boutique in rose silk and ribbons, her orange hair a fluff of spun sugar. "Deary, you're forever in love with lilac."

"My little sister's words precisely," I said, greeting her.

"Where's Papa's locket?" I felt for the missing trinket ashamed for the first time in a year I had not worn it. "Ah, you're off on your cottage affair." She draped pearls around my neck.

"Incorrigible. I battle nerves leaving Papa, Claude's success and closing the shop." I handed her the pearls; she looped them back around my neck.

"You live life on your own, love, nothing wrong with that. But a death in your family may also plague this day." A death brought a piercing cold to my heart and family on a day deserving a shower of sunlight. A man whose name I had not uttered since a child.

"How did you know?" I asked.

Ninette raced to her door, flipped her sign to *Closed*, and rushed me into a private salon in Japanese array. She slipped behind a counter, returning with a crumpled letter and card, tucking them into her sleeve. "Tea, love? Wine? No, I suppose it's too early for a drink."

"What is this? Tell me."

Ninette contorted her face as if the words she would spill tasted bitter. Her eyes already glazing, mine, dejected, sensing today the secret she held was mine. "A stately man walked in last month wishing to buy luxurious tokens for his mistress," she began. "He wasn't the usual, confident sort, pale, nervous—sickly really. After a few jokes to put the bloke at ease, he surprised me with his choice of three fine gifts: my best corset, a black lace fan, and a string of gold beads. We were to deliver them to a quaint apartment on the second floor 99 rue Blanche."

"Ninette, must you whisper your gossip now? The driver waits." The color from her cheeks gone, her tender gaze kept me in my seat. I turned mine to the pink silk tufts on the sofa.

"I broke my rule, Camille. My clerk Eden assists most of my male patrons. Husbands blush buying trifles for their wives, and others, as this monsieur, make the mistake of buying gifts for mistresses I need not know. Do you know why I pass Eden these questionable clients?"

"Why?"

"We share laughs as schoolgirls, but we know the gossip I hear keeps one safe in this city, serves as a warning, sordid as it may be."

"And this man presented you with such a warning?"

"I spied the name on his card, Camille," she whispered. Her body edged closer.

"Someone you know?" I asked, beguiled.

"Bugger, another odd man, Monsieur Valentine, visited months ago for wedding gifts."

"Heavens, to act so bold when I gave him no understanding. The name . . . the name of the woman on the other man's card."

"Françoise Manéchalle. Do you know her?"

I caught my breath choking on the thickness of her sweet perfumes. "No." I rushed to leave. A Japanese screen and kimonos blocked my path. "How do I . . ."

She hurried to pick up a fallen kimono on its form. "Camille . . ."

"I understand. Gossip to protect your friends? I do not know her!" I fell back on the sofa swallowing my tears with a sip of tea. Her bitter brew rose in my throat; I choked it down.

Ninette wriggled her body next to me. "Drink this." She offered wine.

"No." My heart pounded as a mallet on a drum stretched to burst. I laid her pearls on a table, losing myself in the petals of red poppies and violets resting on their edges.

"I didn't say you knew her." Ninette dropped the pearls into a box. "If you did, you'd like to know one thing more—the nervous bloke struck out the first name he wrote on the card, as if to hide her identity, rather poorly. The man could hardly stand. It was Léonie, Camille."

"My mother," I whispered, hiding my face. Her footsteps slid away; she cleared a path for me to leave this private room. A room too sweet with the smell of perfumes and flowers . . . revenge. "Tell me, how did this man know to visit you?"

"He said a girl named Gabrielle boasted of my shop and that she knew his mistress would fancy the things here. As I have said, we both suffer visiting, jealous cousins."

"It has nothing to do with me. I am late."

"Careful, little bird, you soar in the limelight. I saw your portrait. Claude Monet is a true artist. I'll never tell. You're the only friend who refused the whispers about me and gave me a chance in this damned, dark city."

"Do not hate Paris, for it brought you to me." We said our goodbyes, but by Ninette's timid embrace, she had not finished. How I wished I left.

"It was what the man said after his purchase that haunts me . . . this Antoine de Pritelly."

"Monsieur de Pritelly?" I held her hands, bracing for the truth I locked away for years.

"Yes. He said he was dying and that if God might forgive his shame. I don't know why blokes as he confess at a time of purchasing scandalous gifts. It's in rather ill-taste."

I took a deep breath and faced her. "What else?"

"His stepsons would hate him. He disinherited them leaving his fortune to his daughter."

"How lucky, but why is this of my concern, *mon amie*?"

Her finger smeared my tears and her own. "His only daughter— Genèvieve Doncieux."

The joy and fear of my day crashed as ocean waves churning together inside me. The inclination I had since a child swelled to the surface to carry me away, a repeated nightmare only to rise and witness another. My tears fell for the innocence of my sister and the guilt of abandoning her now. "I warned you not to mix with me, a sordid English girl." Ninette dabbed her eyes and mine with a cool cloth. I thought of my baby sister's face slathered in cream. "What will you do?" she asked.

"Leave."

"Good." She toughened up. "It's nothing a child will understand if you make a fuss. These are the secrets of our parents. And yet, no child should ever have to carry a thing as this."

"But we do." A fierce protection overtook my sorrow.

"Geneviève might understand. A child as she might grasp more than we imagine."

"Elise once warned me beauty might be my ruin; it was my mother's. I recall a conversation with a count regarding curses and callings passed through generations until it is accomplished—or snuffed out. In curses, that is the power of a generation, he said, to end them."

"Love, I pray it has ended." Ninette tucked her small box of pearls into my hands.

"So do I."

"*Ma chéri.*" Claude's whisper brought me back to the Salon. "You're pale. What's wrong?" The back of his hand pressed my cheeks and forehead as he did when I tired of posing.

I waved off his fuss with the smile he desired. "An unwelcome chill came to spoil my day. Do not worry about me. Your admirers wait. Celebrate."

"Perhaps you should rest before joining us." He held me until I convinced him to leave.

"I will." I sat at a circular sofa enjoying a moment of solitude. "Monsieur, my dress."

His warmth left my body but his finger traced the curl on my cheek. "*Mon amie*, why are you not posing in the middle of Claude's circle of friends as they applaud your beauty."

I jumped at his kiss to my hand. "Renoir, I have missed you." He soaked in my embrace.

He threw off his hat and scratched his head squinting at me. "Thirty thousand trolls last year. I dare say Monet's *Camille* added a few more." Renoir looked thinner, his scraggly, orange beard overgrown. "*Oui*, I've been away too long lost in love, everything sordid you don't wish to know." He scanned the crowd. "But come, why has my Joan of Arc lost her spark?"

"I wish to know all. How do you do it? How do you see through me?"

He stretched his arms inviting me for a twirl. "I loathe being crowded. Help me clear this room." His body wriggled and wracked in his own dance. I joined him with a hop and a skip into his arms. "An artist is a person who thinks more than there is to think, feels more than there is to feel, and sees more than there is to see—generally in debt and forever in love."

"And has a rich way of repainting a forlorn expression."

"I possess nothing but the hands in my pockets. A debt eats more than a child."

"Horrid words from a horrid man." Marie broke between us slathering Renoir's cheeks with kisses. "Cease love. Auguste is not made for marriage, for he weds every woman he paints."

"I don't apologize for falling in love, ever," Renoir said. A group of giddy women intruded. Renoir's head spun in circles, his body in bows. "Monet's done it, a bold choice for our Joan of Arc—his naming the portrait after you. My lovesick Monet reveals his heart to Paris."

"Too bold," Marie said. "Most artists title a portrait Woman of This, Lady of That."

Renoir's chortle lightened my heart. "The critics hail *Camille* queen of Paris," he said. "I knew it from the start." He bowed and indulged in a soft kiss to my cheek.

"My *queen*," Marie giggled. "I shall meet you with our sisters at the carousel." I nodded, waving my hand in dismissal. Marie chasséd to Albert, dancing in the crowd as at the Mabille.

"I stand as jester." Renoir sighed, studying Claude's portrait. "My paintings, rejected. The Academy's tyranny is at an end. The public is beginning to see such bias."

"The Salon should not be the only venue for an artist to show and sell their paintings to the public. Paris cultivates madness."

"Control. And so, my brave lass flees our Paris?"

"Next year, Claude's *Women in the Garden* will shine the brightest sunlight ever in a French painting. He develops a new technique, a vibrant palette painting outdoors. Oh, visit us. Paint with Claude in the country. Renoir, Claude invites me to dream."

"*Ma chère*, the only thing that counts is what a painter puts on his canvas, and that has nothing to do with dreams. I will paint you no matter where you reside. And if I had not counted Monet as my greatest friend, I would have indeed fallen in love with you." Renoir scattered the crowd marching us into Claude's circle. "Accolades paint Monet's cheeks crimson as the walls."

"We laud our *plein air* nature painter who paints a traditional portrait indoors," Courbet bellowed, rushing me with his embrace. "Our girl smells of lilacs and roses today, my favorite."

"Everything is your favorite," I said, waving to Marie in the next gallery.

"Renoir restored the blush to your cheeks," Claude said, stealing me.

"Monet's eye and salesmanship will make him rich—in time," said Courbet.

"Ah, but Monet will not heed time and expect his notoriety to come fast and easy," Renoir said, wandering into the next gallery. "Bah, battle scenes and portly cherubs—Courbet!"

"I care not if others understand my art; I must understand it," Claude said. Renoir saluted.

Artist and teacher, Eugène Boudin, and the art critic, Zacharie Astruc, greeted me. They supported Claude as a brother. "Monet gives them more than a portrait," Astruc said. "He introduced us to a woman who tells a story, not one who stands frozen in a scene."

"Indeed. The lad makes his way," Courbet boasted. "But we must all heartily support our Monet, for he will devour his fortune in paints and frilly lace blouses."

Théophile arrived, meeting me with his kiss. "Madame Monet," he whispered.

"I look forward to seeing you in Trouville this summer, Camille," Boudin said, leaving with the others. "You will pose for me, no? My Claude misses the sea."

I embraced Boudin. "I know sitting under my parasol at the beach is for your canvas."

Courbet broke through to study Claude's portrait. "Claude's allowance continues and a move to a country cottage in the shadows to paint a radiant Romeo and Juliet garden. Delicious. Now, when the committee hung my paintings poorly in the World Exposition, I withdrew them, exhibiting myself in a hut to great success. The Salon shut its doors to me for *six* years."

"Any wonder? Would any of us like seeing an exhibition of Courbet . . . in a hut?"

We exploded into laughter. "Paintings!" Courbet wailed. "Émile Zola, comic and critic."

A man with slick black hair and a pointed beard swaggered up to our circle dressed in his finest. "Courbet's favorite subject is Courbet," said Zola. "Mademoiselle, you played well the harp at Madeleine's salon." He studied Claude's portrait, me.

"The writer who chased Madeleine's guests for scandal," I said, making them laugh.

"A horrible habit, indeed." Zola twirled his mustache as a vaudevillian villain. "I fancy finding novel characters to inspire my stories."

"Your praise of *Camille* won my family in Le Havre," Claude said, shaking Zola's hand.

"You've riled the rejected Édouard Manet. Many praised him for your work, Monsieur Monet." Zola put on a pair of spectacles. "Did you really complete this work in four days?"

"He did," Courbet shouted, edging his neck out as a peacock.

"I relish its light. I am not for any school and look for a man not a painting. I found him. Bravo." Zola slapped Claude's back as old friends, studying me again. "A lovely model, indeed."

Courbet blew his lips at Zola. "Monet paints no hussies, forgive me Milady, Claude makes us pause feeling moments in nature, across the sea, sunrise, sunset."

"Is this how you explain your art, impressions?" Zola asked Claude, skeptical.

"If I have to explain my art—it is not art," Claude answered.

Claude amused Zola; a friendship formed. Zola scrutinized me. "You are his *Camille*."

"My *wife* is my only model and graces my next work, *Women in the Garden.*"

Zola laughed. "Forgive me, mademoiselle—madame—in Paris, well, an artist's model—"

"Betrothed," I said. "The day makes us all eager to claim fiction as truth. Your novel character: a lady, no mute, treasures and uses her voice despite those who attempt to stifle it."

Zola removed his spectacles tucking them into his pocket soured by my rebellion. "*Oui*, the contentious words of our grisette, as of late, utter women's rights. Wife, mistress, muse— Camille, you impress us all the same."

"Zola!" Claude and Théophile said. Zola held up his hands and apologized.

Courbet stopped me from leaving, puffing his chest at Zola. "Forgive us our foul manners and overindulgence in spirits. A lady of more grace than any in these halls stands with us."

"I have worn out my welcome among you men," I said, slipping away.

"Monsieur Zola," Claude barked. Zola patted Claude's shoulder and turned to me.

"I apologize, mademoiselle," he said, seeing right through me. "Novel, indeed."

"The crowds have thinned. I will sneak another glimpse at my portrait," I said, leaving.

"Mademoiselle Doncieux," Zola said, tipping his hat.

I stopped and scrutinized him now. "How did you—Monsieur Zola." *Had Ninette's secret followed me here?*

≈

I relished the solace of this quiet corridor. "I spied your smirk glimpsing my portrait, Papa. You left before I could greet you," I whispered to myself. "Mamma, see the black curl on my cheek you could never tame; Claude adores it." Tears pooled in my eyes; I blotted them away as Claude did mistakes on his canvas. Loneliness covered me as I viewed my portrait without my family. "Alone in the presence of so many people."

The Parisian queen, the triumphant woman. Henceforth, Camille is immortal and will be called The Woman in the Green Dress. The hour of the Salon arrived. Camille was there dreaming of gathering violets. I admit the canvas that stopped me the longest was the Camille of Claude Monet. His picture tells me the whole story of energy and truth. Regardless of Claude's outward bluster toward the critics, he relished their praise in the papers. His hasty portrait resulted in a triumph beyond our dreams, during the upheaval of our lives.

"You should stand proud." My eyes closed at his soothing voice. "*Camille* is a triumph."

"Frédéric." He offered his tentative greeting, I, my awkward kiss to his cheek. He stood behind me; his breath grazed my ear. "I wondered if you would come."

"If I painted your portrait, I would never leave your side, and yet you stand here alone."

"I suffer boasting and drunkenness." I pointed to Claude's gaggle moving away from us. "Claude fancies the sight of his own brush, Zola the sound of his own voice, Courbet, beer."

Frédéric crinkled his nose at my manner. "Émile Zola has that effect, an art critic and fierce defender of us and the New Art. His glowing review sways Claude's family. And yours?"

"A subject I wish not to discuss." I stared at my bare wrist recalling his bracelet upon it.

"Monet has mad success. His pictures and those of Courbet are the best in the exhibition. Courbet rolls in money. He sells 150,000 francs worth of paintings since the Salon's opening."

"A good shock in Paris attracts the public. I suffer such a shock and fear soon I attract no one." I recoiled at Frédéric's touch, staring into a painting of a forest sunset: an entanglement of trees and gnarled limbs at dusk, a horizon muted with gray and amber. "I look at this path and fear it will swallow me whole, Frédéric. Claude paints a forest path you long to explore not one to avoid. Sunsets should offer one beauty and promise, not pain and finality."

"It made you feel. Théodore Rousseau is a great landscape painter. You look stunning."

"Your musketeer goatee returns—your new play." My eyes lit up at an evening of acting.

"I'm performing it at my uncle's tonight." We wandered into a hall of sculptures. Frédéric offered me the seat next to him on a secluded sofa. "Your throne, my queen."

"You too? I have suffered more jokes from Renoir and Courbet than I care to repeat." I searched the hall for Claude. Alone, I absorbed Frédéric's kindness settling beside him.

"I would welcome your company tonight. My aunt longs to see you."

"You know I cannot." I looked for Claude again; Frédéric's eyes never left me.

"I'm invited to take in the wonder at the Hôtel de la Païva this weekend," he said.

"The courtesan La Païva's mansion? Marie gossips her tub runs milk and champagne."

"The most extravagant new mansion in Paris—Dumas contemplates a play about her. Madeleine refuses; Arsène Houssaye, Gustave Flaubert, and the new writer Zola will attend."

"Émile Zola is everywhere. You know everyone. We leave for our house in the country."

Frédéric slumped over, staring down the empty hall. "*Our* house? A grave mistake."

My posture stiffened. "Can you not be happy for us?" I moved into his sight.

"I wish you well and pray your parents offer consent of the marriage in haste."

I stopped him from leaving. He collected himself, anxious for a rescue in a passing crowd of artists. "And if they do not?" I whispered. "Frédéric, do not look at me so. Not you."

"I never imagined your words would pierce me. Claude's creditors hunt him down threatening to take his exhibition paintings. This is why he leaves Paris. *Camille* would be lost."

"Are you speaking of the portrait or me?" His hand slid away from mine; I took it back. "I am sorry. No fighting. Come with Geneviève and me to the circus this afternoon."

"I have had enough of juggling fire and swallowing swords." We parted. He paused at a window studying the city, shuffling his timepiece. "Camille, how long do you think Claude will go for scrounging? Trouville, the Casino, champagne dinners, Courbet's invitations at the Count de Choiseul's château. You would abandon your family, your faith?"

"Paris judges and so does Frédéric." Three female artists sketching statues in the hall waited for his reply. When they drifted away, he retreated to the sofa. I searched out the window.

"No, *mon amie*." His footsteps shuffled toward the exit and returned behind me.

I spied his sullen reflection in the glass as I watched visitors crowd the fountains and the Palace steps. "You never called me that before," I said. "I leave for more reasons than you know. I choose this. Visit us. Finish your portrait of me—"

"In the chemise?" Shivers chilled my arms as his fingertip brushed my shoulder.

"I am not confused in this."

"I titled it *Young Woman with Lowered Eyes*." He lifted my chin as his model. "I have known about your mother, Camille . . . yet here I stand."

I lost my breath at his confession. "Does Claude?"

"You must tell him." He gazed at me unable to hide his affection and kissed my hand breathing in my fragrance. "I'll visit you on two conditions: apple doughnuts and no Courbet."

With one kiss Frédéric's protection, honor, and desire, a path of shame, daring, obsession might disappear. He noticed my hesitation, my lingering to kiss him back. I let him go, walking away to find Claude. "Will you ever allow yourself to fall deeply in love?" I asked.

"I imagined I had."

"Come, man, we've been awaiting your arrival," Claude called, lunging at Frédéric, breaking us apart. "What have you been doing this whole time?"

Frédéric shook him off and nodded to me his farewell. "Talking about the circus."

"Bazille pontificates platitudes playing in plays," Courbet shouted. "Come, children, the critics wait, but will you swallow their medicine?" "No!" The men howled as boys.

"Apple doughnuts and no Courbet." Frédéric's promise warmed my heart, but at the sight of Marie and Geneviève, the glacial cold of a mother's secret cut through my soul.

44

Camille

A sprinkle of rain at dusk revealed my sister's favorite sky, pink mist against a peach sunset. "It's too early for bed," Genèvieve whined, sitting up as I entered her room.

"Are you feeling better?" I asked, tucking her under the covers.

"The feats of strength," she cried. "Oh, Sister, the prancing horses, a marvelous circus."

"You ate too many sugared apples." I reached for a brush to tame her tangled curls. She pushed it away to stroke my hair. I surrendered; her little hand entangled itself in mine.

"This morning I walked with Papa and told him I'm going to be an astronomer. Papa said I twinkle, no wonder I want to map stars. I know about double stars, two stars flashing as one."

I swallowed the lump in my throat missing my sister's curiosity toward independence as I withdrew to discover my own. "I love a painter of lights, you dream of exploring its origins."

"Papa said my dreams are as fickle as patches of summer wildflowers."

"He told me the same thing when I was ten."

"But I'm nearly eleven now."

"Ten and a few months, I have forgotten." Sun kissed her hair, her pudgy cheeks thinned.

"I have a fine memory. I remember our last lesson. Don't obsess with beauty or coveting a plethora of luxuries; a kind heart is a treasure worth sharing. What's plethora?"

"Oodles." I kissed her forehead breathing in roses.

"Oodles," she giggled. "Camille . . . will I be an old maid the next time I see you?" She pointed to my hidden satchel behind the door. "I tucked cherry foams into your bag."

I swallowed my tears; they fell regardless. "I cannot hide anything from your sharp eyes."

She lowered her head hiding her tears. "Or ears . . . Mamma argues with Papa, and you don't wear Papa's locket anymore. You're still angry with him."

"Hush, it's hidden in my collar." I revealed the locket reminding me of Papa's love and walked to the window. Monsieur Belrose sat outside playing cards with his wife. "Love makes one do foolish things." I sighed, returning to my sister. "Claude will change Paris with his art and he has asked me to help. For a husband to need his wife so is an honor and promise." Genèvieve's stillness and wide attentive eyes softened me.

"Papa says you'll never come back."

"Nonsense. We quarrel that is all and I away for the summer."

"Tilly invited me to Fontainebleau with her family. They have picnics in the forest, go horseback riding, and paint watercolors in nature as Claude. I'll paint him a picture."

Our eyes twinkled together, and I found a measure of comfort knowing my sister might have her first taste of freedom out from Mamma's rule. "I will insist to Papa you go. You must discover more lies beyond these walls. You must dare to dream."

Genèvieve's wide eyes watered with tears; the flood she dammed to make me proud burst upon my shoulder. I closed my eyes relishing her tiny hands cupped on my back, her soft moan as she squeezed and let me go. "But I don't want to go away to school," she cried, letting me wipe her tears. "I want to stay with Papa. He's ill. I hate the new apartment. You're not there."

"I reside but seven miles away. I need the quiet. Do you understand?"

"I understand more than my sister knows. I have always understood."

We searched the ceiling for shooting stars, a game we played before bedtime. "Camille . . . do I have two papas?" She sat up at my gasp, throwing off her covers. My turn to cry. "I'm lucky," Genèvieve whispered.

It's nothing a child will understand if you make a fuss. Ninette's advice reminded me to stay strong. I still could not face her. "You have grown up without me knowing. How?"

"Mamma whispers words about Monsieur de Pritelly that I'm like him. I don't want to be. I don't wish to know anything about him now, and I don't know what's real, Sister."

"Papa loves you and so do I. That is what is real, what matters now."

"Mamma's not herself. Will she be all right, Camille? I'm frightened."

"I cannot explain our mother but hope deep within love abides. She is broken."

"And breaks you?"

Geneviève appeared older to me now in more ways than her ambitions for life. Her big, brown eyes smiled at me with compassion not found in many adults least of all children. I had no tears for my mother. My sister did not know I cried them for a thousand days before this one. "Now who is too serious," I said, pecking her cheeks. "Words for another day, I promise. You need your rest. I will tell you a story." I tucked her back into the covers.

"Your tale about the magical forest," she cheered, finally acting her age. I scooted my chair closer to her side. "Will I see you, Sister?" she asked, tears returning to her voice.

"I will sneak you away to see Claude's work, and we will picnic in the country."

"And take a boat ride among the water lilies Claude fancies? Promise?"

"A hug and a kiss and I must."

"A hug and a kiss and you must."

My sister's love washed over my sadness. "Past the royal palace," I began, "its flower gardens, and orchards, on the first of May the abbess pays the forest dues—a ham and two bottles of wine, setting them on a stone table the Table du Roi." She tugged my arm wishing to snuggle. I held her, whispering my story as her eyes fell heavy. "The Valley of Fairies grows heather as tall as you. Monstrous oaks tickle the clouds in an ancient forest Tillaie."

Geneviève sunk into her pillow. "You'll return, take me on adventures?"

"Soon. Take care of Papa. He will need you now more than ever." I snuffed out the last candle. Dusk lingered casting pink into the room. A last kiss to her forehead, I inhaled her skin laced with rose powder she snuck from my dresser.

"What of your story," she said, sleepy, "*Two Beautiful Sisters*—how can my path fill with flowers without you now?"

Tears streamed my cheeks as she sank deeper into her pillow, her arm falling out from the covers. I held it and said, "You did not know? The story has yet to end." She slipped her hand back into the covers already sleeping. "The sisters' hearts so entwined neither road, sea, earth, or sky could separate their love and devotion. At the mere thought of the other—it rained flowers, and so it rained and rained."

"Now when I see raindrops, I will see our flowers . . . you."

"Forever choose to see pretty things for the unbecoming. A hug and a kiss and you must."

"A hug and a kiss and I will." I set my letter on her favorite book at the window. Tomorrow Genèvieve would read the story of her sister, my love, and promise to return.

⁓

I walked into the shop no longer waiting for Papa's soft steps to meet me at the bottom of the stairs. My trunks overstuffed with garments, his gifted red bonnet on top. "Oh, Papa." The window display—dusty, empty. The lingering scent of freesia and roses whispered revival, a hope Mamma might renew the lease despite Papa's poor health, my leaving.

I caught Monsieur Belrose spying on me. He shuffled to our front door and away. I hadn't seen him move so fast since the day the artists riled him at his outdoor sale. "Child," he called. I raced outside to his door and embraced my old friend, my tears dripping on his dusty shoulder. "There, there. It always works out in the end," he whispered. "You're a good lass. A bit bewildered. A good lass." He pulled out a red silk handkerchief and with his toothless grin said, "I found them among the trappings of a magic man's trade—blue, yellow, green, yours to remember your old neighbor and this . . ." He handed me a tiny birdcage gilded with leaves. "Watch the magic, a novelty to keep a smile on my Beauty. Who tames this beast now?"

"Oh, Monsieur Belrose." A mechanical canary swiveled and chirped lightening my heart.

"You'll come and visit me?" he asked, walking me back into Papa's shop.

"I shall never forget you. *Merci.*"

He snapped a handkerchief and wiped his nose frowning at our empty shop. "Your papa gives in too soon. We do what we must. I may join him. I've never once thought of retirement."

"Never give up your shop, Monsieur Belrose. I will help you dress your window next spring. It will be the finest in Paris. I will visit again soon."

"Good news, child. Where's your papa? He sees his daughter off, no?"

"I hear his footsteps now."

"Then I shall race to my shop. This ornery shopkeeper needs no joust to rouse my heart." His cheerful wave comforted me. He shuffled to his shop and closed the door.

Papa's shoes stomped down each tread. My heartbeat trembled. I cowered near the empty window display, a forgotten fashion plate crumpled on the floor. The door creaked open; his head down, he ambled to the counter. A few bonnets packed in boxes served as his final order. The dress forms empty of summer fashions, a table of lace and ribbons twisted together from a last-minute sale. I searched the dissolving sunset for my first reply watching Papa out of the corner of my eye light a lamp and our crystal chandelier. "Your mother will claim these fixtures," he mumbled. "I fancied hanging them in your new chamber."

"I offered to run the shop, Papa." He shrugged, pretending he hadn't heard, moving to the farthest corner of the shop rattling unwanted parasols.

I peered outside hoping to catch courage, a wave from Monsieur Belrose. A scrim of nightfall muddled my view announcing Claude's impending arrival. Musty damp wood and tobacco replaced freesia and roses. "The doctor said you must give up your pipe for your heart."

"Not the ailment of my heart tonight." He clutched our shop's bell as a priceless relic.

I wrapped it handing it back for his box. "I hope you allow Genèvieve's trip with Tilly."

"I have already arranged it, against your mother's wishes. I visit my brother in London." His hands trembled as he gently folded a lace shawl passing it to me.

"You have given me enough, Papa—dresses for Claude's painting, the beautiful bonnet with the yellow ribbon, the pink parasol."

"Camille desires more . . . always more." At my sigh, his eyes at last found mine. I squirmed as his child, gnawing my lips, twiddling a silver comb. I placed it on the counter; his hand stroked mine. "Take it," he said, walking back to our front window.

"Will Mamma accompany you to London?" He snapped around at my question, appearing frail, hiding his shaking hand in his pocket. A shorter mustache, his posture hunched as the closure of his shop and family secrets deflated his pride.

"She has plans. Her new apartment will never be our home. It fills with ghosts and gold."

"Papa . . ." I bit my lip to keep from crying, but at the heaviness in my heart, my sobs came. I suffered them alone. I held my locket for courage; he noticed but looked away catching a glimpse of Monsieur Belrose sweeping his stoop. "I am not leaving you, Papa."

"You already have. I lose everything in a matter of months, yet the old man across the street carries on. I envy him." Papa tucked umbrellas into a crate stacked with dress forms.

I plucked them out setting them into their own box. "Sit, Papa, you look weak." He wandered to the window again. The coach arrived, my trunks no longer at the curb.

"I suppose I should take orders from my daughter now." He shook his head watching the driver load the carriage with my things. "Claude's using you, *ma fille*."

I sat on the sofa. "My parents do what they wish to gain happiness, why shouldn't I?"

Papa stood taller, swiping at his mustache as he approached. He lifted the black veil from my face taking off my sad hat. "*Oui*, I can cast no judgment, but I am still your papa." He rummaged in one of his hatboxes, revealed a dainty straw hat with a cluster of violets, and set it on my head. I wanted his smile to last forever; in a second, his scowl returned.

"Will we ever speak of her? Where is Mamma?"

"I'm sorry for your mother, the way she treated you. I blame her for you leaving me. The shame you bring on this house, to your sister." He caught his breath and rested on a chair.

"Shame?" Anger blinded me to his pain, focused on my own.

"You believe a snap of your fingers you'll gain my consent, but Claude asks you not."

"I contribute to this cause that must change Paris."

"Cause? He paints pictures. He does not go to war."

"This is beyond art, Papa, the freedom to create, independence from censorship."

"You know nothing of France if you leave your family so. My daughter spoke to me of a rebellion . . . not against me. Artists turn to beggars. What makes Claude Monet any different?"

In a dark corner, a forgotten garment atop a form: the billowy morning dress Claude fancied last spring, the first time we imagined a painting together—his invitation to model, a path away from my family's chaos and secrets. "Claude wants it more. He holds a new vision."

"And you must see him to it." He rubbed his mustache again, glaring as someone else. "Let him prove his worth." Papa stormed to the counter tossing the tangle of ribbons in the trash.

I saved them. "The whispers about this city entangle me as these ribbons! Papa discards beautiful things and speaks of shame, yet never the shame of my mother."

"Silence."

"I remained silent for ten years." I slammed his ledger on the counter. His flush returned.

"I see now what I avoided these months during your deceit with him. You're a disgrace."

My heart cracked, body shaking. "I kept your secrets as a child. A child! I love. Not as you to an empty, unfaithful wife, never as Mamma selling herself to a stranger, a keeper—"

"Camille!" He snuffed out a candle hiding in the dark.

"*I took your side.* I looked the other way. I hated Mamma for you because I saw her with him. I saw her love him more than my own father and leave me to drown so she could save the child she truly loved. I kept your secrets, now you judge mine." My words exhausted him. He steadied himself and surrendered, stumbling into a chair. "You are not Genèvieve's father, are you? And I am the only one who knows. And you let me shoulder this burden . . . a child."

My shame was endless as his tears dripped to the floor as mine had done moments before, alone. I would never lose the image the rest of my days, wishing for Claude's lighted paintbrush to start anew. "Now you become her," he whispered. He flapped a white handkerchief, his final surrender, and wiped his face. "Your mother taught you well, to use shame as a weapon on your father who . . . loved you, this family, no matter the shadows."

"Papa . . ."

"No." He raised a hand to stop me. "Take what's left . . . the driver has loaded your trunks in front of us," he said, indifferent. "There's nothing left for me to say."

I kneeled beside him tugging his leg for attention. "You will not even fight for me?"

He pushed me away. "I lost you months ago, in secrets, distance, and shaming yourself with this man. I do my best to spare my daughter; you mean nothing to him. My daughter once believed past winning and losing. She strolled . . ." Papa no longer held his tears; my shame at the viewing crushed me more than secrets. ". . . with me in the morning and shared her dreams, my modern young lady of Paris. I tamed my angst to let her sail away from me." His eyes on the floor, he stumbled toward the stairs.

"This is how you wish to part?" I stood paralyzed. "You promised to let me fly."

"Not like this. You'll not speak with your mother."

"She will not see me, and I have nothing to say."

"Neither do I." He passed me a thin box wrapped in lilac paper and quietly shut the door his shoes scuffing up each step. They paused at the top; I waited, no resolutions, no embrace.

A box of parasols blocked the front door, a pile of magazines and fashion plates crowned the top and an envelope of money. My hands trembled as I tore into the paper on the box and opened it—a painted fan, the sailboat on the sea. I sat inside the boat, tossing, a wave swelled to swallow me, and yet, I stayed afloat. In a stream of tears, I watched it sail away in the storm, hoping for the sun to bring my family reconciliation in a rainbow.

I turned the knob to her quiet voice shaky with tears. "Camille," she softly called. In my stubbornness and pain, I turned away from my mother as she had done to me throughout my life. I felt no right or wrong, only the numbness of regret and disgrace. "Camille, please. Daughter."

I opened the front door. Claude stood outside waiting. "Are you ready?" he asked.

"As much as I am able."

On any other night, Claude would have taught me about the colored shadows in the moonlight, but I could only see a gray form drifting across the street as a ghost, standing alone on our old shop's sidewalk, yelling my name. And in a glimmer of light, I saw my sister at the window in candlelight, shining as her own star blowing me kisses.

~

Claude unfurled my fingers from my satchel pulling me close. In our dim, quiet house, I took in his embrace. "I love you will not leave me tonight."

"No intruding artists or sneaking home before Papa," I whispered, watching him carry my trunks, dodging Raphael underfoot.

"I have something to show you." We walked outside into a small garden; the sweet scent of gardenias and roses settled me. Everything haunting us in Paris I gladly left behind. My family's heartache still covered my mind. Whatever life Claude dreamed us to live among counts, actresses, artists, and writers—creditors and bailiffs served as a constant reminder Claude was neither renowned nor lord. I showed Claude my envelope of money from Papa. He counted on sales, Courbet, and Théophile's generosity. I lived under Claude's careless philosophy now: when we need it most, it will arrive. Rebellions proved costly in more ways than imagined.

Claude offered no marriage basket of jewels, lace, or shawls as the gifts I helped nervous grooms buy for brides. With one title on a portrait, *Camille*, he proclaimed his love to Paris without apology and introduced me as his wife. He immortalized me in his painting as the woman in green, a proposal in his own way. Camille in the green dress was neither fantasy nor me, but a mingling of the two. A virtuous woman contemplating a life other than one dictated to her by a French code of conduct and morality. A life of adventure, fantasy, and love, or one arranged by parents and priests. The fictions I disdained regarding my mother, I now embraced about myself. Neither muse nor mistress—wife—in the fantasy I imagined when we first met when Claude Monet kissed me and taught me to see the colors in a drop of light.

My boots brushed the pebbled path. Vibrant shimmers surprised me as we entered the garden: the wonder of tiny colored lamps strewn around tree trunks and flowerbeds as at the Mabille. I inhaled minty, wet grass and clover kissed with the scent of roses. "A fairyland."

"Elise and I created a magical garden for your arrival." Claude beamed. "I found such peace in the task; gardening tempts me to trade my paintbrush for a trowel and packets of seeds."

"Now this house is our home." I searched the grass and tree trunks for the colored shadows Claude fancied painting. "Look how the white roses take on lilac shadows."

"And now she sees," Claude said, walking me to a wooden bench Elise's son constructed. "Watch," Claude said, sitting on it excited. The bench glided back and forth as a rocker for two.

"How clever, I am amazed by another's secret talents."

"And secrets, *ma chéri*? How's Genèvieve?"

I sat beside him stargazing as my sister, thousands of twinkling lights and clusters showing themselves in pictures for our pleasure. "Eager for me to come home." He lifted my hand, spinning his ring on my finger. "Do you regret giving me this ring, Claude?"

"Never. Do you wish to leave?"

"No. I wish to wave a wand and make this disappear for my sister. Mamma will buy her dresses and toys. Papa will love her twice as much and take her to carnivals, the carousel, places that help a child forget. Genèvieve will never forget."

"You must help her."

"Love and tell her every moment it is not her fault. It will still hurt, but she will walk a bit taller and the words will soothe the wound. Claude, if I am to live here, you deserve the whole truth about my family." His loving kiss offered permission and safety to confess. "A six-room apartment," I began, "a bust by Édouard Manet's friend, twenty-two copper pots, a mahogany settee covered in velvet, jewels, a house at Reuil, railroad bonds, and six lights decorated with griffon's feet—the horde my mother traded for disloyalty to her husband and children."

Claude stopped me. "It will not matter. I love you."

"Will you continue loving me? Claude . . . I must share, for me. When I was ten, before the flood in Lyon, I heard a noise in our house and ran to Mamma afraid. Papa was away. I saw two shadows loving in a cast of moonlight. Mamma whispered to a man who was not my father. She was pregnant, she told him. The baby was his, she insisted, and my father must never know."

I closed my eyes stifled by the warm air. "I ran to my room. For the first time, Mamma came to me in the night as I cried. 'A nightmare again, my darling?' she asked, her voice trembled with fear, anger. 'You should not wander in this house past bedtime, and now I suffer your mischief, foolish child.' She wiped my tears. 'It was a dream,' she insisted, her breathing erratic. She tightened the dressing gown around her nude body smelling of sandalwood, lilacs, and lemon blossoms. 'Sleep.' Her soft lips kissed my forehead. 'Would you like some warm milk and a bite of cake, the butter cake you fancy sharing with your father? I baked some.'"

Claude sat still and quiet. "I'm sorry, *ma belle*."

"Mamma kept her voice low and sweet, but every word stung my heart. 'Who is he?' I asked. The blood left her face. 'A friend who looks after me when your father's gone. I'm to have a child. I'm very ill, and so he has come to comfort me. He's a rich man and should I die, he promised to take care of you both.' 'What of Papa?' She only glared. I showed no fear at the prospect of her death. She realized her daughter saw through her many fictions and now knew her devastating secret. And so, we fled Lyon, to rebuild not after the flood but a reputation."

"I need not hear another word," Claude insisted, shifting in his seat uncomfortable now.

I stared ahead and continued, 'You'll say nothing to your father, do you understand?' Mamma asked. Her lover's shadow hovered across the entrance to my room. Unashamed, wearing Papa's robe he smiled and begged my mother to come back to him. I cried and carried the sounds of that night and her secret until it followed us to Paris and ruined me."

"Did your father know?" Claude asked.

"*Oui*. Genèvieve, never. She scarcely understands a stranger, Antoine de Pritelly, is her father, and I will never contemplate he is mine. Genèvieve inherits this man's wealth, Mamma will spoil her, and a girl will forget until she matures into a woman and resents us all for this lie."

"She's not you." Claude closed our distance, wrapping me in his arms.

"I chose Papa and Mamma resented me the rest of my life. If you waited for a reason to leave me, now you have it."

"When did I ever choose shadows and darkness over light?"

"What of Paris? The gossip, circles, and salons?"

"If we must live in the country forever it will serve my eyes and paintbrush better. But, if you think Théophile will accept your withdrawal from his salon theatricals, you're mistaken. The people who matter support us."

"What of your father? I am your secret."

"Those who shout morality the loudest hold none. When the time is right, we will wed. And I will leave—not because I abandon you; it is what I must do to paint."

"And I will be alone?"

"Sometimes. Genèvieve may visit and stay with us, Elise and Marie."

"We can scarcely afford this home, the new furniture, food, and the supplies you need to complete *Women in the Garden*. You need your father's support and approval more than ever. And now you must win, not against the Salon, against him."

"I have listened . . . now I wish to tell you what I see."

"What does Claude Monet, the artist, see?"

He rose and took my hand bringing me into the light, studying my face as if contemplating a new work. "A slender nose and a strong jaw I don't have the skills to paint."

"That is not what I mean." We collapsed onto the bench. I settled my body into his welcoming tranquility.

"A strong flower that grows between the rocks. Gilded streets as slick as glass in the rain. Winding roads, patches of green and maze. In the morning, everything washes blue, at sunrise, blush and pink. Afternoon sun glosses the Seine a sheer of chiffon. A lavender sunset grazes the country roads and golden crusts across the plains. Evening, a cobalt sky and a garden of earth in your eyes. I choose to see beauty in an ugly world. This is my solace."

"Teach me." Our hearts knit together in our loving kiss.

In our small, moonlit garden, we stood against the world.

45.

Sophie

May. One week—Paris!

We imagined France in July, sitting under violet skies painting Provence's lavender and sunflower fields. Mom wished for May when Monet's garden in Giverny awoke in brilliant splendor. The empty boxes on my calendar now scribbled with checkmarks and appointments. The holes of my life where Mom fit in remained, making me wonder if I could board the plane to Paris without her. "I don't understand this," I whispered, tears flooding my eyes.

After twenty-four years, faded childhood memories painfully came into focus, secrets locked within, unspoken truths. Each passing day, I promised myself before I traveled to Paris I would face the shadows of my past in the light of my mother's garden.

It's been twenty-four years, and it still hurts. I thought of my last words to Dr. Arnold, more Brian to me now.

"Because you never faced the truth of it," he said.

"Oh, the whole . . . and the truth shall set you free, right?"

"No, Sophia, you set it free."

I stared at the tattered teal diary hidden in Mom's hope chest. The diary I threw away as an over it teen; the one Mom saved until she had the courage to face it with me; the one I now mustered the will to face alone.

Winter collided with spring in a whimsical tease holding mild days captive with snow in April. Sweet romance and reconnection warmed my last days with Philip, but as winter, my heart clung to the bitter cold of my past reluctant to embrace *us*. "Give yourself time, dear," Annabel reminded me. Mom's affairs kept me busy, so did Annabel, inviting me to her bookstore and tearoom for tastings and opinions on Jacey's Victorian décor. Springtime was teatime, and at Annabel's big reveal, the sign read *Josephine's Tearoom &*

Books in honor of my mother. We traded memories and tears over Annabel's now famous English cream tea, the talk of Grandville.

Philip left for Paris with a tempting offer I join him. It was all I could do to make it a matter-of-fact goodbye. He promised to meet me in Paris once I arrived. With work in London, he "hoped" he could make it; at his words, my heart reminded me it wanted more; it wanted Philip. Joe procrastinated closing Faraway Travel. I stayed home painting in Mom's studio, clearing my head to start fresh. I wasn't kidding myself reopening Mom's gallery and completing my second art exhibition required a massive leap. I had enough to do moving into Mom's house, preparing my home for Annabel, and readying my heart for Paris. I didn't mind everything raining down at once, after all it was spring.

I hadn't stepped near Mom's garden in a month with no motivation to care for it in spring. Maudie promised to help; I made perennial excuses for her not to come. Annabel and I raked leaves and added flowerpots and annuals to the front porch. She missed her country cottage and garden in England. I couldn't imagine my aunt moving to the Midwest permanently. "I am giving it a go," she promised. I was thankful the only close family I had left resided here.

May flowers. The anticipated surprise of my mother's garden in bloom overwhelmed me. Honeysuckle, white cherry blossoms, and her flowering crabapple tree Royal Raindrops. I sat in the garden many mornings painting Royal Raindrops, magenta blooms a burst of pink fireworks center sparkling in a flash of moonlight. A bed of cherry roses and lavender geraniums inter-twined with an antique wheelbarrow—a favorite in Mom's paintings, now in mine.

Mom painted a little girl in a sunhat, me, and now I paint my mom among her flowers. In summer, blackberry hollyhocks hugging a brick pillar, the sweet fragrance of English lavender in beds speckled with pink cosmos. A stone path bordered with ivy ended at a white iron table and chairs: a hideaway where Mom and I escaped the world.

I took in her drifts of color reflecting the color harmonies of her Impressionist paintings: blue into purple, red swaying into pink, a burst of yellow. The tapestry of flowers told the tale of my mother's love story with color, light, and nature. Watermelon poppies and pink peonies accented with blue pansies, purple and mauve tulips sprinkled with white forget-me-knots against a white picket fence; the color arrangements and splendor of my mother's garden held the same magic that made me pause as I stood in front of her paintings.

"You painted with flowers." I sighed. "I forgot how enchanting this was." A hummingbird flitted among the asters. *Just wait until the sunflowers bloom,* she whispered in my thoughts. Before Mom became too weak, she spent the last of her days not painting, but tending her garden ensuring it offered its comfort to her daughter this spring. We weeded, trimmed, and pruned together. Mom planted surprise perennials, tucked bulbs into the earth in the fall and tried to teach her distracted daughter last-minute gardening tips for the seasons.

Her Victorian bench invited me to rest. I sat in our favorite spot facing her landscape of blue, mauve, and purple. The teal diary from my youth trembled in my hand. I opened it to the first page. The flowers brought comfort but the air hung thick with regret and caution as I read young Sophie's words.

Sophie's Diary age 15 (almost 16—two more days!)

Mom says I'm an awesome poet, but this isn't for my poems. Her lover Dr. Arnold asked me to write in this journal. He said try. Sixteen and Mom still doesn't want me to know what a lover is. Honestly, I think I raised my mom rather than the other way around. That's what I think today. Tomorrow I might be hiding in the bathroom again blubbering like an idiot. I guess it's better than a babbling idiot someone slaps back to reality. It's awkward all that heaving and crying. I don't like to cry period, but lately I can't help it.

Mom thinks it's getting worse, my anger, nightmares, low self-esteem. I found a scintilla of self-esteem the other day when I beat Henrietta Mancho at tennis, but everybody beats Henrietta Mancho. A ton's stressing me out, my two-faced best friend Megan, missing my boyfriend, I'm not supposed to have—life's hard right now. Having an MIA dad doesn't help.

Well, diary or whatever you are, I haven't written in you since I was ten. I didn't write much. I wrote the word 'why' a lot, 'I wished Dad didn't leave us', and colored pictures of me in a garden with my dad. Ugly drawings like me stabbing him with a gigantic sunflower, me sitting on a bench with a balloon tear, and the one drawing Mom said explained it all: Dad walking away from a garden waving goodbye, a garden on the other side of the world in France. All code for divorce—that's what I told Mom.

I remember Paris. We lived there when I was little. Dad's from Connecticut but he lives with his lover Pauline in London. Mom says she's my stepmom now. To me, Pauline is just "her" and "she." It's the best I can do because she stole my dad away from us.

Mom says she left Dad. Dad says that's true, but from my perspective they left me. "Part of life between moms and dads," Dad said. I've never seen him again so it's not divorce it's leaving. Mom insisted their marriage "ended" and they "fell out of love" whatever the hell that means. All I know, it sucked and it hurt and it was scary. That's pretty much how that diary went.

A year after my parents split, one day I told Mom when I was ten and sat in Monet's garden, I talked to Claude Monet when I was scared. I didn't say God so that freaked her out. I talked to Monet about the Empress tree and his green wooden benches he had carved from the one at Versailles. His pink house with the green shutters in Giverny resembled his home with his wife Camille in Argenteuil. He created the water lily garden for her and loved watching the water lilies dance. But when I tried to see them that day they were all blurry because I was crying and they just looked like flowers floating in dirty water.

Mom's freak-out shifted in high gear until she realized I probably overheard that stuff from the tour guide. Before I knew it, I was drawing and writing 'why' in a diary for a dude with stringy hippie hair named Dr. Arnold.

Mom's the one who encouraged my imagination. Then she figured it out— my imagination saves me. She's been trying to save me ever since Monet's garden which we dubbed the 'divorce incident'. Mom never knew how unfair it was because I never told her the truth.

When I think about my dad, my chest burns, my heart's sick, and that definitely puts Mom's freak-out in high gear. She says holding in anger isn't healthy, but when I contemplate telling her the truth, my heart thumps out of my chest, I can't breathe, and my stomach burns like I swallowed a hot marshmallow, and it's happening to me all over again—my dad leaving.

Sometimes I see clear images from when I was ten. Sometimes I wish I couldn't see them at all. It sucked, Mom. No amount of words in this diary will ever make me tell you I remember. Sometimes I'm convinced I remember it all, and it's not the version you ever told me.

The most poetic thing I'll write is this: Questions exist in life that aren't supposed to be answered. When we dig around in the weeds, if we're not careful we'll get stuck by one of those thorny, bad ones—especially if we're trying to pull weeds in the dark.

Maybe that's the line Mom will say was worth these few pages, the years, because I'm never writing in this stupid journal again. My pages are all warped and wet with tears, and this hurts too much thinking about a dad who never wanted me.

Who never said he was sorry.

I quickly shut the journal. At the last words of wisdom from my fifteen-year-old self, the clear memory of that day played in front of me as I sat breathing in my mother's garden.

46.

Camille

~

April 1867

A year away from Paris . . . time to go home. Home, the idea to Claude appeared as fluid as the paint on his brush. "I offer you no home but a traveler's life—of adventure."

"I understand," I said, clipping his heels. I found purpose modeling for his *Women in the Garden*, learning how to make a home with Claude. In autumn, we left our country cottage for the Normandy coast and its blue expanse of the Seine clear as a sheet of glass. The fishing village, Honfleur, was the town of Claude's youth and mentor, the artist, Eugène Boudin. Claude traded the Fontainebleau Forest for a lighthouse, the boulevards of Paris for shaded dirt roads and farmhouses, our garden for the sea, and fashionable figures for sailboats and steamers. I posed when required, warmed his bed, and prepared meals with Rose, a cook at Mère Toutain's, the one inn welcoming Claude's celebrity, accepting payment by picture.

"Fame is but an exhibition away," Claude promised. "We'll soon establish ourselves."

"Where?" I asked, guilty he made us flee our last landlord leaving unwanted canvases to settle a debt. "I cannot bear the sea. I miss the trees, our garden, Paris."

"How about a villa in Nice as Madeleine," he joked. "A château in Fontainebleau?"

"A pink house in the country, green shutters, a garden, my white iron table and chairs."

"And a bowl of fresh strawberries?"

"And now you see," I snickered.

"Green shutters," he promised. "And a garden . . ."

"Close to Paris so I may visit my sister."

When I threatened to leave when Claude left me, we imagined not paintings but a life together, securing my stay, another month on our own. On nights when Claude traded his sketchbook for a newspaper, the only sounds in the room: the shuffling of his paper, a crackling fire, and my whispers of someday. But as Claude moved closer to his dream, mine drifted away.

Our first flight was an adventure. We landed among the rich and noble along the beach resorts, casino, and racetrack of Trouville, on to the sand dunes and highlife in Deauville, and an invitation to dinner with Courbet at the villa of a count. Paupers dressed as a prince and princess.

The Parisian appetite to appear rich to obtain riches, Papa warned in my thoughts. Madame Rolina was the first of many of Claude's casualties. His hubris inspired him to create enormous works for the Salon again, resulting in spending beyond his means, leaving a wake of debt in each town we stayed. Adventure, what Claude romanticized as flight from bailiffs, promises to repay debts or appease a creditor with a portrait. Claude's charm and paintings helped him avoid bailiffs, other times innkeepers threw us out into the cold. Now, I was a part of this game, left behind to soften innkeepers, bakers, butchers, Courbet, and Théophile's generosity until I became ill. My only hope to recover my dignity and health was my doctor's order to return to Paris to the safety of my family forgoing our vagabond existence.

I sat in the lobby searching out the window, waiting for her carriage to arrive, for her embroidered boots to touch the pavement, her slim form adorned in the finest spring fashion. *Prussian blue*, I imagined. I wandered outside savoring a breath of cherry blossoms and the cool breeze mingled with the Seine, freshly baked bread, and sweet tobacco. I missed Paris. Joy stirred my heart at the choice to abandon the seaport town for the full tide of life ripping down the Paris boulevards.

I drifted back into the lobby catching myself scuffing my heels across the marble floor, absorbing side-glances from the proprietor and a gathering of ladies. I sat on a sofa in a quiet corner next to the window, feeling out of place missing my once modern toilette, wishing I wore a touch of elegance as a new bonnet. I opened my painted fan; the sailboat no longer enticed me. I quickly closed it, unwilling to return to the violent waves and undulating sea.

A young woman holding hands with a little girl skipped past. I missed buying sherbet for my sister, whispers in Elise's flower shop, the Batignolles patisserie where Papa bought our birthday cakes, the chocolaterie where Mamma spoiled us at Easter, and the splendor of spring fashions at the new department stores twittered in Marie's letters. In a year, Paris had changed, so did I, and not a change I ever imagined. *Love was supposed to be enough*, I told Elise during our morning reunion. *But it is hard to love alone.*

Vibrant silks and satins floated in the tearoom at a new café on the rue de la Paix, Paris. I wore an ill-fitting dress in cream with sage embroidery. *A loose jacket and skirt, all the rage*, Elise said presenting it to me, an offering I imagined from Papa. At their whispers waiting alone, I hid myself under my best shawl, the elegant lace wrap Papa slipped to me the day I left Paris. I grew weaker, my mind cloudy, but I did my utmost fixing my hair high in a twist topped with curls and a sprig of pansies wearing the pearl drop earrings Courbet gave me last year. Thoughts of Gustave made me smile; soon embracing him at his World's Fair pavilion prompted courage.

"Lured by the sight of the jetty." At her cackle, passing ladies chattered greetings to my mother, a regular at this exclusive tea room. "Camille, I pray Claude bores with painting old seaport towns and seaweed-soaked rocks so I may enjoy more teas with my daughter."

"Mamma." She offered a dainty hug and pulled us apart with an inspecting eye. A wave of her hand and a young woman escorted us outside to a garden table under red awnings. For the first time in a long time, we traded smiles. *Time softened her.*

"I almost chose the Café Foy at the Palais Royal," she said, eyeing the guests.

"This place is fine Mamma, but I am not properly dressed." I must have missed when she ordered as steaming cups of tea and iced cakes instantly appeared.

"You're forever lovely. Straw hats with buttercups are the rage. Do I wear it well?" Mamma asked, adorned in a fetching silver gown trimmed with bands of red ribbon. She raised a finger to her lips, signaling to her child to stop biting. I pressed my lips together embarrassed.

"I have not followed fashion as of late." She noticed my teacup trembling as I sipped.

"Genèvieve told us you wrote of your dinner with the Count de Choiseul, where his servants wore silver-buckled pumps serving the finest fare on gilt porcelain."

"An extravagant affair . . . a year ago."

"Madame Prost's sells rich toilettes on the rue Lafayette. We'll visit to refresh yours."

Mamma did not often turn quiet as she darted her eyes to me and away. I gave her a moment, admiring the garden. "I am not novel today, Mamma?"

"Look at my daughter. In one year, you grow older, but you lose the sheen to your raven hair, your skin is pink, eyes tired, and your toilette has not the sparkle of Paris. A lesson you taught Genèvieve, no? The world may view French fashions in magazines and papers, but one must come to Paris to see how we wear them."

"I have lost many things."

Mamma took my hand as her child, her familiarity softened my heart, but for a moment. In my state, I longed to trust her. "And so, has my daughter come to her senses? Life on the run with an artist is not as enchanting as the storybooks?"

"We have much to discuss."

"*Bien*, I hoped you would enjoy this new garden, tea on the terrace under the awnings."

"To see and be seen?"

"I'm not one to disappear. Your father knew this." She spit the words as crumbs and greeted a visiting friend. I waved my fan cooling my flush, spying the lonely boat sailing. "I wondered what happened to that fan," she said. "Your father knew you fancied it dreading the day your heart would drift away from his as the boat on the sea."

"I hope Papa is well, busy with new interests. Geneviève wrote he crafts toy boats."

Mamma stared into her teacup, nibbling her cake. "My daughter is beautiful." She chuckled at herself, wiping icing off her lips. "You have put on weight. *Bien*. Geneviève stuffs herself with cake, and yet the doctor claims she's too thin, a weak heart as your papa."

"What's wrong with my sister?"

My mother never wore her hair down in public; she looked younger, flipping it across her shoulder. "We all suffer from weak stomachs, a trait from my mother."

"I had hoped to see Geneviève . . . and Papa."

"Didn't you receive my letter, child?" Mamma asked, offering me a cake. "They visit your uncle in London, but it was good of you to make amends with your father last Christmas."

My heart sunk. I hadn't come for tea, but answers and support. "I had hoped to see him."

"You will in time. What's this rush?" She waved to a woman clutching the arm of a young man, and for an instant the woman's red tresses made me believe it was Camellia, the courtesan in red from the Mabille. "Where's Claude?" she asked, eyeing the woman's jewels.

Quiet, I stared at the tower of treats that failed to entice my appetite. "Perhaps the Café du Grand Balcon engrossed in besting his comrades in a game of billiards. They await news from the Salon." I lied. It came easy now. I knew not if Claude arrived in Paris. I hadn't seen him in a month. He hid away in Le Havre. Where once again, silence was an answer I could not bear, and alone in Honfleur was not a remedy I desired. I needed Paris. "We suffered this winter, Mamma. I could hardly fault Claude for not compre-hending how hard it was for me, surrounded by water, living in an archaic fishing village, abandoned while he explored shores and snow scenes."

"You belong in Paris, not among fishermen and a sea of black dresses at the market. Trouville was lovely, no?" With each idle subject, my mother's confidence lost.

"Claude fancies the sun and is intolerable when it rains. In Honfleur, it rains when it desires in the middle of the afternoon. His moods you see . . . I took ill and spoke about coming home. Odd how he needs me and does not; sometimes I believe he is in love with being alone."

"I warned you," she said coldly. Her indifference no surprise, for it hovered on the surface no matter our tranquil setting or the softness in her voice. "You have Geneviève's disagreeable stomach and are prone to fevers and a cough when you get too much air. And I have come to learn something about you, *ma fille* . . . the declaration you once made to me . . ." She reached her hand across the table, her soft warmth tingled my skin.

I slid my hand away for a sip of tea to keep my tears at bay in this garden. *A strong flower who grows between the rocks*, Claude whispered in my thoughts. How I missed him. How everything had changed in no way imaginable. "That I did not need a man to give me purpose."

"Forward thinking—this issue of women's rights I learned is essential, yet one must understand a lonely path. It's disheartening knowing few hold bravery to clear the path for many. It doesn't seem fair, child. Your health suffers because you have nothing of your own. I know."

"What do you know, Mamma?"

She searched the crowd self-conscious. I didn't have to ask her questions; she knew the answers I desired the moment she saw me. She raised a hand; a waiter hustled to our table, refilling our cups with tea; the handsome young man kept winking at Mamma. She giggled him away, offering me a cake. "Cherry icing," she said, giddy as my sister. I sipped my tea, watching her gain courage. A swirl of yellow and red skirts fluttered at a nearby table; they rose and waved. Mamma waited from them to leave, for us to sit alone.

"A painted swallow soars on the Café Foy's ceiling," she whispered, her voice trembling. "My father told me stories of its origin, how his artist friend painted it impromptu to hide a stain. A jeweler sold trinkets under it, gold swallows on rings, brooches, necklaces, even china. After a visit to this café with your father, he pondered buying you a necklace with a flying gold swallow, a ruby for its eye, as everyone visiting our dress shop took to calling you little bird."

"A pet name my friends use, too," I said, scooting my chair closer.

"He decided on the locket you clutch, hiding it for months, whispering every night how he couldn't wait to see your eyes shine when you opened the package on your eighteenth birthday. Loved . . . I've been jealous of so much I missed treasuring his . . . love."

"Tell me . . . please, Mamma."

$\sim$

"A bitter winter never seen before in Lyon," Mamma began. "Where icy winds blew, my daughter saw sugary snowdrifts and piped icing frosting the branches. No wonder you fell in love with Claude; you two see as no one else. What love does, child, and does not. It gives you sight and blinds you all the same."

We lingered in the tea garden until the crowd vanished; the women she knew no longer waved their hats or bothered. "On such a frozen night I took ill," she said quietly. "Antoine de Pritelly found me on the street. I slipped on the ice, but it wasn't the fall; his palm touched my forehead discerning a fever, and so with you and your papa away, this kind monsieur brought me into his home. His doctor cared for me and for three days, Antoine and I shared all. A lie I told myself. I had fallen and taken ill, but in prior months I had known Antoine for he noticed me."

"Papa did not?"

"I was a child. Your papa was twenty-two years older; I was terrified. My mother, a widow, timid in business and finance swindled out of most of my father's wealth—a distant mother incapable of managing a home or raising a daughter."

"Why you and Papa had no contract?"

"I gave him myself and for nine years I was safe. We had you, a life in Lyon, but . . ."

"You wanted more."

"I wanted the choice that was taken from me. I wanted my father, not a man to marry." Mamma saw the waiter coming out of the corner of her eye and raised her hand dismissing him. I smiled at him; he nodded. I caught him whisper and giggle with a young maid behind the trees.

"And this man stole my mother's soul."

"Don't delight in shaming me, Camille, for perhaps one day you will ache for compassion and understanding at love's enticement, cruelty."

"That day has come. Why Monsieur de Pritelly now? Why were we never enough?"

Her eyes flitted about the garden searching for the distraction of the young waiter; she looked at me her eyes pooling with tears. "I sold my soul to Paris the moment my foot stepped on its soil. I loved your father, a child's ideal of love, for I was a child when we married. My father died leaving a thirteen-year-old girl and widow, his reputation and property, his alone. My mother turned mad with worry caring for me, for I was my father's treasure, as you are to your papa. Perhaps I'm odd, unfit, for most of my life it felt as if I was not made for motherhood."

"You loved this man all these years?"

"Many in life fall in love with the wrong people, mistaking lust for love, but I loved him. When your papa moved us to Paris, that was the end of it, and I was a grown woman lost. Something happened after I had Genèvieve, an ache, pain, emptiness nothing could fill. Antoine found me again in Paris, and the ruse I played attempted to fill a cavern inside me."

"In Lyon, remember the countryside outside our home, Mamma? At night, I would sneak out the back door and roam the meadow under the stars as a fairy. When the fireflies flashed above black summer fields, I flew with them adding a magic glow to wilted wildflowers. I added starlight to treetops and mint to the grassy air. And when I returned, Papa would catch me with a blanket as his butterfly net, dry my toes and tuck me into bed. I never waited for goodnight tales from you. I set myself off on the journey to live in one of my own."

"In time, perhaps . . . I might find your forgiveness."

"When Genèvieve was born the earth shattered—Papa's earth. He quaked as a man broken to his soul. I hated you, Mamma, because you took Lyon away from my happy papa and me and ended my fairy dreams. He brought us to Paris, and when he opened his shop, he let his daughter dance in a different field of flowers among bluebell gowns and sunflower bonnets, a field of green silk, daisy white gloves, and violet parasols. You even took that away from him."

"And what of your father? No husband is innocent in these affairs."

"The mantra of Paris . . . is it impossible to love one? I never believed so."

"And yet, you hardly speak of Claude today. This love steals everything from you without your permission."

"No. You have what you choose. I learned how to live without your love, but now I am sick without Papa's."

"I'm to blame for my daughter living on her own?"

"You had a family . . . but you chose to live for yourself."

"I will not sit here explaining away my life, for now I manage to hold on, as your father, in his words, finds a 'bit of happiness' I stole from him. He tires of it . . . her."

"Elise? Yours is not a marriage but a poorly acted tragedy."

"My daughter who lives with a man unwed lectures her mother on morality, marriage?" Her laugh was odd, another ruse to hide her tears. "We won't divorce—perhaps when your sister is older. Now I start over."

"How many times will this family start over, Mamma?"

"Such disdain . . . I thought you reaching out—why did you call on me?"

"I am pregnant."

At my confession, Claude occupied my thoughts. Mamma gasped and left the table. "I trade tea for iced wine. One moment," she said, fumbling with her purse, nearly spilling her tea.

I watched her skirt ruffle the flowers as she marched down the path. "Mamma?"

"A moment." She rushed away, leaving me to recall my last argument with Claude.

"You see like no other, yet in this you are blind. Give away my child? Deposit a baby at the foundling hospital as if payment to one of your creditors. Whatever you presumed as your good lass; you do not know the Camille you paint, the Camille you claimed you loved."

"Do you not understand our station?" Claude asked, indignant.

"I understood I was beguiled to believe you could take care of me and a child when you care not for yourself. You are no lord, Claude, and yet you ruin our friendships with demands and debts. A wonder we can show ourselves in Paris."

"I don't take advantage. They accept a painting for services, sometimes insisting two, and I do the work. It is the artist's way in France."

"It is your way . . . as is leaving."

"You should have married Frédéric."

"Will you recognize your child? Your hesitation tells me all I need to know about Claude Monet, the artist. What of man, husband, father?"

"Please, I have nothing to offer without my family's support."

"Yet you begged me to leave mine behind. In eight months, I will be of age to marry."

"There is a path many take to offer a child a fine home, no questions, no names."

"No, Claude, a lifetime of questions and names. I possess a modest dowry.

Twelve thousand francs and I will continue to borrow against it until Papa learns this news."

"Perhaps you should return to Paris."

I held my breath. The man I loved was no man. "You will fight for your paintings, but not for your wife and child?

"You are not my wife."

A rush of water over a wet canvas and our imagined portrait of life, lost.

"He will not bend for anyone," I imagined Renoir's whisper, his warnings at the Mabille during a spin. Was I now the woman in red? Yet, neglected, used, tossed aside.

"It's not a matter of thoughtlessness," Claude said, returning in the evening to our little room facing a frozen sea. "What life can our child have?"

"Rather, what life will Claude Monet have with a child?"

"Even if your father wanted to help you, he cannot. He would not bring this shame upon his household, nor would your ill-willed mother."

"The shame falling on us is by you and you alone. You seduced me, telling all I am your wife. I stayed, suffered your distance, carelessness, and moods."

"I warned you many times I often believe I am better off alone."

"I will do this on my own and gain my family's support. They will not abandon me."

"My father and aunt will disinherit me! I could leave you, live without want in Le Havre, but I'm here. I hold no skill other than my art. Success is near. The patrons will come."

"You have none. You are not Courbet or Manet. This fame you seek steals your soul, us."

"Camille?"

"Camille! You could have named her anyone. Now you will not have me. Your inability to provide honorable action in haste speaks clearly. You want me to believe giving up our child is our only remedy because it suits you. It does not me. And so Claude Monet does not win."

"Child," Mamma whispered, her hand fell on my back in a soft caress.

I closed my eyes to erase the memory of Claude's harshness and rejection, but the vibrant image of anger and indifference remained. "Will you help me?"

I was thankful the garden's elegance was ours alone. After confessions,

Mamma slipped us away into her carriage wiping my tears as her little girl. "Child." I heard the tears in her voice; she let them fall, wiping again at mine before hers.

"But you could . . . you could be a mother to me now."

Tucked away in the privacy of her carriage, it drove on I knew not where. "You must know, your father will not be so tolerable this time . . . but I would not be your mother if I didn't help my child now. I will do what I can."

"*Merci, Maman.*"

She tucked me under her arm, her little bird under the safety of her wings. I had nothing now without Claude, but a vision of a mother alone with her child, the hope of Claude's promised commitment, the prayer of my mother's. "A treasured memory you give to me today," Mamma whispered. "Your softness . . . you needing me." I sighed, sitting tall for her, clutching the child inside me. "You are so small. I hardly noticed until you would not eat those sweets," she chuckled. I absorbed her joy as she smoothed her hand over my belly.

"I wish I understood more as a child . . . understood that you loved me."

"I wish to right many wrongs. I pray you are a finer mother than I."

"What I fear most."

"If that is true, perhaps you should ponder Claude's remedy."

"Give away my child?"

"Let us not dwell in darkness today. Think of good things. You come home and gain your strength and we'll attend the World's Fair together . . . if you are able."

"I have people to visit, Mamma. I'm strong enough . . . for now."

"I understand. But you will stay with me until your father comes home."

"What will he do?"

"I don't know, child. It will crush him to be certain. I do not know." She touched the locket around my neck. "But you wear his promise."

"Loved," I whispered.

47.

Camille

"Madeleine lost her voice and moves to Nice to remain utterly quiet," Marie said. "Imagine, silent for six months writing everything on a pad of paper."

"Not one word?" I welcomed a lively carriage ride with Marie to the World's Fair to meet her Albert, while I visited Courbet. Frédéric wrote of his arrival in Paris and news of the Salon. I decided to visit Courbet first to see the wonder of his solo exhibition and garner news of Claude. "You leave me for a four-year engagement in Italy—and you dyed your hair." Marie fluttered her lashes, grinning, fluffing her coppery curls. "Divine."

"Darling, you move more than a traveling circus. Now you have a baby."

"Is my life a circus now, Marie? My child will have an aunt who is eleven." We giggled into the other, not as times past; awkward silence fell between us. She squeezed my hand.

Her eyes glistened. "I don't recall us ever planning that for our lives." Marie's musical laugh, usually contagious, not today. Claude's indecision weighed on my heart, the Salon's verdict, my child's uncertain future. "What will you do if Claude doesn't return?"

"Nowhere to hide in a carriage." I stretched to look out the window at the parade of Parisians flocking to the fair. "He will do what is right," I said to myself.

"You scarcely show," Marie whispered. "A periwinkle gown, oversized jacket—ruffled black buttons, *magnifique*. Our fashions are the rage, but I wear chocolate. Oh, I hear people at the fair wait in line an hour to savor the creations of a bonbon maker."

I sighed at her effort and distraction. "My dress . . . Mamma's gift. Appearances."

"She will not let you live at home?"

"Home . . . their new apartment has never been my home. Mamma's turned leaf drifts in the wind of gossip. I do not blame her. She finally redeems her standing among her friends."

"Her new money helps with that," Marie said, tugging off her gloves.

"It is not proper for my sister. Papa has yet to accept me." I held my tears in a breath.

"Would your parents really abandon you? You'll need many things and your health . . ."

"It is not their scandal; it is mine."

"A father's rejection is a cruel thing, for we have all made mistakes."

"My child will never be that to me, Marie, a mistake."

"*Oui, mon amie*," she said softly. "Augustine gave us tickets. Albert obsesses about a hot air balloon that flies over Paris. I won't ride. Touaillon's bakery, a hummingbird palace, a water lily pond encased in glass, the paintings all tragic. We'll be lost for hours. Will you manage?"

The Salon was not the attraction this year; the World's Fair arrived in Paris. Industries competed for medals under an iron and glass edifice. Visitors roamed world courts and gardens to experience the best in food, art, fashion, furniture, and new inventions. "I promised Frédéric a visit at his studio. I look forward to our evening at Augustine's so I may thank her in person."

"She purchased a store for you and the baby—the sweetest bassinet. Don't tell her I revealed her surprise. Frédéric? Scandalously delicious. Invite him to Augustine's tonight."

"Incorrigible." She helped me out of the carriage. "I welcome this distraction."

"Albert waits in the park, forever waiting. The gardens are the best bit." She skipped away from me as if for the last time. "You look pale. You wish to brave that crowd?" she called.

"Go, before Albert storms this hedge." My cough did not convince her.

Marie sauntered back examining my quiet manner. "Are you certain I should leave you?"

"What will you do?" I asked. "I thought you and Albert would marry."

"Marriage is not the dream of all women. He will visit me in Italy. I will send him away."

"Forever waiting—there I go melancholy in the midst of your cheer."

"I love you, Camille. I command a shower of rose petals and gold dust fall for joy."

"That is not reality, is it?" A mother struggled gathering her four children. Her son raced ahead, his father there to catch him. "I am faced with the harshness of it now."

"Darling, since when did we sign up for the business of reality? I'm an actress and Camille Doncieux is the most famous model in Paris. It *shall* be as we imagine, that is our gift."

"*Merci*, dear friend." I lingered in her embrace breathing in the hope she exuded.

"Look, *mon amie*—a pink cloud in a blue sky your Claude paints as we speak thinking of you." Marie flew into Albert as magnets inclined to the force, stuck together in a loving embrace.

∼

"Gold medals, fine art, progress, and the Exposition's main attraction: a Chinese cook and British sandwiches and beer. I brought you lunch." I waved the delights under Courbet's nose; he closed his eyes breathing in my wrist instead.

"By your soft steps and the mist of rose water and orange blossoms sweetening my pavilion, Camille arrives," he sang. "Glad for it—my hundred and thirty-two paintings stink."

"Nonsense. I detect bergamot and lavender. I am honored, visiting before you open."

"A star, should you let me paint your portrait. I compete with the Salon and win, lass, spending fifty thousand francs on my exhibition. I triumph over the moderns and the ancients!"

"You triumph guzzling mugs of ale." Courbet swayed and staggered trying to focus.

"I'm exhausted," he grunted, "organizing my show—do I not deserve a day of boasting?"

"Gustave Courbet shames the art world. You should crow, you old genius."

"I wish to never grow old in your eyes." Despite our game, Courbet's tenderness revealed he knew. He lifted my hand kissing it. I fell into him with my embrace. "There, there, child."

"A friend told me imagination is our gift, and so we are forever young."

"And handsome." He tousled his mop of black hair, eyes beaming. "Claude reveals your troubles. I'll do what I can. Living in the country saves one from the drinking-shops in Paris."

"Saves you. Gustave, I did not come here for—"

"Hush, child. None of us will judge. For anyone I know who dares, has secret children scattered about like fallen leaves. *Oui*, distasteful, horrendous. Do what is fitting for the child. But come, let me show you my paintings before my fellows arrive."

"The entirety of one's social status hinges on a whisper. I should leave."

"Balderdash! We don't fear whispers in our circle. We embrace them."

"Whispers sell paintings?"

"We don't paint whispers, damn it. One cannot make a living painting quietly."

"I have missed your crass humor."

"Crass? I'm damn funny." He swigged his beer, wiping the foam off his lip, studying me. "You visit Courbet for unpleasant news. The jury slams the Salon door on all who take the new road. Claude, Bazille, Renoir, Sisley, Pissarro, and Manet—refused. Monet suffers most. They claim he assaults the dignity of French art with his paintings." He crumpled the Salon's flyer.

"I do not understand." I swallowed my tears. "*Women in the Garden* is his masterpiece. Singular vision, you said. His effect of light out-of-doors would frenzy the public to his work."

"Child," he sighed, unmoved at the news. "Claude's touch is too hurried and palette too bright. The comte de Nieuwerkerke ensured himself the painting was rejected."

"Why should the head of the committee abuse his influence? Claude makes progress."

Courbet ushered me to a sofa. "Why they reject him. Monet catches their gaze as the spark setting ablaze their guarded tradition. They will not relinquish power for Claude Monet."

"Claude paints from his heart and they hate him for it."

"They said, 'Too many men think of marching into the Salon on this detestable path. We safeguard art.'" He labored to fix a carpet, peeking at me. "The artists of Paris that are of value signed a petition requesting an exhibition of the refused art. It fails, but Claude must not yield."

I toured his gallery, perusing his works—realism in canvas and advice. "I heard whispers Frédéric planed their own exhibition. I never thought Claude—they cannot raise the funds."

"Émile Zola, an important critic, promises his public praise of *Women in the Garden*."

"I cannot escape this Zola," I said. "He pries for scandals. No doubt we fill his stories."

Courbet devoured a sandwich, offering me half. I waved him off at the sight, admiring his painting of a woman and trellis of flowers. "Zola is Zola but he praises Claude's work: 'daring effects, passion to represent his era not the past.' The jury's contempt raises Claude in the esteem of his colleagues and notoriety with the public. Encourage him—in time all will see."

"Who will ensure Claude sees, Master Courbet?"

He replaced my tears with kisses. "In one's defeat, one must patiently strive on."

"I do not care about the Salon's refusals. Claude rejects me and his child for Le Havre."

"Leaving, loving, longing. He will return and he will leave, *ma chéri*. The lad has the most discipline in art I have ever witnessed . . . and none in life and money. An artist travels to see. Claude's eyes seek greater subjects beyond imitation. In time, you will make your home."

"I pray you are right. You are generous in friendship and support."

"Ensure Claude doesn't waste it. I fancy you—you stand up to Monet in life, but not in love. An upside-down tale, my Juliet, I wish not to watch the tragic ending."

I eyed the exit. Courbet agreed, taking my arm, walking me to the door. "I left Paris in scorn and so I leave again," I said. "Have you heard from him?"

Courbet stopped to straighten another painting, sighing. "His father demands he relinquish his wicked ways, but makes no judgment as to Claude leaving you." Courbet arranged a vase of flowers handing me a peony. "Claude confessed you to his father, unheard of, assuring you a sweet child, but Claude's father offers no consent for the marriage." Courbet plopped on his armchair readying his pipe. I took the match from his hand lighting it for him.

"Sweet child," I said. "Gustave . . ." I searched his eyes; a puff of smoke hid them. "Claude asked his father for consent?"

He lowered his head, snickering to himself. I could not be angry, for this was his unruly way. "Your sorrow breaks me down. No doubt—revealing such a situation to his father . . . *oui*, Claude will recognize his child. His conscious would not contemplate otherwise."

"Claude's father refuses to meet me. I am Olympia."

Courbet howled chasing away my sorrow. "What can his father say caring for his own illegitimate child? Ignorant, irate, irony. Bazille intercedes on your behalf. No more tears. Sit on old Courbet's stool and pose. I'll sketch your portrait, making you dwell on happier days while I spew the gossip of the cads who scorn you now. My tales would sell greater than Zola's."

"If you write novels; I shall paint."

"Bah." He blew his lips making me laugh. "Now she grins. Give me the bashful look you do for Renoir so I might paint you in amour not weeping."

I tucked my shoulders back, but I hadn't the will to pose. I sat quietly for a time regardless, and at Courbet's howl at his own scandalous tale, my baby kicked, reminding me my weeping will soon turn to joy.

≈

Dearest Camille,

I return to Paris and find my friends in a sorry state. Beauty, you are the only one who tames the Beast. Claude makes foolish threats, too much at stake for him now. I'll discuss my plan to settle your hearts. Come to my new studio at 22 rue Godot-de-Mauroy forthwith.

Your friend, Frédéric

I walked into his intimate studio. Frédéric held a wooden boat up to the light trying to fix a broken sail. "I am sorry to say Geneviève trades toy boats for bouncing rabbits."

"I've been swindled." He showed the boat's crushed mast; its sail drifted to the floor.

Uneasy, I stood by the door until he took my hand and honored me with his bow. I traded a curtsy for my hug. "You will not break me," I said, squeezing him tight.

"I fancied a twirl." His eyes took me in, catching himself he rushed back to his shipwrecked boat. "Did you know at the Mabille instead of dancing one can view boxing now?"

"Boxing?"

"Renoir holds tickets for an exhibition with Roberts, Pons, and Jacob."

"And I have no idea what that means."

"Neither do I." He laughed, his eyes crinkling in a smile and in a blink to concern. He removed his dusty jacket. I noticed the pile of ashes by the fireplace and the roses on the table. "Theater Lyrique plays *Romeo and Juliet*. The marriage ceremony in the friar's cell is beautiful."

I looked away at the awkward reference, admiring Renoir's painting. "Cinders on your cheek—perhaps, *Cinderella* at the Chatelet?" Our laughter lightened the air. I wiped the soot off his face. Frédéric held onto my hand offering his soft kiss in greeting. "I needed you to welcome me so," I said. "I visited Courbet who readies his exhibition. Claude hides in Le Havre."

"A cruel blow—the Salon rejects us not for poor paintings, rather their insistence it is their duty to squelch our progress. Claude's *Women in the Garden* would have won as *Camille*. "

"A success we counted on. France holds a World's Fair on progress. How is there any progress in Paris? But ah, chocolate appears the season's color— and I run out of small talk."

Frédéric forced a grin offering me a plate of bonbons. I declined amused he stuffed one into his mouth, scrunching his face at the sweet. "A sea of chocolate rippled into my aunt's salon last night at my arrival. I imagined you floating to my chair in yellow outshining them all."

"Red, darling," I snickered, unable to settle my nerves. "I noticed at the fair women obsess with little gold horseshoes around their necks and dangling at their ears."

"Then you will not like my gifts." He waved a box in the air, embarrassed.

"I did not say that." I snatched it.

"Crinoline, no more . . . Paris catches up with our queen."

My joy melted. I looked down at the floor spotting a blue bonnet and a pair of gloves. "Flattery in papers . . . no longer—your queen of Paris has fallen. Please stop looking at me so."

He walked closer taking my hands. "I invited you here so I may help."

I slid away from Frédéric's affection lost in the construction of a broken wooden boat. "Claude claims he is going blind from painting outdoors. Do you believe him?"

"I have no kind words for him now but sympathy for I know you both to be fine."

"The doctor said he may never paint outside again if his condition does not improve."

"No doubt Claude's *condition* will improve with less wine and staring at the blasted sun. Courbet teaches Claude to play a ruse with the public to sell paintings, not with his friends—you. Why do I continue spinning in his madness?"

"Because you all need Claude Monet to succeed."

We walked to an easel, his unfinished canvas of a woman playing the piano, erased with a thin wash of white. "Renoir paints his portraits, I placate my father with a family scene on the terrace, and Monet paints for no one. He is the revolutionary who leads our movement."

"This obsession within him is something we will never understand."

"He's ashamed, Camille, torn apart. I convinced him to walk an honorable path."

I threw my shawl over his green armchair. "Your air makes me angry not your charity."

He retrieved it, bundling me back underneath it. "It's not charity. I care for you both." Frédéric led me to the sofa. My knees buckled; he steadied my steps.

"I am so tired, Frédéric, and have no more tears."

He left and swiftly returned, handing me a glass of water and plate of grapes. Silent, he walked to his desk retrieving a card from the drawer. "I employed Ernest Cabadé, a doctor friend to care for you and deliver the baby." He tucked the card inside my palm.

"The strapping, quiet fellow fond of sonnets? I bested him at Balzac."

"*Oui.* You can trust him. Lucky, he fancies Claude's work."

I enjoyed the sweet grapes savoring more Frédéric's care and attention.

"*Merci.*" I drifted at his words. "Mamma worries about the baby; I must stay bedridden this summer. I disappoint you."

"The apartment is small, two blocks from your family." He fussed with the boat again. "The doctor will do as you wish. A good family can give the baby a fine life," he said coldly.

"Frédéric." I stormed to him tearing the toy from his hands. Tears burned my eyes. He stood defiant. "Loving Claude, I chose this path. I will not tread a step on that road."

He wiggled the boat from my hands and set it on his windowsill, broken, used. "I will help you move but I soon leave Paris on holiday for Montpellier."

"Stop this." A chill came over me; sweat drenched my body. "I am not desperate as your conscious requires a dose of a good deed." I caught my breath, struggling back to the sofa, my hand trembling as I sipped my water my other hand steadying it. Frédéric sat beside me; his eyes searched mine. He pressed a cool towel to my forehead calming me until my breathing stilled.

"I wanted to take care of you," he whispered, his lips against my cheek. I turned away.

"Théophile hires a nurse." My hand slipped from his. "He sees to my health, my pride."

"I don't mean to shame you, *mon amie*. I would never."

"Strange . . . to have a father who would do anything to keep me safe, silent now refusing to see me, and a mother who abused my love, offer compassion now. She does not abandon me."

"I have only known a loving family," he said, taking my hand. "I tried to save you."

"This is why you purchased Claude's *Women in the Garden*?" I asked in a whisper. "Twenty-five hundred francs, a great sum for a painting."

"Not any painting—a Monet." He smiled, my breathing stilled, our frayed bond mending. "It is Claude's finest work. That painting is our beginning. None of us will quit now."

Quiet, I opened his gift. Tiny gold horseshoes dangled on a chain and earrings. I kissed his cheek. He placed it around my neck, his fingertips grazing my skin. My tears could not stop.

"I pay him in installments, fifty francs a month." He wiped my eyes, adjusting the horseshoe dangling next to Papa's locket. "From the first day we met . . . I wanted nothing but to be yours."

"I will always remember you wanted me as I am. I could never let you quit your art."

"I would."

"I would regret it forever." He leaned in and kissed me. I savored our last. "Will you let me see my portrait when you finish?" I asked, holding him.

We paused and let each other go.

He walked to a covered canvas rocking on his heels. I followed him. He lifted my hand to do the honors. The cloth fell away and she sat before me reminding me who I was.

He captured every curve of my face, the angle of my thin nose and open smile of my lips, my black lashes, swept up hair, feathered brows, and the precise moment I closed my eyes, enraptured. He illuminated my skin with innocence; my cheeks blushed at his advances, misguided love in a studio on a winter day, an attempt to warm the other. Now, he stood before me guided by perfect love—his portrait of me retrieved my soul, my dignity.

"You gave me more than a painting today," I said. "I do love you." I held onto him finding strength in his compassion. "Never give up on submitting to the Salon. Keep fighting. We will win with an exhibition of our own one day, I am certain."

"We?" He grinned, tinkling the little gold horseshoe at my ears. "Claude follows no one. My fellows mock him now for painting copies in the Louvre to earn a few francs."

"Frédéric, Claude copies not in the Louvre. He paints his views of Paris."

"If that is true, he will be the first to do so from a tower inside the Louvre, a grand sight I cannot wait to see." I gathered my things and walked to the door. "Camille," he called. "The more one judges, the less one loves. I could never judge you for my love is great."

"Balzac and Bazille." With one last embrace, Frédéric sent me off in the carriage, his cologne lingered on my skin; sweet tobacco reminded me of Papa. How I missed him.

48.

Sophie

Petite Fille du Jardin: Little Girl of the Garden.

I crumpled the twenty-four-year-old newspaper article in my hand. My tears smeared the words in vintage black ink as I unfolded it soiling my hands to read:

Authorities questioned two Americans, a mother and father, in the incident involving their daughter on Friday evening in which they claim they lost Petite Fille du Jardin at the garden until closing. A sunhat thrown into the water lily pond by the little girl had authorities fearing the worst until they found Petite Fille du Jardin safely under an Empress tree playing and crying inside our beloved Giverny garden with her imaginary friend, Claude Monet.

An eleven-year-old boy with messy brown hair and green eyes handed me a pink rose. I remember green eyes; they matched the green benches in the garden, Monet's garden. He held my mother's hand. *Philip.*

Visitors circled flowerbeds and trailed off into rows as ants to a melon rind. *Dad, that artist is wearing a sunhat like me.* My little eyes noticed everything: dragonflies flitting across the garden, a wooden bird feeder tucked inside a crabapple tree. A yellow climbing rose Mom called Mermaid, swimming under Monet's second-story bedroom window. And sunrise, the mist over the Seine floating to Giverny transforming Monet's garden into a fairyland.

We walked among little red cups of nasturtiums under the Grand Allée, Monet's tunnel of roses, to a green gate: the entrance to Monet's water garden. "Mom has an old wheelbarrow in her garden at home, too," I said to myself while Dad stared at his shoes. I closed my eyes at the autumn breeze, sniffing the air laced with sweet perfume and spices.

September. The only kid in school on summer vacation in the fall, the only time Dad could "work it out." "Monet's garden will burst into roses and water lilies," Mom promised. She didn't have to shake me awake on this trip. I was a ten-year-old in Paris sleeping in a hotel that screamed Cinderella's castle. We visited the Eiffel Tower, drank the chocolate I remembered as a child. Mom pulled me along the cobblestone streets as a wooden duck on wheels. "Remember, *ma fille?*" she asked. I nodded as a girl in a cuckoo clock until I couldn't walk another step.

The next day, a visit to the Musée de l'Orangerie and Tuileries Garden, lunch at a café—Dad couldn't make it, an unexpected meeting in London and another. "We can't take an important vacation without an interruption," Mom said. "This isn't working, Lewis."

"Something we should have figured out ten years ago," Dad mumbled. He caught me listening, shaking his frown into a smile, tugging my earlobe to make me laugh.

Mom tucked me into bed before their whispered brawl of the evening. "We will paint the sunflowers, *mon trésor*. If you search for them, patches of lavender crocuses pop up in the grass in secret spaces. Soak in all you can, and when we share our stories back home, it will feel like we're sitting in Claude Monet's garden sipping tea, *oui?*"

"*Oui*," I whispered, kissing her goodnight. "I hope it's sunny so I can find the crocuses."

"And if it's not?"

"When I don't see something I like . . . repaint it." I closed my eyes giddy at her laugh.

"My girl will make a marvelous artist. Sweet dreams, *mon trésor*."

The next morning wasn't so magical. Mom skipped September for Halloween dressing me as a mini Dorothy from *The Wizard of Oz*. "I'm too old for this dress," I whined, popping the elastic accordion suctioned to my waist. "But I like the sunhat."

"Josephine, let her wear pants," Dad moaned, holding his chin as *The Thinker*. He did that around Mom as if the pointy end of his chin would fall off. "We're flying."

"You're not *flying* our daughter to Giverny. You're riding the train like everyone else. You promised," Mom huffed, tying hideous knots over my shoulders.

"Give on this one, Jo. I gave on everything else."

Mom walked to the window, twirling her licorice waves into a ponytail glaring at Dad. "The big show won't save you this time, Lewis. It won't save you from what you have to do." She widened her eyes at him as if it was his turn to give me the spoonful of medicine. My parents had separated, I knew. Our trip to Paris was his last chance at being her husband, my dad. Mom stared into Dad; he focused on the ceiling. With all the cherubs and carvings up there, we all ended up staring at it. "Fine," she said, throwing her arms in the air. "Sophia, wear the slacks and pink blouse." I rushed into my bedroom to change.

The roomful of fairy-tale distractions helped me deny the day wasn't as magical as Mom planned. She mentioned something about tickets and lunch. Dad plopped on the fake Louis armchair rubbing his chin. Mom stared out the window sipping her tea. "Thanks for painting my fingernails pink, Mom. They match my blouse." I learned two interruptions in rapid succession worked at changing subjects and filling nervous, quiet spaces.

"Bring your sweater, *ma petit chère*. Behave for your father. I will see you soon." By her scowl, I didn't have time for a second tantrum. I sucked in my lips to keep from crying.

"We were going as a family," Dad said, his voice trembling. "We came all this way—"

"For Sophia. Damn it, Lewis. You knew I had this show. You've known about my exhibition for two months. *You* decided to change our plans and go to Giverny today, not me."

"I don't have time, Josephine. I told you, London—"

"London. *Oui*, London!"

"Mom, is my sunhat on right?" She stared at the rug, Dad the door. "We don't have to go today, Dad," I said, catching his frown. Mom growled. Dad was tired. No one laughed.

Fake the flu, I thought. But I wanted to wear my new sunhat, see the water lilies dance as Mom said they did for her years ago. Wisteria curtains, water sunsets; an Empress tree sounded magical all by itself. Mom painted her first water lily painting for me, the moment she first saw them, the second the sunlight turned the petals from white to lemon. The past year felt strange alone with my dad. He changed. He cursed more; smoked again, sported a new haircut Mom said he thought made him look younger while she grew older.

"Sophia, go with your father and enjoy Monet's garden. I'll meet you at the Empress tree by closing. I promise. We'll soak in a sunset and sneak off for pastries and cream in Chailly, maybe Versailles on Thursday. Would you like to see where King Louis XIV lived?"

"*Oui, Maman.* I'll wear a dress to Versailles. I promise." I held her, kissing her cheeks.

"You always keep your promises, *ma petit chère.* I can depend on my girl to be brave, *oui*?" she asked, straightening my shoulders.

"I can't do this, Jo," Dad said. "You're supposed to go with us."

"You will do this, Lewis. You will take your daughter to Monet's garden and have a wonderful time." Their faces flashed a convulsion of secret code: blinks, headshakes, and two nose rubs from Dad. He looked like a baseball catcher signaling pitches Mom refused. Today she threw him a curveball he wasn't prepared to catch.

~

I didn't complain about skipping the train ride. Dad rented a car. He gave up the reins on flying us from Paris. He gave up the reins on everything: my education, moving to California, separating from Mom, her thriving career. Nothing sat well with my father.

I fought sleep to the hum of the tires. Dad stared ahead bemused by thoughts prompting odd smirks. I lost myself in the countryside until I assaulted the silence with a sneeze.

"We would have had a good time in the air, little bug. Clear skies," he said, sputtering out a breath like a dying balloon. Sweat pooled above his lip forming the mustache Mom insisted he shave. Mom insisted a lot this trip. Lunch at a restaurant I couldn't pronounce, painting together. *The Empress tree, don't forget Sophia will love the Empress tree. No, wait for me. I want to show her the Empress tree.* Monet's garden was just a garden with my dad. Instead of trudging around with a tour guide, speaking for my dad so he wouldn't have to, Mom would name the flowers Monet painted, eager to plan her own canvases, inviting me to imagine them with her.

Monet's blue china and banana dining room—I wanted Mom here now. Dad hadn't said a word other than, "Wow, do you smell that? I thought there would be more roses. Geraniums are so common. Really? We came all this way for geraniums?"

I wondered where Monet sat for tea in the morning before he painted. Mom would know. His studio flooded in sunlight—I refused to see Monet's studio without Mom. Then my dad said it. In the middle of the tour guide's most inspired speech . . . by the water lily pond.

"Sophia, we're getting a divorce."

My heart ripped away from his hands. I turned my back on him staring at muted colors and weeds. I saw weeds in Monet's garden, ugly, dirty weeds.

"Sophia, you have to choose who you want to live with . . . your mom or me. You're probably better off with your mom, little bug. You can pick. It's up to you. You'll have to like London. You won't like London if your mom's set on California. Damn it, Josephine."

His words jumbled inside my ears. Ignoring Mom's forecast for sunny skies, my eyes produced a storm cloud of rain. I kept quiet, pulling my sweater. I wanted to throw my sunhat into Monet's water lily pond and run away. I did.

My sunflower hat landed on a lily pad, a water lily dressed the rim. I drifted with it.

Windmill arms, wading, sinking; water filled my nose and ears. A scrim of bubbles hid the wonderland. I fanned them away and held an endless breath; marveling at cloudy roots balancing lime lily pads as spinning plates on a stick. Mossy water shimmered with light under an aqua, rippling sky. Monet painted me with brushes of cobalt, rose, and lemon. I swirled his colors through my fingertips until I saw the flickering glint at the pond's edge. A hand reached for mine, muddy boots planted near the shore. A stranger held me. My father vanished.

I started a laugh, a taut expression turned to fear, anger. I ran away. Streaks of blue and pink followed. The sky turned sage and gray as I fell under an apple tree, hiding inside dry reeds of irises withered past their season, rolling over in the grass, scratchy and cold. I watched clouds crawl across the sky imagining an airplane's fumes writing my name in the blue. *Sophia, Sophia.*

I had entered Monet's painting, me floating as a mermaid among his water lilies. For one moment, under the spell of his magical garden, I didn't care if my dad left me—the story I told myself to fall asleep on the lonely nights thereafter. The memory I used to replace the nightmare he gave me, the story standing in front of me now.

I fell asleep on Monet's grass and wilted flowers, crushing them under my body, faintly hearing the calls in French, "*Petite fille! Petite fille!*" The sun dried my clothes, my hair. I found the Empress tree, playing catch now with bounding breath. I sat alone waiting, my sandals sweeping blades of grass. Waiting. When I opened my eyes, my father left, the water covered me, and I saw nothing I could grab onto to reach the shore, to feel safe.

"Sophia!" he shouted, waking me.

I searched the crowd blurred with tears, clapping my ears at their gasps, squinting at their shocked expressions, shaking heads, and pointing fingers. I needed to find the Empress tree, hoping I wasted enough time with Dad, Mom waited for me. It wasn't nearly enough time.

I ran away down a dirt path leading to the tree. My dad stood at its end and barreled the reverberating shout all kids hate. "Sophia Noel!"

I stopped.

He wasn't gentle, his face turned red as the apple I hoped to pick with Mom. He forced a fake grin as onlookers gawked. His nose kept twitching, more chin grabbing—I wanted to yell, it's there. Your chin's still there! He grabbed my arms and set me on the green, wooden bench under the Empress tree. The one Mom promised we would sit on together. "I wanted to see this with Mom. "You ruined everything!" Oglers whispered in French. My father waved them away.

"Sophia . . . I can't do this. Look at me, Sophia. Sometimes mommies and daddies . . . it doesn't work out." I counted blades of grass. Spotted a dead one and gasped. A dead blade of grass in Monet's garden, I killed it. He walked in circles and contemplated lighting a cigarette, shoving it back into his pocket. "Your mother . . ." I turned my back to him. "It's not easy. Shit! Damn it, Josephine." He scratched at his buzzed haircut, whispered cuss words, the big ones.

And walked away. *It has nothing to do with me, say it, Dad. It has nothing to do with me.* He dropped my wet sunhat and turned back, arms in the air. "What am I supposed to do?" Words recited to wives not children. I stared at my sunhat, dead on the ground. The brim soaked with moss and dirt.

Quiet tears fell. They wouldn't stop. I didn't want them to. I wanted him to regret every single one. He wouldn't pick up my sunhat or offer me a hug. He stood there, staring at me, his daughter, expecting me to solve the grown-up problem. I stared into his eyes to offer my answer and said slowly, softly, "I hate you. I knew you'd leave. I hate you."

He held a fist, massaged, and warmed it, biting his lip to thwart his own tears. Tears I was happy I gave him. My dad never hit me. He pushed me once and grabbed my arm, but he would never hurt me. He was killing me now. "You're not giving me a chance."

"You don't deserve it. I want Mom. *Maman! Maman!* Give me my sunhat. You killed it!"

He left. He left me there. He said he was going to find my mother and left me there. Five seconds, five minutes, five days, a kid doesn't know about time.

My father abandoned me in Monet's garden.

49.

Sophie

I didn't see my dad after that day for four years. Barely saw him at thirteen; never saw him until twenty, and finally at thirty-three in a coffin. And we never talked about it, not until after college, a coded conversation. He claimed I misremembered. He had to step away to think, check his rage because *I* had made him furious. *I* embarrassed him. *I* didn't make it easy. *I* wanted him to leave me alone. *Nothing was going to happen. I didn't leave you. I . . . stepped away.* Stepped away for twenty-two years. *Come on, Sophia, the Giverny story again? We came back to talk to you, remember? You were a mess. How embarrassing.*

I wanted to believe him, so I did, after he flew me to London to meet my new stepbrother Georgie, paid for my summers with Aunt Annabel in England, after we found our laugh years after I married Blake. Before my father's death, *I* made peace. He never did.

I wanted to believe my dad hadn't abandoned his daughter at the Empress tree in Monet's garden for any strange tourist to grab. I wouldn't believe my dad left me there—but he did.

He did.

Alone. Afraid. Angry. Sad. Destroyed.

He did.

I sat on Monet's cold, green bench hugging my sweater, my wet sunhat, crying, waiting, closing my eyes, trying to breathe in Monet's garden, but all I could smell was my musty, wet hat. In quarantine, I hogged Monet's circle of benches the tourists wanted to visit. The tour guide asked me why I was alone. At least someone did. "I'm waiting for my mom," I lied. "She'll be here any minute and told me not to leave this spot. She's an artist."

The freckled-face guide believed me and began her next tour. "All right, you're safe with Monet," she said. "He'll take care of you. I thought you would like a sunflower, mademoiselle, and a cookie." Before she left—my mother's shoes, I saw Mom's floral heels on the stone path, her footsteps crunching pebbles pinging as her strands of pearls. She lifted my chin and held me.

"He did it to get back at me, Sophia," she said. "I'm so sorry he hurt you. It's over. We must be grown up now. I must see my brave little dear. Can you be brave?"

Can I be brave? Can a ten-year-old be brave after her father dumped her on the other side of the world in Monet's garden? Can a *ma petit chère* grow up in a few seconds, paste a smile on her face, and walk back to that water lily pond to apologize to the tour guide? Sit for a while with *Maman*. The *Maman* I screamed for hours before. Mom or dad—I would have to choose.

"Go to London," he said. "Help me with the plane. Wouldn't I like London instead of being stuck in an art gallery in jerky California, nutty California?"

"It's settled, Lewis," Mom warned. "We agreed. You left her. You."

A taffy pull, that's where I lived the next year, twisted and stretched until pliable and shiny between cold metal bars. How would Mom and I make it? Dad wasn't around, but he was still dad. What would he be now?

"Come, Sophia. See." Mom walked me to the water lily pond, a strange boy following on our heels. I felt foolish meeting a French boy for the first time with my sad, red eyes until he kissed my cheeks making me blush and Mom smile. She never liked crying in front of me. It took everything for her not to grab me and leave. That wasn't my mom. She sucked in a breath of fresh air as if it held her up preventing her from imploding.

The water stilled. Mom saw my sunhat floating amidst the water lilies. I had thrown it back into the pond and hid myself in the garden until I decided to wait for her under the Empress tree. I spotted the lavender crocuses in the grass and picked one. I figured the garden owed it to me for being an accomplice to my unhappiness. I picked an apple, too, wondering how long they would search for me. When the police came, I hid inside the sunflowers and fell asleep in a shady cove with the withered irises. Minutes? Hours? It felt like days. I hadn't a plan to run away and live in the garden, so I rushed back to the Empress tree, hoping Mom would find me.

A gardener noticed us as Mom and I watched my sunhat wobble and drift in the pond. Mom tried to hide her smile and nodded to him; he waved. He stepped into his boat and floated toward my sunhat to retrieve it. He stroked the water with a long rake. Dad and I saw him fishing out vegetation hours before, but this time it was a girl's sunhat spoiling the composition of Monet's water lilies. "I ruined it, Mom. I'm sorry."

"You're not seeing, Sophia. Look how they dance."

"How what dances, *Maman*?"

"The lilies. Did you see them teeter like this before your hat drifted by to say *bonjour*?"

"No."

"They have you to thank for their waltz today."

I looked down ashamed. "I didn't mean to throw it in there. I was mad at Daddy."

"I know *ma fée*. So was I, and I shouldn't have left him . . . left you."

"I made him leave. He'll never come back."

"That's not true."

"Why did he leave me here? Why didn't he come? I waited. I waited for the Empress tree to show me magic. Daddy wasn't there, you weren't either. No one was."

Without a word, my mother grabbed me, squeezing me into her body. She held and rocked me until I made her let go. This time I dried her tears and turned to catch the boy skipping stones across the grass. He tried swinging on a tree branch until a passer-by stopped him. "Madame, is this your child? Please keep watch," the woman said. Mom didn't hear. She brought me into her chest again, and we turned together, my mother and me in Monet's garden watching water lilies dance between watery ripples of orange sunlight.

～

I opened my eyes; my memory complete. I didn't need Mom's words to fill in the blanks. The truth sat inside me waiting for me to set it free.

I dropped the worn teal diary in the grass. "It's over," I said, turning the page in my lavender journal, the one beginning the next chapter of my life. "A few blank pages left, for Paris." I sighed. "It's time."

Blame.

I muddled mess of color.

Its path leads to nothing beautiful.

I cannot blame my mother for my father's actions, and I cannot blame myself. I have unspoken words and missing pieces, but I'm not afraid to find them now. Their watery pain will no longer seep into the fabric of my life weakening it, but making it stronger.

Philip rescued me. A man left me, a boy found me. I don't know how long it will take for my heart to trust in love again. No time limits, forgiveness—the missing piece to the puzzle of me.

I closed my journal barely wanting to touch the old one. My breathing shallow, sweat washed my skin. "Too many shadows in this garden today."

"No, Madame, the light is splendid. The tulips and asters make a good—"

"You abandoned me," I whispered to no one. *Little bug,* my father sighed in my thoughts. "Dad," I said quietly, searching the sky. "I used to tell Mom it felt like you stuck a porcupine in my heart—the sting of a needle every day, every moment I thought of you. Why did you give me that memory? Why couldn't you give me hugs, kisses goodbye . . . your explanation? I wouldn't have cared. I would've been angry, but I deserved an explanation."

"Madame, it's heartless to torture a man for his sins when he has asked for forgiveness."

"You never asked for forgiveness! You erased every trace of wrongdoing."

I spent the rest of my life making amends for that, Paris, England, the water lilies . . .

"I never wanted your water lilies; I wanted you. I'm thirty-five years old still waiting for you to come home, Dad. You chose to lose me. I didn't choose to lose you."

I'm sorry, little bug.

"I imagined your apology my whole life."

I watched Monet—my father—pack his things and leave.

"No more excuses. No more escapes."

"I wanted to kiss you goodbye," he once confessed. "I couldn't, little bug, so I painted you in my mind's eye."

"You're no Monet, Dad. You can't paint away the fact you devastated your daughter and never said a word."

His salute—the last portrait of my dad. *"I love you, Dad,"* I whispered in *his ear. "Roger that," he said, smiling. "I love you too, little bug."* He appeared ill, but we didn't speak of it or our painful past. It didn't matter now. We held each other tight, my head on his shoulder, and we gave each other a loving, last goodbye.

I sighed away the past and opened my eyes to my mom's garden blooming with hope. "I'm thankful, Dad, I never told you it was too late. You died without giving me your apology, but I forgave you. I forgive you now."

I cried into no one, falling to the grass as the day my husband died. I wished to see the shoes of someone but it was all right I saw only my own. I trusted again in simple prayers and Mom's last wish: for her daughter to see . . . see beyond subjects, colors, and heartache . . . see that I am never alone and unconditional love extended a hand through real friends. *Take it,* I told myself, promising to call Jacey, Annabel, Philip, and Joe.

In a few days, my shoes will walk the cobblestones of my youth in Paris and welcome new memories in Monet's garden. "I'm ready to see something other than pain, take in flowers instead of breathless sobs, and twirl at sunset instead of hide under overcast skies."

I picked up my tattered teal journal. It was time to bury that sad girl with questions, no one on her side. I found a garden trowel, laughing to myself and crying, pretending to plant a seed of faith believing perhaps next spring something unexpected and beautiful will grow. *You don't have to wait,* I snickered at Mom's imagined whisper, staring at the lemon tulip streaked with red. *Triumph,* she called it. *It signifies perfect love and eternal happiness.*

"*Merci, Maman.*" I soaked the ground around the tulip, carefully digging up the dirt and its bulb as she taught me, and set it in the hole covering my teenage journal. "Triumph and a sprinkle of rain." I laughed turning to my cell phone buzzing on the bench where I left it. "Grow," I whispered to her flower, swiping dirt on my jeans.

I smiled at the text from Philip: In London. Thinking of you . . . us. I miss you.

I miss you too.

Philip: Would you let me in again? You game?

I'm game.

50.

Camille

~

Étretat, France 1868

A careful observation of Nature will disclose pleasantries of superb irony. She has for instance placed toads close to flowers. "Papa, no doubt you would fancy this quote by Balzac," I muttered to myself, closing my book. "I wish I could tell you in person."

In this quiet village by the sea, I swallowed more ironies than fine dinners. No outings with the Brohan sisters at the Grand Hotel or parlor games in stunning array, no twirls with rebellious artists at an outdoor ball, and no need for a studio meticulously ordered with tables of custom brushes and tube paints. The sapphire sea, fishing boats, and a magpie on a snow-covered fence replaced me as model for a time, a paintbox in nature—Claude's studio. I assured myself Claude's isolation resulted until I grew stronger, my skin radiant and youth restored. *Will I ever return to Camille Doncieux of Paris, Papa's ma fille, the defiant Parisian shopgirl of his Elegance Shop who sold well the finest fripperies on the rue de la Paix, Batignolles?*

I gave birth to my son in a one-room apartment on the Impasse Saint-Louis, under the care of a doctor Claude paid with a portrait. Jean Armand Claude Monet was our lifeboat now, my fair-haired cherub, the Beauty that tamed the Beast. I suffered in Paris alone while Claude lived without want in Le Havre keeping me and our baby secret. His father refused to meet us, but Claude recognized his child despite his family's threats. "I choose you," he assured.

Another spring, I prayed Papa's frostiness would thaw and love and forgiveness blossom in his heart to receive his daughter and grandson. "Give him time," Mamma said. "Your little doll will mend all our hearts." My baby started with mine as healing and forgiveness overcame me watching

Mamma nestle my son. From inn to inn, debt to debt, the passion of young love and adventure ceased. Claude's letters bemoaned patience, leaving me again for Le Havre in a hamlet recommended by Zola—Bennecourt. By summer, the novelist, Émile Zola rescued his nerves and "Monet's bird who cries rivers," paying my travel to reunite with Claude at a cottage in Fécamp, elated we left the fishing village in autumn.

Claude returned with a silver medal for *Camille* at the Le Havre exhibition. Arsène Houssaye, Madeleine's former director of the Comédie Française, purchased *Camille* funding our final move to Étretat, a fashionable seaport town, with its old church, quaint shops, and chalk cliffs rising from the sea. Villagers draped honeysuckle over doors bidding good fortune to travelers. I breathed them in and all the hope they extended.

Serenity greeted us in the abandon resort that returned to a fishing town at season's end. Fashionable bathers vanished, and washing women caught the spring water on its way to the sea. Claude painted vessels on the bay, the pebbled beach, and thatched-roofed fishing boats. He promised to make me fall in love with the water in our own houseboat, a floating studio to paint the water lilies we left behind in Bennecourt, Ville d'Avray, and Giverny.

For the rest of the year, we could at least call Étretat home. Claude found the sea's rhythmic roar at night comforting, the tide's rush and ripple lapping the shore come morning as pleasant as birdsongs as he walked the shingle seeking motifs to paint. I missed the bustle of Paris, the morning cabs, the aroma of hot chocolate and baked bread, Geneviève's giggles, Marie's gossip, and Madeleine and Augustine singing my name.

I missed modeling for Frédéric and Renoir, how disheartened my rebels acted now. "We lose this battle, but our war continues," Claude promised. A year later, the Salon made it clear: freethinkers posed a threat to their existence. "Everyone is beginning to appreciate Claude's search for true tonality," Boudin encouraged. "They take the bread from our mouths," Claude said. "The more original I become, the more they reject me."

"You must show the world you do not need them," I said.

The Salon's rejection was a blow to our purse but a reminder of our purpose. This year, the Salon accepted only one of two paintings Claude submitted, an insult to a rising artist. They hung Claude's painting and the works of his comrades poorly in a gallery exhibiting inferior artists. A final disrespect, and so the Seine River carried us away from Paris again to the Normandy coast, and I made peace with the sea, for this time we journeyed as a family.

I wrapped my seashell gifts for Genèvieve. My favorite part of the day; our letters offered a connection to Paris. I held hers taking in the scent of lavender from the paper. "Come, Raphael." He danced for a place in my lap. "What does Sister write us today?"

Dearest Camille,

Today I learned a violently rouged face looks disgusting. A puff of powder poorly applied—unfortunate. At Thomas's birthday party, Jeanne said I looked like I crawled out of a flour bag. I confess, I borrowed Mamma's cream suffering a horrendous rash and imagined smearing my cheeks with disgusting rouge wouldn't harm. Oh, I harmed everything.

Thomas still asked me to walk in the Parc Monceau. Don't tell Claude, but I fear his favorite water lily, the white with red petals, suffered Thomas's stick, so his rump suffered my boot. This only made Thomas fancy me more! Jeanne whispered Thomas might kiss me under an ugly, old oak planted by his great-grandfather. Not a first kiss I could imagine, a great-grandfather spying on us from Heaven. I don't believe walking with Thomas under any trees is in my best interest, do you?

Your seashell pretties help me sleep and dream of you. How is my fat nephew? I giggle as I write picturing his puffy cheeks. Papa said the recipe you sent Mamma for baked fish is delicious and wanted me to tell you. Good news, no? Lastly, I spied in Mamma's gossip paper Paris buzzes about a Russian prince who will soon wed the daughter of a seamstress. Do you think I should ignore Thomas and hold out for a prince?

Your loving sister, Genèvieve

Dearest Genèvieve,

You are wise beyond your years and hold the title aunt, but you are most definitely too young for a first kiss. Thomas Maywheel seeing you as beautiful, with or without war paint, is no surprise. I warned you about

Mamma's potions. Elise has a salve to calm your rash, and now I imagine you drop this letter begging Papa for a visit.

How I miss Papa. I hope to see you soon under a star-filled sky to share fairy stories and pray Papa joins us as when we were younger. The picture of you dancing in Claude's cottage garden has carried me through many lonely days since my departure. You were such a beautiful aunt to baby Jean at his baptism at Sainte-Marie des Batignolles. Marie, Frédéric, Julie Vellay and her companion the artist Monsieur Pissarro would not stop talking about your chocolate curls and ruffled plum dress. I imagine you will live in it now.

Théophile promises to help us travel to Paris next spring and fancies you believe he is the Count of Monte Cristo in Dumas's novel. Courbet writes he will soon visit us with his friend Alexandre Dumas; I will finally meet the famous author of The Three Musketeers.

Claude calls me to walk the cliffs and scout the beach for his next painting. But we must write often so it does not seem we are apart. Lastly, I have no doubt the water lily suffers no harm from a stick and will surprise as it blooms next summer. Claude never runs out of a supply of flowers to paint. Pass to Mamma a recipe for English teacakes our worthy cook has passed to me. Claude cannot stop eating them.

I love you forever, Camille

SALLY LUNNs. A pint of cream, lukewarm, a piece of butter, dash of salt, a tea-cupful of yeast, 1 1/2 lb flour; mix them together, let stand three-quarters of an hour; bake them an hour.

"You're crying again, *mon amour*," Claude said, entering the room.

"A letter to my sister." I cuddled Raphael.

Claude unfolded his handkerchief and dabbed my tears. "Come, now. I arranged care for the baby. He's asleep. I have something to show you."

"You are not dragging me to play dominoes at that café, are you?" I fanned my letter into a mist of orange blossom water.

"No. Do you wish to spend time with me?" Claude asked, dejected.

"I have been waiting a long time for you to ask."

"We'll mail your letter." He tucked me into my cloak as I readied my package. "Another prize for your sister—she'll have a roomful of the sea."

"Precisely," I said, holding my tears. "Am I posing?" I asked, excited.

"No, but I decided to paint two works of you and the baby and submit them to the Salon. The first time I undertake this composition. I wish the world to see my loving family."

"Your news makes me happy."

"Come, before it turns cold and the sun sets." We took our first walk alone since arriving, scuffing stones on the pebbled path to the cliff. Claude rarely discussed serious matters as he absorbed his nature, but arriving at the church on the hill overlooking the sea, chapel of Notre-Dame, he spoke of regret, I, forgiveness. "The cliff on the right is called the Cote d'Amont," he said. "Where I paint my view of the arches and rock formation rising from the sea." He pointed to a wooden bench yards in front of the church's door. We inhaled the sea.

I stared out at the horizon of blue and the foamy tide rolling over the shoreline. We stood high above the beach, the town below and tree-lined hills beyond. "I see why you relish this spot. It looks like a fairy village from up here, villagers flitting about their tiny gardens."

"The stone-faced fishermen I've met don't flit about tiny gardens."

"Indeed." I looked back at the winding path we traveled, our feet dodging star thistle in the lush grass. Silver streaks grazed the meadow with the breeze as angels soaring above. Every birch, willow, and orchard we passed, Claude promised to paint and cover our walls with canvases to bring to Paris and make a showing at the next Salon. *Always the Salon*, I thought. Claude tugged my hand, shifting my attention to the sea.

He walked toward it as if it called him. "Most deem the cliff on the left, the Cote d'Aval, provides the most charming walk," he said. "I say this view presents the whole beach, horizon, and the white chalk cliffs. Is it not magnificent?"

I joined him offering the warmth he needed. We lost the approval of our families, and in such moments, love was our salve for the wound of rejection. Nature freed Claude, it never judged him, it offered no guilt, and in these towns that knew us not, he frequented its old church to find himself again, chase the moods that raged between us, the doubt that hindered his progress, and regain confidence in his art. "This is where you slay the monster doubt," I said, taking in the effects of light and shade on the grass-covered cliffs.

"*Oui*," he whispered. "Give me a garden and carpet of grass beneath my feet, a field of red poppies at sunrise and streams of white light across the blue sea at sunset."

The view of Étretat was breathtaking here; the church grounds quiet from visitors as if our home. The town sat in a valley between two hills, houses, villas, and gardens, patches of farmland, the hills beyond, and the crescent-shaped beach before it. Fishermen docked their boats on a natural bay between the cliffs, a shingle of pebbles on the beach, clouds riding the sea and sails swollen with the wind, captivated Claude for months. Seeing it now, I understood why we moved here, why Claude desired to share his deepest feelings and impressions of soul and spirit in a painting, to bring a glimpse of nature indoors and a moment of serenity to the viewer.

The view enraptured Claude's brush, the blue sea brought him back to me, its snowy foam crashing against the cliffs quieted his own tempest. "The wind is still today," he said. "Why I wished you to come. I had to tie everything down last week. Winter arrives early."

"I missed our time alone, the open air. I enjoy a seaside resort in autumn."

"You don't miss the balls and concerts at the casino?" He laughed.

"No. You will never paint a beach strewn with parasols and pantaloons as Boudin." A rustle of colored leaves swirled at our feet. I saved a plum leaf for my sister. Claude grinned, returning his gaze to the sea. "Geneviève would claim fairies sprinkled diamonds across the sea."

"Few will paint this view."

If he held a sketchbook, Claude would draw me on this hill, my blue scarf flying in the breeze. I left him to his panorama, listening to the waves crashing against the rocks. "A cymbal at the end of an overture, Frédéric would say."

Claude chuckled. "You miss him."

"I miss all our friends."

He sighed and tapped on his pipe, thinking better of it he slipped it into his jacket, bundling me in my scarf. "Why do you suffer me? I'm jealous, bitter, wicked, and angry for my friends will arrive in Paris with an abundance of canvases."

"Papa used to say if you keep looking back at what should have been, you will miss being thankful for what is in front of you. We find fortune now with your patron Monsieur Gaudibert."

"And so, you forgive my absence and lingering in Le Havre?"

One of many, I thought but did not speak on it yet. "Free from worry you now fancy watching the stormy sea from this cliff, lingering at a café where the only topic of debate: dominoes you play for hours sipping brandy. When you cannot sleep, you walk with your lantern as the fishermen on the shore and visit this old church where its doors are always open. Until you must return to our red and white brick cottage to face we fled to another village, not for new motifs, but away from the gossip and creditors that chased us from Paris. I am tired of running, missing home." Losing strength, I stumbled to the bench; Claude rushed to my side. "It is nothing, a dizzy spell from the wonder of your view."

"From the hell I put you through. I am sorry, Camille."

I caught my breath, watching the flight of a seagull in the distance. How still and lonely it felt sitting next to him. "I need to understand," I said softly. "What is it about being alone? I will not hurt you. I will not leave." Claude turned to me, the sea washing over his eyes. He stroked my cheek, offered his soft kiss, lifting my chin to make me smile as if posing me for a painting long overdue. I bit my lip as that nervous child waiting for his answer. *Did he love me as I loved him? Did he need me?* His lips brushed over mine settling my fear. I pressed him, but no matter our fresh start, I would always dread waking to his absence.

"I go to a place that has nothing to do with trees or water. No matter my threats to quit, this passion reappears not as a weed but a perennial flower."

"What good is this place if you reside in it alone?"

"I paint as I must breathe. When I hide my easel, store away my brushes, I paint pictures in my mind, my fingers brush across my leg in swirls. What makes a man so I do not know. A gift that chases him until it's accomplished. Fame no longer appeals to me for I failed to survive its sting. I only hope the reward for my obsession is change. I wish to paint as a bird sings. Other men fight for more noble causes; I was made for this."

"Now you have a son."

"Who saved me."

"Brought you back."

"*Ma belle*," he sighed. "Mine is a dog's life. I walk for hours on the beach, in the country to find a sight to excite my eyes to paint like no other. I support a family now, and my painting is frenzied, unsure. But I'm convinced I'll find my way."

I followed his gaze to a flower growing between the rocks. "A sliver of blue, glint of white in the belly of the yellow petals, a circle of peach on the rock."

Claude raised an eyebrow and plucked the flower offering it to me. "My wife should walk with me more often to sharpen my sight."

I kissed his fingertips stained with blue. "I wish to be your wife by law and regain my father's favor and respect. I need Papa's love, Claude, as you need the sea. You are enchanted with being alone I am not."

He pitched rocks over the cliff. "You lament we've replaced dinners in wealthy salons to meals by a fire and champagne for homemade cider. It's easy being influenced by what you see and hear in Paris. My work here will at least have the merit of looking like no one else's."

"This is what you do when our conversation turns unpleasant. Why bring me here . . . to soften your rejection of marriage with the beauty of nature?"

He puffed out his chest, reminding me of when I corrected Papa misquoting Shakespeare. I called him to sit beside me. "The older I grow, the more I realize we never dare express directly what we feel," he said. "What can I offer? No marriage basket of lace, jewels, shawls."

"Since when has Claude Monet heeded the traditions of France? I have Mamma's sapphire ring longing to wear it as your bride. Living well offers other meanings. Your son bundled safely in his cradle, a wife who cares for you waiting to hear stories of your travels come evening and admire the wonders you paint. Thank God you painted your way out of debtor's prison and your freedom was at the disposition of your creditors."

"They understand."

"They do not understand an artist who fights France. They support their families."

"Frédéric suggested I walk to Le Havre and chop wood."

"What does Frédéric Bazille know of sacrifice as he naps in his mother's greenhouse, sips his father's wine in his smoking room, and devours grapes and peaches in January on the terrace?"

He laughed. "You've found your fight and scowl. Has Bazille lost your favor?"

"No. Frédéric is your son's godfather and supported us even at the cost of his own debt."

"I will purchase *Women in the Garden* back from him someday."

I tampered our coming argument with a kiss. "I already counted on that. I miss eating breakfast in our cottage garden at the white iron table you bought me for my birthday."

"*Ma belle*, in time we will settle in our own home."

I broke off the stem of the flower I held and tucked it into his buttonhole. "I have learned something over the years, Claude Monet never settles."

"I fight the reality, next year, we must move closer to Paris so I may sell my paintings and influence progress."

"It shall be as we imagine," I said, thrilled. "That is our gift. Where? The country! Ville d'Avray or Giverny? The garden you imagined and water lilies you desire for your own."

"Argenteuil, the spot of Sunday outings and pleasuring boating. I'll spoil you with Sèvres china, rosewood furniture, and wooden floors of your own to call the *frotteur* to shine them."

"A new stove to make your *pot-au-feu*. You have not tasted mine, beef, savory stock, carrots, celery, no cabbage, and cloves in the onion served with a sprinkle of nutmeg."

"Winters warmed by a steady fire with sweet-smelling wood."

"A yule log and in spring, a berry luncheon for my friends, white hyacinths and violets a centerpiece for my table and bonbons of strawberries dipped in white chocolate."

Claude's laugh roared as the sea. "You have made me hungry."

I looked to the church unable to hold my tears. He waited for my words. "You must promise me—never leave us again." He took me in his arms. "I am twenty-one, the legal age to marry. I do not know if my dowry is still mine, but I give to you everything that is me."

I missed his attentive eyes, discerning love not regret. "I will do more than that." He kissed me with passion; it had been so long. With the rush of the ocean below, he turned my gaze to the horizon. A sunset painted a streak of peach and lavender across the sky reflected in the watery glass below. A gold path stretched toward a fallen sun. "Marry me," he whispered. I clung to him, my breath as erratic as the waves against the cliffs. "We'll make plans next year."

Next year. I forbid my spirit from sinking. I had plenty to do: Papa's consent, the contract, ceremony, all teetering on Claude's success at the next Salon. "A honeymoon in Trouville."

He offered his hand. I garnered the strength to walk home. "I love you with so much of my heart, that none is left to protest," he said, grinning.

"You have memorized quotes from our British cook who indulges my game of reciting Shakespeare. I write my sister tonight."

On our walk home, Claude would not let go of my hand. "*Ma chéri,* don't think too much. It will happen . . . everything as we imagine."

We strolled the path soon returning to our cottage on the hill—a fire aglow, the baby's nurse knitting a pair of mittens waving to us at the window. "I wish I could paint our life into a pretty portrait where there is not a shadow to be found," I said. "We have walked in the shadows. I never thought you would wish to paint them, stormy seas, black ships fighting against the sea."

"We see light and darkness, but rarely admire what is in between."

"What is that?"

"Tranquility of shade, mystery of shadow, stillness of twilight, and the possibility of dawn."

"Claude Monet, I live with shade, shadow, twilight, and dawn."

"I never promised to be one thing or another."

"A square of pink." I kissed his nose. "A sliver of blue." I showed him his fingers.

"Now you see. Go, write your sister, and tell her of our news."

∼

Dearest Genèvieve,

I begin with a confession. I taught my sister false instructions on beauty. Beauty exudes from your heart, how you act, not merely what you see or wear. I love a man, an artist, who views the world as beautiful in times we cannot and expresses himself in freedom so we might glimpse beyond. I also live with a man whose faults bring out the ugliness in this world, as does your sister's. How can one hold such shadow and paint such light? We must care for our nature more than our outward appearance. The color of a flower does not make it any more beautiful than the next. Is it not its fragrance, the sight of its blossom come spring after a flowerless winter that brings us happiness? Goodness, kindness, and doing what is right are flowers we must cultivate inside for others to see. When I hold my child, I see true beauty.

People who claim to possess beauty above all, show more ugliness than any horror in nature. Papa has yet to understand my circumstance, though harsh and at times ugly in the light, shines more beauty than a million dress shops or jeweled windows. Geneviève, life may not always appear as beautiful as you wish, but you have the power to change your vision and see. It is the reward after a long journey, to see beyond pain, listen past the noise, open your eyes after a lonely winter, and take in the joy of spring's rebirth. This is the beauty I see; our family is no longer broken as before, no matter Papa's distance—and secrets do not keep us safe, but entangle us into a darkness that will steal everything if we so allow. Only the light cleanses as we banish secrets from our midst vowing to protect them no more.

Now, words Papa imparted when I was your age when a flood tried to wash our dreams away and a ruinous love invaded ours. Your voice is important, imagination limitless. You are not inferior because of your sex but better for it. Dreams come from hearts, not men. No man or woman is without fault, and love is not a guarantee your heart will not break but is the salve that mends it. Sorrows will come, but they shall not be the end of you.

My son will grow up to witness his father become the greatest artist in France, and so my news: Claude and I will marry. Next spring, I visit Paris to assure Papa and pray for his consent. I will be with you again. A hug and a kiss and I must.

I leave you words to share with Papa, a game you surely play with him now. A quote from Balzac to remember, "When you doubt your power, you give power to your doubt." Your power, my sister, is your light and perfect love. It would not be a game with Papa if I did not also offer a quote from Shakespeare, words from The Merchant of Venice that encapsulate my sister: "How far that little candle throws her beams! So shines a good deed in a weary world."

With all my heart and forever love, Camille

I will write further on the wedding, love, and how my news made little Raphael dance.

~

Claude peeked in on me as I finished my letter. I sat grateful for a modest room to myself, a desk to write, a stack of stationary and the trinkets I purchased to send my sister. "Rose water this time." I waved her letter in a mist of fragrance, breathing in sweet roses and new beginnings. Tonight my heart swelled with thanksgiving for my family, our cottage by the sea, and our walk on the cliff. I folded my letter, tucking the flower from the rocks inside and placed it on my desk ready to mail come morning.

Claude's light steps entered the room; the flicker of his candle danced upon my shoes. His hand brushed the stray hairs across my neck sending a chill up my arms. I absorbed the love in his kiss and smiled at the paintbrush he placed before me. "Time for your lesson," he said.

"Oh, I am tired. It is too late. Could we not enjoy our sleeping baby and the fire?"

"You cannot miss this lesson." He tugged my arm, pulling me to my feet.

"Geneviève will be surprised at our news." We entered the main room, our table aglow from the fire. Claude had arranged a loaf of bread, plate of grapes, and a vase of stunning, fragrant peonies. "Where did you find these?" I asked, as he offered me my smock, positioning me in front of my blank canvas on its easel.

"Look harder," he snickered.

"Lovely." The candlelight flickered across the petals, large peonies too fine for any shop in Étretat. At closer inspection, my heart skipped at the sight of pink rosebuds tied with a lavender ribbon. I closed my eyes, a film of tears trickled down my cheeks. "White blooms with a hint of yellow and a rose perfume . . ."

"That will fill my studio with the sweet scent of roses."

"Madame Lemoine peonies? The only shop I know to find them—"

"Madame Lemoine shall fill your need for a sturdy peony to shift about when working," Claude mocked. "How the light will dance off those petals. Who else would you recommend to watch our child while our nurse visits her family, and I take my Camille for a walk at sunset?"

"Elise!"

"Perhaps," Claude crooned, teasing me.

"A nice surprise. You remember the morning at Elise's flower shop where we first met. I recommend her pots of hydrangeas. They hold a shade of blush that brightens in the light."

"I could never forget you. I had planned to return for them. But now—"

"I apologize for my boldness, monsieur," I said, enjoying our play and memory.

"Never apologize for your boldness, mademoiselle."

"Oh, I cannot wait to see her . . . and could I hope, might I . . ."

The front door creaked open. "My bounty is as boundless as the sea. My love as deep. The more I give to thee. The more I have, for both are infinite." At the soothing voice, Claude caught me but could only hold me for a second.

"Papa!" I had no words but flight into his arms.

He held me as if his little girl had fallen on the ground and lifted me up into his strong arms. "I believe your tears have caused the tide to escape its banks," he whispered. "But do not fear, for I am here. I am here." I huddled into his arms as his child, restored, renewed. I hadn't a care for our next words, of being right or wrong. For this was the twilight Claude spoke of . . . neither light, nor darkness, admiring what is in between.

I close my eyes and see the meadows of Lyon. White tiny flowers Papa and I cannot name fill the countryside come spring, violets, too. Fuzzy, pink blooms intrude upon our path, sticking to our fingers as spun sugar. Papa and I run through the fields warmed by the sun with my little dog Raphael. Raphael is only a pup, a white fluff bouncing in the field of green; I can always find him. And then . . . the water comes, and Papa saves us all.

51.

Sophie

~

Paris

A Paris breath. Spun sugar, hot bread, candied ginger, white tea, orange blossoms. Sunrise, its pink sheen washes the cobblestones I remember as a child. I see every shade spilling in cracks, over corners. Dusk. The Seine counters sunset's blush rippling in olive and gold. The world's city where one imagines losing one's self in reinvention and love.

One more step to move through. One, two . . . twenty.

Annabel and I strolled down the Paris boulevards, family memories awakening until our feet could wander no more. Secret gardens, romantic tearooms, museums, lunches, pastries, chocolate in cafés, the best places I remembered. We traveled by train to Giverny in silent reflection. I hesitated in front of the gate. The sight of Claude Monet's pink house and the green shutters pricked my skin with excitement and dread. Annabel thoughtfully arranged our visit on Monday, Painter's Day, when Monet's garden sprouted canvases and artists channeling inspiration and genius to paint his palette of flowers.

"Tomorrow, we'll wake before sunrise and catch the mist outside these walls, over the hills ablaze with poppies, and hovering over the river valley below. You'll want to paint, my dear. I'm certain of it," Annabel said, squeezing my hand.

I clutched my canvas, paintbox, Mom's journal, my own. It was the closest thing I had to Mom standing here with me. We met the guide and toured the house and studio; new memories collided with old. For an hour, I avoided the two places my heart feared the most: the Empress tree and Monet's water lilies. "Shall I leave you to it, Sophia?" Annabel asked.

Quiet, I breathed in the garden, the damp earth, spices, and sweet floral fragrance—I was ten. My tears answered for me.

Annabel whispered to our tour guide; the guide patted my shoulder and left us alone.

We walked to the circle of benches under the Empress tree. "It's bigger," I said softly, taking in its lilac blooms. "My mind is at peace, my emotions have no idea I'm thirty-five years old right now," I said to Annabel, slowly placing my things on the ground, sitting on the bench clutching Mom's journal.

"This is what Josephine wanted, Sophie," Annabel whispered, her voice trembling.

"Thank you for arranging this quiet day."

"The less tourists the better . . . for this."

My stomach dropped as I stared at the lavender envelope in her hand—Mom's stationary, Mom's writing. I swallowed, unwilling to take it. "I don't think . . ."

"This, my dear, will be the hardest obstacle you face to moving through."

"What obstacle?"

"The truth."

I held up my mother's journal biting my lip, my breathing staggered. "This was supposed to be it." I searched Annabel's eyes, the ones I looked to for comfort. She darted them away, up to the tree and back. Her loving, gray-blue eyes glistened.

"It's up to you," she said. "I can't force you. But this is how she wanted it. She tried . . ."

I took the envelope in my hand and opened Mom's journal to the last page, my fingers tracing its spine, the ragged edges of missing pages. "What do they say?"

"This is your step, Sophia. I'll leave you to it, but I'm right here. Right here." Annabel walked to a nearby bench talking quietly to the guide. They strolled away. I watched her leave. She waved, assuring me she would remain. They paused, Annabel listening, to the guide's history lesson on Claude Monet's garden.

The clouds vanished revealing a sunny day, the lavender envelope resting on the slat of Monet's green, wooden bench. My sandals no longer dangling, my tired soles skimming the gravel below as I stared at the letter. My soul warmed to the words hidden inside, but the memories overcame me too fast to absorb.

I turned to Monet's garden, the Empress tree and the magical lilac blooms softening to lavender as the sun hid behind a cloud. "Damn it, Mom," I whispered. I opened my journal to its final page and wrote a single promise: *I will forgive.*

I slipped my journal back into my tote, took in a deep breath for courage, and let the birds sing me to a soothing place. I held in my lip and the coming tears as I stared at the shaky writing of Mom's tired hand. "Why now?" I whispered to no one, to her, opening the letter to read my mother's last words.

52.

Josephine de Lue

My Sophia,

Thousands of stories sit hidden on shelves inside the library of us. I wish I maintained the strength to write mine. Family stories hold magic like no other, heartache, too, *ma fille*, with one difference: after their telling, we hold the power to write our own ending.

I hope with all my heart you are sitting in Monet's garden under the Empress tree, a fragrant breeze caresses your beautiful face, and the sun kisses your cheeks for me. You never doubted my love, and I pray your faith in that love remains as you read a chapter of my story.

My mamma used to say, "Secrets between mothers and daughters out-number the stars." Oh, *ma fille*, one glance into your grandmother's eyes, she knew your secrets. "Who can we blame? A talent mothers pass to daughters, *mon rêve*." My dream, she called me. "In my generation, men carried their indiscretions as a trophy toward manhood, but when a woman sins, the sound of her sin: a perpetual hiss, a clanging bell rippling water, a ripple forever touching unexpected souls." I learned forgiveness mutes sin's noise, but fear convinced me I need only ask God for forgiveness, not you. I am ashamed I have no more years to wait, courage to seek, or time left to imag-ine the day I confess to you my secrets. My silence is a sin I pray you forgive.

Mamma mentored my art and paved the way for us as a heroic girl during World War II in Occupied France. Secrets ensured our family's survival. Mamma was tough, but she loved her only child keeping me close. My parents dreamed I would stay with them always, working in our small art gallery in Paris. "Josephine, strive to work for yourself. Never depend on anyone," she insisted. Ironic, my mother rescued by many as a child, embraced such a lonely view of the world. Your grandmother survived the war, *ma fille*, but was terrified to live.

When I met your dad, I was young, rebellious, and eager to conquer Paris with a dream to study art in America. "The American and Gypsy within you lure you away from Paris," my grandmother snickered. My grandmother survived an unimaginable period in history when the Nazis invaded France. "Much suffering, little Josephine," she cried, rarely speaking of the horrors she and Mamma witnessed and endured. A vital family story tucked away for another day written in the journals saved for you in my hope chest.

With this history, I understood my parents' strict boundaries. "Many died for the freedoms you enjoy," Mamma said. She arranged my education and career as an artist, but didn't count on her enlightened daughter coming of age during the most electrifying and socially permissive generations in Paris, the sixties. Marriage wasn't a priority, and despite contempt for women's art, I made noise. Once I tasted success and independence, the page of my story turned.

At nineteen, I met a band of friends who followed me throughout my lifetime. My dearest friend, Annabel, six years older, a spirited Englishwoman and Shakespearean actress. Annabel married Henry, fifteen years her senior, a theater owner. And Annabel's younger sister we called timid Pauline. "American men fancy mousey girls," Annabel assured her. I knew the opposite. My father was the timid American, Mamma a bold, independent Frenchwoman.

My final year in college, two handsome American men joined our group of friends: Lewis and Johnny, Air Force pilots stationed in London often visiting Paris and Annabel's summer parties. Annabel introduced me to Johnny; Lewis and Pauline made an awkward pair. Lewis, the braggart, exuded mystery. Johnny, all swagger, tall, handsome; his dark hair and blue eyes matched mine. Johnny believed in me, my art, and promised to take me to America.

My last summer in Paris, my troupe of friends and I celebrated a long farewell. "You, dear, are an artist who falls madly in love with falling in love," Annabel warned me. I stretched away from Mamma's rule and by summer's end fell in love with two men: Johnny and Lewis. "Two bulls in a flower garden." Annabel predicted the end of my story before it began.

I was a game to Lewis. Johnny proposed. No matter my success, Mamma refused to support my leaving Paris. Immature, afraid, I withheld my answer to Johnny's proposal until events one evening decided for me. On this night, silly with champagne and each other, the enchanted glow of a carnival and its carousel changed our friendships forever.

We toasted the end of our carefree summer, splurging at a fine restaurant when an American friend of Johnny's, Tristan, arrived. Nouveau riche and charming, Tristan and his date Jillian showered us with champagne at dinner. A lover's spat; Jillian left. Tristan joked their ritual and joined us at an evening carnival where we all overtook the carousel. Annabel favored ending our night. Johnny insisted our party continue, upset I hadn't mentioned his proposal.

I often wished we passed that carnival, sat at the café across the park debating our futures. Lewis and Johnny showed off at a throwing game; I noticed Tristan take pills. Tristan flirted with Pauline, me. We played along—not Tristan. Drunk, he started his own game mocking us with gossip. "Playboy Johnny is unworthy of Josephine's affection." He laughed. "Unfaithful Lewis is secretly in love with Josephine using clueless Pauline." Tristan shouted everyone's secret but mine until he whispered, "And Josephine, the great artist, is going to have a baby." Carnival shouts, my laughing friends, ceased. Johnny's glare warned us he would silence Tristan. What happened next haunted us forever.

I giggled away Tristan's lie with champagne and flirted with Lewis, angry at Johnny's silence and for inviting Tristan. Johnny watched me, then Lewis. Lewis eyed him until we all jumped onto the carousel ride. Pipe organ music rang through my body. Johnny walked away to watch the empty, spinning carousel. "It's late," he called, disappointed with me.

"Now you demand we go home, *mon amour*?" I asked. "We say no!" At the cheers of my friends, Henry shook Johnny into a jollier demeanor. I closed my eyes; my anger kindled against him, myself. "It shouldn't be this complicated, Johnny," I shouted. "Love should be easy."

"It is, dear." Annabel laughed. "You're too bloody stubborn to grab hold or let go!"

Carousel music stirred me awake, champagne flooding my head. "When the carousel stops whoever catches me, wins me," I foolishly shouted. The carousel slowly spinning, I teetered from horse to horse. Lewis called for me, hiding in the dark as the carousel began its ride. Tristan made his way around the carousel, leering, frightening me. The carousel took flight.

I hid behind a horse, startled at the stroke of a finger tickling my wrist. Tristan stood behind me. He pulled me into a sleigh. We tucked ourselves into it, the ride spinning faster. He laughed, whispering in French how beautiful I was and that Johnny didn't deserve me. Tristan held me innocently enough until his hands wandered behind my back, across my stomach, my thighs. My head spinning, desire raced over me, and in a whirl, Tristan kissed me.

I closed my eyes, laughing at our drunken game. Tristan decided I wanted more. Johnny couldn't hear me above the clamoring music. He hadn't hopped onto the ride, but I caught him through the trees searching for me as the carousel spun round and round past him. With nowhere to go, Tristan turned forceful. Lewis heard my scream. He found Tristan on top of me, picked him up, and kicked him off that spinning carousel. "Johnny!" I cried.

The music faded.

I clung to a horse as a child until the carousel stopped. With every turn, I saw Tristan's lifeless body, his violent landing, anger in Lewis's eyes. A terrifying minute, Tristan wobbled to his feet. We stormed off the carousel. Johnny looked at me, tears streaming down my face, my clothes disheveled. He grimaced at Lewis and punched Tristan. We left Tristan behind. No one spoke on the drive home. The next morning, we received the tragic news: Tristan died.

Jillian found him slumped over on his kitchen table, a bottle of pills, alcohol. "He had a range of problems," Johnny said. "I tried to save my brother so many times." The police questioned us. Tristan died of an overdose. Guilt covered us, especially when we learned Tristan was Johnny's younger brother.

"He wasn't good, but I wanted him to be." Johnny blamed himself. I hoped we could put that night behind us in time, marry as Johnny planned, and leave for America. In the preceding months, I learned the truth—I was pregnant. Tristan's death changed Johnny. He loathed Paris, no longer prepared for our future, marriage, or leaving London as Lewis had promised. A week after the death of his only brother, I never saw Johnny again. He left for London. He left me.

Frightened, alone, pregnant I could never face Mamma. It was nothing I was proud of, but I had Lewis. I was so young, *ma fille*. Lewis and I were together on occasion when Johnny flew back to London unsure of us. I was tired of being alone, and I had a baby to consider. Annabel was right; I abused the love of two men. Tristan's death made us all rethink our lives. Lewis proposed, my chance to leave Paris, heartache, and travel to America where my baby would have her father, and I wouldn't have to do this alone.

Before you became my happy ending the next few pages of my story rivals any storm we endured. My daughter deserves the truth, the ending of my story so she can write her own.

I traded Mamma's rule for Lewis's. We married at Annabel's cottage in England and left for America. I lasted a little over a year, how I missed Paris. I carried the weight of Tristan's death until you were born. My little girl healed the divide with my parents. We lived in Paris for five years until Lewis transferred back to the U.S., California. I joined an artist group; my career blossomed. Lewis and I walked a stormy path, and I locked away my secrets, so I told myself.

Lewis traveled often to London. I learned alone wasn't awful; I had you. Your dad and I separated. When Lewis mentioned he saw Pauline during a stay in London—I knew. Lewis desired the simple life I took from him years ago. Pauline was that life. Perhaps he knew the truth, ever since that night at the carousel. Lewis moved back to London carrying his own secret. We tried reconciling when you were ten, one last trip as a family to Paris and Monet's garden.

A trip that wasn't a fresh start but a painful goodbye.

Where I excelled in passion for art, I failed in courage for life. "Mom, we're an unbeatable team," my sweet daughter would tell me. I believed in us so much I kept your dad away from you to keep you safe. I could never tell you Lewis wasn't your father. My little girl knew with every question I selfishly ignored under the guise of protecting you. When Lewis left, it wasn't fair, but in my broken heart, I decided there was never a reason to tell you this truth. But if Lewis and I had a chance to save our marriage, I had to confess. I didn't know it was too late. During our last family trip to Paris, I told him the truth; it devastated him.

The day of our visit to Monet's garden, I had an exhibition in London where I discovered Lewis had a young son with Pauline, an affair hidden for years. Philip's parents worked with me, suffering through their own divorce. Philip was so upset I invited him to meet you at Monet's garden. When I realized I left you with Lewis in his state, I raced to Annabel. She always provided the answer—Johnny. All I could think of was you sitting there with Lewis without me. So you see, *ma fille*, your dad never left you at Monet's garden, I did.

Johnny flew me to Giverny. I raced to find you, Philip holding my hand. I longed to rewrite that day, the years, but I could only hold you. After my divorce, an angel to us all, Annabel found Johnny again. Years ago, Annabel warned me about Lewis, but who warned him about me? I aimed to protect you from my mother's life of cruelty, a Gypsy child who grew up fatherless in whispers and hatred during a time where suspicions and secrets resulted in death.

At thirteen, he saw you at the carousel here and sees you still. He watched you grow up, cried when you cried, cheered, provided for your needs. He moved to Grandville to watch over you, keep you safe until you left for college, married. He moved I knew not where, but I always felt him watching over us; that's what Johnny did. Every birthday, I longed to tell you. I was happy you reunited with Lewis after college. He loved you, Sophia, but London kept him distant.

You are a grown woman now. It has taken the end of my life to share my secret. A good, loving man came to me again a year ago—your father Johnny. You know him as Randall.

Randall accepted a position here to stay close, aware I was living my final days. We shared beautiful, secret days planning to see you. Oh, Sophia, time left us; your heart was so fragile, *ma fille*, losing Blake, your own difficulties so young and vast. I made peace.

I broke my promise to my mamma never depending on or needing anyone. I needed them all to save my daughter: Annabel, Philip, Jacey, Joe, Mr. and Mrs. Elders . . . Randall, even Megan. Words my grandmother lived by during the war championed my cause: How many hearts does it take to save one? Many. Many hearts, Sophia.

I do not doubt in his own way you have met your father by now. And if you haven't, I will tell you who he is and hope, with all my heart, you give him the chance I never did. A man I wished I treasured, genuine, loving, honest, and forgiving.

Open your heart to Randall. You can trust him. He loves you and desperately wants to be in your life, to win back the lost years I stole from him, you. We saw him once at the art museum. Remember? I rushed to leave unable to do it in my state. A beautiful day with my daughter, but my mind was unclear, body weak. I am so sorry for this pain. I could forever fill pages with I'm sorry, but rather fill them with love and the knowledge my precious daughter holds a forgiving heart. My daughter's grace made me well, a better woman than I could have ever been alone. How many hearts does it take to save one, *ma petit chère*? As many as are willing. Live, my daughter. Live.

All my love, *Maman*

53.

Sophie

"Sparrow?"

I turned to his rich, soothing voice. "Cowboy." I ran into Randall's arms. "This is the memory I wanted." I held him tight.

"So did I." We clung to each other letting lost years and the weight of sordid secrets slip off our backs. Nothing mattered but the smell of blossoms, his tender kiss to my cheek, and the comforting eyes I had learned to trust so easily. "There's much to say," he whispered.

"There is." We released each other. He stepped away, admiring me, wiping his tears as I tucked my mother's letter inside my journal. "It's a lot to take in." I felt ten again, surrounded by Monet's garden, but this time . . . I wasn't alone. "The carousel," I cried. "It was you."

He lifted my chin, offered his handkerchief wiping my tears as a father I longed to know. "Your mom thought it was time for us to make a new memory at a carousel. A good one . . . too few, but I held on to them, you." He showed me two photos. In one, I was a child in Mom's arms on a carousel in Paris. The other, thirteen in jeans and a flannel shirt riding a carousel horse like a rodeo queen. "My girl's beautiful smile helped me through a lot over the years."

My girl. I sighed at his words. "I wish I remembered, known about you." I stared into the photos and handed them back. "I wanted to know my dad, I needed to understand."

"I didn't stay away. I wanted to be there for you always, but I promised her."

"You would have married?"

A smidgen of distance at his sidestep, memories flashed across his eyes as he stared into mine. He bit his lip and said, "It doesn't matter now. We were different people then, so young."

"I'm so sorry about Tristan."

Randall snapped around surprised at the mention and slowly backed away, his thoughts hidden as he searched the sky. "I wonder what they're talking about now?" he asked himself, chuckling. "Rough memories to contend with, Sophie . . . your mom and me, we're from a different generation. We don't discuss it. We never have. We just . . ."

"Move on."

"Yeah." He swiped his face embarrassed at his truth and picked up a stick avoiding my stare, squirming away from my need for answers. A loving man, his painful past behind him, but here I was as a careless gardener digging up tender roots striving to grow among the weeds.

"It's wrong . . . moving on, walking away." I stared at the empty benches under Monet's Empress tree. "You're right," I said, my courage failing. "It doesn't matter . . . because Mom's not here." I fell into his arms. I couldn't imagine I had any tears left missing her. He cradled me and walked me to the green, wooden bench. The one I wished she could fill. I gathered myself, burying my journal into my tote, wiping my eyes. With a deep breath in and out, he scooted closer, his hand over mine. "It's easier moving on, it is," I said quietly.

"But it's never right." Randall cleared his throat and faced me, my hand covering his now. "Lewis came back here for you, Sophie," he said, his voice shaking. "It doesn't excuse what he did to you, but he came back." I pulled away. He wouldn't let me go. "He felt like such a coward; he thought he should stay away for good so he couldn't hurt you anymore."

"How do you know this?"

"He was my best friend. We were all a mess, Sophia."

"So am I, but a child doesn't understand what that means; no child should ever have to." Randall stayed quiet. I looked to the clouds as if the Scrabble game Mom and I played would spell out answers to my whys, directions on what was next, an outline on how to heal a broken heart, move through . . . move on. *Your father's here now, Sophia. Don't lose him again with the need to be right.* "That's how we lose people we love. I'm sorry, Randall. It doesn't matter now."

"A child should never have to walk through what you suffered. I'm sorry, Sophie."

I looked up at the Empress tree, clusters of glittering lavender jingled in the trees. Randall returned my grin. "I waited my whole life to hear those words. Thank you."

"You deserve a lifetime of I'm sorry's. Maybe it's time we both let go of what's past and try living today. Will you try, Sophie? Will you try . . . with me?" Randall's gentle, blue eyes took me in, asking me to trust him, offering his love.

"I'm shaky on embracing the present these days. I'll do my best—but, Randall . . . you have to promise me one thing."

"Anything."

"Never leave."

"I'll never leave you, Sophie. I will never leave."

I held him tight, taking in the words I waited my entire childhood to hear, soaking in his promise, making one of my own. *I will open my heart to my dad, Mom. I will. Merci.*

I turned to the bustle of a crowd behind us to the welcoming sight of true friends. "What?" I shouted, rushing to them. "Oh. My. Gosh!"

Randall let me go, but it would take more than a group of friends to lose him. He stayed on my heels, his shadow covering me. I watched his form shelter mine; hazy childhood memories came into focus. The form of a loving man I never knew, the one who longed to stay and never leave; one who shook my tiny hand at Mom's exhibitions, who waved to me from the audience at my first play, and the one who blew me kisses and laughed as I made faces riding the carousel. *He loves you, ma fille, and wants desperately to be in your life, to win back the lost years I stole from him . . . from you.*

My mother's final wish settled my heart and filled the empty spaces with love. I sighed and looked at Randall and the welcoming sight of friends.

"Your mom bought us all tickets!" Jacey said, running to me.

Joe shined his Hollywood smile. "Your mother didn't want you to be here—"

"Alone," I said, squeezing him tight.

"Alone," Annabel, Randall, Joe, and Jacey chimed together, a beautiful note.

"This doesn't happen to people like me." I hugged them all again.

"Well, dear," Annabel said, draping a cherry and lemon chiffon scarf around my neck, "because you think you've made up your mind to be alone. That wasn't good enough for us."

"We're real, Soph," Jacey sang. "Real."

How I welcomed her song.

"Life is messy, *oui*?" Philip joined the crowd with a manly shove to Joe. "Let it be messy, Sophia," he said coming closer.

My friends scattered.

"I'll be right over there," Randall said, winking, pointing to Annabel taking photos of a bed of irises. He wrapped her in his arms making me laugh.

I took in the moment watching my friends. Joe threw a tentative wave. Jacey slipped her arm into his as they strolled down a stony path. "You're all here, in Paris!"

"Technically, Giverny," Philip said, holding my hands together into his. "Messy can be perfect."

"What's the point if everything in your life is in order?" He greeted me with kisses to my cheeks as that timid boy. "Never allowing a surprise to happen, an unexpected friendship to blossom . . ."

"Or love?" He pulled me under the shadow of the Empress tree, shafts of light flickering across our skin. I closed my eyes to his kiss, soaking in his affection. "I missed you."

"I promised myself if I was lucky enough to score a second chance, I would kiss you properly . . . here, in this garden."

"A do-over?"

"A do-over."

"I wore my sweater."

His finger brushed my chin. "I didn't bring my pocket watch."

"I thought you always carried it."

"I didn't want to jinx this."

"That day wasn't a jinx. It was . . . a surprise." We searched the garden and looked to each other; Philip's wide grin turned mischievous as the boy in Monet's garden I met years ago. "Life is so strange, isn't it, Philip?"

"No."

I laughed. "Let me guess," I said with a smile. "It's a wonderful life."

"*Oui*. Come, *mon ange*. We both have new memories to paint."

~

Annabel and I stayed behind in the garden until closing while Philip showed my friends around Giverny no doubt catching up sipping coffee in a charming café. Annabel and I lingered among the flowers in silence until sunset.

One last place to visit.

Monet's water lily pond was more magical than I remembered the pink sky rippling across the water. "I didn't appreciate this as a girl," I said to Annabel. "I couldn't see the magic."

"You're not that girl any longer. I wager you see much clearer now." Annabel studied the pond, me.

"When I was a child this pond frightened me," I said, "now it's serene. It hardly moves. I threw my sunhat into this pond, and if it wasn't for the gasps of horror from onlookers, I think Mom would have painted it drifting across the water."

"Now you will paint it." I relied on Annabel's encouraging words, her belief in me remind me of my mom's. "I've never seen Randall so happy, Sophie."

"Strange, how buried memories from years ago suddenly surface—good memories."

"An unlocked door you had the courage to open. It's hard to take in the words of your mother." She patted my hand. "We were all so young and foolish." She forced a smile keeping her tears in check.

"I know, Aunt Annabel . . . I miss her, too." She fluffed my scarf and draped a strand of hair behind my ear, her gray-blue eyes, the loving eyes of my mom, glistening with love. "But, Annabel, I have a dad, here . . ."

"*Oui.*"

I stretched my face toward the sun letting its warmth wash over my cheeks, imagining my mom's kiss at bedtime as a child. *The last of the sun makes room for the stars and fairy tales*, she whispered in my dreams. At the click of the light switch, speckled, white spots drifting across my eyes in the darkness, transformed into fairy rides, bubbles racing through a forest of green. *"Whimsical sprites spin and twirl, upsetting the master of the evergreen. 'We must work', he orders,"* she tells her story laughing, *"though happily, while fairies and sprites fly about, dusting flowers with magic shimmer and setting pearls on blades of grass."*

I never heard her endings. I fell fast asleep.

Write your own ending. Your own story, Sophia, she reminds me.

I drifted to a familiar spot, the place where I stood for the last time with my father. "I understand," I said, to the squeeze of Annabel's hand, her light footsteps exploring in the distance.

I searched the sky's gray wisps for the answers I needed to leave here. A leaf tumbled across the grass reminding me I wasn't alone. "No more ghosts," I said to no one. "No. More. Pain."

I took in this spring canvas, no longer afraid of shadows or the light.

Birds and frogs trade songs; the sweet smell of wisteria parading as jasmine mingles with roses. Red and yellow tulips burst forth above the evergreen, lilac and white irises rise under the shade of an apple tree, and soon, water lilies—floating, teetering on beds of waxy green.

A little girl's sunhat no longer drifts inside my mind, but the sight of a father found and the friends that brought me here.

I turned to the last page in my journal, a small space ready to fill.

The greatest loss we may ever experience is that of ourselves.

I found that thing I lost along the way, Mom. At first, I thought it was Randall, but it was so much more. I found me.

It's far from settled and perfect. I'll have to remind myself often, but I found the family I lost. I found my way back home in a garden across the sea.

I closed the journal, my ending yet to be written, a new chapter of my story just beginning. *See, Sophia,* my mother's imagined whispered covered me with love. The water tranquil and silent, I searched Monet's pond. "What did you see?" I asked him quietly. *You won't see anything beautiful unless you let go,* I thought. I closed my eyes. The scent of mint invades the marsh. I begin to smell the dahlias, sweet and spicy and a hint of rain fattening up the clouds. I exhale, feeling the warmth of forgiveness wash over me now. "It wasn't mine to carry, Dad. It was yours." I opened my eyes to the water lily pond, letting my thoughts drift on clusters of lily pads. "Look at you."

I gazed one last time . . . for now . . . leaving the pain of abandonment at the bottom of the pond, under earth, far under earth. The lily pads floated effortlessly in unison with the breeze. My sigh commanded the past to fall off my shoulders, and in a harmonious show, the breeze blew the gray clouds revealing golden sun through the willows.

I looked up to catch a stream of pink drifting across the sky of blue, the sunset's show on the horizon. "It's beautiful today, Mom. *Mon rêve.* My dream."

And near the edge of the pond, an unexpected flower, a water lily flashing pink, showing before its time. I glimpsed a dragonfly, my ear faintly hearing the call to leave. The dragonfly flickers above its lily. The lily remains stoic, serene.

One last glance at the coral sky now streaked in vanilla and peach.

The dragonfly flits between unfurled chiffon petals of its lily.

"Sophie, it's time to leave," I heard it as a whisper.

I closed my eyes picturing the dragonfly and its lily: he, encircling the rosy mist about her, she, scarcely beginning to move. In a great splash by an unruly frog—I saw the lily dance.

How it danced.

I saw it dance.

ACKNOWLEDGMENTS

Special thanks to one of my favorite dreaming places, the Saint Louis Art Museum and to Simon Kelly, Curator of Modern and Contemporary Art. When you opened Monet's *Water Lilies* exhibition, you had no idea I needed that space to sort out all things loss, love, and second chances. *Merci*.

I am grateful to the librarians at the Saint Louis Art Museum's Richardson Memorial Library, and Washington University's Kenneth and Nancy Kranzberg Art & Architecture Library for assistance and access to your special collections and databases. To the Claude Monet Foundation for your invaluable resources on Claude Monet's garden, house, and studio in Giverny, France. Thankful for the archives and my time writing at the Monet exhibition: *Impressionism, Fashion & Modernity*, at the Metropolitan Museum of Art, New York, where I met Camille.

Hugs and ginormous thanks to three book rock stars, spectacular friends and trusted first readers: Betty Taylor, sweet Jenny Belk, and my heart sister, Susan Peterson. Your kindness, giving and cheers overwhelm me. Thank you for your selfless efforts to encourage authors, readers, and those around you!

To my husband Michael, the champion of all things imagination Michelle. Your love and relentless support lift me higher. I dream, write, imagine because of you, your sacrifice, unwavering faith, prayers, and love. I love you forever . . . never letting go.

My mom taught me everything I know about being kind, loving people, forgiveness, courage, dreaming big dreams, and allowing my imagination to take me wherever it will. We were going to paint together. I miss we didn't get the chance. Her daughter believes she is fully happy painting sunsets in God's sky, and they are beautiful.

To my AWESOME readers—friends, I am humbled by your thoughtfulness, encouragement, and this chance to share my heart with yours. When I write a novel, my heart's hope is that you will not only be entertained but comforted with a word of encouragement or two in an imaginative, thought-provoking story, an escape. You, too, hold dreams, gifts, talents. Remember, even in the smallest of ways, a smile, an encouraging word you make a difference to the people around you. Never give up. Never believe the lie you do not matter because you do to me and every heart around you. Thank you from the bottom of my heart.

Lastly, to every heart that may be hurting from loss. My husband whispered these wise words to me when my heart was broken into a million pieces, and again while writing this story: Remember, your tears are a testament to the relationship you had with your loved one. You are never alone. Someone will always listen. We do not *move on* from grief; we move through it. Time, trusting others, opening your heart *will* heal wounds. Banish the negative; remember the good. Let go of the hurt, the lost I'm sorry's you should have received, embrace the new, purpose to see beauty in the ugly things. Do not believe the lie you are done. You have so much life to live—this gift. You are strong, brave, whole, and healed, and you will come out the other side. I promise.

AUTHOR'S NOTE

An unfinished concrete wall in my basement turned into the blank canvas that helped me move through the loss of my mom. Two months after she passed away, I found the set of acrylic paints I bought for her birthday. The paints I hoped would reignite her dream of being an artist. Before I knew it, I was slashing my concrete wall in a dim room in my basement with angry globs of cobalt blue, slashes of emerald, and swirls of pink. Somehow, in the end, I imagined it would vaguely resemble the center panel of Claude Monet's masterpiece, *Water Lilies*. As my effort continued, it didn't matter what it looked like; I was painting.

With every brushstroke my tears fell at the reminder, my mom wasn't here to see my effort. Every night for two weeks, I painted until my wrist and shoulder gave out, but I wasn't painting a wall I was avoiding missing my mom, picking up the pieces of my heart, and trying to understand this alien thing called grief.

After the death of my mom, a casualty to a national drug shortage for a chemotherapy drug to extend her life she could not get, I had to follow my heart and write this novel as a dedication to her. My mom was a 1960s wife who dreamed of becoming an artist, but she set that dream aside to raise her children. Though she never realized her dream, art resided in her soul, art, and creativity she gifted to her children. And so, for a few pages, my mom was a famous artist: Josephine de Lue.

When I lost my mom, I wasn't prepared for walking through *how* I lost her. Well-meaning people stamped a time limit on my grieving process. No amount of time passes that takes our tears away in missing loved ones we lost—AND THAT'S OKAY. It gets better, the tears come less; you get stronger, but who said we have to suck them all in? If water makes flowers grow, I think tears make us grow. I rather cry more, than feel less.

The tranquility of Claude Monet's paintings always captivated me. I was astounded when I learned of Monet's secret struggles, selfish, careless nature, censorship of his art, his unyielding dedication to paint and see like no other, the aim behind his rebellion, and the darkness, including deep self-doubt, this painter of lights endured while he produced serene masterpieces.

How do you whittle fourteen years of the most famous artist in the world and his mysterious first wife, eighteen moves spanning three countries in twelve years, and the support of their friends, stars of Paris, the Impressionists, into a few scenes for a novel? When I set out to write *Water Lily Dance*, I had no idea the monumental task of research required regarding the birth of Impressionism, its many artists, their "new" Paris, and the lives of a trailblazing couple surrounded by famous friends and patrons.

Each thread unraveled a mystery and heartache surrounding Monet's early life. In the end, I realized *Water Lily Dance* held many rebellions: Claude Monet, Camille Doncieux, Sophie Noel, Josephine de Lue—every character has a story, a fight.

And there was Camille, a mysterious and misunderstood figure in art history. We know little of her background because Claude Monet destroyed all letters, photographs, and diaries relating to her existence, with one exception: the eighty portraits he and his fellow Impressionists painted of Camille, many Monet kept and repurchased from previous buyers in his private possession until his death despite his remarrying. This fact alone began my quest to dig deeper in archives, hundreds of letters and 19th-century French records and publications to find more about Camille Doncieux and her family and I did.

Though the historical account regarding Camille Doncieux is fictional, I was thrilled when I discovered new information regarding her family's connection to wealth and art, never before discussed. This thread enabled me to paint the layered life of this intriguing woman, an important figure in the Impressionist art movement I believe in more ways than we will ever know.

I consulted several online catalogs, art museum archives, auction house records, numerous books, 19th-century French documents, and letters regarding the history of Monet and his friends. To learn more about my references, the history and reasons behind *Water Lily Dance* please check out my blog and visit me at my website at: www.MichelleMuriel.com.

ABOUT THE AUTHOR

MICHELLE MURIEL is the award-winning, bestselling author of *Water Lily Dance* and *Essie's Roses*. She holds a Bachelor of Fine Arts, magna cum laude, and worked as a professional actress, a member of Actors' Equity and The American Federation of Television and Radio Artists for twenty years, doing theater, voice-over, and commercial work. She is also a songwriter and musician. Michelle lives in Missouri with her husband and two quirky Border collies. Connect with Michelle at MichelleMuriel.com.

Made in the USA
Monee, IL
07 February 2022

90842568R00247